art
30i ....nal Category for *First Grave on the Right* and the 2012 RITA
awards for Best New Book.

She lives in New Mexico with her husband of more than 25 years and two
sons, the mighty, mighty Jones boys.

Visit Darynda Jones online:

www.daryndajones.com
www.facebook.com/darynda.jones.official
www.twitter.com/Darynda

Praise for Darynda Jones:

'Hilarious and heart-felt, sexy and surprising, this paranormal has it
all . . . An absolute must read – I'm already begging for the next one!'
J.R. Ward, No.1 *New York Times* bestselling author

'From its unique premise to its wonderfully imaginative characters,
Jones's award-winning Charley Davidson mystery series, from *First
Grave on the Right* onward to this fifth delectable installment, will
continue to attract and delight a broad spectrum of readers'
Booklist (starred review)

'Jones perfectly balances humour and suspense . . .
will leave readers eager for the next instalment'
Publishers Weekly

By Darynda Jones

First Grave on the Right

Second Grave on the Left

Third Grave Dead Ahead

Fourth Grave Beneath My Feet

Fifth Grave Past the Light

Sixth Grave on the Edge

Sixth Grave on the Edge

Edge

Darynda Jones

piatkus

PIATKUS

First published in the US in 2014 by St Martin's Press
First published in Great Britain in 2014 by Piatkus

Copyright © 2014 Darynda Jones

The moral right of the author has been asserted.

A CIP catalogue record for this book
is available from the British Library.

ISBN 978-0-349-40345-8

Printed and bound in Great Britain by
Clays Ltd, St Ives plc.

Papers used by Piatkus are from well-managed forests
and other responsible sources.

MIX
Paper from
responsible sources
FSC® C104740

Piatkus
An imprint of
Little, Brown Book Group
100 Victoria Embankment
London EC4Y 0DY

An Hachette UK Company
www.hachette.co.uk

www.piatkkus.co.uk

For Michael and Cathy,
who make Saturday nights more entertaining
than a night at the Comedy Club

Acknowledgments

First, thank *you,* wonderful readers, for braving another adventure into the world of Charley Davidson. Once more unto the breach, my friends. May this journey bring you joy, laughter, and lots of warm, fuzzy feelings.

A special thanks (and my undying gratitude) as always to my incredible agent, Alexandra "The Powerhouse" Machinist, my amazing editor, Jennifer "The Genius" Enderlin, and to all the teams at St. Martin's Press, Macmillan Audio, and Janklow & Nesbit Associates. I'm ever so grateful to have you! And thank you to the ultra-talented narrator of the audiobooks, the lovely Lorelei King.

And a note to Loren . . . LOREN! . . . who left me for another writer. Or, well, a lot of other writers. But it's okay. No, really, *sniff* I have Nick now. It's all good. But I wish you the very best, mister!

Thank you to Eliani Torres! How you put up with me and my constant overuse of certain words that I'm not going to list here for fear of sending you into cardiac arrest, I'll never know. Thank you so much for your wonderful, mad skill. And to my betas, Theresa, Cait, and Rhiannon. Your input and ideas were invaluable. Theresa, I owe you big-time! Thank you for coming through with such flying colors during that initial crunch.

Thank you thank you thank you to my extraordinary Grimlets! Your generosity is insane. Please know how much you mean to me. And a special thanks to Jowanna, aka Mama Grimlet, who makes me giggle in all the right places.

To all of my family and friends for your love and support. Where would I be without you? (Don't answer that.) And a special thanks to my writing buddies, the incomparable Jacquelyn Frank and the super hot CL Parker. And since we're on the subject, thank you *so* much to J.R. Ward for talking me down off the ledge seconds before I toppled over. Love you all!

And last but not even close to least, to my assistant Dana, the torrential, exuberant, effervescent, gale-force whirlwind beneath my wings. You amaze and inspire me to be the best I can be every single day.

Sixth Grave
on the
Edge

1

A blank is the only thing I draw well.

—T-SHIRT

"A girl, a mocha latte, and a naked dead man walk into a bar," I said, turning to the naked dead man sitting in my passenger seat. The *elderly* naked dead man who'd been riding shotgun in my cherry red Jeep Wrangler, aka Misery, for two days now. We were on a stakeout. Sort of. I was staking out a Mr. and Mrs. Foster, so I was definitely on a stakeout. No idea what Naked Dead Man was on. Considering the fact that he looked about 112, probably blood thinners. Cholesterol medication. And, judging from the state of his manhood, which I couldn't stop seeing *every single time* I turned toward him, Viagra. If I were to hashtag that moment, my status would read something like #impressed.

I gave him two thumbs up, then looked back at the house again, happy to be sitting in Misery. The Jeep, not the emotion. I'd just picked her up from the car hospital two days earlier. She'd had several surgeries to fix her broken girlie bits because a raving lunatic rammed into her. He'd knocked her into a state of mangled disrepair and me, as I was in the driver's seat at the time, into a state of oblivion. I stayed in that state long enough for Mr. Raving Lunatic to cart me off to a deserted bridge to kill me. He failed and died in the process, but Misery had paid a high price for his nefarious machinations. Why did bad guys always try to hurt the ones I loved?

And this one had succeeded. Misery was hurt. Bad. No one wanted to work on her. Said she couldn't be saved. Said to give her over to the scrap yard. Thankfully, a family friend with a body shop and a few incriminating photos, which just happened to have found their way into my possession, agreed with great reluctance to try.

Noni kept her for two long weeks before calling to tell me that he'd almost lost her a couple of times, but she'd pulled through with flying colors. When I got the green light to go pick her up, I tore out of my apartment so fast, I left a dust trail behind me, along with a flummoxed best friend, who'd been telling me about the couple in 3C. They were apparently newlyweds, if their energy to do it—her words—all night every night was any indication. I hurried back to her, however, because I didn't have a car and I needed a ride.

When we picked up Misery, Noni tried to tell me everything he'd had to do to her to get her up and running, but I held up a hand to stop him, unable to bear it. This was Misery he was talking about. Not some random Wrangler off the streets. This was *my* Wrangler. My best friend. My baby.

Holy cow, I needed a life.

I had to hand it to Noni, though. Misery was good as new. Better than I was, anyway. Ever since that night, I'd been having problems sleeping. I suffered from debilitating nightmares that left me screaming into my pillow, and I jumped every time someone dropped a feather.

But at least Misery was okay. Like, really okay. It was weird. Her cough was gone. Her sluggish response time was no longer an issue. Her reluctance to wake up in the mornings as she sputtered in protest every time I tried to fire all engines was nonexistent. Now she started on the first try, no groaning or whining, and she purred like a newborn kitten.

How Noni had managed to fix her insides as well as her outsides I'd never know, but the guy was good. And Noni was my new best friend. Well, after Misery. And Cookie, my real best friend. And Garrett, my kind of, sort of best friend. And Reyes, my . . . my . . .

What was Reyes? Besides the dark and sultry son of evil? My boy toy? My love slave? My 24/7 booty call?

No.

Well, yes.

He was all those things, but he was also my almost fiancé. All I had to do was say yes to the proposal he'd written on a sticky note, and he would be my fiancé for reals. Until then, however, he was my almost fiancé.

No, my soon-to-be fiancé.

No! My *nigh* fiancé.

Yeah, that'd work.

I turned back to the naked dead man, stuffed a couple of Cheez-Its into my mouth, and confessed my latest sin.

"I'm just kidding," I said through the crackers, regretting the fact that I'd tempted him and now had no follow-up. No punch line. "I don't know any 'girl, mocha latte, dead man' jokes. Sorry to get your hopes up like that." He didn't seem to mind, however. He sat staring straight ahead as always, his gray eyes clouded and watery with age, oblivious of my charm, my clever repartee, and my intellectual wit. He was ignoring me!

It happened.

"Cheez-It?" I offered him.

Nothing.

"Okay, but you have no idea what you're missing here."

I could only hope that one day he'd actually talk to me; otherwise, this was going to be a very one-sided relationship. I dusted Cheez-It gunk off my hands and went back to a drawing I'd been working on. Since he didn't talk, I had no way of finding out his identity. And in my attempt to avoid eye contact with Naked Dead Man's penis over the last couple of days, I'd also avoided several key clues as to said identity. First, he had a long scar that ran from under his left arm, over his rib cage, and down until it ended at his belly button. Whatever had caused it couldn't be pleasant, but it could be vital in identifying him. Second, he had a tattoo on his left biceps that looked very old-school military. It was faded and the ink had spread, but I could still make out an eagle with its talons gripping a United States flag. And third, right underneath his tattoo was a surname, presumably his: ANDRULIS. I'd taken out my memo pad and pen and was drawing the tat, since I had yet to find a camera that could photograph the departed.

I did my darnedest to draw the tat while simultaneously balancing the Cheez-It box against the gearshift, within arm's reach, and keeping an eye on the Fosters' house. Sadly, I sucked at two out of three of those tasks. Mostly at drawing. I'd never gotten the hang of it. I failed finger painting in kindergarten, too. That should have been a clue, but I'd always wanted to be the next Vermeer or Picasso or, at the very least, the next Clyde Brewster, a boy I'd went to school with who drew exploding walls and houses and buildings. No idea why. Alas, my destiny did not lie within the lines of graphite or the strokes of a paintbrush, but at the whim of dead people with PTDD: post-traumatic death disorder.

Oh, well. It could have been worse. Clyde Brewster, for example, ended up in prison for trying to blow up a Sack-N-Save. Thankfully, he was better at art than at demolitions. He'd asked me out several times, too. #Dodgedabullet.

"I know you're not really into baring your soul," I said, eyeing Mr. Andrulis's bare, naked soul, "figuratively speaking, but if there's anything you want or need, I'm your girl. Mostly because not many people on Earth can see you."

I added a shadow on the eagle's face with my blue ink pen, trying to make it look noble. It didn't help. It still looked cross-eyed.

"And those who can see the departed usually see only a gray mist where you might be. Or they'll feel a rush of cold air when you walk past. But I can see you, touch you, hear you, pretty much anything you."

Maybe if I added highlights on its beak, it would look more like an eagle and less like a duck.

"My name is Charley."

But I was using a pen. I couldn't erase. Damn it. I had to think ahead. Real artists thought ahead. I'd never get into the Louvre at this rate.

"Charley Davidson."

I tried to scratch off some of the ink, bracing the memo pad against my steering wheel. I tore a tiny hole in the paper instead and cursed under my breath.

"I'm the grim reaper," I said from between gritted teeth, "but don't let that bother you. It's not as bad as it sounds. I'm also a private investigator. That's not as bad as it sounds either. And I shouldn't have given your eagle eyelashes. He looks like Daffy Duck in drag."

Giving up, I wrote the name underneath the eagle-ish-type drawing, consoling myself with the fact that abstract art was all the rage before pulling out my phone and snapping a shot of my masterpiece. After angling it this way and that, trying to get the focus just right, I realized the eagle looked better when turned on its side. More masculine. Less . . . water fowl.

I saved the best one and deleted the rest as a car pulled up to the Foster house. A nervous thrill rushed up my spine. I put down my pen and memo pad and took a sip of my whipped mocha latte, forcing myself to calm as I waited to see who was driving the gold Prius. I was spying on the Fosters, who lived in a modest neighborhood in the Northeast Heights, because I'd been asked to by a friend of mine. She was a special agent with the FBI, like her father before her, and this had been his case, one of the few that went unsolved under his watch. I was trying to help her solve it, though *solving* might be a strong word. If my hunch was correct, and I liked to think it was, I had insider information that my friend's father was never privy to. Mr. Foster owned an insurance company, and Mrs. Foster ran the office of a local pediatrician. And approximately thirty years ago, their son was taken from them, never to be seen again. I was about 100 percent certain I knew what happened to him.

I eased forward and pressed against the steering wheel, angling for a better look at the driver when my aunt Lil's voice wafted toward me from the backseat.

"Who's the hottie?" she asked, her blue hair and floral muumuu solidifying around her as she materialized in my rearview.

I tossed a wink over my right shoulder. "Hey, Aunt Lil. How was your trip to Bangladesh?"

"Oh, the food!" She waved a hand extravagantly. "The people! I was in heaven, I tell ya. Not literally, though." She cackled in delight at her joke.

Aunt Lil had died in the '60s, a fact she'd only recently discovered. So, she couldn't have actually eaten or interacted with the native population. At least, not the living native population. I'd never thought about her visiting the departed when she traveled. Now, *that* would be fascinating.

She hitched a thumb toward my newest friend and wriggled her penciled brows. "You gonna introduce us?"

The garage door rose and the driver pulled inside but didn't close the door. It gave me hope. I just wanted a glimpse. A tiny peek.

"He's not very talkative," I said, squinting for a better view when the driver's-side door opened, "but I think his last name is Andrulis. It's on his tattoo."

"He's got some ink?" She leaned forward and spotted Mr. A's package. It was hard to miss.

"Good heavens," she said, her eyes rounding in appreciation.

Before I could get a look at the driver, the garage door started closing. "Darn," I whispered, tilting my head in unison with the descending door until it completely blocked my view.

I'd seen a woman's foot as she stepped out of the car before the door closed completely. That was about it.

"He's certainly been blessed," she said.

I laid my head against the steering wheel and expelled a loud breath as disappointment washed over me. I'd been handed a file that could hold many answers to the puzzle that was Reyes Alexander Farrow, my nigh fiancé, and the Fosters were a big piece of the puzzle. Their first son had been kidnapped while napping in his room. Because there was never a ransom demand and no witnesses, the trail went cold almost immediately despite a massive search and public pleas from the parents. But the FBI agent assigned to the case never gave up. He'd always believed there was more to the case than just a kidnapping. And so did his daughter. We'd worked a couple of cases together in the past. She knew about my rep for solving difficult crimes, and she'd asked me to look at this cold case that had been the bane of her father's existence.

And that was the day that Reyes Farrow's kidnapping fell into my lap. *He* was the child who had been abducted almost thirty years prior. I glanced down at the file stuffed between my seat and the console. So much potential there. So much heartache.

"Don't you think?"

I blinked back to Aunt Lil. "Think what?"

"That he's been blessed."

"Oh, yeah, I do." I couldn't help another glance. "But it's just so . . . there. So unavoidable." I tore my gaze away and pointed to his tat. "So, the name Andrulis. Does that ring any bells?"

"No, but I can do some investigating. See what turns up. Speaking of which, I have an idea I want to run past you."

I shifted around so I could see her better. "Shoot."

"I think we should work together." She jammed a bony elbow into my side encouragingly, her arm passing through the seat to poke me.

"Ooooh-kay," I said with a light chuckle.

"Ha! I knew it was a good idea." Her face brightened, the grayish tones of life after death lightening just a little.

It could work. We could be the Dynamic Duo. Only without capes, sadly enough. I'd always wanted to do good deeds in a red cape. Or, at the very least, a mauve towel.

After taking another sip of my now lukewarm mocha latte—which was better than no mocha latte any day of the week—I asked, "Are you planning to draw a salary?"

"The way I see it, we should split the take fifty–fifty."

I stifled a grin. "That's the way you see it, huh?"

"Oh, and we probably need code names."

Her suggestion made me choke on my next sip. "Code names?" I asked through the coughs.

"And code phrases like, 'The sun never sets in the east.' That could mean, 'Switch to plan B.' Or it could mean, 'Let's grab a bite to eat before the men come over.'"

"The men?" She'd really thought this through.

"Or it could mean, 'How do you get blood out of silk?' Because as PIs, we'll need to know stuff like that."

"I'm sure you're right." The file caught my attention again, and I turned back to the Foster house. "Blood can be stubborn." Maybe I should just walk up and knock on the door. I could say I was helping a friend with an old case. I could ask if there were any new developments we hadn't been informed of. I could ask if they knew that the man recently released from prison after doing ten years for a crime he didn't commit was their son. I could ask if they knew what he'd been through, what he'd suffered at the hands of the man who raised him. But what good would adding guilt on top of guilt do anybody?

"Are you okay, pumpkin cheeks?"

I shook out of my thoughts. "Yeah, it's just . . . well, two hours down the drain, and for what?" I gestured toward the Fosters' house. "A foot in a sensible shoe driving a sensible car."

She looked across the street toward the house. "What were you hoping to see?"

Her question took me by surprise. Even I wondered what I was really doing there. Did I simply want to see the woman who might have given birth to the man of my dreams? Did I want a glimpse of the man who may have been his human father?

Reyes was the son of Satan, forged in the fires of hell, but he'd been born on earth to be with me. To grow up with me. He'd done his homework and chose a steady, professional couple to be his human parents. He'd planned for us to go to the same schools, shop at the same stores, and eat at the same restaurants. Sadly, even the best-laid plans go awry.

"I'm not really sure, Aunt Lil." What had I been hoping to see? A glimpse of Reyes's past? Of his future? What he would look like in the years to come? Since it had been only a few days since a crazy man tried to kill me, I was trying not to rush terribly headlong into any situation, no matter how innocuous it might seem on the surface. I'd decided to take the week off. Reckless behavior would just have to wait until I'd healed a tad more.

"Goodness, that won't do. You can't just call me Aunt Lil willy-nilly. We'll definitely need code names. What do you think of Cleopatra?"

I chuckled softly. "I think it's perfect."

"Oh! Trench coats! We'll need trench coats!"

"Trench coats?"

"And fedoras!"

Before I could question her further, she was gone. Vanished. Vamoosed. I loved that woman. She took eccentric to a whole new level. Still, I had work to do, and sitting at a stakeout just to catch a glimpse of the Fosters was ridiculous. I started Misery, then picked up the Cheez-Its and stuffed a handful into my mouth the very second the phone rang. Naturally. Because when else would it ring?

I hurried and chewed before answering my bestie's ring. Cookie worked cheap, which made her the best receptionist in all of Albuquerque, in my humble opinion. But she was also very good at her job. I'd set her on the task of finding everything she could about the Fosters. She was as fascinated as I was.

After another quick sip to wash down the crumbs, I finally answered. "Do you think if I lived on Cheez-Its and coffee alone, I'd ultimately starve to death?"

"They had another son," she said, her voice full of awe.

I had no idea what that had to do with my question. "Does he eat Cheez-Its?"

"The Fosters."

I bolted upright. "Can you repeat that?"

"The Fosters had another son."

"No way."

"Way." I heard her fingernails clicking on the keyboard as she worked her magic. "Very much way."

"After Reyes?"

"Yes. Three years after the abduction."

"Do you know what this means?" I asked, my awe matching her own.

"I certainly do."

"Reyes Farrow—"

"—has a brother."

#Holyshit.

2

I sat stewing in a foggy kind of astonishment. Cook did, too. We sat in absolute silence, broken only by the sound of Cheez-Its crunching between my teeth, for several tense seconds.

"Are you still on your stakeout?" Cookie asked at last.

I swallowed. "Yes. I think Mrs. Foster came home, but her garage door closed before I could catch a glimpse. I have, however, bonded with the naked dead man in my passenger seat."

"Well, there's that."

"Right? He has a tat. I'm sending you a picture."

"Of his tat?" she asked, surprised.

"Of my drawing of his tat. Hold on." I sent the pic with the caption *Don't judge* underneath it. "Okay, how are things back at the fort?"

"A Mr. Joyce came in and insisted on seeing you today. He seemed really agitated. He wouldn't leave his number or anything. I told him you'd be back this afternoon. Is this a new kind of Rorschach test?" She was referring to my drawing.

"Turn it sideways."

"Oh, okay. Andrulis."

"Do you know him?" I asked, my voice edged with hope.

"Nope. Sorry. I knew an Andrus once. He was hairy."

I checked out Mr. A. "This guy isn't that hairy. He is well endowed, though."

"Charley," she said, appalled. "Get your mind out of the gutter."

"Dude, it's right there. It's not like I can miss it."

"Oh, poor man. How would you like to be walking around naked for all eternity?"

"You just described my worst nightmare."

"I thought your worst nightmare was that one where you are eating a hot pickle and it burned your lips and they swelled until you looked like you'd had injections."

"Oh, yeah, there's that one, too. Thanks for bringing all that back up again. I should sleep beautifully tonight."

"Did you call your uncle?"

My uncle Bob, a detective for the Albuquerque Police Department, had the hots for Cookie, and Cookie had the hots for him—but neither one would make the first move. I got so tired of watching them pine for each other that I decided to do something about it. I set Cookie up on a date with a friend of mine to make Uncle Bob, or Ubie as I liked to call him in my therapy sessions while trying to explain why I had a debilitating fear of mustaches, jealous. Maybe a little competition would light a fire under his ass. The same ass Cookie had a major thing for.

"Sure did. How's our plan coming along?"

"You mean *your* plan?"

"Fine, how's *my* plan coming along?"

"I don't know about this, Charley. I mean, if Robert wanted to go out with me, he'd ask, right? I'm not sure trying to make him jealous is a good idea."

It always took me a minute to figure out who Robert was. "Are you kidding? It's a fantastic idea. It's Uncle Bob we're talking about here. He needs motivation." I gave one last glance to the Fosters' house before driving off.

"What if he loses interest?"

"Cook, have you ever lost interest in a pair of shoes because someone else was looking at them?"

"I guess not."

"Didn't it make you want them even more?"

"I wouldn't go that far."

I turned onto Juan Tabo and started back toward the office. "Okay, I'm headed that way. How about lunch?"

"Sounds good. I'll meet you downstairs."

My office was on the second floor of the best brewery the Duke City had to offer. It'd recently undergone a change of ownership when Reyes bought it from my dad. The idea of Reyes as a business owner warmed the cockles of my heart. Whatever those were.

"He has a brother," I said, still stunned at the possibilities of it all.

"He has a brother," she agreed.

This I had to see.

I wound around tables and chairs to get to Cookie. Fortunately, she'd grabbed us a spot before the mad rush hit. Ever since Reyes took over, the place had been jumping. Business was always pretty good, but with a new owner who was also a local celebrity— Reyes made national news when the man he'd gone to jail for killing was discovered alive—and the addition of a brewery in the building adjacent to the bar, patronage had tripled. Now the place was packed with men who wanted the fresh brews and women who wanted the brewer himself. Hussies.

I walked stiffly past the worst hussy of them all: my former BFF, who'd apparently decided to move in. Jessica had been at the restaurant every day for over two weeks. Most days more than once. I knew she was hot for my man, but holy cow.

Clearly, I'd have to say yes to Reyes soon. This was getting ridiculous. He needed a ring on his finger—and fast. Not that that would stop them all, but hopefully it would thin out the horde.

A tatter of giggles erupted from Jessica's table as I passed. She was probably telling them the tale of Charley Davidson, the girl who claimed to talk to dead people. If she only knew. Then again, if she were to die soon, I'd totally ignore her. She'd want me to talk to her then.

"You brought me a flower," Cookie said as I plopped down across from her, collapsing into the seat with a dramatic flair I usually reserved for the evening cocktail hour.

"Sure did." I handed the daisy over to her.

"So, a homeless guy?"

I nodded. "Yeah. He was at the corner up the street and walked through traffic to hand it to me."

"How much?" she asked, a knowing smirk on her face.

"Five."

"You paid five dollars for this? It's plastic. And filthy." She shook it to get the layer of dirt off. "He probably stole it off someone's grave."

"It was all I had on me."

She shook her head in disappointment. "How can they always pick the suckers out of a crowd?"

"No clue. Did you order?"

"Not yet. I was just glad to get a table. That man came back in, Mr. Joyce. He's still agitated and was not happy you wouldn't be back to the office until one."

"Well, he'll just have to hold his horses. PIs have to eat, too."

"And I see your bestie is back again."

I glanced back at Jessica's table. "I think she should have to pay rent."

"I concur wholeheartedly."

A slow warmth spread over me as I spoke. The heat that forever surrounded Reyes curled around me like smoke. I could feel him near. His interest scorching. His hunger undeniable. But before I could seek him out, another emotion hit me. A cooler one, harder though no less powerful: regret. I turned and watched as my dad made his way to our table.

"Hey, Dad," I said, nudging a chair with my foot.

He pushed it back to the table. "I just came in to finish up the last of the paperwork." He looked around Calamity's. "I think I'll miss this place."

I was sure he would, but nostalgia was not the emotion I felt emanating from him.

"Why don't you sit down, Leland?" Cookie asked.

He snapped back to us. "That's okay. I have a few errands to run before I head out."

"Dad," I said, my lungs struggling for air underneath the oppressive sadness and regret pouring out of him, "you don't have to go." He was leaving my stepmother for a sailboat. Not that I blamed him. A sailboat would at least be useful. But why now? Why after all these years?

He waved off my reservations. "No, this will be great. I've always wanted to learn how to sail."

"So, you start by planning a trip across the Atlantic?"

"Not across," he said, his smile a ploy to set my mind at ease. "Not all the way."

"Dad—"

"I'll take it slow. I promise."

"But why? Why all of a sudden?"

He released a hapless sigh. "I don't know. I'm not getting any younger, and you only live once. Or, maybe twice in my case."

"I had nothing to do with that."

"You had everything to do with it," he countered, and placed a hand over his heart. "I know it. I feel it in here."

He swore I'd cured him of cancer, but I'd never healed anyone in my life. It wasn't in my job description. I dealt more with the other side of life. The after side.

"Don't leave her because of me. Please." If he was leaving my step-mother for my benefit, because of how she treated me, he was a day late and a dollar short. He should have done it when I was seven, not twenty-seven. I could handle her. I'd learned how the hard way.

Cookie pretended to be studying the menu as Dad shifted uncom-fortably.

"I'm not, pumpkin."

"I think you are." When he dropped his gaze to the sugar jar instead of answering, I added, "And if that's the case, you're doing it for the wrong reason. I'm a big girl, Dad."

When he looked back at me, his expression held a desperate passion. "You're amazing. I should have told you that every day."

I put my hand over his. "Dad, please sit down. Let's talk about this."

He checked his watch. "I have an appointment. I'll come see you before I leave. We'll talk then." When I narrowed my eyes on him, he added, "I promise. Take care, pumpkin." He bent and kissed my cheek before head-ing out the back door.

"He seems very sad," Cookie said.

"He's lost, I think. Consumed with regret."

"Are you okay?"

I drew in a deep breath. "I'm always okay."

"Mm-hmm." The doubt in her expression only fueled my need to mock her in public.

"So, what made you think fuchsia pinstripes would look good with yellow?"

"You're deflecting."

"Duh. It's what I do. What's today's special?"

"True. But really," she said, straightening. "Does this look bad?"

She looked fantastic, but I could hardly tell her that.

I'd felt Reyes near me, watching the interaction with my dad. I spotted him when I looked toward the board that listed the daily special. He was wearing an apron and had a towel in his hands, drying them as he pushed off the bar and strolled toward us.

Cookie saw him, too. "Holy mother of all things sexy," she said, her eyes drinking him in.

"Right there with ya."

"Will I ever get used to that sight?" she asked me, not daring to take her eyes off him.

"The adorable sight of Reyes Farrow in an apron?"

"The adorable sight of Reyes Farrow period."

A giggle escaped me before I said, "Well, you know what they say: Practice makes perfect."

"Exactly. I'll need lots of practice."

"Me, too."

A table of women old enough to be his grandmothers waved him down before he got to us. He stopped and listened to them gush over his cooking but kept his sparkling gaze on me. It stole my breath. Everything about him stole my breath. From the way he dried his hands on that towel to the way he lowered his lashes shyly when they propositioned him.

They propositioned him!

What the bloody—!

"We're very limber," one of them said, pulling on the apron string Reyes had wrapped around his waist and tied in front.

Cookie was in the middle of taking a much-needed drink of cold water and burst into a fit of coughs at the woman's brazenness.

When Reyes looked back at me, he caught me with my mouth open in astonishment. I slammed it shut, hoping I hadn't in any way resembled a cow. But he turned back to the women as though suddenly interested in the wares they were peddling. As if.

Cookie wheezed beside me, trying to get air through her abused esophagus, but I couldn't worry about that now. I had to win my man back from these silver foxes. One of them had a walker, for goodness' sake. How limber could she be?

"Excuse me, busboy," I said, snapping my fingers in the air to get his attention.

He ignored me, but I caught the grin he was wearing. I also felt the pleasure my attention gave him. It radiated from his essence and brushed over my skin like hot silk.

"Busboy," I repeated, snapping more loudly. "Over here."

He finally apologized to the flirty foxes, explaining that his heart belonged to another before he strolled to our table. "Busboy?" he asked, stopping in front of us and leveling a look of concern on a red-faced Cookie.

She took another sip and waved a hello.

I gestured to his apron. "You look like a busboy."

"In that case, can I clean anything for you?"

"You can clean your dirty mind," I said, teasing him. "Having fun?" I indicated the table with a nod.

"They were complimenting my cooking." He leaned in very close. "According to consensus, I'm really good at scrambling things."

They'd nailed that one. He was really good at scrambling my insides. My emotions. My girlie bits. "That's wonderful," I said, pretending not to care, "but we need lunch."

"Didn't you hear? I've been demoted to busboy, so you'll have to ask your server about lunch. I don't think busboys can take orders."

I pulled the apron string in much the same way as the flirt did. "You'll take my order, and you'll like it."

A soft, deep laugh reverberated out of him. "Yes, ma'am. Can I suggest the Santa Fe chicken with Spanish rice?"

"You can, but I'll have the margarita chicken with fries smothered in red chile."

"I'll have the Santa Fe chicken," Cookie said quickly, so falling for his ploy. He'd probably ordered too many chickens from Santa Fe and now had to hand-sell them to get rid of them. How different could chickens raised in Santa Fe be?

He flashed her a grin that was so beautiful, my heart skipped several pertinent beats. "Santa Fe chicken, it is. Would you like iced tea with that?" he asked me. When I hesitated, trying to decide between tea and an extra-large nonfat mocha macchiato with caramel sauce on the bottom and a dollop of whipped cream, he said, "It's a yes/no question."

I almost burst out laughing. Ever since he proposed to me on a sticky note, he'd been asking me a lot of yes/no questions to reiterate the fact that his proposal was also a yes/no question.

I shrugged. "Sometimes it's not that black-and-white."

"Sure it is."

Cookie, knowing where this was headed, decided to study her menu again.

"Then my answer is yes."

He stilled, waiting for the punch line. He knew me very well.

"Yes, I'll have tea with my lunch and an extra-large nonfat mocha macchiato with caramel sauce on the bottom and a dollop of whipped cream after."

Without missing a beat, he said, "Tea, it is."

He started to turn, but I stopped him with a hand on his arm.

"Are you okay?" I asked. "You seem—" I lowered my voice. "—warmer than usual."

"I'm always okay," he said, mimicking what I'd said to Cookie earlier. He caught my hand in his and brought the back of it to his lips, kissing it softly. The heat from his mouth was searing.

It wasn't until Reyes walked away that I realized the room had grown silent. Every eye was on us. Well, every female eye was on us. I glanced at Jessica and our gazes locked for an uncomfortable moment. She was jealous, and that fact didn't make me happy. Why was she jealous when she didn't have any claim to Reyes? Then again, jealousy was in a whole category by itself. One that sat right between instability and insecurity. But her jealously raked across my skin like fingernails.

Jealousy from Reyes was one thing, but jealousy from humans had a different taste, a different texture. It was hot and abrasive, like putting on scratchy burlap clothes right out of the dryer.

"When are you going to answer him?" Cookie asked, drawing my attention.

"When he deserves an answer," I volleyed.

"So, saving your life countless times doesn't warrant an answer?"

"Sure it does, but he doesn't need to know that."

One corner of her mouth tilted mischievously. "True."

And that was one thing I never felt from Cookie. Jealousy. She was just as hot for Reyes as anyone, but she was never jealous of our relationship. She was happy for me, and therein lay the heart of a true friend. I'd thought Jessica was my best friend, but looking back with my 20/20 hindsight, I realized I'd felt jealousy radiate from her on several occasions in school. That should have been a clue, but I'd never been accused of being the brightest bedspread in the hotel.

"Okay, how are you going to get him over?"

"Well, since he lives right next door, I thought I'd just pound on the wall."

"Not Reyes. Robert."

Who was Robert again? Oh, right. "You let me worry about Uncle Bob."

Cookie was getting nervous for the seven millionth time, so I went through my plan again from beginning to end. I loved going over it anyway. Mostly because it was brilliant, but also because if Cookie didn't go along with it, all that brilliance would go down the drain, kind of like my self-esteem every time I ran into Jessica.

"This first date is just the primer. I'll get him over right as your date is picking you up. He'll be so blindsided, he won't know how to react. What to say." I giggled like a mental patient at that. "I'll explain to him that you joined a dating service."

"What?" Cookie balked. "He'll think I'm desperate."

"He'll think you're ready for a relationship."

"A desperate one." She fanned herself with the menu, her doubt evident in every swish.

"Cook, lots of people join dating services. It doesn't have the stigma it used to."

"Then what?"

"Then you'll go on another date."

"With the same guy?"

"Nope, a different guy."

Fear caused panic to spike inside her. "What? Who? You said this would be quick and painless."

"It will be. I'm not sure who date number two will be. I have only so many friends who will let me use them unscrupulously."

Cookie groaned.

"This will work, Cook. Unless you want to do something really crazy and just ask him out yourself?"

"I couldn't," she said, shaking her head vehemently. "What if he says no? And then it would be really awkward between us for the rest of our lives. We'd have those awkward silences that make my eyebrows sweat."

"Oh, yeah, those are pretty awful. Anywho, it's date number three that will be the clincher. If he doesn't ask you out before then, we may have to hire an actor."

"An actor?"

"Cook, we've already been through this. Why are you questioning everything?"

"I think I've been in denial. But now that it's really happening, I feel like those people who say they can bungee jump, but when they're actually standing on the bridge, the reality of the situation hits them in the face."

"Yeah, never bungee jump. Reality isn't the only thing that hits you in the face."

"At least the bungee rope didn't leave a scar."

"Thank goodness. So, for date number three, we need someone good. Someone who can be sexy and a butthead at the same time. Someone—" It hit me before I even finished the thought. "I got it."

Cookie lunged forward. "Who?"

A slow, evil grin spread across my face. "Never you mind, missy. If we get that far, you'll know soon enough. In the meantime, I have some bargaining to do."

A loud bout of laughter echoed around me, and I glanced toward Jessica's table. She was with the same three friends she was always with, and it made me wonder what they did for a living. They came to lunch here together almost every day. And were often here in the evenings as well. Did none of them have families? Responsibilities? A life?

I thought back to our big blowup in high school. Jessica had said some pretty nasty things. She'd turned on me so fast, my neck hurt. As well as my heart. A fact that she seemed to revel in. When I confronted her and asked her point-blank why she didn't want to be friends, she told me I had no redeeming qualities. What the hell did that mean?

Cookie noticed where I was looking. She patted my hand to draw me back.

"Do you think I have redeeming qualities?"

She curled my fingers into hers. "You're totally redeemable. You're like a thirty percent–off coupon. No! A forty percent–off coupon. And I don't say that lightly."

"Thanks."

Again, I felt Reyes's heat before I saw him. He brought out our food personally, a service Jessica and her friends didn't receive. Neither did the silver foxes, though they didn't seem to mind. They kept winking at him, and one licked her lips suggestively. It was so wrong.

"Oh," I said after he set our plates down, "I forgot to ask you. If you were a utensil, what would you be?"

He straightened. "Excuse me?"

"A utensil. What would you be?"

He crossed his arms over his chest, then asked suspiciously, "Why do you want to know?"

"It's for a quiz. It's guaranteed to let us know if we are compatible. You know, for the long haul."

"Really?" he asked. He pulled out a chair, turned it around, and straddled it to sit with us. "You have to take a quiz to see if we're compatible?"

"Yes," I said, trying to recover from that last move. He was just too sexy, straddling that chair, crossing his sinewy arms over the back of it. "Yes. This stuff is important, and they have a ninety-nine percent success rate. It said so." I dragged out my phone, brought up the online quiz, and held it out to him. "Right here. See?"

He didn't even spare it a glance. Cookie was busy cutting into her Santa Fe chicken and fending off an inappropriate smirk.

"You can't trust anything on the Internet."

"Can, too," I said, completely offended.

"So, if I posted a comment saying I was an Arabian prince from Milwaukee?"

"Yeah, but you're a big fat liar. You don't count. I mean, look at your dad. Pathological liar *numeral uno*. Lying is in your genes."

He leaned forward. "There's only one thing in my jeans right now."

"Are you going to take my question seriously or not? This could be the key to our futures."

"I have a key in my jeans pocket. You could search."

He was completely blowing off our chance at happiness. "What are you, twelve?"

"Centuries, maybe."

"You're twelve centuries old?"

He winced. "You know how older women say they are twenty-nine?"

"Yeah."

"Well, I'm kind of doing that."

"No, really, how old are you? Wait!" A thought hit me. Hard. Like a baseball thrown from the pitcher's plate at Wrigley Field. "How old am I?" I hadn't really thought of it in those terms. I was supposedly from an ancient race of beings from another universe, another plane of existence. How old was I?

"A machete," he said, getting up and righting the chair.

"What?"

"If I were a utensil."

"Does that count as a utensil?"

He winked at me. "It does in my world."

"Okay, fine. I'd be a . . . a spork! Wait, what does that mean? I'm not sure a machete and a spork are very compatible."

He took hold of my chin and lifted my face to his. "I have a feeling a machete and a spork can work very well together."

Before I could argue, he bent and pressed his mouth to mine. The heat scorched at first, then penetrated my skin and spread through me like warm honey. The kiss, barely a peck, ended too soon as he rose, surprised Cookie with a quick kiss on her cheek, and went back to the kitchen, giving me a spectacular view of his ass.

Cookie gasped and touched the spot where Reyes's lips had brushed, stars bursting from her eyes. "I want that," she said, suddenly determined.

I looked back toward the door Reyes had disappeared through. "Well, you can't have it. It's mine."

"No, not that. Not him." She shook out of her stupor and said, "I mean, yeah, I'd take him in a heartbeat, but I want that. I want what you two have, damn it." She set her jaw. "Let's do this. Let's set up that stubborn, rascally uncle of yours until he begs me to be his girl."

"Yeah, Cookie," I said, raising my hand for a high five, but she floundered. "Don't leave me hangin'."

"But what if he doesn't ask me out?"

After waving toward a couple I didn't know who'd just stepped in the front door to save my dignity, I lowered my hand and said, "I think the more important question is, do you think a machete and a spork are very compatible?"

"Charley, you have to quit taking those ridiculous quizzes."

"No way. I have to know."

"Fine, but why a spork?"

"Because I'm versatile. I can multitask like nobody's business. And I like the way it sounds. It's so . . . sporky."

3

Coffee doesn't ask silly questions.
Coffee understands.

—BUMPER STICKER

We weren't back in the office ten minutes before the door to the front entrance opened. I'd expected Mr. Joyce, the agitated man with the issues. Instead I got Denise. My evil stepmother. Thankfully, Mr. Joyce was right behind her. He afforded me the perfect excuse not to talk to her.

Her pallor had a grayish tint to it, and her eyes were lined with the bright red only the shedding of tears could evoke. I honestly didn't know she had the ability to cry.

"Can I talk to you?" she asked.

"I have a client." I pointed to the man behind her to emphasize that fact.

Giving her chin a determined upward thrust, she said, "You've had clients for two weeks now. I just need a minute." When I started to argue again, she pleaded with me. "Please, Charlotte."

Mr. Joyce was holding a baseball cap, wringing it in his hands. He seemed to be growing more agitated by the second. "I really need to talk to you, Ms. Davidson."

"See?" I pinned Denise with a chastising scowl. "Client."

She turned on the man, her face as cold and hard as marble. It was an expression I knew all too well. "We just need a minute," she said to him, her tone razor sharp. "Then she's all yours."

He backed off, raising a hand in surrender as he stepped to a chair and took a seat.

My temper flared to life, and I had to force myself to stay calm. I was twenty-seven. I no longer had to put up with my stepmother's insults. Her revulsion. Her petty snubs. And I damned sure didn't have to put up with her invading my business and bullying my clients. "That was not necessary," I said to her when she turned back to me.

"I apologize," she said, doing a one-eighty. She turned back to Mr. Joyce. "I'm sorry. I'm in a very desperate situation."

"Tell me about it," he said, dismissing her with a wave. He clearly had problems of his own.

With all the enthusiasm of a prisoner walking up to the hangman's noose, I led Denise into my office and closed the door. My temper flaring must have summoned Reyes. He was in my office, waiting, incorporeally.

Then I remembered. He didn't like Denise any more than I did. Blamed her for most of my heartache as a child. Of course, she'd caused most of it, but Reyes could be . . . testy when it came to my happiness or lack thereof.

"Want me to sever her spine?" he asked as I sat behind my desk.

"Can I think about it and get back to you?" I asked, teasing. Kind of.

Denise looked toward the wall he was leaning against, the one I was looking at, and naturally saw nothing. But where her usual response would be to purse her lips in disapproval, she wiped at her lapel and sat down instead.

"What do you want?" I asked her, my tone as cold as her heart.

"I'm sure you know that your father has left me."

"At last."

She flinched like I'd slapped her. "Why would you say such a thing?"

"Are you really asking me that?"

"I love your father." She almost came up out of her chair. "I've always loved your father."

She had me there. She'd always been an attentive wife to him. Of course, *attentive* included her agenda, which was manipulative, conniving, and venomous. I couldn't believe that I could dislike someone so much, but Denise had always been that splinter in my relationship with my father. She did everything in her power to keep us apart. Her jealousy was bizarre and childish. Who on earth was afraid of a father's love for his child? It just made no sense to me. It never had.

And yet she was never that way toward my sister, Gemma. In fact, she and Gemma were fairly close. I had a feeling Dad's leaving Denise affected Gemma much more than she was willing to admit. She knew how I felt about our stepmonster, and the fact that she couldn't go to me when she needed support made me a very bad sibling. But the truth was, she couldn't. I had no warm and fuzzies where Denise was concerned. She'd made sure of that from day one.

"I—I need you to talk to him. He's been sick and, and he's not thinking straight."

"And what do you want me to say?"

She leveled an exasperated glare on me. "I want you to convince him to come back home where he belongs. He's still weak. He still needs medical attention."

"I'm sorry," I said with a soft, humorless chuckle, "you want me to convince my father to stay with you? The bane of my existence? The woman who made my childhood a living hell? After everything you've put me through, you want my help? Are you insane?"

Too bad Gemma, a licensed psychiatrist, was at a conference in D.C. I'd call her and schedule an appointment for Denise ay-sap.

"What have I ever put you through?"

My temper flared again, and I bit my tongue, literally, to keep my emotions under control. When I lost control, the earth shifted beneath me. An earthquake in the middle of Albuquerque would do no one any good.

Reyes straightened as though worried I'd lose control as well. I closed my eyes and took several gulps of air. This wasn't me. I didn't hate people. I didn't make them pay for their misdeeds. Too many departed had crossed through me. Too many times I'd seen what people went through, what they'd endured that made them become the people they were when they died. Until I'd walked a mile in her shoes, I could not judge Denise so completely. That would make me no better than she was. I opened my eyes to her stone face, the face that brought nothing but hurt feelings and knotted stomachaches. Maybe two miles.

"I just have one question," I said, trying to hold the resentment from my tone lest I sound like her. "Why?"

"Why?"

"Yes, why? Why did you hate me from day one? Why did you treat me like a thorn in your side? What on God's green earth did I ever do to you?"

She sighed in frustration and let her true colors show through. Her impatience with me, with anything I had to say. "I did no such thing, Charlotte. I don't hate you. I never have."

I leaned forward and gave her my best Sunday smile. "I'll tell you what. When you can admit that you hate me with every fiber of your being, I'll help you win back Dad. How does that sound?"

"I will never say such a horrible thing."

I'd offended her. Sweet. "So you can feel it, you just can't admit to it?"

She squeezed the pocketbook in her lap, her fingers flexing involuntarily. "Charlotte, can we talk sensibly?"

"Wait a minute," I said as understanding dawned. "You're here because

Dad is fed up with the way you treat me, and you're thinking that if we become besties, he'll come back to you."

"I'm here because I want us all to get into counseling together. Not just Leland and me, but all four of us, including your sister." Reyes crossed his arms over his chest and went back to holding the wall up while I stood simmering in my astonishment.

She was a piece of work. "How about you go into counseling for you? Get over yourself. And when that happens, when you can be honest with me, we'll talk again." I was being so mean. I wanted to applaud myself. I wasn't a mean person by nature, so it took a lot of energy to bring out the beast in me and stick with it for more than thirty seconds. Damned ADD. But I was so proud of myself. No more being a carpet for someone else to walk on. I was my own girl, and no one was walking on this carpet but me.

"Charley," Cookie said through the intercom.

I poked the button. "Yes, Cookie?"

"Um, are you almost done? I need coffee."

"Oh, sorry! I'll get it made and bring you a cup."

"Thanks. And can you bring me the box of Nilla Wafers while you're at it?"

"Can do." I jumped up and headed for the Bunn. "Priorities," I said to Denise. "That's what life is all about." I filled the tank with water and scooped coffee into the basket. "And coffee. From now on, I am my own priority." I picked up the box, fished out a Nilla wafer, and stuffed it into my mouth so I could talk with it full. "No more Chawley cawpet." Or, well, mumble with my mouth full. Denise hated that shit. "Chawley—" I swallowed. "—Charley carpet has been ripped up, and the only thing left for people to walk on is cracked, splintered wood." God, I was good at metaphors.

"I tried," she said, rising and perching her purse strap on her shoulder.

"Yes. Yes, you did. And a noble effort it was." I gestured toward the door, hoping she'd take the hint. "I'm not sure what all this is about, anyway. It's not like we could really go into counseling. He's leaving soon for the open sea."

She turned back to me, her face full of surprise. She blinked and I felt an understanding wash over her; then she plastered on a fake smile, one full of pity with a heaving sprinkling of contempt. One I had seen far too many times in my twenty-seven years. "And here I thought you could detect lies."

She strode to the door and opened it before I could stop her. "Wait. What lies?"

"I'll tell you what," she said, turning the tables, reveling in the power she'd just acquired. "When you can grow up and take a little of the responsibility for our failed relationship, I'll tell you what your father's really up to."

Without another word, she walked out, leaving me speechless.

What my father was really up to? What did she mean by that? Unfortunately, I didn't have time to investigate now, but Uncle Bob and I were going to have a long talk the minute I was finished with Mr. Joyce. In fact, that would be my excuse to get him to go over to my apartment that evening. Nothing like killing two birds with one stone. But that sounded so bad. What did those poor birds do to anyone? I decided to change that particular cliché to "Nothing like killing two bad guys with one bullet." Better. Maybe it would catch on, become accepted worldwide. A girl could dream.

Mr. Joyce was already standing, waiting his turn with the impatience of a kindergartner waiting for his afternoon snack.

"Come on in," I said to him, gesturing to the chair across from my desk as I headed to the Bunn to complete my promise to Cookie. She'd need CPR if I didn't get her a cup soon. "So, what can I help you with?"

I poured Cookie's cup, knowing full well she was interrupting my "meeting" with Denise only to save me from her. I adored that woman. Cookie! Not Denise. After taking the coffee to her and handing her the box of wafers with a wink, I started to close the door between our offices as she took a sip of the piping fresh brew. She rolled her eyes until I saw only white. It was kind of creepy. We were kindred spirits to the core.

"It's a little embarrassing," Mr. Joyce said after I offered him a cup, poured my own, then sat behind my desk. Reyes had disappeared as he was wont to do once any immediate danger was dispelled.

"Why don't you start from the beginning?" I felt the agitation he was sporting externally, but I also felt anxiety and extreme fear. Like gut-wrenching fear.

"Um, okay." He twisted the baseball cap in his hands before pinning me with his gaze, taking a deep breath, and blurting out, "I sold my soul to the devil and I need you to get it back for me."

That was new.

I blinked a few times, took a slow sip, then asked, "Did it fetch a good price?"

"What?" he asked, surprised by my reaction.

"Your soul. What'd you get for it?"

He bit down and charged forward. "Ms. Davidson, I'm not kidding."

"I can see that."

"I've talked to a few—" He glanced around, worried we'd be overheard. "—*individuals* in your field, and they all recommended I hire you. Said if anyone could get it back, you could."

"Really? And what kind of individuals are in my field?"

"You know," he said, setting his ball cap on my desk and easing forward to whisper. "The supernatural kind."

"Ah. Right. Because they're on every street corner. So, this demon you sold your soul to—"

"Devil," he corrected, punching the air with an index finger. "He was the devil."

"Okay, first of all, the *devil* is never on this plane this time of year, so if the guy who bought your soul says he's the boss man himself, he's lying."

"Seriously?" he asked, surprised. "Well, maybe he didn't say he was the devil, but he had powers, you know? He had an intensity I felt every time he looked at me, like the weight of it alone could crush me. And he has my soul. It's gone. I can't feel it anymore." He patted his clothes as though searching for his wallet.

Wonderful. Mr. Joyce was crazy. I took out a pen and pad. "Okay, can you describe your soul in detail? I'll put out a BOLO."

He leaned back, annoyed with me. It happened. "I thought that you of all people would understand."

I put down my pen. "Why me of all people?"

"I know what you are," he said. "He told me."

"The devil told you?"

"No, the guy." He raked a hand through his hair. "The guy who took my soul. Maybe he just took it for the devil. I don't know."

As entertaining as this was, I needed to call Uncle Bob and ask him what was going on with my dad. No way did I call Dad. If he didn't want me to know something, I damned sure didn't know.

"Okay, well, thanks for coming in, Mr. Joyce, but—"

"Hedeshi!" he shouted, remembering a name. A name that I knew well.

"Hedeshi is dead," I said, wondering how he knew the name of the demon sent to kill me. Thankfully, I had the son of Satan and a guardian departed Rottweiler named Artemis backing me up, or I wouldn't have been there at all.

"Right, he told me about Hedeshi. Said he was dead. During the card game, he'd—"

"Card game?"

"The poker game," he said, growing more agitated by the second. "The one where I lost my soul."

I clasped my fingers together. "Let me get this straight. You gambled your soul away?"

"Well . . . no. Not exactly. I needed money. He knew it. Used it against me." Shame washed over him in one bright-hot wave. "It was for a good cause. I needed money and he had the highest game in town, so I took a chance. I hocked everything we had just to get a seat at the table, and then I lost every penny." He scrubbed his forehead, embarrassed. "When he saw how distressed I was, he made me an offer I couldn't refuse, so I said yes. I sold him my soul."

"Of course you did. Hedeshi," I reminded him.

He squinted his eyes, trying to remember. "The guy, the dealer, said there was a grim reaper in town wreaking all kinds of havoc on his brethren. Said you managed to kill one of the top generals from hell, a man named Hedeshi."

How on earth did some dealer from an illicit card game know that? "And how do you know I'm this grim reaper?"

"Because everyone told me," he said, his voice getting louder. "Look, can you just go talk to this guy? Just get it back? I'll pay you."

"I thought you didn't have any money. That was why you were at the card game in the first place."

"Yeah, well, I got some. I got a lot. Selling one's soul is very profitable." He bowed his head, and the heartache that spread through him stung the backs of my eyes. "Turns out even money can't cure cancer."

Son of a bitch. The big C. My most hated enemy.

"Look, I just need my soul. He can have everything back. I just need my soul to be with her. I promised."

So, a woman he loved had died, and now he wanted his soul back so he could be with her. That was also new.

"You're the only one who's ever stood up to one of these guys. No one else will even try."

"There's a good reason for that. They're rather deadly."

"I'll do anything. You can have it all. The money. The cars. Everything. My husband and I are devastated."

And once again, I was taken aback. Just when I thought I knew what was going on. "Your husband?"

"Yes. Paul. We got married in Massachusetts the minute they legalized it."

"Then who is this 'she' you promised to spend eternity with?"

The huge tears shimmering in his eyes as he looked up at me stole my breath and my heart in the same moment. "Our daughter. She was only three when she passed away from neuroblastoma. I got her the best medical care money could buy, but it made no difference." He took out his wallet and retrieved a picture out of it. Two actually. Handing them to me, he asked, "Do you know what it's like watching a three-year-old girl die of cancer? She was so brave. She only wanted one thing—our promise that we'd be with her in heaven someday." His voice broke as I studied the pictures. A gorgeous girl with blond ringlets and huge blue eyes graced the first one. The second one had been taken after a few rounds of chemo, her bald head, no less beautiful, shining in the sun as she flew down a slide, her smile as wide as the New Mexico sky. "We both promised her we'd see her again. Paul doesn't know what I did for all of this. He doesn't know I can't keep our promise."

I wasn't sure if it was his sorrow or mine that formed a lump the size of a softball in my throat. Either way, I couldn't stop the emergence of tears as I gazed at the angel in her fathers' arms. "When did she pass?" I managed to ask, my chest tightening.

"Yesterday." And with that, he collapsed into a mass of tears, sobbing into his hands uncontrollably. I rounded the desk, wrapped my arms around his shoulders, and sobbed with him. This was the part I didn't handle well. The people-left-behind part. Their sorrow was like a boulder on my chest.

I felt Reyes, felt his heat before the door opened and he stepped inside. He didn't interrupt. He stood back and watched over me as I let the pain of death crush me into dust.

4

My boyfriend called me a stalker.
Well, he's not actually my boyfriend . . .

—STATUS UPDATE

I led Mr. Joyce to the door and promised I'd do whatever I could. I still had no idea if he was crazy or not, but I planned to find out.

"What have we got?" Cookie asked, her voice soft.

"We have a client who sold his soul to the devil."

"Another one?"

She knew just what to say. A little embarrassed, I graced her with the best smile I could conjure under the circumstances. "Exactly. When will these guys ever learn?" I looked over at Reyes, who'd stood watch the whole time. I was more than a little embarrassed that he'd witnessed my breakdown. "Is that even possible?"

"It's possible," he said. I felt genuine regret emanating off him.

"Then I have a card game to go to."

He pushed off the wall and followed me as I grabbed my bag and headed out the door. "You're not serious."

I stopped and leveled a determined gaze on him. "I'm as serious as neuroblastoma."

He bit back a reply, knowing it would do him no good. He was learning.

I paused at Cookie's desk. "You're not wearing that tonight, are you?"

"What's wrong with this?"

"Nothing. If you're running away to join the circus."

She gasped, then narrowed her lids threateningly. "I should have locked you in your office with your stepmother instead of using these ridiculous intercoms you insisted on buying at that horrid estate sale and coming to your rescue."

It was my turn to gasp. I also jutted out my index finger accusingly for dramatic flair. "That estate sale rocked. Who doesn't love a good taxidermist's collection?"

She shivered at the reminder.

"And those intercoms aren't half as ridiculous as that outfit."

Her expression hardened and I felt the weight of sorrow lift. God bless her. I winked knowingly then strode out of the office to prepare for tonight.

But first, Uncle Bob.

I accepted a card that read LIVE FREE OR DIE from a homeless man with leathery skin and several missing teeth. In return, I gave him what little change I had in my pocket as I walked across the parking lot to my apartment building. And it was literally *my* apartment building. Reyes had bought it for me. I had no idea what to do with it, but I loved that it was mine.

"You aren't going to that game," Reyes said as he stalked behind me.

"Sure am."

Heat from his anger rose around me. A lot of heat.

I whirled around to face him. "What is the problem?"

He kept coming until he was only inches away from me. "You. It's like you search out the worst, most dangerous situations to go into, then rush to get there without a second thought."

"I have second thoughts," I said, and turned to continue my journey to the building. "And sometimes I even have third and fourth thoughts, too."

He grabbed my arm before I'd taken two steps. "This isn't funny."

I made a pointed effort to look down at his hand, the one holding my arm, before refocusing on his face again. "No, it isn't."

He let go of my arm. "You can't save every desperate soul out there, Dutch." When I started toward the building again, he stepped in my path. "You're going to get yourself killed if you try, and I'll be stuck here alone, all because I'm in love with a bleeding heart who'd rather risk her life for strangers than listen to anything I have to say."

I shifted my weight to one leg, jutting out a hip. "You're in love with me?"

He stepped close again and rested a hand on my jutting hip. "You know I am."

"I know. But the heat of your anger is going to burn you alive."

He ran his tongue along his lower lip as he studied me. "Maybe I have a fever."

Suddenly worried, I reached up and felt his forehead. Blisteringly hot, but when wasn't he?

He tested his forehead himself. "See? I probably need a sponge bath," he said, turning playful.

As sexy as that lopsided grin of his was, I was starting to get worried. I felt his forehead again. "Do you really have a fever?"

"Ever since the first time I saw you."

I couldn't help but giggle at that. "Seriously, Reyes. Are you feeling bad?"

"Only when you're not near me."

"Do you get sick?"

"Every time we're apart."

This was getting me exactly nowhere. He was deflecting on purpose. "Fine. But I'm going to that card game. I totally have a plan," I said, side-stepping past him.

"Because your plans always work so well." He followed me inside and up the stairs.

"That's not fair."

"Dutch, I'm not kidding. Dealers are not what you think."

"Dealers?" I stopped on the stairs and gaped at him. "You knew about him? You knew he was here?"

"No, not exactly, but I do know they exist. And if he really is a Dealer, he's very, very clever. He could convince a mother to sell her children into slavery for a dime."

"I can't believe a being like that actually exists. So it really is possible to sell your soul to the devil?"

He nodded. "And you don't even have to go to the crossroads to do it."

"Holy cow. How do I not know these things?" I continued up the stairs while foraging in my bag for my keys.

"It's not really what you think," Reyes added. "There's a lot you don't know, and there's a lot you don't need to know, like how to handle a Dealer."

"So, what are they, exactly?"

"They are demons. The Fallen."

"Like Hedeshi?"

"Very much like Hedeshi, only they've gone rogue."

"Rogue?" I stopped on the landing. "What does that mean?"

"It means they're demons who've escaped from hell and are living on earth as humans. They owe no allegiance to my father. They simply live here, feeding off the souls of others."

"Please tell me you're kidding."

"Wish I could, but they have to eat just like you and I do."

"You mean to tell me souls are their sustenance?"

"Exactly, but they can only get a soul if the donor willingly gives it up."

"Why would someone willingly give up their soul?"

He shrugged. "Power. Money. Health."

"I just— I'm so floored by this." I slid my key into the lock, but stopped again, trying to absorb this new turn of events. "Is there a contract? Like in the movies?"

"No. No contract. That's Hollywood's version of a Dealer. In real life, they are much cleverer than that."

"Then how is the bargain sealed?"

"Upon the human's word, the Dealer marks the soul. Then, when he's hungry, he calls it forth. Believe it or not, a person can live without their soul. Not very long, but it can be done."

"What about Mr. Joyce? Did he still have his soul?"

"No. He was right. His soul was gone and probably has been for at least a couple of months. He won't last much longer. He's been so absorbed in his daughter that he didn't realize what he was feeling was the illness that happens when the soul is gone. The body withers away."

Damn. I hated to hear that. "Okay, answer me this: Is it possible to get one back after the demon has fed off it?"

"It depends on how long he's had it, if it still has any energy left. They can live off one soul for months if they have to." He stepped closer to emphasize his next point. "And yours," he said, his tone warning, "he could live off for hundreds of years. A millennium, even. Getting your soul would be like winning the lottery of feasts, which is why you aren't going anywhere near him. He has to trick you out of it, and trust me, a Dealer can do exactly that. They are often called Tricksters in your mythology for good reason."

"Thanks for your faith in me."

"Dutch, it's not my lack of faith in you. It's my certainty that you would do anything to get this man's soul back. I've seen it a hundred times. You risk everything, every part of yourself, for complete strangers. It's . . . disturbing."

He had a point.

I opened my door and stepped in. "Again, I ask, how do I not know these things?"

Reyes crossed his arms over his chest and leaned against my doorframe as I tossed my bag onto my kitchen table and headed for Mr. Coffee. "Because you're you," he said, teasing me.

"Don't you have to get back to work?" I asked, nodding in the general direction of the bar.

"Son of a bitch." He gritted his teeth. "I do, actually, but I won't be long. Don't do anything without me."

"Okay," I said, hiding my crossed fingers behind my back.

He stepped to me. "Dutch, I mean it. Don't you dare go try to find this guy."

"I won't. Pinkie swear." I held up my pinkie. He didn't hold his up so we could entwine them and swear our allegiance. Left hanging for the second time that day. "But," I added, pointing said pinkie at him as menacingly as I could, "I am going to that game tonight."

He bit down, the muscles in his jaw contracting with the movement. "Then we need more of a plan than your usual fare."

"What's my usual fare?"

"Rush headlong into any situation that could get you killed, consequences be damned."

"That plan has worked beautifully for me in the past," I reminded him, frowning in reprimand.

"I apologize," he said, but the insincerity cut to my core. He totally didn't mean it. "I tend to forget how beautifully your plans work when each and every one goes awry, including the one that left you stranded on a deserted bridge with a man who had every intention of burning you alive."

He did not just bring that up. "You're still mad at me about that?" When he only glared at me, his eyes shimmering in the low light, I crossed my arms over my chest defensively. "That wasn't a plan. That was a surprise attack. And I told you, I tried to summon you. I couldn't. I was concussed." I pointed to my head to demonstrate. Not with my pinkie, though.

He was in front of me at once, the animal inside him rearing reflexively, and kept going until I'd backed into the cabinets and could go no farther. Bracing his hands on the countertop on either side of me, he moved even closer, his heat spiraling in blistering waves around me. "You can summon me whenever you desire," he said, his warm breath at my ear, brushing down my neck. "I am but a thought away."

"Are you saying I didn't summon you on purpose?"

He leaned back to look at me. "You tell me."

"I thought you had to go to work."

He bit down again before checking his watch. "I mean it. Nothing until we can come up with a better plan. Promise me."

"I promise. Geez." He was so untrusting.

First things first. I hunted down my phone and dialed Uncle Bob.

"Hey, pumpkin," he said, clearly in a good mood.

I was about to change that. "I need you to come over tonight."

"Sure thing. What's up?"

"Dad."

"He's there?" he asked, seeming surprised.

"No, but Denise came to see me. She is under the impression Dad isn't going on a trip into the wild blue yonder. You wouldn't happen to know anything about that, would you?"

"Not really." He paused a long moment, then added, "But I've suspected."

"You've suspected what?" I asked in alarm. "What's going on?"

"I have a meeting in two. We'll talk about it when I get there. What time do you want me over?"

While I wanted him over right then and there—this was my dad we were talking about—I had to consider the plan Cookie and I—mostly I—had dreamed up to get Ubie to ask her out. Honestly, it was like pulling teeth with this guy. "Around six?" That should give Cookie enough time to get ready and her date enough time to get over from the West Side. He had to work until five, so . . . "Yeah, six will work."

"That'll work for me, too. Do you want dinner? I can pick something up."

Though I should have felt at least a twinge of guilt—I was setting him up, after all—I couldn't quite manage it. The setup, or as I liked to call it, the Get Cookie Laid Plan, was a necessary evil. Uncle Bob was usually so confident, so straightforward, but throw Cookie into the mix, and he became a spineless wiener. Not that wieners had spines to begin with, but really. It was Cookie. Our Cookie! What was she going to do? Bite him?

Okay, that was a strong possibility, but that'd come after the fruits of our endeavor had been delivered. Cookie could be sassy like that.

"Sweet," I said, astounded at my acting skills. I should've gone to Hollywood when I had the chance, but when that old man offered to take me that one time at an abandoned gas station in the middle of nowhere, I wasn't sure I could trust him. Mostly because he had rope, duct tape, and lots of condoms in his backseat. Still, I'll never know what could have come of it. How far I could have risen. *C'est la vie.* "I love it when you buy dinner. How about Italian from that really expensive place that I never go to because it's too expensive?"

He chuckled. "Can do. Would you just like me to order the most expensive thing on the menu?"

"Duh. See ya then." Right before I hung up, I said, "And don't be late!"

"Please. It's Robert Davidson you're talking to."

Who was Robert again? Oh, right. That always threw me. "Fine, *Robert,* just don't be late."

"I'll try."

I hung up and realized Mr. Coffee was ready for me. A sharp thrill ran up my spine with that knowledge. It was weird. I hurried over to him, gave him a saucy wink, then poured a cup of joe, dumping all kinds of artificial thises and thats in with him, wondering why he was called Joe in the first place.

Then I turned and stared at my walls, realizing I suddenly had nothing to do. Actually, I did. I could mull over ad nauseum the fact that there was a demon out there feeding on the souls of the living. Or I could ponder the fact that cancer was a stone-cold bitch who needed to die a slow and painful death, over and over for all eternity. Or I could think about the fact that Reyes had a human brother. A biological one. But none of those options appealed to me. Since Reyes had thwarted my plans to scope out the Dealer Mr. Joyce had described to me, I was at a standstill. In my apartment. With absolutely nothing to do! It was weird.

I supposed I could stare at Mr. Wong, my apartment mate. He'd actually lived there first, hovering with his nose in one corner of my living room when I'd first scoped out the place, but I'd loved the apartment. No, I'd loved the building. It seemed to lure me inside. To woo me with its old-world architecture and cultured lines. Either that or I'd had one too many margaritas that day.

And while I talked to Mr. Wong all the time, I'd never really tried to communicate with him. To get the lowdown on his story, his life. Maybe I didn't want to. I often did my best to avoid the more painful aspects of life, even though it didn't always help; witness my physical and emotional breakdown with Mr. Joyce in my office only an hour earlier.

But maybe Mr. Wong was like Mr. Andrulis in my passenger seat.

Maybe he was just lost, wanting to cross, to get to heaven, but he didn't know how. I'd never really examined Mr. Wong for markings or tattoos of any kind. Perhaps if I found out who he was, what his story entailed, I could lure him out of his stupor and help him to the other side. Wasn't that my job, after all?

I pulled a chair over to Mr. Wong and sat down.

"I'm here for you," I said, taking the slow and easy approach. His back was rigid, his shoulders straight, his short gray hair a bit mussed and in need of a trim. "If you want to cross, you can, you know."

Wait, what if he did? What would I do without him? I'd grown so used to having him around to talk to, to commiserate with, I wasn't sure how I'd handle the place without him.

"Can you at least tell me your name? I'm fairly certain it's not Mr. Wong." I'd only called him that because . . . well, because he kind of looked like a Mr. Wong. It was the first thing that popped into my head.

When he still didn't answer, I put my cup down and stood by him. His head, even though he was hovering about a foot off the ground, still did not pass mine. He couldn't have been more than five feet tall. His gray uniform reminded me so much of the pictures I'd seen of Chinese internment camps. The people starving, made to work until they dropped. Literally.

Maybe that was why I'd never really tried to communicate with him. Maybe I didn't want to know his story, what he'd gone through. As surprising as this might seem to the average observer, I did not handle that stuff well. My heart broke all too often. Even when people passed through me who'd gotten past their hardships, their heart-wrenching pain, and had lived long, full lives, seeing that part of them still cut me to pieces. So, maybe all this time I'd been hanging with Mr. Wong, I was really putting off the inevitable, the truth, not for his benefit, but for my own.

I was so amazingly selfish, sometimes I astonished even me.

I reached over and took his hand into mine. It was the first real contact I'd ever had with him. I was always afraid he'd up and vanish on me.

Dead people tended to do that. But he didn't move. He let me fondle his extremities as I searched for any kind of tattoo. Any mark that might lead me to his identity. It was probably too much to hope that he'd have a tat with his name on it like Mr. Andrulis.

I carefully lifted a sleeve. Nothing, though he did have a lot of scars, mostly thin wisps across his fragile skin. The same with the other arm. I bent and lifted a ragged pant leg. Again, scars, though not so many, but no other markings of any kind.

I heard Cookie open the door as I was looking at his right leg.

"What are you doing?" she asked, heading straight for Mr. Coffee. I'd suspected those two for some time now. Cookie seemed suddenly very concerned as to his whereabouts, his everyday activities, how long it took him to brew. She was eyeing him, sizing him up; I could tell. It could have something to do with the fact that her own coffeepot died after a long bout with congestion. I think its fuel pump went out. But she needed to keep her eyes off my man if she knew what was good for her.

"I'm fondling Mr. Wong," I said, dropping his pant leg and rising. "Did you find anything out about our Mr. Andrulis?"

"Sure did."

I peeked around Mr. Wong. "Seriously? And?"

She stirred her cup, rinsed the spoon off, then walked over to me and handed me a paper. "Is this him?"

I looked at the clipping. It was a photograph of several veterans from a local VFW event. She'd circled one of them, and underneath was a list of their names, including a Charles Andrulis. I squinted, trying to bring the picture into focus. "You know, that might be him. It's hard to tell. He's so naked now."

"According to the obituaries," Cookie said, taking the chair I'd pulled up to Mr. Wong, "he died about a month ago and is survived by his wife of fifty-seven years. But she's not doing well."

"Maybe that's why he's still here," I said, pulling up another chair and retrieving my coffee cup. "Maybe, I don't know, maybe he's waiting for her."

Cookie sighed in romantic bliss.

"But wait. Why is he freaking naked?"

"Oh." She scoured her bag until she produced a stack of papers. "Okay, I called the home where he and his wife were living, and according to a Nurse Jacob—who sounded quite yummy, I might add—they were giving Mr. Andrulis a shower when he collapsed. He died instantly of a heart attack."

"Oh, man. Poor guy."

"I know. It's really sad. Nurse Jacob said his wife doesn't know he's gone. Even if they told her, it would sink in for only a few minutes before she was asking for him again, so they haven't told her. They just keep telling her he's coming right back."

"You know what?" I said, rising and pacing the floor space. All two feet of it. "I've had it. I don't want to be around death anymore." I was holding my cup with one hand, but my other flew all over the place in indignation. "I'm done with sad stories that leave me whimpering and fetal."

Cookie straightened. "But aren't you the grim reaper? I mean, isn't death your job?"

"Yes." I strode to my desk and took out a piece of paper. "Yes, it is, and I quit."

She relaxed and sipped on her coffee a bit before asking, "So, what are you doing?"

"Writing my resignation letter. How do you spell *disestablishmentarianism*?"

"First of all, I'm not sure you know what that word means if you are using it in a resignation letter."

I paused and examined my letter. "Really?"

"Second, I'm not sure you can quit."

"Oh, yeah?" I went back to writing my letter, throwing in a few curse words to get my point across. "Watch me."

I signed it with all the flair I could muster, then folded it into thirds, tried to stuff it in an envelope, pulled it back out and refolded to make the thirds more even, tried again, pulled it back out. "Oh, my god, how do you get a letter into a freaking—?"

"Would you like to hear my third point?"

I blew a lock of hair off my face and turned to her. "Sure."

"Third, just who are you going to send that letter to, exactly?"

Damn. She had a point. But I was busy looking at Mr. Wong's back. I saw something I'd never noticed before through the threadbare material of his shirt. Dropping the letter, I strolled over to him, stood on my tip-toes, and peeked down the collar of his gray shirt.

"Holy cow," I said. His entire back was covered in tattoos. "I think Mr. Wong may have been triad."

"Triad?" she asked, standing slowly. "Aren't they kind of dangerous?"

"From what I hear, they are." I reached around him and unbuttoned the top couple of buttons of his shirt. "I am so sorry, Mr. Wong. So, so, so, so sorry."

After I'd unfastened enough to pull the shoulders down, I carefully peeled back the shirt and examined the artwork. It was stunning, but not what I'd seen in the movies that would link him to any underground organized crime syndicate, Chinese or otherwise. It was Chinese characters, beginning with a straight line across, then more characters falling from there and forming vertical lines of text. Only, I couldn't read them.

I'd been born knowing every language ever spoken on Earth. Part of the gig, I guessed. Even though that didn't include the ability to read and write said languages, I knew just enough Mandarin to be dangerous.

Cookie was standing back, watching me with nervous anxiety. "Well? Is he triad?"

"No. I mean, I don't think so. I'm not sure what he is. It's just words.

Chinese characters. But I don't recognize them. I can't read it." A thought hit me, and I turned to her. "Aren't you supposed to be getting ready for your fake date?"

She pulled her bottom lip between her teeth. "I'm not sure, Charley."

"Cook," I said, righting Mr. Wong's shirt just in case he was triad and could put out a hit for my head to be brought to him in a plain, brown package, and stepped to her. "You have to snap out of this." I took her shoulders and gave her a little shake. I didn't slap her, though. That might be taking it a bit far. "You want this, remember? For reasons known only to you and God above, you have the hots for my uncle."

She drew in a deep breath and nodded. "You're right. It's for his own good."

"Damn straight, it is. And it'll be funny to watch him squirm. I can't wait to see the look on his face—"

"Charley!"

"But that's not the only reason I'm doing this! I swear."

"You are such a bad liar."

I chuckled and led her to the door. "Go get ready for your fake date. Ubie should be here around six. Ish. You never know with him."

She nodded again, handed me her cup, then headed across the hall to her own apartment. I said a quick prayer, asking for divine intervention in her fashion choice, then went back to Mr. Wong. Some of the lines of text went all the way down his back and disappeared into the top of his pants, but no way was I going there. I had to leave him at least an ounce of dignity.

I could try to draw the tats, as I had with Mr. A, but that would take me forever, and I just wasn't that good. Time to kill two bad guys with one bullet. I summoned Angel, a thirteen-year-old departed gangbanger who'd wanted to see me naked before he'd agree to become my investigator. I was happy to report he had yet to see me naked and he was indeed my investigator. I'd blackmailed him. It was how I rolled.

"Hey, Charley," he said, popping in behind me. Very close behind me.

I stepped away from him and gave him a good once-over. "You're being very nice today," I said, letting the suspicion I felt show. "What gives?"

"What?" he asked. He stepped to Sophie, my sofa, and fell back to land softly on her soft cushions. "I can't say hey to my favorite grim reaper?"

Oh, wow. Something was definitely up. I strolled over to him, turned around, and plopped down on his stomach to incapacitate him. Then I proceeded to tickle him until he begged for mercy.

"Okay, okay," he said, laughing like a schoolkid. It was nice. "I give up."

"What's up with the nice act?" When he hesitated, I went back in for the ribs.

"No! Okay, I'll tell you. I'm just happy. My mom's doing really well."

"Yeah, thanks to the raise I gave you. So, she fell for the 'dead uncle left her money' thing?"

He wiped his eyes as I let him up. "Seems like it. She's just happier now. Something has changed."

"Angel, maybe she's happy because she's figured out you're still around."

His disposition went from light to dark in a flash. "No, she's not. I told you, I don't want her to know."

"I know. Geez. I didn't tell her anything. But she suspects. You know that, right?"

He sat back down and rubbed the peach fuzz on his chin. "I know. As long as she doesn't know for certain, she'll be fine."

"Well, either way," I said, going to warm up my coffee, "I'm glad she's doing well."

"Yeah, me, too."

"I have two jobs for you."

"Okay, but I've decided I need weekends and holidays off."

"Why?"

"I don't know. It just sounds good. And I need benefits."

I gave him my best deadpan expression. "Isn't it a little late for medical?"

"No, I need other benefits. Like seeing you naked. But only sometimes. I'm not greedy."

"You are not seeing me naked. Now, do you want to know the jobs or not?"

"Sure. Why not? I'm only dead. It's not like I can argue."

I curled up beside him, and he put an arm around my shoulders. "Can we make out?"

"No. Can you draw?"

He shrugged. "I used to be pretty good. Haven't tried it in about thirty years."

"But you can manipulate objects sometimes. I've seen you."

"Yeah. Do you need a nude portrait done?"

"Yes, actually, I do."

He rose slightly. "Really?"

"Yes. Of Mr. Wong's back."

Disappointment lined his handsome face. "That old guy? I'm not sure that's a good idea."

"Why?"

"I don't know. He's . . . *escalofriante*."

"Angel Garza," I said, leaning away from him. "Mr. Wong is not creepy. Why would he give you the chills?"

"He just does."

"That's not nice."

"Whatever you say, *'jita*."

"And you can't call me *'jita*. It's wrong. I'm older than you are."

He still had his arm on my shoulders when his full mouth tilted playfully. "You are not older than me. If you'll let me see you naked, I'll prove it to you."

The way Angel talked, the departed could have sex. But really? Could they? I wasn't about to find out with a thirteen-year-old. "You are not seeing me naked. I need you to draw the tattoos on his back."

"I can try, but I don't think he'll like it. What if he's ticklish?"

I pursed my lips in reprimand. "I don't know what else to do, unless you can talk to him and find out who he is."

"I've already told you: I'm not a ghost whisperer. And if you could see what I see, you wouldn't even want to know who he is."

I bolted upright. "Why? What do you see?" Then I remembered something. When I was hurt and almost burned alive, I'd seen Reyes's darkness, the flames that forever engulfed him, the scars from his past. Reyes said I was looking at him from another plane. Now I just had to remember how I did that.

I looked back at Mr. Wong and concentrated. Then I squinted. Then I squinted harder until he became a blurry patch of gray.

"Is it working?" Angel asked, a soft laugh escaping him.

I gave up with a hopeless sigh. "No."

"You're the grim freaking reaper. You can do anything. You just haven't figured that out yet."

"Dude, how do you know more than I do? Are my abilities, like, common departed knowledge?"

"No," he said with a shrug. "You kind of learn things as you go. It's like on-the-job training."

"That's exactly how I feel. So, like what? What can I do that I don't know about?"

"I just told you. Pretty much anything."

"That's so helpful. Thanks," I said, giving up. Again. "What do you see?"

He looked at him, studied him a long while, then said, "Power."

My eyes rounded. "Power? What do you mean? What kind of power?"

"That's it. Just power. You'd have to see it to understand. *Me da mala espina.*"

Well, that was a huge help. "Something ominous is coming, huh? When isn't it? I want you to try to draw the tattoos on his back onto this paper when you can." I pointed to my sketchpad.

"Okay. Most likely the pencil will slip through my fingers, but I can try right now if you want."

"Nope—right now, you have another job."

"Okay. I get paid time and a half for overtime, right?"

"No. I need you to go check out a demon posing as a man."

"I don't like demons."

"I don't either."

"That's funny, since you're sleeping with one."

"Reyes is not a demon."

"Keep telling yourself that, *mijita*. He is the most notorious demon of them all."

"Are you going to go check this guy out or what?"

"Sure, but when the prince of hell turns on you and decides to engulf the world in a blazing inferno, don't say I didn't warn you."

"Deal," I said, plastering a smile on my face.

5

I'm only here to establish an alibi.

—T-SHIRT

I told Angel where he could find the Dealer, with instructions to just get a feel for him. For his power. "But don't get too close, else he'll sup on your soul," I'd added, after which he'd rolled his eyes. He could be such a drama queen.

I looked back at Mr. Wong and studied him. Power. I just didn't see it. Duff!

I bolted up again. When Duff, a departed man who'd followed me home from a bar one night—long story—first saw Mr. Wong, he seemed . . . surprised. Like he knew him. Or recognized him.

Mission for the moment: Find Duff.

I went to the last apartment he'd lived in. He moved around a lot, but the last time we'd talked, he told me he was back in with Mrs. Allen down the hall. She had a vicious poodle named PP. To PP's credit, however, he did try to fight off a pack of demons for me. I had a soft spot for him now. Super soft. Like Twinkie guts, only not so marshmallowy delicious.

I knocked on Mrs. Allen's door, waited a bit, then knocked again. PP was yapping up a storm from behind it, but it took Mrs. Allen a bit to travel that distance, even though her apartment was smaller than mine.

She cracked open the door, the chain still on, until she saw me and took the chain down to let me in.

"Hey, Charley," she said, and I realized immediately she didn't have her teeth in.

"Hey, Mrs. Allen." One thing I didn't think to come up with was an excuse for being there. "Um, I was just wondering how your . . . heating system was working. Mine is on the fritz."

"My heating system." She practically shoved me inside. "It's awful. Never works right, and poor PP feels the cold. Breaks my heart."

She hobbled to her thermostat. "See, it's on seventy-five, and I know it's not a degree over seventy-three in here."

"Okay," I said, searching for Duff. According to the talk on the streets, I could summon any departed, as I had with Angel, but I didn't know Duff that well. I didn't want to just drag him away from whatever it was he was doing. Come to think of it, what did the departed do all day?

"Duff?" I whispered, sidestepping a snarling PP and hurrying over to a bedroom door to peek inside. Nada.

"And this stove still hasn't been fixed. I told that lazy, good-for-nothing landlord about my stove weeks ago."

I turned back to her. "Your stove isn't working?" I tried to walk over, but again had to sidestep PP. I glared down at him and the one fang he had left that protruded out of his gnarly mouth. "And here I thought we were friends." He snapped at me to make sure I understood the truth of it, so I quickly made my way past. Vicious little shit.

No one in the building besides Cookie and Reyes, including the current manager, Mr. Z, knew I was a proud new owner of a run-down apartment building, so Mrs. Allen didn't know she was talking to the person responsible for all the repairs.

"No, ma'am, it's not. See?" She turned on all the burners, and none of them heated up. "How am I supposed to make stew?"

"Well, I'm not sure, but I'll write that down and go talk to Mr. Z about it."

"Lazy good-for-nothing. He won't do anything about it."

He would now. I'd make sure of it.

"Okay, well, thanks. I'll let you know what I find out."

"Thank you, honey. PP always liked you."

PP snapped at me again, barking until I could take it no longer. I rushed out the door and back to Cookie's apartment. I knew that Duff had spent some time crashing there, too. I'd never told Cook. It'd only freak her out, and as fun as that was to do, I didn't want to hear how every noise in the apartment was the dead guy. Her imagination would have run rampant.

I went in without knocking, under the guise of checking on her. She was in her room, changing clothes, and from the state of her closet and drawers, she'd done that a lot.

"I just don't know what to wear," she said, tossing aside a nice burgundy blouse.

"That would have been great."

"No. I don't like the way it fits."

"How does it fit?"

"Wrong. What about this?"

"You probably shouldn't wear orange and purple together on a first date. Just thinking out loud."

"But it's a fake date. Who cares?" She picked up a glass and downed half the contents before I smelled the alcohol.

"Cookie, what the hell are you drinking?"

"I made a frozen margarita with Amber's slushy machine. Don't judge me."

I stifled a giggle and looked at my watch. "Oh, my gosh. It's almost six."

"Oh, good heavens. I haven't been on a date in years."

Cookie put down the drink and started trying on blouses again while I looked for Duff, who was missing in action here, too. She tossed the fifth blouse aside when I walked back in.

"What was wrong with that one?"

"The color. You just said—"

"Right, right. But at this rate, you're going to be late for January. Get a move on, missy!"

She glared at me. It was the alcohol talking. I could tell. "Hey, do you have any repairs you need done? I'm making a list."

"Oh." She straightened and started ticking off a list with her fingers. "My refrigerator is making a funny sound. The faucet in the bathroom leaks."

"Hold on." I ran back to my apartment and returned with a pen and paper. "Okay, fridge, faucet."

"Yes, and the floor in the living room squeaks. Amber's window lets in a lot of cold air. The ceiling still needs to be painted after that disastrous pool party you tried to have on the roof."

"That wasn't my fault. And it was a kiddie pool, for goodness' sake."

"Oh, and those bar things in my closet need to be rehung."

"Bar things . . . in clos . . . et," I said while writing. "Is that it?"

"I'll think of more. I forgot you're now responsible for all that." She blinked in thought. "That's kind of scary."

"Tell me about it."

I hit the rest of the building, under the guise of making a list of demands for the new owner on what repairs needed to be made. Of those who were home, which was only about half—and excluding a woman on the first floor, who kept calling me Bertie and throwing ramen noodles at me—I now had a list of about seventy-two items that needed to be replaced or repaired. Seventy-two! This ownership thing could become a hassle. Luckily, I had a man who was apparently made of money. He bought the building for me in the first place. Making good on the purchase was the least he could do in my worthy yet humble opinion. But Mr. Z was the one who'd actually do the repairs.

I'd make one last stop at his apartment, also on the first floor. He probably told that lady about me. I'd never even seen her before. Maybe that was the problem. Maybe she was a shut-in who didn't like people invading her turf. I could understand that, but why Bertie?

After all that, no Duff. I was worried I'd have to summon him whether he wanted to be summoned or not, but first, I needed to see the resident manager slash maintenance man. Mr. Zamora opened his door wearing a pair of overalls and a graying T-shirt, the TV blaring in the background. Instead of a greeting, he pursed his lips—the ones that resided directly under a thick mustache—in annoyance. I took that as my cue.

"Hey, Mr. Z. I have a list—"

The door slammed in my face before I could finish. Right in my face.

I stood there in a shock a solid minute before I tried again, knocking harder this time to let him know I was not going away.

He opened the door again, eyed me up and down, then started to slam the door.

I stuck my booted foot in it, preventing it from closing completely.

"I'm off," he said, swinging the door wide. "Can't you see I'm having dinner?"

I looked inside, and sure enough, there on the table sat a feast fit for a king. If that king was really fond of hot dogs and potato chips.

"I'm sorry to bother you, but I have a list of repairs that need to be made to various apartments in this building."

"Oh, yeah?" he said, taking the list from me. He read it over, then crumpled it up in his hand and tossed it at me. "I can't do any repairs without prior authorization. You have to go through the management company."

The paper had hit me in the chest, and after I got over how amazingly rude he was being, I decided to file assault charges. I grabbed my chest and doubled over, moaning in agony as he looked on.

"Are you about finished?" he asked, completely unmoved. "My show is on."

I hopped up to see over him. He was watching a rerun of *Breaking Bad*. At least he had good taste in television. "I love that show," I said, trying to look past him to see which one it was. "I take Misery to their car wash all the time."

"So, you're okay? You didn't get a paper cut, did you? Should I call an ambulance?"

"Okay, fine, be that way. Just tell me exactly what the procedure is to get repairs made." I picked up the paper and smoothed it out on my stomach.

"I told you. You have to go through the property management company. I work for them now. They work for the owner."

"I'm not sure you should be treating tenants like that."

"Like what?" he asked, offended.

I leaned in to him. "Like slamming doors in their faces."

"I'm off. I told you."

"It doesn't matter. These are tenants. These are people who make it possible for you to draw a paycheck. They deserve a little respect."

"Listen, Charley. If you want respect, you gotta show some."

"What?" I asked, my turn to be offended. "When have I ever been disrespectful to you?"

He squared his shoulders. "You're loud. You throw parties. You invite strange people over at all hours. And you call me Mr. Whiskers behind my back. It makes me sound like a friggin' cat."

"I most certainly do not. I call you that to your face just as often as I do behind your back. And I haven't had a party in months."

He pressed his mouth together. "Look, no matter, you gotta go through the proper channels for me to fix anything on that list. But I gotta warn you. We have a new owner. I'm not sure what he will do with all that." He pointed to my list.

"I'm not sure either." I didn't think about that. I needed working capital. I needed a sugar daddy. Or Reyes Farrow. Either way.

"Fine," I said, folding my note and stuffing it in my pocket. "I'll just go to the new owner directly."

"You know him?" he asked, surprised. Of course he would think the new owner was a him. Reyes bought the building before transferring ownership over to me, a fact that still boggled my mind. Giving me an apartment complex was like giving a twelve-year-old a Fortune 500 company and saying, "Now, take good care of it."

"I sure do, and I plan on giving him an earful of how I've been treated here today."

"Yeah? And I'll tell him about the ostrich."

I gasped. "That was *one time*. And she pulled through it just fine."

"Mm-hm. Can I finish my dinner now?"

"Yes." I turned and stalked off to show him how angry I was. Ostrich, my ass. She was fine once the vet removed the Tupperware.

As I made my way to Reyes's apartment, hoping he'd be home from work, I called out to Duff. Darn him. One minute I can't get the man out of my hair, and the next he's impossible to find. Like a ghost.

Laughing at my own sense of humor, I knocked on Reyes's door. Someone had to laugh, and I was pretty much the only one who got me. It was a lonely life.

The door opened, and a seemingly annoyed Reyes stood on the other side. What'd I do now?

"Hey," I said, about half a second before the door slammed in my face. What the—? I knocked again, this time pounding.

The door opened wide as he leaned against the frame and crossed his arms at his chest. He really liked that pose. I really liked that he liked that pose.

"What was that for?" I asked.

"Why didn't you use the key?"

"Because." I'd thought about it, but I still had a hard time just barging in on him. I handed him the list. "I thought you were at work."

"Was. I'm not now."

"A man of few words. Well, I got a few words for you." I pushed it into his hands. "I need working capital."

He scanned the list. "What will you do for a new stove in Mrs. Allen's apartment?"

"Jump around and sing 'Oklahoma'? How do I know? It's a stove."

"I'm going to need some kind of incentive program if I'm going to fork out this kind of money."

I held back a laugh. "Incentive program, huh? So what's a stove worth these days?"

"Depends. Do you have a nurse's uniform?"

I raised a mischievous brow. "No, but I have a Princess Leia slave costume."

A deep hunger flashed in his irises. It caused a warmth to flood my abdomen, and only partly because he knew what a Princess Leia slave costume consisted of.

"That'll do," he said. "And this is already taken care of." He handed me back the list. "Just give this to the management company."

"They won't give me the runaround?"

"Not if they want to remain your management company." He had a point. "Are you still insisting on paying the Dealer a visit?"

As he spoke, a shadow nearby caught my attention. Sometimes ADD was a good thing. I turned in time to see Duff appear by my door, then disappear just as quickly.

"Hold that thought," I said to Reyes as I spun around and scanned the hallway. "Duff!" I called out. "Show yourself this instant."

He did, but he materialized at the other end of the hall.

"What are you doing?" I asked him.

"N-n-nothing. J-j-just s-standing here," he said, his stutter more pronounced than usual. But he wasn't looking at me. He was keeping his watchful gaze on Reyes and resembled a rabbit ready to bolt.

"Look," I said, walking toward him, "I just have a few questions. I wanted to talk to you. Will you come here?"

"I-I'll s-stay here, thank you v-very much."

Aw, he was sweet. "You're so welcome. But, really, I need to talk to you—"

I'd started to gesture to my door when I caught Reyes's scowl in my periphery. I turned back to him. "What are you doing?"

"What?"

"You're intimidating him."

"I'm standing here."

"Yes, intimidatingly."

One corner of his mouth lifted playfully. "And just how should I stand?"

"For starters, you can stop scowling at him."

He let his gaze travel back to Duff, slowly, menacingly, then said, "But it's fun."

"Reyes Alexander Farrow." I marched back to him. "Can you be nice to the departed or not?"

He lowered his head, pretending to be repentant, then looked at me from underneath his long lashes and said, "But Duff here isn't just any departed, are you, boy?" He leveled another cold stare on him, and Duff disappeared.

"Damn it," I said, backhanding Reyes's shoulder, albeit lightly. "How do you know him?"

"Duff and I are old friends. He used to come visit me in prison."

"What?" I glanced over my shoulder, but he was still gone. "Why?"

"He was keeping an eye on me." He reached out and let his fingers glide along my stomach.

"Why would he do that?" I asked. I was always out of the loop.

"He was worried about you. Seems he's smitten."

Oh, man. Seriously? "He's a departed, Reyes. It's not like we can actually have a relationship."

"If any human could have a relationship with a departed, it'd be you. And he knows it." He slid a finger into my belt loop and tugged.

"Reyes, he's harmless. Be nice to him."

He ran a hand around to the small of my back, the heat of him almost too much to bear. It soaked into my skin and my hair, and caused goose bumps to lace over me, it was so hot. "I love that about you," he said, picking up a lock of my hair and rubbing it between the fingers of one hand while pulling me closer with the other. "Your inability to see the bad in people until it's too late." He was being awfully flirtatious, almost as though he were trying to change the subject.

"Are you saying Duff is a bad person?"

"I'm saying you're too good for him."

I finally molded to him, letting him press against me. "I'm too good for you, too," I said, teasing. But he didn't take the bait.

"Agreed," he said instead, a second before he lowered his mouth to mine, fusing us together like an arc welder. He wrapped his arms around me, the hold viselike, unyielding. The heat was blistering and surreal at once, and I felt it all the way down to my toes. He broke off the kiss and nipped at my ear. "I guess it's a good thing you can have a relationship with a departed," he said.

"Why's that?"

"We can still see each other after I die."

I tried to lean back to look at him, but Reyes went from cruising at a solid twenty-five miles per hour to flying faster than the speed of sound. In an instant, he had me pinned against the wall, the long fingers of one hand bracing both wrists above my head while the other slipped beneath my sweater. His hand slid around my waist and up my spine, his fingertips tracing the hollow line of my vertebrae.

"Probing for a weak spot?" I asked him softly, well aware of his penchant for severing spines.

"I know exactly where your weak spots are," he said, and he proved his point by slipping his hand underneath my bra and cradling Will Robinson, teasing her crest with a soft squeeze.

Arousal leapt inside me so fast, I felt the world spin.

"And I know exactly where to probe," he continued. He pushed my legs apart with his hips and pushed against me, the friction of our jeans causing a nuclear heat to build in my abdomen.

I tore one wrist free of his grasp and planted my hand on a steely buttock to pull him closer. He let a husky growl escape him. The deep sound reverberated through my bones, crashing like spilled wine against them. And like wine, the effect was intoxicating.

Someone, a man, cleared his throat nearby.

It took me a moment to realize we had company. When I did, I broke our hold with a startled jump. "Uncle Bob," I said, smoothing my clothes and straightening to face him. "You're early."

"I'm late, actually." He stood there in a brown suit and loosened tie, looking both uncomfortable and cautious.

I glanced at my watch. It was 6:10. "Oh, wow, the time must've slipped away from me."

"Must have," he said before raising the bag he was carrying. "Hungry?"

"Famished." I looked back at Reyes, who was back to scowling, this time at Uncle Bob. "What about you?" I asked him. "Want to join us?"

"No, thank you," he said, stepping back into his apartment. A burst of cool air rushed between us with his absence. "I ate at the bar."

"Okay, well, we can discuss our business for tonight later?" The card game didn't start until nine, so we had some time to come up with a brilliant plan that would keep us both alive. And hopefully one that would let us keep our souls as well.

I didn't want a demon supping on my soul.

Uncle Bob's timing could not have been more perfect. Right as we turned to go into my apartment, Cookie's date rose in the stairwell beside us. He nodded to us and went straight to Cookie's door to knock. Uncle Bob stopped in his tracks. He surveyed the man from the top of his neatly trimmed head to the tips of his wing tip toes. It was funny. Kind of. On one hand, I felt sorry for him. On the other, it was his own fault. Cookie wasn't going to wait around forever. She needed snuggle time.

He turned back to us as he waited for Cookie to answer the door. I winked at him. Barry was an old friend from college. We'd had a couple classes together, including one on jazz appreciation. We'd bonded over the fact that going in, neither one of us was particularly fond of jazz, but we'd learned to love it. Especially the history.

I stepped to my door and turned the knob slowly, taking my time, waiting for Cookie to answer hers. When she didn't answer immediately, I began to get a little worried. But when she did answer, all my fears dissipated. She looked fantastic. She wore a dark burgundy pantsuit with a cream-colored throw around her shoulders. If that didn't get Uncle Bob's attention, I didn't know what would.

Uncle Bob made a point of speaking to me in a louder-than-necessary voice. He asked me once again if I was hungry.

I chuckled and said just as loudly, "Why, yes, I am, Uncle Bob. Like I said before. But thanks for the recap."

"Oh, hey, Cookie," he said, pretending to just notice her. As if his eyes didn't almost pop out of his head the minute they landed on her. He was so bad at this flirting gig.

Cookie offered him a brilliant smile as she shook Barry's hand. "Hello there yourself, Robert. I see you brought dinner. I'm sorry I'll miss it."

Uncle Bob followed me inside, almost stumbling when I paused at the threshold of my apartment to give him more time. He cleared his throat in embarrassment and said, "I'm sorry, too."

Barry led her to the stairs, taking her hand as they descended them. Uncle Bob noticed. I thought he would break his neck, trying to watch them walk all the way to the next landing.

"So, what do you know about Dad that I don't?"

He pulled out two trays from the bag: one with spaghetti and one with lasagna. I dived for the spaghetti before he could get to it.

He shrugged, took his lasagna, and headed for my kitchen table. "I probably don't know much more than you do. But I've noticed a distinct change in his behavior."

At first I just kind of stared at Uncle Bob, not sure what he was doing. Then I realized he was using a kitchen table for its intended purpose. Weird. "Well, duh. I could have told you that. His bout with cancer and his sudden remission made his telling me he was going on a trip plausible. He said he was going to learn to sail. But Denise seems to think otherwise. What could he possibly be up to?"

I sat beside Ubie at the table. It felt strange. I'd never eaten at my kitchen table. This was an experience for me.

"I hate to make assumptions," Uncle Bob said as he stabbed at his lasagna. "But if I were to guess, I'd say it had something to do with you."

"Me? Why me?" I twirled spaghetti around my fork.

"Didn't you notice how, after going to all the trouble of having you arrested just to try to get you out of the PI business, he seemed to give up pretty easily?"

"I noticed him trying to shoot me. The rest is kind of a blur."

"I'm just finding everything he's done lately pretty suspicious. If I didn't know better, I'd say he was investigating something. He'd get like that in the old days. When he was on the scent of something big, he'd get secretive. Defensive. I haven't seen him like that in a long time."

"But what kind of case can he be working? What can he possibly investigate? He's not even a detective anymore."

He put down his fork and extended me his full attention. That meant he was about to tell me something I probably didn't want to know. "Let's just say he's been asking a lot of questions about your boyfriend."

I put down my fork, too. "Reyes? Why would he be investigating Reyes?"

"I don't know, pumpkin. I'm probably wrong. So, Cookie has a date?"

At last. I was wondering when he would bring her up. "Yeah. I think she joined some kind of online dating service. From what I understand, she's very popular. She has a date every day this week."

"With a different guy?" he asked, appalled.

"With a different guy."

After that, Uncle Bob seemed to lose his appetite. He barely touched his lasagna and left with a grim expression on his face. We definitely got him thinking, contemplating what his lax attitude toward a delicious creature like Cookie was costing him. Now I just had to worry about one thing: Uncle Bob's penchant for investigating. If he figured out what we were doing, he'd disown me. And possibly sell me to a Romanian count.

6

Sometimes I wrestle my demons.
Sometimes we just snuggle.
—BUMPER STICKER

Duff finally showed after Uncle Bob left. He seemed embarrassed, and I wondered if he'd heard what Reyes said about him. That he was bad. But how bad could he possibly be? The way I understood it, if someone was very bad, they went straight to hell when they died. So, no matter what Reyes said, Duff couldn't have been that bad of a person.

"S-sorry about that," he said, hanging his head in shame. "I didn't m-mean to r-run out on you. Reyes and I don't r-really get along."

"Reyes and a lot of people don't really get along," I said.

I'd made another pot of coffee and was in the middle of pouring when he popped in. I'd need all the energy I could muster to face this Dealer guy. Which was a cool name. Any demon living off the hard-earned souls of humans didn't deserve a cool name. It was like when the media gave cool names to serial killers and terrorists. They didn't have the right to anything cool, in my opinion. Of which I had many.

"Reyes told me you used to visit him in prison."

If I didn't know that Duff had exactly zero blood pumping through his body, I would've sworn he'd blushed. "Oh, th-that. I was just k-keeping an eye on him."

"Why?" I asked, sitting back at my kitchen table. It was nice there. Homey.

He drew his shoulders in, unable to look at me. "B-because. H-he kept going to s-see you."

That baffled me more than a little. Flummoxed, I asked, "You mean, incorporeally?"

"Y-yes. He shouldn't have."

"Why's that?"

"B-because he's n-not a nice person."

Interesting. "That's funny. He said the same thing about you."

His gaze shot up in surprise. "He d-doesn't know me. He w-wasn't there."

This was getting more intriguing by the moment. "He wasn't where?"

"At my h-house. Where it h-happened. But because of it, they took me away and th-that's how I m-met Rey'aziel. I didn't know he was the d-devil's son when I m-met him, though. He was j-just an inmate. Like me."

"You were in prison?" I asked, more than a little taken aback.

I could tell by his expression he was waiting, no hoping, that the world would swallow him. His shoulders concaved even more. His chin tucked in shame. "Y-yes, Charley, I was in p-prison. I knew Rey'aziel w-wasn't like the rest of us, but I d-didn't know how different until I died."

I wanted to ask him why he'd gone to prison, exactly what happened, but if Duff had wanted me to know, he would have told me. I didn't want to push him, but I did want one thing. "Did you die in prison, Duff?"

"Y-yes. Kind of. I had b-been paroled and was j-just about to leave when it happened."

That explained why he was in civilian clothes when he passed. "Do you want to talk about it?"

"N-no. It won't change what happened. B-but you were l-looking for me?"

"Yes, I was. I wanted to ask you about Mr. Wong." I pointed to the new subject of our conversation as he hovered in the corner. "When you first saw him, when you showed up a couple of weeks ago, you seemed to recognize him."

"N-no, I don't know him." He took a step back like he was going to leave.

I stood and put an arm on his shoulder. It was a show of encouragement, but that's all it was. A show. I really did it to keep him there. I'd recently learned that as long as I had physical contact with a departed, he or she couldn't vanish. It was great. But the moment I lost contact, they could disappear before my eyes and I had no way of getting them back. Or so I thought. Angel swears I can summon any departed I want to at any time. It was an interesting concept. One I'd try someday, but today, I just wanted to know more about Mr. Wong. No idea why the urge suddenly hit me. It just seemed important. His story seemed important.

"Duff, I'm not trying to make you uncomfortable. I just want to know what you know about him."

He glanced over his shoulder toward my roomie, then shrugged at me. "I don't know anything except what I see."

"What do you see?"

He drew in a deep breath and let it out slowly as he studied him. "I see a f-force, like a thick shield around him. It's powerful. I c-can see that, too. Power. Strength. Like he's m-made of it."

Man, I needed to learn that trick.

"Can't you see it?" he asked.

"I wish. I've tried. I'm just not sure what to do."

"I—I could help you," he said, stepping closer.

Maybe Reyes was right. Maybe he had a crush on me. Then again, maybe he really could help me.

"Then," he continued, his expression full of hope, "you could see what Reyes is."

I felt Reyes's heat flare to life around us. Duff jumped back in surprise.

"Duff," Reyes said as he materialized in the doorframe, "are you trying to get me in trouble?" He was doing his menacing bit again.

Duff didn't say anything. He dropped his gaze to the floor in submission. Or fear. I wasn't quite certain which.

"Reyes," I said, my tone warning, "I'm just asking him about Mr. Wong. No one seems to know anything about him except he has a power or a force around him."

Reyes glanced over, barely interested. "I didn't notice before, but, yeah, I guess he does."

Duff laughed.

"You have something to share with the class?" Reyes asked.

I was just about to warn him again to be nice when Duff said, "That was a mistake."

"What was?" Reyes asked.

"You not noticing."

Reyes frowned. He seemed confused when he looked back at Mr. Wong. Then even more so when he turned back to Duff. He suddenly wore a mask of suspicion. Wariness.

I began wondering a lot of things, not the least of which was why Duff had suddenly lost his stutter.

I had a lot on my plate: A naked dead man riding shotgun everywhere I went. A mysterious Asian man hovering in my corner who was made of something powerful, whatever that meant. Another man who sold his soul to a demon who was indifferent to the fact that it was for a good cause. A demon who was going around tricking people out of their souls so he could eat them. Which, ew. A rascally neighbor who'd proposed to me and was expecting an answer sometime this century. And an ongoing child-abduction case that had led me to believe that my man might have a brother he either does or doesn't know about. I was so not good at tying up loose ends. And to top it all off, I was one step closer to getting my BFF slash receptionist laid by my uncle.

That was so wrong. No matter. Life was good.

Until I lost seventeen million dollars in a card game.

I looked across a table set in the middle of a dark, smoky back room of a warehouse and studied the Dealer. The demon who supped on souls in his spare time. He was not what I'd expected at all. Then again, what did one expect when meeting a demon? This guy was terribly handsome, if a little too Goth for my tastes, and much younger than I'd imagined. He couldn't have been more than nineteen or twenty, and he looked like he came straight out of a vampire novel, with shoulder-length black hair, a white ruffled shirt; and a six-inch top hat that he never took off. There was something horridly attractive about him. Maybe it was his confidence. His perfect skin. His long, pale fingers. Or his penetrating bronze eyes—a color so rich, so vividly chromatic, I'd never seen anything quite like it. I'd found myself caught in his mesmerizing gaze on several occasions throughout the evening.

But I had to remember, this wasn't really the demon. This was the unfortunate human the demon had chosen to possess. So the beauty that encased him was stolen, just like the souls from which he took nourishment.

He seemed just as fascinated by me. He'd focused all his attention on me the moment I arrived, and rarely looked away. At any other time, that kind of constant inspection would be unnerving. Tonight it was intriguing.

The only thing that broke the spell was a darkness that even I could see. It escaped him when he turned his head too quickly or leaned forward too abruptly. The darkness, the demon inside him, would hesitate a microsecond too long and leave a smoky trail of its essence, like a child coloring, unable to stay in the lines. I had to keep one thing in mind at all times: Underneath all that charisma and spellbinding charm lay the heart of a demon who stole people's souls.

Reyes didn't exactly like the plan I'd come up with, but I didn't give him much say in the matter. I was here for the soul of my client, Mr. Joyce. Not for Reyes. And as far as I knew, Reyes's soul was fine. But I did as he'd asked. I'd dropped my hand beside my chair the moment I sat across from the Dealer and summoned Artemis, my guardian Rottweiler who liked nothing more than ripping out the throats of demons. She rose up out of the floor until her head lifted my hand. Normally she'd roll over for a belly rub, but she sensed the demon in the room instantly and had been keeping an eye on him ever since, waiting for my command.

I patted my boot to make sure Zeus was still in there. I'd brought the knife Garrett Swopes hunted down, the one that could supposedly kill any demon on Earth. Including Reyes, which explained why Garrett had hunted it down in the first place. I felt better knowing it was close. I knew what a demon was capable of. I'd felt the slice of their needle-like teeth as they slid across my skin. I'd felt the stab of their razor-sharp claws as they dug into my flesh. I'd felt the icy chill of their breath as they readied to rip me to shreds. Zeus was definitely nice to have around.

I patted my boot again.

Three other players joined us—all men, all desperate, all searching for something they couldn't get at a card game. Did they know what the Dealer was? What he could do for them? Did they know how much it would cost them in the long run? It was one thing to die. It was another to lose one's soul. To come to a complete end. To exist no longer.

I nodded when Angel showed up. He stuck to the shadows at first, but once the game got under way, he went to work.

This was a game of luck and skill. It took total concentration. Damn it. I sucked at concentration. And I wasn't all that lucky either.

Artemis watched the Dealer like a leopard watched its prey. Anytime he leaned close to deal or to gather cards or chips, a low rumble escaped her chest. No one there could hear it, of course, except for the demon. But to his credit, he never flinched. He pretended to be oblivious, but surely he could see what I was. He could hear Artemis and Angel. He didn't seem particularly worried, though. Angel sucked at cards as bad as I did. I was down a cool seventeen mil. Or seventeen hundred. Probably seventeen hundred. I'd lost track a while ago and was now waiting for him to bargain, to offer to forgive the debt if I'd just give up my soul. He had yet to make that offer, but the night was young. Really young. We'd played only one hand.

Even with Angel walking around the table, telling me what everyone's hands consisted of, I lost. Probably because knowing what everyone was holding didn't matter. I had no idea what constituted a winning hand. If two pairs beat three of a kind. If a full house beat a straight flush, two poker terms that always reminded me of a house full of people with only one toilet. Not sure why.

"You gotta get better at this shit, *mijita,*" Angel said. "You only brought two thousand dollars and you just lost seventeen hundred. In one hand."

A minuscule smile played about the Dealer's mouth as he watched me. He could clearly hear Angel. Could probably see him, too. But I wondered if he could feel Reyes. The human body he'd inhabited may act as a barrier, making him unable to feel the heat that engulfed the room as Reyes watched without materializing. It was impossible to be certain.

"If you're going to send a boy to spy on me, make it a boy worth my time."

So he was ready to drop the charades. I was cool with that. I never could remember the difference between the gestures for words and syllables, anyway.

Angel was offended. Naturally. "Are you talking about me, *pendejo*?"

The Dealer spared him a humorous glance. "I could feast upon your soul, little one, and still have room for dessert."

I leaned forward to get his attention back on me. "You can't have his soul. You can't take a soul unless it was handed to you willingly while the person was still alive. I know the rules, asswipe."

"Such colorful language, Reaper. And you did your homework. I'm surprised. It's not your style."

The other men exchanged sideways glances, confused, wondering if they'd missed something as the Dealer studied me. "Is that really what I think it is, in your boot?"

My hand went to the dagger instinctively.

When I didn't answer, he asked in awe, "You found it. I didn't even know if it was real."

"It's real. Very real. But how did you know I had it?"

"Its glow, of course. You can't see it?"

"No." This not being able to see what other supernatural entities could was getting old.

He absorbed that, his expression calculative, then explained, "Let's just say it makes an impression."

The Dealer gathered the cards, getting a little too close to me, and Artemis let out another guttural growl. The hairs on the back of my neck rose. Thank goodness she liked me. I couldn't imagine what the demon was thinking.

He shuffled and said casually, "Call off your dog."

I reached down and caressed her ears. "She's fine right where she is."

"Not that one." He began dealing. "Rey'aziel."

He did feel him. And he clearly knew who he was.

"He's fine right where he is, too."

He finished dealing, his long fingers nimble as they handled the cards like a seasoned pro. Then again, he probably was a seasoned pro. "Show yourself," he said to Reyes.

And Reyes materialized behind me. I looked up at him. "I'm not doing well."

"I can see that."

The other men at the table were now completely confused. This was poker. *High-stakes* poker. Not the strip poker I usually played. I sucked at that, too. And the Dealer and I were talking crazy. Poker did that to people.

"Rey'aziel," the Dealer said without looking up from the cards. "It's been a long time."

Reyes stepped to the side and leaned against the wall. "Funny, I don't remember you."

The statement seemed to sting him. He flinched—so quickly, I almost missed it. "You wouldn't."

Surprise flashed in Reyes's expression. He pushed off from the wall and seemed to be staring straight through the Dealer. I looked again but saw nothing.

"You're marked," he said, astounded. "You were a slave."

The barest hint of a smile lifted a corner of the Dealer's mouth. "I was."

"You're Daeva." Reyes scoffed as though suddenly disgusted by the creature before him. "You were created from the souls of my lost brethren. You never fell from heaven."

The Dealer cast him a pointed stare. "And neither did you, or have you forgotten?"

"Not at all. I just thought I might have a fight on my hands. This shouldn't take long," he said as he stepped forward.

The Dealer stood, his chair scraping against the floor and falling back as he faced the son of the man who'd apparently created him as well. The light illuminated his face a bit more, and he let a wide, brilliantly white smile spread across it.

Angel grabbed my arm and pulled. "Charley, let's go."

"Still don't recognize me?" the Dealer asked Reyes.

My nigh fiancé laughed softly in surprise, but it wasn't a humorous laugh. It was filled with astonishment and, if I had to guess, an ounce of reverence.

"You escaped?" he asked as though that surprised him the most.

Angel tugged again.

I pulled him to my side and kept an arm locked around him protectively.

"We should go," he said, whispering in my ear.

The Dealer's chin went up, proud of his accomplishment. "I did. Of course, I didn't have a map to get me through the void like you." He gestured to the tattoos that lined Reyes's upper body, the ones that made up a map to the gates of hell. "The gates of hell proved a bit tricky, but here I am."

"And here you'll die."

He lifted one shoulder, unmoved. "I figured as much. I just need to have a conversation with the reaper, then we can finish this."

Reyes stepped to my side at once, his expression hard. "I wouldn't."

Angel squeezed tighter, wanting out of Reyes's reach and wanting me out of harm's way.

"You're in love with her," the Dealer said. It wasn't a question but a statement that held both wonder and admiration. I wasn't sure why he would feel either. "It all makes sense now."

"Don't forget who I am," Reyes said, his tone razor sharp, his stance rigid like a cobra about to strike. "You don't need anything from her."

One brow shot up, implying that the Dealer was so unimpressed, he didn't know what else to do. "No, Your Highness, I don't. But you do."

Reyes stepped closer. "And what would that be?"

"Victory." When Reyes remained silent, he continued. "It's what I do, if you'll remember. I win. And now, more than ever, you need a win."

The air crackled with tension, the friction it caused creating a vortex of heat, Reyes's anger was so palpable. He started for the Dealer, but I put a hand on his arm to stop him. Angel jerked out of my grip. I was too close to Reyes for his comfort. He stepped away from the melee, but to his credit, he didn't disappear.

Reyes stopped at the feel of my touch and glanced down at me. It wasn't a nice glance.

"Why do we need you?" I asked the Dealer, ignoring Mr. Grumpy Britches.

His intense gaze landed on me again, but the moment it did, Reyes growled. He looked back at him before answering. "Because there's only one way to beat your father, and she holds the key." He gestured to me with a nod of his head. "If she doesn't live through this, Earth will become a very dark place."

"Live through what?" I asked, but the Dealer didn't look at me that time.

He kept a watchful eye on the predator. The more immediate danger. "The Twelve have escaped," he said to Reyes, and though I had no idea who or what the Twelve were, Reyes seemed to have no trouble figuring it out.

His expression changed to one of astonishment. It wasn't easy to astonish him.

"If they get to her," he started, but Reyes recovered and interrupted before he could finish, much to my chagrin.

"They won't."

"They will if you don't keep a very close eye on her. She gets into enough trouble without the Twelve making an appearance. They will rip her apart and make you watch while they do it."

Reyes bit down so hard, I could hear his teeth grind. "They'll try."

"You need my help, and you know it."

"This is like the prophecies Garrett found," I told Reyes, patting his arm, trying to convince him to listen. "You and I are the key, remember?" I looked back at the Dealer, who didn't dare meet my eyes.

But before I could question him any further, Reyes asked, "And why would you help us?"

"Why else? I want him dead as much as you do." He leaned in, his mouth twisting into a snarl. "Even more so, I'd wager, and if you want to win this thing, you'll listen to what I have to say. There's only one way to bring him down. We can't risk the reaper because of your pride."

I started thinking back to when I'd first arrived at the game tonight. The Dealer didn't seem the least bit surprised when I walked in. Surely he knew who I was the moment I showed up, like he was expecting me.

"Why am I here?" I asked him. "Did you arrange this?"

He lifted one shoulder. "I simply encouraged Mr. Joyce to seek you out through a few connections I have. He was desperate enough to do it."

I released Zeus, pulling out the knife and holding it toward him as steady as I could. Which wasn't very steady. I was shaking. And I had to pee.

"You're still on my turf, stealing the souls of good people. And you stole that body you're living in."

"I didn't steal anything. I was born on Earth, just like the prince."

I gaped at Reyes. "He can do that?"

After a long hesitation, he nodded. "It's a complicated process, but yes."

"Wow, okay, but you've still stolen souls."

He shrugged helplessly. "Man cannot live on bread alone. And I steal nothing. Whatever I take has been handed over to me willingly. I pay a very high price for the souls I take."

"Not high enough."

"You forget, they come to me and they are getting what they want in return. It's a win–win." When I only glared, he added, "I am not your enemy. We have a similar agenda."

"I want Mr. Joyce's soul returned to him."

He threw his head back and laughed, and I sensed a genuine enjoyment in his reaction, as though I were entertaining to him like a fly might be to a spider. So that was annoying.

"And then," I continued, letting my mouth lift into a patient smile, "I'm going to take this dagger, push it into your heart, and watch you die."

"Well, then, that's not a very good incentive for me to do what you want, now, is it?"

"You need to be brought down. I'm sorry, but it has to be done."

"I believe you," he said, surprised. "I think you are sorry, even if just barely. What if I only bargained for the souls of bad people? You know, murderers and child molesters and people who cut in line at the theater snack counter."

There was a thought I could live with. Well, not the snack-counter thing, but . . . "You could be like the demonic version of Dexter."

"Exactly," he agreed.

"But how many have you taken in the past? How many good souls do you have to compensate for?"

He raised a helpless hand. "I've been on this plane in human form for more than two centuries," he said, surprising me to my core. "If I had to guess, I'd say more than a few. Surely you won't hold my past indiscretions against me."

I stepped closer and his chin went up. He watched Zeus carefully, like one would watch a venomous snake poised to strike. "No more," I said, my tone low and even. "Never again. And I want Mr. Joyce's soul returned to him. I don't care what kind of bargain he made, I want it canceled."

"As you wish, but I want something in return."

"Do not bargain with him," Reyes said.

Of course, I ignored him. "What?"

He gestured toward Zeus with a congenial nod of his top hat. "The dagger."

I snorted. "You've got to be kidding. The only way you're getting this knife is when its blade slides into your chest."

He shrugged. "It was worth a shot. Then how about you let me help you with this little Twelve problem, and it's all his."

"You can do that?"

"Dutch," Reyes said, but I shushed him with an index finger. A very powerful index finger, it would seem, because he let me continue.

"You can return it to him?" I asked. "Good as new?"

The Dealer winced. "*New* is a strong word, but once it's back in place, how it fares is up to him."

I raised the knife again, but he stood his ground, albeit warily. "And no more, right?"

"No more, right. Only bad people."

"No snack-counter line-cutters, either. They have to genuinely be bad, as in harmful to the human race."

"Not a problem. I know a rapist down the street. I can live off him for weeks."

"And I want Joyce's soul returned immediately."

He snorted. "Do you think me a fool?"

"I think you're all kinds of a fool. There's no telling when, or even if, these twelve jokers will show up."

"Clearly, you have trust issues. I'll give him back his soul when the favor is returned."

"I'm returning it now by not burying this blade in your chest."

He paused in thought, but only for a split second before saying, "You think that a favor?"

I wasn't sure what he meant, so I deflected. "I think I'm bored. Leave Mr. Joyce's soul alone."

With that, I turned and walked out, completely unsure if I'd accomplished anything at all.

7

*I lost my virginity,
but I still have the box it came in.*

—T-SHIRT

Though I couldn't be 100 percent certain, I got the distinct feeling Reyes was angry. He sat in Misery, his back rigid, his gaze averted, his jaw set to the consistency of marble. And he was still incorporeal. He could have vanished but didn't. Did he want me to know how angry he was, or was he worried about this Twelve-pack? When he cast me a glare from underneath his lashes as we headed home, I glared right back.

"What?" I asked, my adrenaline level still high. My disbelief even higher. He wasn't worried about the Twelve. He was angry with me. Me! What had I done now?

He shook his head and returned his attention starboard. When he spoke, his voice was low, calculated. "You did exactly what I said you would."

"What? I have my soul. And my dignity. He didn't get either one."

"That's debatable. You made a deal with him."

"For the survival of humankind," I said defensively. "Or something like that. Who are the Twelve?"

It took him a while to answer. Brooding did that. Took its time. Meandered. Wandered around, oblivious of the needs and impatience of others. It was kind of like a small child that way. Just when I was about to fill the uncomfortable void of silence with the theme song from *Gilligan's Island,* he answered. Disappointment washed over me.

"The Twelve are most commonly referred to on my plane as the Twelve Beasts of Hell. But here on earth, they are most often referred to as hellhounds."

"Hellhounds?" I asked, astonished. "For real? They're hellhounds?"

"Yes. They were imprisoned centuries ago. It would seem they've escaped."

I let a whistle slip through my lips. "Honest-to-goodness hellhounds. That's unreal. Why were they imprisoned?"

"Have you ever met a hellhound?" He worked his jaw. "They're unruly. Uncontrollable. They kill anything and everything in their paths. They were one of my father's experiments gone bad."

My fingers tightened around the steering wheel. "He created them?"

"Yes."

"Like he created you?"

"No, not really. My father created me from his own flesh, which is why I am his son. He created no other being like me." He gave me a sideways glance. "That's not arrogance. It's simply fact. One I'm not proud of."

I was still busy trying to wrap my head around the whole hellhound thing. "Wait, what about the Dealer? You said he didn't fall from heaven."

"He was a slave, one of millions, also created by my father."

"You called him Daeva."

"Many scholars on earth believe Daeva and demons are one and the same. They are wrong. Demons, true demons, fell from heaven. They are the Fallen sons."

"So, like, they're purebred while the Daeva are, I don't know, clones?"

"They are slaves. Period."

I didn't like that word unless I was using it to refer to Cookie. "You know, traditionally, slaves are simply an undervalued race of people. They are every bit as good and worthy as you or I."

"Daeva are not a race," he said, his voice hardening. "They are a creation of my father's."

"Why do you feel so much animosity toward them?" I asked, surprised.

"Who says I do?"

"Reyes, come on."

"It's complicated," he answered at last. "When God first created the angels, they were referred to as the sons of God until he had one true son, created to lead humans, to clear their paths into Heaven. In that same sense, when my father first created the Daeva, they were called the sons of Satan until he had a one true son. Me. Then they were nothing but Daeva. They were not Fallen. They were not the sons. They simply were. And just as some angels became enraged by what they perceived as injustice from God's favoritism of man over his own creations, some of the Daeva felt slighted when my father sought to create me. It complicated matters."

"But you knew him? The Dealer?"

"Everyone knew him. He was a champion. He was the fastest and strongest being in hell, but he was a slave, destined to always be a slave. It was a position he didn't care for."

"I can't imagine why," I said, letting the sarcasm drip off my tongue. Then Reyes's words sank in. "Wait, was he faster than you?"

Without looking at me, he nodded. I sucked in a soft breath of air.

"Stronger?"

After a lengthy pause, he said, "Yes. We never fought, but if we had, he would have won."

I wouldn't have been more surprised if a two-by-four appeared out of nowhere and slammed into my face. "So, really? He can beat you?"

"I believe he could have, yes, but that was in hell. This is a different plane with a different set of rules. Who's to say what he can do here?"

"But why did you try to go up against him? If he's that dangerous, why risk it?" When he didn't answer, I pushed him, growing angry that he would risk himself so frivolously. "Reyes, why would you do that?"

"I'm too stunned to answer that right now."

"What? Why?"

"I am astonished that you would ask me such a question."

"Really? Do you know me at all?"

"Well, this has certainly been a day of revelations," I said as Reyes and I walked from Misery into the apartment building together. He was apparently not leaving my side. "So, the Twelve beasts, huh? I'll bet they're fun at parties."

"Not unless you like massacres," he said, scanning the area as we walked.

"Not really. We probably shouldn't invite them to our engagement party." When he glanced at me in surprise, I added, "You know, if we have one."

He followed behind me on the stairs. "Probably not."

"I want to know more about the Dealer," I said over my shoulder. "I mean, I didn't even know they had slaves in hell. That place has to be bad enough without throwing the title of indentured servant into the mix."

"My father has millions. He can create them from the remnants of lost demons."

"Like from their DNA?"

"Something like that."

"So, this Dealer was a champion? Of what? Volleyball?"

"Think more along the lines of gladiator."

"Seriously? They play gladiator games in hell?" It just seemed unfathomable.

"We had a lot of free time."

I stopped on the landing and turned toward him as he ascended behind me. "Reyes, I want you to give him a chance. I think he really is out to help us. You can be mad at me if you want, but I just think he really does want to see your father fall."

"Sure he does. Wouldn't you want to see your captor fall? It doesn't mean we can trust him."

"I think you're letting your prejudices get in the way," I said, turning to ascend the next flight.

"Dutch," he said, taking my shoulders and urging me to face him, "you can't ever trust Daeva. No matter how much they help. No matter what they do for you, they simply cannot be trusted."

"I understand the generalization, but he's different. There's something very special about him, and I have a feeling we are going to find out what that is someday."

"Not if you're smart, you won't."

"I'm not stupid," I said, growing tired of his questioning everything I did. "I do use common sense."

"You have to have common sense to use it."

I stiffened. He did not just say that. "You did not just say that."

"When it comes to humans, Dutch, you are blind. You do things for them that no other person alive would do. And if you believe even remotely that this Daeva will help you in that endeavor, you'll lose everything to him."

"No person alive would do for me? That just goes to show how well you know humans. You may have been one for the last thirty years, but you know nothing of our spirit. Of our generous nature. It's different for everyone, but most humans are kind and giving. And we care about our fellow man. And woman."

"I know enough about humans to realize not one person on this earth would risk his life to save yours."

"You're wrong. And if my suspicions about the Dealer are right, you'll be eating those words before all this is over. We allegedly have twelve very nasty creatures to fight, and I'd bet my last dollar he will be with us to the end."

"At which point, he will trick you out of your soul and grow fat and old on you."

I unlocked my door and shouldered my way in to block his entrance. "I'm tired. I'll see you tomorrow."

He offered me an angry nod, then turned toward his own apartment. I shut my door softly. He slammed his.

Cookie came in later than I did. I could hear her familiar footsteps on the stairs. She knocked softly before opening it, which was so not like her. "Are you still up?" she asked.

"I sure am. How'd it go?"

She still looked great and had a fresh glow to her face.

"Wait, you're not falling for Barry, are you?"

"Oh, heavens no. But we had such a good time. It was fun to get out."

"I'm glad."

"Did Robert, I don't know, ask about it?"

I giggled. "He did. It was great. He was dying to ask me, but it took him a while. Did you see the look on his face when he saw Barry?"

"Yes. Charley, I feel guilty."

I pursed my lips. "Cook. I can feel emotions, remember? And it's his own fault."

"Oh, right." She grinned. "I think this could work. He was stunned speechless when he saw my date."

"Honey," I said, putting a hand on hers, "he was stunned speechless when he saw you."

"You think so?"

"Absolutely. I don't think he's into men."

She dismissed that with a wave.

"You know what I mean."

She had stars in her eyes. I guess I'd never realized how much she liked Ubie. I mean, it was Ubie. Who could've guessed that?

"So," she said, easing up to the bigger questions of the night, "how was the card game?"

"I lost my ass. And, well, have you seen my ass?" I patted it to emphasize my point.

She laughed at first, then sobered. "Wait, really? You lost money?"

"Nah, I convinced the Dealer it would be in his best interest to let that one slide."

"Oh, good. So, was he really a demon?"

"Yep, or as they are called, a Daeva. A slave demon."

"They have slaves in hell?"

"Apparently. Crazy, huh?"

"Daeva. I like it."

I explained to her what happened in great detail, mostly because I was having a hard time wrapping my head around everything myself. When I finished, she just kind of sat there. And stared. For a really long time.

I looked over at Mr. Wong. "I think I broke her."

"No, I'm okay, but holy cow, Charley. This just gets deeper and deeper. I mean, when you told me you were the grim reaper, I thought, 'What more can there be?' But it just goes so much further than that. And now the Twelve? Seriously? It's endless."

"I know, and I'm sorry. You didn't sign up for any of this."

"Are you kidding? I love this shit. I wouldn't trade my life for the world. Well, maybe the world. Is the Dealer in the market for a slightly used, thirty-something-year-old soul with a few dents in it? I could use a mansion in the Keys. And a Bentley. With chrome rims and a killer sound system."

I laughed, partly out of relief. "I figured you more as a Rolls-Royce kind of girl."

"I'd take either."

"I bet he'd take you up on that offer. I liked him," I added, picturing his face.

"The Dealer?"

"Yeah. I mean, he was so young. Or, well, he looked young."

"You have such a soft spot for kids. Are you sure that's not what you're feeling?"

"I love kids. They go great with fries and a shake."

She chuckled. "How does Reyes feel about him?"

"He would rip out his spine if I let him."

She patted my knee. "I would expect nothing less from the son of evil incarnate. He's a good guy."

"Yes, he is," I agreed. "Even though he has a tendency to annoy me to the lowest levels of hell. Where there is no coffee."

"But he looks amazing in an apron."

"Right?"

We both fell into a dream state for a few seconds.

I snapped out of it first. "Okay, well, go to bed. We have a lot to do tomorrow. No rest for the wicked, and all that crap."

Cookie was right. Reyes was a good guy. He'd done so much for me. And put up with so much from me. Then again, I had to put up with his alpha-esque personality. Lucky for him, I had excellent self-control. Otherwise, I'd end up kicking his ass every other day, leaving him fetal and whimpering, and then where would we be?

I got ready for bed and changed into something more comfortable, namely a T-shirt with a pair of bottoms that said, PEEL TO REVEAL PRIZE. After weaving my hair into a soft braid, I curled onto my most fabulous mattress, the one I got at a going-out-of-business sale, and snuggled into the thick folds of my Bugs Bunny comforter.

But even insulated, I could feel Reyes's heat. It leached through the wall and surrounded me in a gentle, soothing warmth. He'd been living next door for a few weeks now, and I wondered if I'd ever get so accustomed to being enveloped in his delicious heat that I wouldn't notice it. Probably not. Standing next to him was like standing next to an inferno—to me, anyway. And pretty much only to me. If Cookie had been there, she wouldn't have felt it, which made no sense. Humans could feel the cold of the departed when they were near. Both the departed's cold and Reyes's heat were supernatural occurrences. Why could they feel one and not the other?

But the fact that Reyes's heat could penetrate walls had surprised me the first time I noticed it. Our beds butted up against the same wall, and I could tell the minute he crawled into bed every night. And not just because I was with him about half the time when that happened. Even in my own apartment, I could feel him. He was always hottest when he first crawled into bed. As he drifted to sleep, his heat dissipated a bit. He was still unnaturally warm even in slumber, but not so much as when he was awake. And especially not so much as when he was angry. Or, well, in the throes of passion. *Scalding* would be an appropriate adjective for that.

But the heat wafting toward me now had the consistency of anger. I lifted a hand and placed my palm on the Sheetrock that separated us. It was scorching, almost painful.

Yep, anger.

He'd been lying in bed, probably thinking of the best way to dispose of the Dealer. I would have to convince him otherwise for the time being. The Dealer was different from other Daeva. He'd been born on earth. He was, in every sense of the word, human. Partly, at least. And very much like Reyes himself.

So if Reyes was going to stew in his own anger, fine. I did what I had to do, and he would just have to learn to live with it. We were nigh affianced. He had to take the good with the bad. And besides, I could give Reyes Alexander Farrow something much better to think about.

I wondered if he could feel my emotions through the wall, because his heat grazed over my fingertips and along my palm as though purposefully. As though it had an agenda.

Reyes could do amazing things with his essence. He could send it out. He could skim it over my skin. He could bury it deep inside me until I writhed in ecstasy. I wondered if I could do that, too.

I'd left my body before. I'd killed a man in the process, but from that experience, I knew it was possible, but could I control it the way Reyes could? He'd come to me hundreds of times, even when we were growing up, before I knew who, or what, he was. And now I'd done it. My essence, my spirit, had left my body. Could I do it again? The first time was under extreme duress. I wasn't duressed at the moment. A little stressed, maybe. A little befuddled at what had happened with the Dealer, with everything he'd told us, but not duressed.

Still, I was the grim reaper. I had to get a grip. Figure this shit out before I was ripped apart by a hellhound. I had to learn what I could and could not do, and I had to learn to control it. What better test subject than someone who was almost indestructible? I could be like a mad scientist, and Reyes could be my experiment. What could go wrong?

Closing my eyes, I ran my hand farther up the wall. The sensation of fire grew stronger as I brushed my sensitive fingertips over the texture. I let it. I welcomed it, urged it closer, absorbed it until it penetrated my skin, soaked my bones to the marrow, and pushed up my arm. It touched my neck, tingled along my cheek like a soft caress, laced across my collarbone, down over my chest and flooded my torso with a tart warmth. Danger and Will struggled against the confines of my T-shirt, their crests jutting out, the texture of the material only serving to harden them more. The friction sent a jolt of pleasure straight to my core, rippling through me, pressing down until the heat dipped low in my abdomen, until it consumed every molecule in my body.

But it was my turn. I was the mad scientist in this scenario. I wanted to do the same to him, to penetrate his body and soul the way he'd penetrated mine. I fought the unimaginable pleasure coursing through my veins and I focused. I pushed. I sent out my energy, let it glide along my nerve endings and up through my arm until it broke through the wall between us. I still couldn't actually see Reyes, but I could sense him and feel him. I could very much feel him.

I let my energy wash over him. Let it explore the hills and valleys of his muscles as they contracted and released under my touch. I felt the smoothness of his skin, the hardness of the muscles underneath, the tautness of his abdomen. Lower and lower until I was rewarded with a telltale rush of blood.

He sucked in air through his teeth when I grazed his erection. The sense of accomplishment was heady, but I wanted more. I wanted inside him like he'd been inside me. I wanted to make him come from the inside out. I wanted to make him writhe in ecstasy. Beg for release. But he'd put up a guard. A mental block of some kind. Always wary of what I might see if he let me in.

That was hardly fair.

I sharpened my touch. Let my fingernails bite into his flesh. Coaxed and urged him to let me in. His arms were resting above his head, and he curled his hands into fists. Clenched his jaw.

"Dutch," he said in warning.

I said nothing back. I wasn't sure if I could. But I pushed again, opening his legs, and let my energy pulse over his body in electric waves. He threw back his head, pressing it into the pillow as his fingers became entangled in the sheets around him.

And he lowered his guard.

The moment he did, I entered him. Our energies collided in a rush of sensuous elation, the atoms pushing and pulling until the friction built to nuclear levels. He arched his back and fought me, each of us struggling to get the upper hand, to send the other over the edge first.

At the same time I was exploring him, he was exploring me. It took me a moment to realize part of what I was feeling was my own skin being caressed. My own fires being stoked. His energy brushed over me and around me and into me like liquid smoke, fusing with every particle in my body as he stirred the arousal crackling inside me. I felt his hunger, hot and urgent between my legs, raw and powerful. The air in my lungs thickened as a series of aching spasms grew stronger with each beat of my heart, siphoning me closer and closer until a white-hot orgasm burst inside me, crashing and tumbling and reeling.

I'd gotten lost in my own swelling desire, but it seemed my climax was all Reyes needed to release his own firestorm. His muscles tensed around me as I felt the sweet sting of his climax spill onto his stomach, the evidence warm on his abdomen.

I felt him claw at his sheets as the orgasm coursed through him, ebbing only for a microsecond until it spiked again in time with his racing pulse. After a few agonizing moments, it slowly ebbed, leaving only Reyes's labored breathing in its wake. He'd had a death grip on his sheets. He disentangled his fingers and ran them over his face before covering it with one arm.

He spoke to me then, his deep voice husky, spent. "Come sleep with me."

When I didn't answer, again unsure if I even could, he rose to clean himself off. I could see him more clearly now, but my touch was still more sensitive in this state than my sight. Something I'd have to work on, would have to strengthen like a muscle.

I stayed with him until he crawled back into bed and dragged a sheet haphazardly over his bottom half. Then he pressed his hand against the wall, and his lids drifted shut almost immediately. Just before I left, he whispered it again. "Come sleep with me."

But he was out. It was odd sensing everything about him and yet not actually seeing him with my eyes but only in my mind's eye. I could suddenly understand why, when he was growing up, he never knew if I was real or not. He'd thought I was a dream. That was exactly how this felt. Dreamlike. Real and yet not real. Tangible and yet untouchable, as though he would slip through my fingers if I actually tried get hold of him. But I'd done just that. Touched him. Caressed him. Milked him until he came.

I fell asleep immersed in his essence, in his taste and texture and earthy scent. I also fell asleep with my hand against the wall, his heat warming my palm not six inches away from his.

8

Clothes? sufficient
Keys? found 'em
Coffee cup? full
Sanity? sanity?

—T-SHIRT

I woke up what seemed like seconds later to a hand over my mouth, and that's just never a pleasant way to wake up. Alarm spiked so fierce and so fast, Reyes was there instantly, incorporeally, engulfed in his black robe. It grew like a tidal wave around me, and I heard the sing of a blade being drawn. But I didn't know what was happening. I held up a hand to stop him, trying to gain my bearings. A man in a black ski mask stood over me, a gun in his right hand, the tip of which was lodged against my left temple. A fact that made me very uncomfortable.

Reyes growled, and I could feel his visceral need to slice through the man, to overtake him. He pushed it back. Swallowed it down. But it wasn't easy, and his control wouldn't last long. Which meant I didn't have long.

I forced myself to relax, to control my reactions, and sought the intruder's intentions. Did he want me dead? If so, I was about to un-leash an enraged son of Satan on his ass. But I recognized the reason for his presence instantly. He was carrying out orders. I could feel obligation, along with a disturbing sense of enjoyment, rush through him. He was a messenger, a fact that raised the question, whom was the message from?

The man laid a piece of paper on my chest, then used that hand to clutch my throat. "You have forty-eight hours to find out where they're keeping her or your friend dies." He shoved into me, crushing my larynx and jamming the barrel into my temple as a warning. "And no cops." He shoved again, pushing off me; then he was gone.

Only as he was leaving did I realize there were two of them. They bolted through my bedroom door, having no idea how close they'd come to having their spines severed.

I coughed and drew in a deep breath as Reyes's robe disappeared. He rushed to me. "Who the fuck was that?"

I held my neck, tested my throat with a quick swallow. "I have no idea. But I'm okay."

"Like hell you are."

"Wait, my friend?"

Dread sent a rush of adrenaline shooting up my spine. I jumped up and ran to Cookie's apartment. She'd locked it, thank God. I pounded on the door, then went back for my key, but she opened the door before I could find it.

"Charley!" she said, hurrying forward. "What happened?"

"Are you okay?"

"Yes." Cookie glanced around, wondering why she wouldn't be.

"Amber," I said a second before scrambling to Cookie's apartment to check her room.

Cookie was right behind me, as was a flesh and blood Reyes Farrow. He'd thrown on a pair of jeans and come out of his apartment. I opened Amber's bedroom door and turned on the light. She was sound asleep, her long dark hair tumbling over her pillow like a princess from a fairy tale.

Cookie whispered behind me. "Charley, what? What's going on?"

I turned off the light and closed the door. "I'm so sorry, Cook. Two men just broke into my apartment."

"Why the fu—?" Reyes began, his voice loud enough to wake Amber.

"Reyes," I said in a breathy hiss, "not here." He was angry with me once again. Men and their mood swings. Women had nothing on them.

I led them both back to my apartment, and the minute I closed the door, he tore into me. "What the fuck was that?"

He wasn't wearing a shirt, and the button on his jeans had yet to be fastened, so it took me a minute to respond. "What? They threatened a friend. They said if I didn't find some chick in forty-eight hours, my friend was dead."

"And?" he asked, getting closer to me. His anger undulated around me, hot and pulsing.

"And if they are holding a friend of mine, I couldn't have you severing their spines, now, could I?"

He whirled away from me with an angry growl.

Cookie was holding a hand to her chest, not sure what to make of everything. "Two men broke in?" she asked, glancing around.

"Yes. Oh! The paper." I hurried back to my room and brought out the paper he'd practically stabbed into my chest. It was a picture of a woman with a name underneath. That was it. "Okay, I have forty-eight hours to find this woman or my friend dies." I shrugged. "Like I only have one. Which friend?"

"I don't know," she said, lowering herself onto a chair. "Maybe we should call everyone we can think of. Make sure all of your acquaintances are okay. I mean, did it sound like they were actually holding a friend of yours?"

"Kind of," I said, thinking back. "I'm not sure. It happened so fast."

Reyes was busy pacing like a caged animal, and I couldn't help but note the fact that he was becoming more attuned to my emotions. He'd appeared the moment alarm rose within me. It was uncanny.

"I'm sorry, hon," I said, walking to him. "I just couldn't take the chance. I needed to know why they were there before I sentenced them to life in a wheelchair."

I stopped talking when I noticed the look on his face. He was still angry, but his expression had softened.

I reached up and tucked a lock of hair behind his ear. "What?"

When he spoke, his voice was hoarse, ragged. "You called me hon."

A soft laugh escaped me. "It's a term of endearment."

He blinked as though he didn't know what to think.

"Hasn't anyone ever called you hon before? Honey? Sweetheart?"

"No."

I wondered what his human parents had called him when he was a baby. "I bet you have, you just don't remember."

"You should have let me rip them to shreds."

"That may be and I may regret that later—in fact, if my track record holds true, I'm fairly certain I will—but for now, I'm fine."

He ran a finger down my forearm, not wanting to show too much in front of Cook, most likely.

"Shouldn't we call the police?" Cookie asked.

"They said no cops. I'll call Uncle Bob and fill him in tomorrow morning."

She nodded and rose to go back to her apartment.

"Yes," I said, following her out. "Go, get some rest."

"Rest?" She pointed to Mr. Coffee. "You start the coffee and I'll get dressed. We'll start making phone calls immediately."

God, I loved that woman.

We called every friend I'd ever had since the day I was born. Not really, but it felt like it. My friend Pari, a tattoo artist who'd been banned from computers for hacking, complained for twenty minutes that I'd woken her. After an eternity, she finally shut up long enough for me to ask her if she was being held hostage by a group of men in ski masks. Then I had to suffer through another twenty minutes of what a stupid question that was.

"It wouldn't have seemed stupid if you really were being held hostage by men in ski masks," I'd argued. Either way, that was the last time I'd call her at four in the morning.

By six, I was pretty much out of people that I could call friends. Not that it took me that long to go through the list. It just took that long for people to answer their phones. We had to call some repeatedly, a fact that they did not appreciate one bit.

Next time, I'd just let the bad men keep them.

Uncle Bob came over around six thirty, and we explained what had happened. He kept checking out Cookie, worried about the events but dying to know how her date went. I wasn't about to tell him.

"I'm hitting the shower," Reyes said, nodding to Ubie.

"Don't hit George." I scowled at him. His shower was magnificent. I'd named him George because he just didn't look like a Tom, Dick, or Harry. "What did he ever do to you?"

Despite Reyes's rocky disposition, his full mouth showed traces of a smile that reached all the way up to his sparkling mocha-colored eyes, the green and gold flecks brilliant even in the artificial light. He offered me a soft kiss, his mouth brushing across mine before he took it farther, showering tiny kisses along my cheek until he came to my ear. His warm breath stirred my hair as he whispered, "George misses you." Then he stood and winked playfully.

But what he did next surprised everyone in the room. He bent down, kissed Cookie on the cheek, and whispered something in her ear, too. I sat stunned. That was the second time he'd kissed her cheek in as many days. After a curt nod to Ubie, he strode out the door.

"Is there something I need to know about you two?" I asked Cookie.

It took her a moment to travel back to Earth. When she did, a soft pink glow suffused her face. "He thanked me for being a good friend to you."

I put a hand over my heart. That guy. "He can be the sweetest thing when he's not killing demons and shit."

"True," she said.

The kiss affected Ubie even more than it did Cookie. I could feel a tinge of jealousy in the mix of emotions radiating out of him. Among them were insecurity, worry, and doubt. Poor guy. If he'd just ask Cookie out, all this would be over. It would only take one of them to be bold enough to make the first move. Freaking wusses.

"Yeah, I'll go now, too," he said, clearing his throat as he stood. "I'm going to send over a uniform—"

"Uncle Bob, you can't. They said no police. Just find out what you can about the woman in that picture. We have lots of protection right here."

Ubie cursed under his breath, then said, "I'll send over a plainclothes. I know just who to send. He can be your nephew, Cookie. Do not let him leave your side." He took a minuscule step closer to her. "Promise me."

"Thank you, Robert. I promise."

"I'll come back by this evening to check on you girls."

"Oh, well, you could," I said, thinking ahead, "but Cookie won't be here. She has another date. Like I said, popular." I winked at him.

"Are you sure that's wise?" he asked. "Considering the circumstances."

Cookie was busy giving me the evil eye when she pasted on a smile and turned back to him. "Right, yes, I do. I almost forgot. But if you want to drop by, I could cancel."

"Oh, no," I said, waving a dismissive hand, "Uncle Bob wouldn't want to ruin your evening just to come by and talk shop—right, Ubie?"

It took him a moment to force the words past his clenched teeth. "Right. No, you're right. You go have fun." He started for the door. "I'll call this evening to make sure you're okay."

"There's really no need," I said to him. My sentence was followed by a slight squeak when Cookie kicked me in the shin. I waved to Ubie, then turned on her. "What are you doing?"

"What am I doing? What are you doing?"

"What do you mean what am I doing? I asked you first."

"He was coming over," she said, pointing toward the door. "He wanted to spend time with me."

"BS, Cook." I got up and took my cup to the sink. But only to rinse it out and pour a fresh cup.

"BS?"

"Yes, BS. He comes over all the time. He practically lives over here some weeks, but has that gotten you two anywhere? Are you any closer to dating? To making out on my couch? To having hot monkey sex in the bathroom stalls at the Sizzler? I think not."

Her shoulders deflated. Slowly. Like a balloon with a tiny pinprick that made the slightest of squeaks as air escaped it. Only she didn't squeak. "You're absolutely right."

"I am?" I stopped and thought about it. "That doesn't happen very often."

"I know. Enjoy it while it lasts." When I gaped at her, she said, "What? Everyone knows I'm the brains of this here operation."

She had a point. "Okay, I'm going to shower the residue of smoky back rooms and men in ski masks out of my hair."

Cookie got up and started washing my dishes.

"Oh, no, you don't have to do that. Please, stop." I added a touch of melodrama to be more convincing. "Really, Cookie."

"Okay, I'll stop."

"I'm just kidding. Wash away. Someone's got to do the dishes, and

God knows Mr. Wong isn't pulling his weight." I glared accusingly at him before heading to the bathroom.

"I'll just wash these while Amber finishes getting ready."

Amber, who was doing her hair at my kitchen table because Cook refused to leave her alone after our most recent adventures, protested. "I could've gotten ready in my own bathroom, Mom."

"We have to get a move on," she said, ignoring her offspring, "or you'll be late for school again." She quirked a quizzical brow. "It's weird how much that annoys them."

I shook my head, befuddled as well as I entered my bathroom and closed the door. Then and only then did I let the tremors wash through me, did I acknowledge the blurred vision and rapid heartbeat that hit me every time I thought of those men in my room, of that gun to my head. I looked in the mirror. I was better than this. I could overcome it. Fear would not take hold of me again. Not ever.

I took out my toothbrush and squeezed a line of toothpaste over the bristles. But I was shaking, and the tube caught on the bristles as it glided past. When they bounced back, they flung a speck of toothpaste in my eye. Mint-flavored toothpaste with fluoride and tooth-whitening grit and shit.

I screamed and covered my eye with both hands, falling back and knocking my Little Mermaid figurine off the shelf. "My eye!" I cried, trying to focus past the pain. "My left eye! It burns!"

Before I could regroup, the door to my bathroom was ripped open and Reyes was standing on the other side. He stood there panting, his alarm causing adrenaline to rush through him in hot waves.

"Holy mother of God," Cookie said, her hands encased in plastic yellow gloves.

That was the exact moment I realized Reyes was as naked as the naked dead man sitting in my Jeep. And he was wet. Very, very wet.

Reyes turned to her as she gaped at him.

"Oops," I said, realizing what I'd done. I'd practically summoned him with my screams of agony.

He just stood there like an anointed god, not even trying to cover his junk, and said, "I was in the shower."

"How is George?" I asked, but before he could answer, we all turned slowly to the fairy princess standing behind her mother.

Amber stood with jaw dropped and eyes like saucers. Huge, happy saucers. Cookie dived toward her and attempted to cover said eyes with those big yellow gloves, but Amber was quick. She stepped to the side and easily thwarted her mother's plans, receiving a full frontal of the son of Satan for a solid twenty seconds.

That was dangerous on any level.

I bolted into action the minute I could tear away from his perfect physique: wide shoulders, steel buttocks, and that ever-popular dip in the hip. But I had a job to do. I rushed in front of him and couldn't miss the playful wink Reyes gave Amber as Cookie ushered her out. She blushed and giggled under a cupped hand.

"Holy crap, Reyes," I said in my best scolding tone. "You can't just expose yourself to twelve-year-old girls."

Cookie hurried back in to grab her things. "That's right," she said, fumbling with her list of things to do for the day while trying to avoid Reyes's sleek, naked body sparkling in front of her.

I rolled my eyes, retrieved a towel, and wrapped it around his waist. He smirked as he watched me from underneath his lashes, not bothering to help in the least.

A hopeless sigh slid through Cookie's lips as she finally looked at him. "You've set the bar too high now. No one will live up to—" She gestured to all of him. "—all of that. You've ruined my daughter."

"Sorry," he said, but he wasn't. I could tell.

A smile broke across Cookie's face. She pointed an accusing finger at him. "No, you aren't."

He shrugged. "Yeah, not really."

"Rascal," she said before she closed the door behind her. Or tried to. It just kind of hit the doorframe and bounced back. She tried again with the same result. Then again. And again.

"Cook, it's okay," I said, peeling the injured door out of her hands, which were still covered in yellow rubber. "I'll get the door." When she nodded and started across the hall, I added, "I'll need those gloves back."

I examined my door. It was fine. The doorframe, however, had seen better days. "Did you do this?" I asked him. "How can I lock my door if I can't even close it?"

"That is a problem." He'd come up from behind and reached a long arm over my head, imprisoning me. "Guess you'll have to stay at my place."

I fluttered my lashes. "Or Cookie's."

He handed the towel back to me, a wicked expression on his face as he walked back to his apartment. Naked. All shimmery and sleek. Cookie had nailed it. Holy mother of God.

After the plainclothes got to Cookie's apartment, I let him walk her over to the office while I sought out Misery. Cook would have a busy day with everything I'd thrown at her, and I had enough to do to keep me busy for minutes. Probably half hours.

I needed a man. A man I could push around and shout orders to like a military commander. I needed a man named Garrett Swopes. He was the only one of our group who'd visited hell. Besides Reyes, of course. I excavated my bag for the keys to Misery, which were brand-new and not like my old keys at all, and headed that way. I unlocked Misery with the fob. That was new, too. Misery had never had remote anything. She'd been old school. Stick the key in. Turn. I was surprised I didn't have carpal tunnel with all the sticking and turning. But now, I just pushed a button. It was so *Jetsons*. I made that whirring sound every time we took off down the street.

After opening the door, I tried to climb inside. I would have succeeded, too, if an eighty-pound Rottweiler hadn't been sitting in the driver's seat.

"Artemis," I said as she panted happily, her stubby tail wagging as fast as bumblebee wings flutter, "you can't drive. The last time you drove, we almost killed a mailman."

She whined and put a paw possessively on the steering wheel, her huge brown eyes pleading.

I leaned over and checked Mr. Andrulis. He didn't seem to mind Artemis. I rubbed her ears. "Okay, look, I know traditionally your species and the mailman variety of my species have never really gotten along, but we can't kill them. We can't target them." I was never sure if she did that on purpose or not.

She let out a loud bark, indicating something just over my shoulder. I let my gaze wander in that direction and realized we had company. A man in his early thirties dressed in a gray hoodie and fatigues stood watching us. Well, me, since he couldn't see Artemis.

I nodded congenially before turning back to Artemis and saying through gritted teeth, "Seriously, girl, you have to move."

"I'll wash it for you," the guy said, taking a couple of steps forward. I'd recently had a gun to my head and wasn't in the mood for any more shenanigans from the penis-endowed gender. I reached into a side pocket of my bag as nonchalantly as I could and wrapped my fingers around Margaret, my Glock.

"I'm sorry?"

If he was homeless, he hadn't been for long. He was clean, his clothes almost new.

"Your Jeep. I can wash it. I have a side business." He took another step toward me and handed me a homemade business card. It'd been printed on regular paper, then cut out with scissors. Apparently by a preschooler.

"Well, thanks, we're good for now."

"You wouldn't happen to have a couple of bucks on you?" he asked, sniffing into a knit fingerless glove.

"You take a few steps back, and I'll look."

"Really?" he asked, excited. "Thanks." He stepped back, and I once again excavated my purse for a wallet as I let my gaze slide past him.

I'd been having a lot of odd encounters with homeless people of late. Well, lots of my encounters with homeless people were odd. Especially the one where that guy threw a mustard burger at my windshield as I sat at a stoplight. I didn't even do anything to that man. He was all screaming through my plastic window.

But maybe these encounters were a sign from God. Maybe he wanted me to work with the homeless. Or, and I was thinking outside the box with this one, maybe they were all some kind of elaborate setup to take pictures of me with these people, so that they could later blackmail me into doing something illicit. Normally my thoughts wouldn't have veered in quite that direction, but they did this time. Probably because there was a man sitting in a beige sedan parked down the street with a wide-angle camera pointed directly at me.

Oddly enough, I'd been seeing that same beige sedan a lot lately, too.

He seemed to have snapped the shots he wanted. He lowered the camera and was scrolling through the shots when I knocked on his window. Hard.

He jumped and flailed a bit at being surprised.

"Who the fuck are you?" I said, practically screaming at him. I was not going to take being set up lying down.

Of course, there was an added benefit to screaming. With any luck, it would garner the attention of anyone who happened to be close by. If he came at me, I'd have witnesses.

I took two quick seconds to scan the area. Probably something I should have done before provoking a stranger who could've had an AK-47 stashed in his undies, for all I knew. Luckily, there was a man taking out the garbage of a little café that sat beside Calamity's. He paused from his task to look on with mild interest.

No Reyes, though. I guess the only thing he sensed, the thing that called him to me, was a spike in adrenaline. I tried to stay calm so as not to summon him. He'd had a busy night what with all our sexual energies colliding like atoms in the sun. And then there were the men in masks. Add to that the whole toothpaste debacle, and Reyes should be about as exhausted as I was.

I refocused on the paparazzi. "What the fuck, dude?" I yelled when he turned to put his camera on the passenger seat. He put his key in the ignition, and for some reason—my reflexes being so catlike and all—I tried to open the door. I had every intention of dragging him out by his hair and beating the truth out of him. Thankfully his door was locked, because at some point during my walk over, I lost all sense of reality. His engine roared to life, and before I could utter another curse word, he peeled out, narrowly missing my toes.

I stood stunned for a solid minute. He was not just on some mission to set me up—as he drove past, I saw his jacket in the backseat. It had a badge clipped to the pocket. He was a cop.

9

Son of a bitch.

Were the cops setting me up?

I hurried back to Misery, hoping to catch the other guy, as he was clearly part of whatever was going on—but he was gone as well. I slammed the door shut and cursed under my breath before realizing my bag was still there. The guy could so easily have taken it. Thank God for small wonders.

When I opened the door again, Artemis had moved to the backseat. She stared straight ahead, pretty as she pleased, as though she'd really wanted the backseat the whole time. "I'm sorry, girl," I said as I climbed in. "Mr. Andrulis, I don't usually yell and slam doors, but being surveilled in what clearly is some kind of setup makes me cranky."

He didn't answer and I was really starting to feel bad for the guy. He had to be chilly.

I started up Misery, let her idle a solid five seconds—which was four seconds longer than usual—then backed out of the parking lot in search of a man with an inferiority complex.

When I stopped by the bond enforcement agency Garrett Swopes most often worked out of, the receptionist told me he was on a sting to apprehend a fugitive. I asked the pretty girl, who was far too young to be working at a bond enforcement agency, where that would be.

"Oh, I can't tell you that, Ms. Davidson," she said, popping her gum. "My uncle would kill me. He told me so. Said he'd cut my throat in my sleep if I ever gave you any information on any of our cases."

"Wow. That's a little harsh. Your uncle, huh?"

"Yeah. He hired me temporarily to see if I'd work out."

"Do you?" I asked, giving her the once-over. "I mean, you look like you do."

She blinked, trying to grasp my meaning. "Do I what?"

"Work out."

"Oh," she chuckled. "Yeah, they warned me about you. But I can't tell you where he is. You won't get anything out of me."

She went back to popping her gum and filing her nails, and I nodded. "I think you'll work out just fine, honey. Swopes wouldn't happen to be at an apartment complex on the corner of Girard and Lead, would he?"

Her mouth dropped open. "How—?"

Well, that was all I needed. "Thanks, hon. Tell your uncle hey for me." I waved as I went out the door. Poor thing. She had all the details written in triplicate in front of her. I didn't have the heart to tell her I could read upside down.

Hopefully she'd figure it out eventually. She'd have to learn fast if she planned on working for her uncle. He was quite the skiptracer himself in his day. He'd had a rep for having hard knuckles and a jaw made of steel.

Sadly, his nose was not made of the same indestructible substance. It'd been broken more than once and sat slightly to the left of his face, but he was a cool guy.

Still, why would he tell his niece not to give me any info? We'd been friends for a long time. And I'd apologized for that whole pineapple debacle months back. He really needed to let it go. Resentment like that tended to fester. He'd get an ulcer if he wasn't careful. That was kind of my specialty, though. Causing ulcers. Everyone had to be good at something.

I pulled in behind Garrett's black truck and turned off Misery. I'd lost Artemis somewhere around Central and Juan Tabo. She saw a cat. Garrett was standing at his tailgate with two other men. They all wore badges around their necks identifying themselves as bond enforcement agents. I quickly realized one of the men was the receptionist's uncle, Javier. And he'd told her not to give me any info. I hoped I wasn't getting her in trouble.

They turned toward me en masse. Garrett Swopes was a tall drink of water with mocha-colored skin and sparkling gray eyes. He also had incredible abs. Not that I was interested in him, but it was hard not to notice his abs when he answered his door shirtless all the time. That could be because I'm always showing up at his house in the middle of the night. Weird how I always needed him around four in the A.M.

He'd been in the middle of pulling on a bulletproof vest. This guy must be bad. It took a lot to get Swopes to wear Kevlar.

It took a moment for Javier to recognize me. He frowned and said something to Garrett, pointing toward me repeatedly. Garrett let him rant, nodded, then waved me to him. The third guy I didn't know. He was at least part Asian and looked like he'd been in one too many bar brawls. But really, who needed all those teeth? It was overkill if you asked me.

I climbed out of Misery and sauntered over to them with a nonchalant smile.

"How did you know where we'd be?" Javier asked.

"I didn't. I just knew where Swopes here would be and I need to talk to him. You are just a bonus." I batted my lashes at him.

His brows snapped together. "You didn't bring any C-4, did you?"

"Javier, you have to let that go. Let bygones be bygones."

He pulled his sidearm and clicked off the safety. "I'll show you bygones."

"Now, now," Garrett said, wrestling the gun from him. "Charley brings out the worst in all of us. It's not her fault."

"He's right," I said. "I have a condition."

"See?" he said, consoling his boss—though truth be told, Garrett ran that business and was the reason it was so successful.

"We have a job to do, Swopes," he said before stalking away.

I turned to Garrett, grateful that he had my back. I was growing on him. I could tell. I was a lot like mold that way. "I can help," I said, offering my services.

Javier heard me and came stalking back. He'd planned on arguing with me, but he changed his mind about halfway back. I could see it in his expression. "Yeah," he said, looking me up and down. "You can. Go up to apartment 504 in that building and knock on the door. Tell them Crystal sent you."

Garrett chuckled under his breath and checked his weapon. His arms were all sinewy and muscly when he did it. God, I loved arms. "We can't send her up there."

"Sure you can," I said. "I'm here to help out anyway I can, because that's what friends do for each other. They help each other in times of crisis. They have each others' backs."

He lowered the gun and gave me his full attention. "All right, what'd you do now?"

"What?" I asked, appalled. "Me?"

"We doin' this or not?" the third guy asked. "I have in-laws at my house. They're trying to convince my wife that I'm no good. That she should leave me and go back to Puerto Rico with them. I have to get home before she realizes they have a point."

I laughed and shrugged. "I would make a great distraction. Wait, Crystal isn't a pimp, is she?"

"No idea," Javier said. "But something like that would go a long way in erasing my memory."

"So would tequila. But I'll help. I'm ready. Send me in, boss."

"I'm not your boss."

I frowned at him.

"Okay," Garrett said after Javier showed me a picture of Daniel, the guy they were apprehending, and told me exactly what to do. We were walking hand in hand to the apartment building, and deep down inside I prayed Reyes wouldn't show up. The guy's temper lately—well, always— was kind of iffy. "What do you need?"

I laughed again, trying to sell the star-crossed lovers bit as Javier and the bad husband took up position, flanking the building and readying to invade. "I need a million dollars, but from you, I need to know how far you've gotten with that book."

"The prophecies?" he asked, surprised. "Dr. von Holstein is still working on the translations, but he's had a couple of exciting break-throughs."

I had to force myself not to giggle every time he said the doctor's name. It was just funny. I needed to name something von Holstein. Too bad I'd already named my couch. Maybe a chair. Or the saltshaker. I could name her Heifer von Holstein.

"Is that it?" he asked as we rounded the corner to the entrance.

"Not even. Is there anything about the Twelve in there?"

He slowed his stride, just barely, but enough for me to know I'd hit pay dirt. "There is, actually. Several stanzas center around the Twelve and their role in the shit storm to come."

My heart kind of sank. I usually did my best to avoid conflicts with beings that escaped from hell for the sole purpose of ripping out my jugular and presenting my lifeless body to their master. Especially when said master defined the phrase *evil incarnate*.

I held up a brave hand. "Don't sugarcoat it for me, Swopes."

"I wouldn't dream of it."

"God forbid I get a decent night's sleep."

"We couldn't have that."

"Do we win?" I asked. We got to the elevator, which looked about as safe as that guy on the street earlier handing out free samples of blue candy in little Baggies.

Garrett pressed the UP button. "What do you mean?"

"The shit storm. The Twelve." I waved a hand to demonstrate the vastness of it all. "Do we defeat them?"

The doors slid open. We stepped inside; then he pushed the button for the fifth floor while offering me a look of mild confusion. "Why would we fight them?"

"Because they want my head on a platter."

Keeping my hand in his—though I wasn't completely sure why, since no one was in the elevator with us—he asked, "Why would they want your head on a platter?"

"Because," I repeated, growing impatient, "they're the Twelve. It's apparently what they do."

"Charles, you need to stop watching late-night movies. The Twelve are good. They're sent to protect you, the daughter."

"What? They're hounds from hell. How can they—?"

"Hounds from hell?" When I nodded, he asked, "Literally?"

I nodded again.

"Then we're talking about a different Twelve. The Twelve the prophecies mention say they are all spiritual beings."

"That can't be right," I said as we stepped off the elevator. The dreary halls were paved with stained carpet that had the acrid scent of urine and chemicals. I covered my nose and mouth, trying to guard against the telltale aroma of illegal drug production. I wondered if Daniel was a cook or just a distributor. But the worst aspect of the entire scenario was the cries of a baby down the hall. Why was there always a crying baby down the hall?

We stepped over old fast-food bags, empty bottles of both soda and beer, and a pair of ripped jeans before we found Daniel's door. Garrett took up position around the corner that led to the stairwell, his sidearm drawn.

When he gestured that he was ready, I stuffed a piece of gum in my mouth, raised my hand, and almost knocked.

Garrett questioned me silently with an urgent shrug.

I leaned toward him and whispered, "Why were we holding hands downstairs, playing star-crossed lovers, if I have to go in here alone?"

The grin that spread across his face was so full of mischief, I almost laughed.

"You are a dirty, rotten scoundrel," I said, teasing him.

He winked as I straightened my shoulders, then really knocked.

"What?" a male voice yelled out, clearly annoyed at having been disrupted.

But I'd knocked too soon. I forgot that the only gum I had was the super-duper sour kind. The kind that promised a pucker with every piece.

I blinked back tears, tried to realign my eyelids to the same width, and said, "Crystal sent me," in my best New York accent. No idea why.

He wrenched open the door before I could get my lids completely realigned. I could feel one squinting against the powerful atomic mixture squeezing my cheeks together like an overzealous aunt. The kind with too much lipstick and sharp nails. He paused a moment to take me in, during which time I forced my lids to chill, smacked the gum as annoyingly as I could manage, and winked. He nodded a greeting with his big head. It sat atop his big shoulders only to be outdone by his even bigger belly and what had to be size 14 shoes.

After he surveyed every inch of me in much the same way I'd surveyed him, he glanced up and down the hall. When he was satisfied no one had taken up position around the nearest corner—Garrett was good—he gestured me inside. "Muffy's in here."

"Muffy?" I asked, following him inside. I was going to have to pretend to want to have sex with a girl? A girl named Muffy? What the hell kind of name was Muffy? If I were a prostitute, I'd go for something cool and exotic like Stardust. Or Venus. Or Julia Roberts.

From my periphery I spotted Javier round the corner, at the opposite end of the hall, narrowly escaping the observant gaze of Daniel the bad guy. Garrett eased forward as our target closed the door, sealing my fate like a ziplock bag sealed in freshness. I could only pray they'd hurry. If I had to kiss a prostitute dumb enough to call herself Muffy, I was going to demand compensation. She couldn't possibly practice good dental hygiene.

"The shampoo's under the sink," Daniel said. "Try not to clog it up."

Okay, this was getting way kinkier than I'd expected. I'd need therapy when it was all said and done. No, wait, I already needed therapy. Never mind.

As my overactive imagination conjured all kinds of scenarios of why Muffy and I would need shampoo, an adorable Yorkie yapped at me from behind a recliner. "And do her nails," Daniel said as he plopped into a creaky recliner. "Last time the girl didn't do her nails."

Wait? Was he serious? I thought I was supposed to be a prostitute or something.

I scanned the area for other occupants, but he appeared to be alone. "Okay, I gotta text Crystal and let her know I'm here, ya know?"

"Fine, whatever." He picked up the remote and turned off the mute. A game of some kind was on, the sound of a cheering crowd blared through the room. Good thing. The noise would muffle any ruckus the guys made.

I scooped up Muffy to keep her out of harm's way, then texted Garrett the situation: *One male. Alone. And a Yorkie. Count to thirty.* I wanted to get Muffy into another room before they broke down the door.

"I ain't seen you before," Daniel called out to me. "You work with Crystal long?"

"Um, yeah, you know."

He muted the TV. Damn it. What'd I say?

"How long?" he asked. He stood again and came into the kitchen just as I sent the text.

I stuffed my phone into my pocket. "Only a couple of months. She needed someone while Valerie was out."

"Who the fuck's Valerie?" he asked, easing into the kitchen. Keep it simple. Keep it simple. But before I could answer, he asked, "Is she that skinny chick that ran off with Manuel?"

I laughed and shrugged. "I don't know. I never met her."

"That chick was psycho, man. You should have seen what she did to Muffy's ears. She just needs a trim, okay? I don't want no sissy-ass do with bows and shit. Fuckin' Valerie. I told her that, and she still gave her pink highlights."

You could give a dog highlights? "Okay. No bows. No highlights. Got it."

"Okay. Just so we're—"

The front door crashed open, and I took a dive with Muffy. I couldn't keep the term *muff diver* from popping into my head as I did so. Daniel wasn't stupid. He didn't hesitate a second before he went for the large kitchen window. He slid the dirty pane up and scrambled headfirst through the thing, his large body deceivingly quick.

"Swopes!" I called out, tossing Muffy onto her pallet and hurrying through the window after him.

What I didn't realize at the time was that Daniel was a planner. A suspicious sort. He knew if anyone came at him from anything other than the front door, they'd have to take the fire escape up to his apartment, so he'd loosened the rails. No one could come up without it collapsing, and only he knew where to step to get down safely. The poor man's alarm system.

I never got the memo. Thus, the moment I basically fell through the window, following him onto the rigged fire escape, the railing gave beneath our weight and toppled over, secured to the exterior wall only by the bottom bolts. Daniel clung to a set of bars he'd installed, probably for that very purpose, but without a stable foothold, he couldn't hang on for long. The railing swayed, metal clanging against metal as the third guy from our party stood in the alley at the bottom, his eyes large as he watched. Daniel grunted as his hands slipped, and he fell onto the rocking fire escape, his weight causing another bolt to go.

In an instant, we dropped a perilous foot. I had a death grip on the bars, my feet dangling as I tried to get a foothold. I looked down again before I remembered the old adage: Never look down. Five stories was freaking high!

"Charley!"

Garrett was hanging out the window above me.

"What?" I asked. "Get me off here before I plummet to my death."

But he was gone. Seriously?

"Having fun?" Reyes asked me. My adrenaline had spiked, and he was there. It was kind of nice, but he was incorporeal. He couldn't really help me. Or, well, I didn't think he could. He was sitting on the railing, his full robe waving like the sails of a flagship in the wind. He pushed back the hood, then let the robe settle around him and disappear.

"Not really." I heard sirens in the distance.

"Son of a bitch," Daniel said, trying not to make the metal contraption sway. He was more on the top part of the escape and I was more on the bottom part, hanging on by my fingertips. Memories of the elementary school playground flashed before my eyes. I sucked at monkey bars. I was always the girl who got blisters and fell into the dirt halfway across.

"Any ideas?" I asked him.

"You could climb up," he said matter-of-fact.

I was literally hanging by my fingertips. Climbing up from this position would require way more upper body strength than I currently possessed. "You're not putting any weight on this metal thing, are you?"

"I don't think so. I can go if you want."

"No!" I shouted.

"Bitch, what?" Daniel said. "I didn't do a damn thing to you."

I groaned. I had to be stuck on a collapsing fire escape with a guy who could give a sumo wrestler a run for his money.

"I could help you," Reyes said, and I felt my fingers slipping, the wetness of my palms making the bars slick. "Do you want my help?"

Clearly we were playing games. I gave him my best death stare.

He chuckled and said, "It's a simple yes/no question, Dutch."

Before I could say anything else, a sheet floated down from overhead.

"Grab hold!" Garrett yelled, but I couldn't let go. If I did, I would fall.

My fingers slipped a centimeter more, and I heard Reyes at my ear, his voice as deep and as beautiful as he was. "Let go."

"I can't," I replied in a whispered strain.

"Of course you can."

But before I could argue any further, my hands slipped again and the bar disappeared from my grasp entirely.

10

I used to be indecisive.
Now I'm not so sure.

—T-SHIRT

My reaction was instantaneous. Adrenaline spiked hard and fast. Sound ceased. Gravity let go. And time slowed to a stop. The blood pumping in my ears was replaced by a thick, odd feeling of pressure all around me like a vacuum.

I looked up. The sheet floated over my head as though it were rising instead of falling. I could just see Garrett as he stood at the window, holding the sheet, his expression severe. He'd cut his hand. Blood that had been dripping off his palms was headed back to where it came from as time not only slowed but reversed itself.

Amazement consumed me. I literally felt the shift of gravity. The pull of the earth beneath my feet became a soft, subtle push in the opposite direction.

I was flying!

Or, well, floating. But before I could get too happy and lose the precarious hold I had on the moment, I felt Reyes's strength surround me like a force field, his hand wrap around my wrist as I took hold of the sheet.

"Ready?" he asked, but the moment he said it, time bounced back in place with a vengeance. It crashed into me in one giant wave. Sound rocketed through me and gravity staked its claim, jerking back toward the earth and almost wrenching the sheet out of my hand.

I slammed against the building and struggled to hold on as Garrett pulled.

"Hold on!" he said from between gritted teeth.

He didn't need to tell me twice.

I tucked my errant hair behind my ears as Garrett walked up. "What the fuck was that?" he asked, raising my ire. "We had a guy waiting for him below. You didn't have to go out the window."

"I didn't know you had a guy down there. Nor did I know Daniel over there was so paranoid that he disabled the fire escape. You might have shared your plan with me."

"Are you okay?"

"Yes. I'm fine. Except my fingernails hurt. How's your hand?"

"It'll heal. Especially when it's holding a ten-thousand-dollar check. So, I guess it's your turn: What did you want to talk to me about?"

"Oh, right, the Twelve. My sources say the Twelve are a group of im-prisoned demons who escaped hell and are coming here to rip me apart."

He stilled.

"No, wait, to rip me to shreds. I think that's what he said."

He leaned against the tailgate with me, testing the bandages on his hand. "Dr. von Holstein told me there were several mentions of the Twelve. I'll ask him to look closer at that."

"Sounds good. In the meantime, be really really really really care-ful."

"Any particular reason?"

"Yeah, some men broke into my apartment and said I had to find this lady within forty-eight hours or my friend was dead." I took out a photocopy Cookie made me of the picture. "The problem is, I have no idea which friend it is."

"I didn't think you had any friends."

"I have you," I said, petting his manly biceps. "You don't happen to know her, do you?"

He shook his head. "Sorry. But I can look into it."

"Thanks. And just so you know, I have no intention of finding this woman. It could get sticky."

"Sticky works." He put the folded picture in his back pocket. "So what happens when the Twelve get here?"

"Oh, that. Yeah, we all die a horrible, painful death. Or I could use the dagger you found. I figure I'll just talk them all into throwing themselves on it, one at a time."

"Your plans suck."

"People keep telling me that."

"I had a thought recently," he said.

"Just one? Don't strain your brain."

"I think we should work together."

Another partner. First Aunt Lil, now Swopes? Was there something going on I didn't know about?

"You have a job," I pointed out.

"Yeah, but I want to broaden my horizons."

Well, I already had Aunt Lil on board. We could be a threesome, I guessed. We could be the Terrific Trio. It could work.

"I'll think about it. Do you have any references?" I asked.

"None that would really impress you."

"Hmm, we can work around that."

"We should grab a bite. Talk about it."

A woman in a yellow halter and cutoffs walked around the corner, took one look at the plethora of cop cars and the ambulance, and turned back the way she'd come. I wondered if she was the girl sent by Crystal. "What about Muffy?" I asked Garrett.

"Who's Muffy?"

"Daniel's Yorkie."

"Well, okay, but only one. I'm not that hungry."

"She needs a home."

"Don't look at me," he said, horrified I'd looked at him.

"Swopes, I can't take her. I'm never home."

"And I am?" When I glared, he said, "Fine, I think I know someone who will take her. But you'll owe me. Again."

I snorted. "I don't owe you. Just because I got you shot a few times and sent to hell doesn't mean I owe you." He didn't answer. We were at a stalemate. An impasse. A standoff. I caved first. It never took long. "Fine. What do you want?"

He looked at the activity around us as he spoke. "Do you remember that woman who kept coming over just to have sex? Marika?"

"Yeah, sure. You said she had a son. He might be yours."

"Yeah, well, I want to know for sure."

That should be easy enough. "You want me to ask her?"

"No. She put her husband down as the father. She'd never tell you the truth."

"Ah, but that's my specialty. I can tell when people are lying, remember?"

"Doesn't mean she'll give you the name of the father. And I don't want her to know I'm looking into it. If someone starts asking around, she'll get suspicious."

"Okay, what, then?"

"I'll let you know later," he said as Javier walked up to us. "Until then, do you know any good Yorkie recipes?"

"That's not even funny."

"It's a little funny. We should still grab a bite. Talk about our future together."

"Don't get any ideas about us, Swopes. I'm nigh affianced. And I only put out for coffee."

"I read your status updates," he said. "I know the score."

I frowned. "I could cook *you* for dinner, instead. Roast you over an open pit of flames."

One side of his mouth slid north. "Been there. Done that."

I winced at the reminder.

After answering questions from the APD and taking a tongue-lashing from the owner of the apartment building, who was very particular about his fire escapes, I said my good-byes to Mr. Garrett Swopes and headed downtown, Mr. Andrulis and I driving until we came to an ever-familiar mental asylum. It wasn't familiar because I'd spent time there or anything. This mental asylum had been abandoned in the '50s and housed one of my favorite people on planet Earth, the Rocket Man.

The last time I saw him, I'd behaved very badly. I hadn't been back since, mostly because I'd threatened to rip his little sister, who was five, to shreds if he didn't answer my questions. Shame consumed me at the memory. I had driven here more than a few times in the last couple of weeks, and each time I couldn't bring myself to go in.

I sat in front of the building for ten minutes before I realized I was not going in this time, either. Well, that and the fact that a car had followed me for several blocks and was now parked down the street doing the same thing I was doing. Sitting and waiting.

At first I thought it might be the guy from that morning with the camera, but it was a different vehicle and the driver had dark hair. I pulled out the telephoto lens I'd recently acquired from a guy selling telephoto lenses and Chia pets out of his trunk. I bought it so I could be a real PI and take photos from a distance instead of just on my phone. Way too many instances where I had to get really close for a money shot, only to be chased down the street by men trying to scam an insurance company for a neck injury that kept them from being able to walk at all. Those guys could book it. I took a few shots over my shoulder, trying not to scare the guy away. And/or convince him to come after me. Car chases were never as fun in real life as they looked in the movies.

When I scrolled through what I'd shot, mostly the inside of my Jeep, I picked up my phone and dialed the office.

"Davidson Investigations," Cookie said. That sounded way more professional than my greeting, which often mentioned flavored lubricant.

"Yes, ma'am, can I get a pizza, thin crust, extra pepperoni?"

"No."

Gah. Testy much? "I think someone is following me."

"Is he in a white coat and carrying a butterfly net?"

Odd that she would say that while I was sitting in front of a mental asylum.

"No, but I know who it is. And I know who sent that cop to take pictures of me this morning."

"A cop took pictures of you this morning?"

"Yes, I posed for the annual Daughters of the American Revolution dessert calendar. You'd be surprised at how good cupcake pasties look on me."

"Doubt it."

"You saucy minx. Actually, I think I'm being set up, and I just want it on the record that whatever it is they're going to say I did, I didn't."

"Well, nobody can say life with you is boring."

"Thank God."

"Any idea who's behind it?"

I glanced down at the camera screen again. "Sure do. He's tall, wears a uniform, and seems to come out of nowhere."

"Superman?"

"Captain Eckert."

"The captain?" she asked with a soft gasp. "Why? What does he have to gain?"

"I'll find out soon enough. I'll be paying the captain a visit very soon. Until then, what do we have?"

"Okay, the woman in the picture is the sole witness to a murder by none other than Phillip Brinkman."

"The car salesman?" I asked. "His commercials are ridiculous."

"The word on the street is that the car dealership is a front and that he is really a drug kingpin."

"Seriously? Isn't there a TV show about that?"

"He allegedly beat a guy to death in a fit of rage. When he realized his girlfriend was still in the house and saw the whole thing, he tried to kill her, too. She barely escaped and is now in WITSEC."

"Witness protection? What the hell? What makes these guys think I can find out where she is? WITSEC is tighter than my skinny jeans."

"I don't know, but I do know that the person in charge of the case is your friend Agent Carson. Seems the FBI had been investigating him for a while on separate charges. They can't make anything stick, so they're trying to get a conviction on this murder."

"So, what's the problem?"

"They don't have a body."

"Oh, wow. That makes it difficult. Okay, anything else?"

"Yep. I'm not sure if you want this now, but the Fosters' son has moved back home and is living with his parents while he finishes up his master's degree at UNM."

"Really? He's there? Did you find a picture of him?"

"Sure did. Several, in fact. He's on Friendbook."

"Perfect. And?" I asked, curiosity burning inside me. Either that or I'd already had too much coffee.

"He looks nothing like him," she said, the disappointment in her voice undeniable. "Seriously. Like there's not even the slightest resemblance. Are you sure the Fosters didn't adopt this guy? He's really . . . white."

I burst out laughing. "I'm sorry."

"No, I mean like albino white without the actual condition. Which is fine, normally. I just expected him to be more Reyes-like. Have you seen pictures of the Fosters?"

"Well, no. That's why I really wanted to get a glimpse."

"This is a big fat disappointment, I don't mind telling you. I mean, he's nice looking. He's just not Reyes. Not even close."

"Look at it this way: You can see Reyes all the time now that he's in our building. And sometimes you can even see him naked. As can your twelve-year-old daughter."

She let a forlorn sigh slip through her lips. "That's true. I'll send you the Friendbook link."

"Perfect," I said, holding back a giggle. "Thanks."

"Sure. Anything else?"

"How's your escort?"

"Cute and married."

I chuckled out loud that time. "I need to go talk to Special Agent Carson and get the lowdown on Sleazy Car Guy. I think I'll head that way."

"I think that's a good idea. So, about the pizza—you were kidding, right?"

"I was kidding. I'll be a while. Grab lunch when you can."

"Will do. Reyes is making his famous green chile chicken quesadillas." Damn him. "Enjoy."

I hung up and clicked on the link.

With the noon hour fast approaching, my stomach decided to do its gurgle-and-growl thing. I watched Captain Eckert in my rearview for a while. And as entertaining as that was, I needed to go see a good guy about a bad guy and figure out why Sleazy Car Guy thought I could help him find his ex, the woman who allegedly saw him commit murder. Sucked when that happened. Lunch would have to wait.

But I still couldn't figure out why the Men in Black thought I could find her. The only connection to the case was my friendship with Agent Carson, but that was a pretty slim connection. It wasn't like we hung out socially or anything. How would anyone know we were connected?

I dialed her number. Got her voice mail. Waited for the beep. Then I did my best creepy kidnapper voice. "This is a ransom demand," I said, my voice raspy. Kidnapper-y. "Deliver one hundred boxes of Cheez-Its to the unmarked—ignore the license plate—cherry red Jeep Wrangler sitting in your parking lot by noon today, or you will suffer the consequences." I paused to cough. Raspy was hard on the esophagus. "They will be dire."

I hung up. That was my way of letting Agent Carson know to expect a visit. She could have been out of the office, but I'd just have to take that chance. She usually ignored calls when she was in meetings, which meant she should be at the FBI headquarters. Thus, with sound logic guiding me, I headed that way.

Much to my surprise, however, she called me back almost immediately.

"Hey, girlfriend," I said in lieu of hello, hoping it would bring us closer.

"You might want to block your number when making ridiculous ransom demands."

"That demand was not ridiculous. Have you ever thought about changing your name to AC? Or SAC since you're a *special* agent."

"Charley—"

"We could call you Sack."

"I'm kind of the middle of something."

"Sorry. Sorry. I just have one question."

"Shoot."

"Do you have any friends in the Secret Service?"

She hesitated before saying, "No."

"Darn it. I was hoping you could smooth things over a bit. I seemed to have ruffled some feathers. They're very sensitive."

I could hear her run a hand down her face. She did that a lot when I was around. "What'd you do now?"

"Nothing, I swear. They just get really nervous when you butt-dial the president. Over and over. Like seventy-eight times. These jeans are really tight."

"Charley, is this conversation going anywhere?"

"I hope so or I'm wasting my gas for nothing. Can we meet for coffee?"

"Sure. Meet me at the Flying Star on Paseo."

"Paseo?" I asked. "As in Paseo del Norte? What are you doing up there?"

"I am a field officer, Charley. I go out into the field and investigate."

"Oh, right." I scratched that whole "she should be in her office" thing and did an amazing seven-point U-turn. Not many appreciated my driving prowess. Or the fact that I stopped the flow of traffic in several lanes. "A woman's life is at stake here!" I yelled out my window. Or I would have if it'd been down.

I walked into the café, ordered my usual fare, which often had the word *mocha* in it, a tuna melt with sweet potato fries, and a slice of their salted caramel cheesecake—because YOLO—then sat down with my almost good friend.

No. My soon-to-be good friend.

No! My nigh good friend.

I seemed to have a lot of relationships at the moment in that very fragile "nigh" stage.

Meeting in a public place was a good idea. If I were being followed—by someone other than the captain—no one would see me walk right into the FBI field office. It worked out beautifully.

"Hey, Sack. Can I call you Sack?"

"No." She sipped her coffee, her short brown bob perfectly coiffed, her navy business suit perfectly pressed. I felt very slobbish next to her. Oh, well.

She was reading the paper, completely ignoring me. It was awkward.

"So, how's work?"

"Great." She closed the paper. "Did you look into that case?"

The Foster baby abduction case. How did I tell her I knew exactly who and where that baby was? I didn't. Not yet. I needed a little more info before I cast that stone and caused any lasting ripples in the universe. Tossing out the fact that I'd known all along where that missing baby ended up could crack our fragile bond. But if I went to her with irrefutable proof of her dad's suspicions—mainly that there was more to the case than met the eye—our bond would be cemented like that time I accidently superglued my fingers together. That was an awkward week. One never appreciates opposable thumbs until one no longer has them.

"Sure did," I said, taking a sip myself. "I still am, actually, but I have a strong lead."

Though her pretty expression remained impassive, her emotions spiked inside her. She really wanted to solve that case for her father. And I wanted that for her, but I had a more pressing case at the moment.

She was reaching for her coffee again when I said, "Emily Michaels."

She paused and looked up at me, but before she could say anything, a server brought my food over.

"Aren't you eating?" I asked her.

"No. I didn't know you were eating."

"I'm eating. You should order something."

"What did you get?"

"Tuna melt."

"Is it good?"

"Emily Michaels," I reminded her. I felt like she was changing the subject on purpose.

"Why do you want to know about Emily Michaels?"

"Because."

Her lips thinned. "Why?"

"I can't tell you. The man who held a gun to my head said no cops."

Her mouth dropped open. I totally considered tossing a fry into it just to see if I could, but this was probably not the best time.

"Can I talk to her?" I asked.

"No."

"Can you set up a meet?"

"No."

"Can you tell me where she is?"

"No."

Damn, she was tough. The FBI probably taught her how to withstand interrogation. I'd never met such resistance. Such pure determination. Maybe if I asked nicely.

"I won't actually use that information," I said, as though that would help. "I just need it as a backup. They said they are going to kill a friend of mine if I don't get it."

"Then give them a fake address and call me. I'll have a team there to intercept. You can testify against these men. Wham bam."

"And then what? Go into WITSEC with Emily? No, thank you."

"Well, if you think there is even the slightest possibility that I'd give you that location, you're wrong."

I figured as much. "Why did they choose me, though?" I asked aloud.

"Probably because they know our connection."

"What connection?"

"We're friends, for one thing," she said with a shrug.

Score! "Right. Of course." I knew we were friends. I could now die happy. "And for another?"

"You're a PI. They probably thought you could set up a lunch with me and just ask me to hand over that information."

I snorted. "Crazy people. Who would think such a thing?"

"I wonder," she said, her expression deadpan. "I do need to report this, Charley."

"You can't. No cops, remember?"

"Sorry. I can't keep that kind of information to myself. If Brinkman's men are getting that desperate, we're getting close. We could use this to our advantage."

"What about my advantage? And my friend's advantage they are supposedly going to kill, though I'm beginning to think they don't really know who my closest friends are."

"Finish up," she said, nodding to my sandwich. "I'll need you to come to my office to make a statement."

"Sack! No way."

"I'll sneak you in through the back. You can leave your Jeep here."

Son of a bitch. "I'm sorry," I said, rising from the table, "but I can't risk it. If they get a whiff of an investigation where this is concerned, things could go very south very quickly."

Her expression changed to one void of all emotion. "I'll cuff you, Charley. I can arrest you on charges of obstruction of justice and hold you until you cooperate."

I sat back down. "And I thought we were friends."

"We are, which is why I'm going to get all the information on this that I can and investigate. It's what I do. Let me help you for once."

Surely I had smoke billowing out of my ears. "You've always trusted me in the past, and I've solved a couple of pretty big cases for you. Or have you forgotten?"

She rubbed her forehead. "Son of a— Okay, here's what we'll do. I'll make a preliminary report stating there is a strong probability of an attempt on Emily's life. You have forty-eight hours."

I knew she'd let me do this my way. Hopefully things wouldn't go south.

"But if this turns south, we are doing it my way."

Sometimes I wondered if Sack could read my mind. Really good friends could do that.

11

It's a beautiful day.
I think I'll skip my meds and stir things up a bit.

—BUMPER STICKER

After convincing one of my best friends on the planet to give me some time on the Men in Black case, I headed over to the Fosters' house since I was on that side of town anyway. I was now as curious as Cookie about what they looked like. Were they fair skinned like their son? If so, how was Reyes so dark? So exotic?

One possibility that came to mind was, naturally, did he look like his real father? Did he look like Lucifer? If so, and he'd chosen the Fosters to be his human parents on earth, did he not consider their fair coloring when choosing a potential family?

Of course he did. Reyes was too smart not to.

I pulled up to an empty house that was for sale and pretended to be a potential buyer, looking this way and that before settling in and checking my phone. There was also a yard sale a couple of houses up, yielding a steady flow of traffic, so I blended right in. I knew Mrs. Foster would be home soon, so I sat outside, checking my e-mail and doodling in my memo pad. My doodles turned to words that eventually turned to names. *Charley Farrow,* I wrote, liking the feel of it, the look of it. *Charley Davidson Farrow.* Or should I hyphenate it? What were women doing these days? *Mrs. Reyes Farrow.* Farrow. I could get very used to that name.

I glanced up just in time to see a Prius pull into the Fosters' garage. The door came down before I could see her, just like before, but I'd see her soon enough. I took out the case file Agent Carson had given me, the one of the kidnapping almost thirty years ago.

I glanced at my sidekick and made a mental note to carve out some time to go see his wife, Mrs. Andrulis. The poor guy needed to be done with whatever it was he'd left unfinished. I couldn't have him running around naked forever. It just seemed wrong.

"I'm having a hard time not looking at your penis."

"I get that a lot."

I jumped in response to the voice coming from my backseat and slammed my memo pad closed. Reyes popped in, very hot and very . . . corporeal. He seemed more solid now than he used to be. Less incorporeal. The departed were always solid to me, but they didn't look solid. And while Reyes had always had more color than the actual departed, he was still incorporeal. Not quite flesh but not quite spirit. Something in between. Lately, however, he was leaning toward the flesh.

"What are you doing?" he asked.

"Nothing. I was going to a yard sale. I'm in need of a new yard and—look! There's one for sale."

He looked across the street straight at the Fosters' house. "Okay," he said, and I felt a tinge of anger rise in him. "So, what are you waiting for?"

"I'm scoping out the situation," I said, hoping he'd believe me but knowing deep down inside I'd lost the game before it ever began. With my plans foiled, I decided to go to the yard sale anyway. I'd show him.

I climbed down from Misery and shut her door, leaving my nigh fiancé in there to simmer and stew.

Three women who'd been arguing were still arguing when I walked up. Their disagreements seemed to center around the items in the yard sale. Two were dressed to the nines in mid-twentieth-century apparel. I guessed them to have died in the 1950s or '60s. The third one, and the smallest, was in a fluffy pink robe with a *V* embroidered on the chest and tiny house slippers.

"Oh, I remember that music box," she said, looking on as a young girl picked it up and opened the lid. "Daddy made it. He gave it to you, Maddy, on your sixteenth birthday."

"No, he didn't, Vera," the tallest of the three said. "He gave it to Tilda on her twelfth birthday." She gestured to the third woman, who nodded in agreement.

The first one, Vera, was having none of that. "Madison Grace, I remember that box, and I remember the day he gave it to you."

"He gave Maddy a picture frame on her sixteenth birthday," Tilda said.

"No, he gave me a picture frame on my fifteenth birthday."

"Was it your fifteenth?" she asked, looking skyward in thought. "I thought that was the year you were sent to your room for sneaking a kiss with Bradford Kingsley in the broom closet."

"I never kissed Bradford Kingsley," Maddy said, appalled. "We were just talking. And besides, he liked Sarah Steed."

All three heads dropped in unison, apparently remembering their friend fondly.

"Poor girl," Vera said. "She had such bad breath."

They all nodded sadly before Tilda added, "If only she could've outrun that rooster, she and Bradford may have eventually married."

I watched the three reminisce with no one the wiser. The tiny one, Vera, seemed to be the oldest, with Tilda second and Maddy bringing up the rear. Watching them was kind of like watching a sitcom. And since I rarely had time for TV anymore, I stood back and took complete advantage of the entertainment.

They started arguing again about a paint set as the little girl took the box she'd found to her mother. The woman's eyes sparkled with interest. "How much is this?" she asked a man sitting in a lawn chair.

"I'll take two and a quarter."

"Two and a quarter?" Vera yelled, rocketing out of her melancholy. She shook a fist at the man. "I'll give you an even five square in the jaw. How's that?"

"Don't get your hackles up," Maddy said, eyeing her elder sister.

Vera cupped her ear and leaned forward. "What?"

"Oh, for heaven's sake, Vera Dawn, you can hear me just fine, now. We're dead."

"What?"

Tilda shook her head and looked over at me. "She does that to annoy us."

I laughed softly and scanned the small crowd to make sure no one was paying too close attention. "Would you like to cross?" I asked them.

"Goodness, no," Maddy said. "We're waiting for our sister. We all want to cross together."

That was new.

"That sounds nice. You know where I'll be when you're ready."

"Sure do," Vera said. "You're kind of hard to miss."

I spotted an old piece of equipment sitting lopsided on a card table. "What is that?" I asked, my eyes glossing over in fascination.

"Not really sure," the man in the lawn chair said.

"Maddy, your grandson always was a dirty scoundrel." She looked at me. "His poor mother hasn't been in the nursing home a week, and he's selling everything she ever owned."

"Everything any of us ever owned," Tilda said. "And that's a lie detector. Our father worked for Hoover, don't cha know."

"That Hoover was an odd man," Vera said, her nose crinkling in distaste.

Maddy frowned at her. "How come you can suddenly hear?"

Vera cupped her ear again. "What?"

I stifled a giggle. "A polygraph machine? For real?"

"What?" This time it was the dirty scoundrel of a grandson who'd asked.

"Does it work?"

"No idea," he said before lifting a beer.

"Does it work?" Maddy asked as though I'd offended her. "It works like a dream. I used it on Tilda once when she went out with my boyfriend behind my back."

"That wasn't me, Maddy. That was Esther. And because you had no clue what you were doing, the results were inconclusive."

"How much?" I asked the man.

He shrugged. "I'll take twenty for it."

"Sold."

"Twenty? Twenty dollars? That should be in a museum, not in a yard sale. That boy needs his hide tanned something fierce."

I paid the guy, then walked back over to them. "I agree. If this is original FBI equipment, I bet I can get it to the right people."

"You can do that?" Maddy asked.

"I can try," I said with a shrug.

"Thank you," Vera said.

I nodded and took my prize.

"I did too know what I was doing," Maddy said as I walked off. "I just chose to be the bigger person."

Tilda snorted and the arguments began again. I almost felt sorry for their sister Esther. She had a lot of baggage waiting for her when she passed.

I decided to drop off the polygraph machine at home before checking in at the office. If Agent Carson and I were still friends, I would give it to her with explicit instructions to get it to the right people. Surely there was an FBI museum somewhere, and it could earn me brownie points. I was a firm believer in brownie points. They were like Cheez-Its. And Oreos. And mocha lattes. One could never have too many.

As I was driving home, however, an elderly woman appeared out of nowhere in the street ahead of me. Reflexes being what they were, I swerved to the right, narrowly missing a herd of parked bikes and side-swiping Misery against a streetlamp.

I screeched to a halt, hitting my forehead on the steering wheel

The woman had been in a paper-thin nightgown, both the gown and her hair a soft baby blue. Though I'd only seen her a second, it was enough to register the fear on her face, in her fragile shoulders. She looked nothing like Aunt Lil, but I couldn't help but compare the two. If Lil was scared and lost, I would search the world over for her. That was the impression I'd gotten from this woman.

Thankfully, the area I was in at the moment wasn't super busy. No one noticed my little mishap. I glanced over to check on Mr. Andrulis. He was still staring straight ahead, nary a care in the world, so I scanned the area for the woman. She was gone.

Left with no other choice, I pulled back onto the street and started for home again, only to have the woman appear again. In the middle of the road.

It took every ounce of strength I had to curb my knee-jerk reaction and slam on the brakes. Swerve to the side. Hit something. I bit down and braked slowly as we drove through the woman. After checking traffic, I pulled into an empty parking lot and got out. She was gone again.

No way was I playing this game all day. I'd kill someone at the rate I was going. So I crossed my arms, crossed my ankles, and leaned against Misery in wait. After another minute or two, the woman appeared again. She materialized right in front of Misery, looked around as though trying to gain her bearings, then disappeared again. I rounded the front of my Jeep and waited. This time when she appeared, I gently took hold of her arm.

She blinked, then furrowed her brows, squinted her eyes, presumably against my brightness, and looked up at me.

"Hi," I said softly about a microsecond before she hauled her foot back and kicked me in the shin so hard, it brought tears to my eyes. I let go of her, took hold of my shin, and hopped around, cursing under my breath. After gathering myself, I turned and glared at her. "That had to hurt your toes." She was barefoot, after all. "Please tell me that hurt your toes."

"Where are you taking him?" she demanded, her wrinkled face, like cracked porcelain, puckering in anger. She raised a fist at me, reminding me very much of Vera from the yard sale.

"Your name isn't Esther, is it?" I asked. She could have been the sister they were waiting for.

"My name is none of your concern, hussy. You give him back this minute."

Hussy? "Hashtag color-me-confused," I said her. "And this week's insanity award goes to the crazy lady with the blue hair."

"I ain't crazy, and you give him back. I heard about women like you." She eyed me up and down like I repulsed her. I was horridly offended.

"No. I'm not giving him back." I leaned in and said through my teeth still gritting in pain, "You can't have him." Then I frowned in thought. "Who?"

"Like you don't know."

I had a thousand comebacks, but none of them made sense. One can only say things like *Your mama* and *Stick a sock in it* in certain situations. So I gave up on the smart-ass route.

"Look, little crazy lady, I have no idea who you're talking about."

She focused on something over my shoulder, and I looked back at Mr. Andrulis.

"Wait, Mr. A? He's yours?" I asked, suddenly hopeful.

Her anger evaporated the minute she looked at my naked dead man. "We were married over fifty years ago. And I catch him in a car with a hussy. After all this time!" She broke down and sobbed into her fists. In the span of sixty seconds, she went from angry to nostalgic to grief-stricken.

"You didn't happen to be on medication when you died, did you? Perhaps something in an antipsychotic?"

Her gaze slid up over her fists. And back to anger.

"Look," I said, putting a hand on her shoulder. "He's only here because he's been waiting for you." That was an educated guess. He'd never told me why he was there. Wait, maybe it was to get away from his spouse. Maybe he'd come to me seeking refuge. That would suck since I just handed him over to her.

I walked her around to the passenger door, suddenly realizing to my utter mortification we had an audience. Correction, since the onlookers could hardly see the little crazy lady, I and I alone had an audience. Wonderful. I opened Mr. Andrulis's door and put a hand on his arm to hopefully draw him to me. With his wife close by, it could work this time.

And it did. He slowly turned toward me, then glanced over at his wife.

"Charles?" she said.

Luckily I realized she was talking to him and not me before I answered.

She stepped closer and I moved out of the way. "Charles, what are you doing with this hussy?"

Oh. Em. Gee.

"After all these years—"

Dawning realization and a knowing smile crept across his face. He lifted a hand and wiped a tear off her cheek.

They didn't say anything else. They embraced and hugged for several minutes as I surveyed the damage to the side of Misery. Freaking light pole came out of nowhere. Fortunately, the scratches were very superficial. Surely they could just be buffed out.

My audience, which consisted of three kids on Huffy bikes, stood waiting for me to explode again and argue with air, their phones at the ready. I so did not want to go viral. Praying they hadn't thought to record my earlier confrontation with Mrs. Andrulis, I went about my business, ignoring them. But any second now, I was going to have to explain to the Andrulises who I was and what I was and let them know they could cross through me if they wanted to. I'd have to pull the talking-into-the-phone routine. But before it even came to that, they were through.

It happened so fast and unexpectedly, it made me dizzy. I sank onto one knee as their memories flashed in my mind. Charles Andrulis was born in Chicago and stationed at Kirtland Air Force Base for two months before he was blindsided by a redheaded concession worker at the local movie theater. It was love at first sight, but he was so afraid to ask her out, so afraid she'd say no, that he simply stole her employee-of-the-month picture off the wall. He was sent to war a week later, but he carried that picture with him everywhere, cursing himself for being so stupid, vowing to ask her to marry him the next time he saw her. If he made it back alive.

He did and he did.

He made it back alive albeit a bit roughed up, but by the time he got out of the hospital and back to New Mexico, the redhead no longer worked at the theater.

But she'd been good friends with a couple of the employees there and he found her the next day, working the reception desk at a local law office.

Taking no more chances, he walked straight up to her—or, well, limped up—in full dress uniform, struggled to get to one knee in front of her, and proposed. At which point, the feisty redhead slapped the ever-lovin' crap out of him. But not before she, too, fell in love. They were married a week later and what followed was a whirlwind of children and grandchildren, of long workdays and short family vacations, of struggling to survive and loving each other through the worst of times.

When I blinked back to the present, the air cool against the wetness on my cheeks, I realized something that had never even occurred to me before. Life really was short. The Andrulises' lives were rich and colorful, even the bad parts. But it was worth every second. Charles had never once regretted marrying . . . Beverly. Her name was Beverly.

I liked her.

I carried the heavy polygraph machine up the two flights of stairs to my apartment, vowing to get an elevator installed the first chance I got. How expensive could they be? My phone rang the minute I sat it on my kitchen table. The convent where Quentin lived on the weekends appeared on the caller ID. Sister Mary Elizabeth, a very interesting woman who could hear the conversations of angels, was on the other end. I could tell something was wrong the moment she spoke.

"Charley?" she said, her voice quivering.

"Hey, Sis, what's up?"

"It's Quentin. The School for the Deaf called. He left campus this morning and has been gone all day. He's never done this. Have you seen him?"

Alarmed, I asked, "Have you tried his phone?"

"Yes. I've texted him several times and tried to do a video chat with him. Nothing. He's not picking up."

The alarm level rose. That was so unlike Quentin. He was the sweetest kid on the planet. Well, most of the time. He was a beautiful blond-haired, blue-eyed sixteen-year-old whom I'd met when his physical body was possessed by a demon. The demon was ripped to shreds by my handy-dandy Rottweiler guardian, and Quentin had been a friend ever since. He had no family and lived at the convent with the sisters when he wasn't at school. I wasn't sure how the Catholic church felt about that—but so far, so good. At least he hadn't been kicked out yet, but if Quentin started misbehaving in any way, I couldn't imagine the church would let him stay there much longer.

"Okay, let me see what I can do."

The moment I hung up, Cookie rushed upstairs and barreled into her apartment. I walked across the hall and watched her as she searched it.

"What are you looking for?"

"Amber," she said, diving for her phone. "I went to pick her up from school and she wasn't there. The office said she was marked absent all day. Why didn't they call me?" She was panicking, but I was amassing an all-consuming kind of dread.

Surely they wouldn't have.

Before I could tell Cookie about Quentin, my phone rang again. "It's Amber," I said to her, then put an index finger over my mouth to shush her before answering. I had a feeling I knew what was going on. And I had a feeling I knew why Amber was calling me instead of her mother.

"Hey, kiddo, how was school?" I said, unable to resist.

"Aunt Charley?" she said, her voice quivering more than Sister Mary Elizabeth's, and that dread I'd felt rose like a tidal wave inside me.

"Pumpkin, what's wrong?"

"We're at the top of the tramway. Something happened. I need you to come get us."

"Are you hurt?"

"No, we're . . . okay. It's just, Quentin is kind of freaking out. He won't talk to anyone but you. He's really scared. We were supposed to be back before school let out, but we got up here and he just lost it. I'm so worried about him."

Relief washed over me so completely, my knees almost buckled. "Stay on the line. I'm leaving now."

"Please don't tell my mom."

Damn it. I knew she'd called me for a reason. "I won't. Stay right where you are."

Cookie pawed at me, frantic for information on her daughter. I covered the phone while retrieving my bag and keys. "They're okay," I said to her quietly. "They decided to skip school and take the tram to Sandia Peak. But something happened with Quentin."

"Oh, my goodness, what? Is he hurt?"

"No. She said he's scared. Either he has a fear of heights he didn't know about or something else happened. Something supernatural."

She grabbed her bag. "I'm going with you."

"No, she didn't want me to tell you, and you have to pretend I didn't."

"What? Charley, this is no time to be the beloved aunt. She skipped school. Anything could have happened. She is going to be grounded for the rest of her natural-born life if I let her live that long."

"I just promised her I wouldn't tell you. Besides, you have a date to get ready for."

"A date?" she screeched. "You've got to be kidding. I can't go on a date."

"I went to a lot of trouble to set this up. You can't leave me hanging, Cook. And this is just as much for Amber. You need to act like you know nothing about this."

"Why? So you can be the hero? I am perfectly happy with being the bad guy in this, Charley. She will be punished for skipping school and pulling something so dangerous."

"I know," I said, putting a hand on her arm. "And she'll do the right thing. You watch. But let her be the one to tell you, Cook. If she knows I told you, she'll never trust me again."

"I can't be worried about your relationship with her—"

"She tells me everything, Cook," I said, trying to get my meaning across. "She asked me the other day about contraception."

After an absorption rate of approximately twenty-four bytes per second, taking into account the limited RAM we were working with, Cookie screamed at me. "She's twelve!"

I winced and pressed the phone against me harder, hoping Amber hadn't heard. It did sound bad when I said it aloud. "I was going to tell you, I swear." Then I beamed at her. "She told me she wants to wait until she's married to have sex."

Cookie calmed instantly.

"But she doesn't know when she will want to have kids, so she was asking me the best methods."

"And you fell for that?"

"I have a lie detector built into my genetic code, remember? She hasn't done anything. I promise. And in case you're wondering, Quentin is a virgin, too."

"I so don't want to know how you know that."

"I scrolled through her texts one night when she was over," I explained regardless. "I had to make sure there was nothing going on. I'm the one who brought him into your lives. It would kill me if something happened to Amber that you'd resent me for."

"Charley, Amber is her own girl. I would never blame you—"

I heard Amber talking into the phone and held up a finger to put Cookie on pause. "I'm here. I'm headed that way now."

When I pressed the phone to my shirt again, Cookie just said, "Go."

I tore out of the apartment and ran to Misery. The tram was only about fifteen minutes away from me, then another twenty-minute ride to the top. I prayed Quentin would hold on.

It didn't take me long to figure out what the problem was, why Quentin wouldn't take the tram back down the mountain. There simply weren't many things creepier than a dead girl in rags staring you down. She must have picked up on the fact that Quentin could see her like she did with me. She stood in front of me, her long dark hair in matted strings over her face, hiding most of it. But her eyes shone through the strands. Especially when she got close, as in an inch from my nose, and glared, her eyes completely void of life. It didn't matter which direction I turned, she was there, nose to nose, staring me down like a gangsta. She'd probably crawled out of a TV screen at some point in her life. Or death. Either way.

But I had to give it to Quentin. He was right not to want to come back down. She was creepy as heck. I didn't want to take the ride back down either.

I'd taken out my phone and tried to talk to her, but she just stared. Not really seeing. I couldn't even look out over the gorgeous landscape. If I turned to look out a glass panel, she'd appear in front of me, hovering outside the rail car, creeping me out even more.

"Look," I said to her, gripping my phone harder, "cut this crap out and cross through me." Everyone quieted and shuffled their feet. I couldn't blame them. My one-sided conversations with the departed often sounded weird even on the phone. But I couldn't help that now. "You are scaring people. Are you doing it on purpose?"

Nothing.

We were nearing the top of the tram, and I didn't know if I could get Quentin down the mountain if she was still hanging around. Maybe I could make him close his eyes. But it would be better if she'd just cross.

I lowered my head and gathered my energy. I'd never tried something like this, but maybe I could make her cross whether she wanted to or not. I waited until the energy inside me calmed, then sent it out, softly, coaxingly, to lure her in. It seemed to be working. She moved closer to me. And ran smack into my face.

Wonderful. Now I was standing in a car full of people with a dead girl stuck to my face. This was so wrong.

As Angel was about to tell me. "That looks so wrong, *pendeja*. It's creeping me out."

I spoke through clenched teeth. She clung like a magnet. I couldn't shake her off without looking like a complete spaz. Not that something like that ever stopped me, but still.

"Join the club. How do I get her off?"

He laughed, enjoying my agony. Her right eye was practically touching my left one. Our eyelashes met when I blinked. When I moved, she moved. When I stepped back, she floated forward. It had been a long time since I'd been this creeped out.

"You look like Siamese twins."

"Conjoined twins," I corrected him, "and for the love of pancake syrup, get her off me."

"I ain't touching that. She's like that girl from the movie."

"*The Ring*?" I asked, surprised that he'd seen it. He died long before it was made.

"No, the movie where that girl who gets possessed turns her head all the way around."

"Oh, *The Exorcist*."

"That movie was messed up."

"Yeah, I can see the resemblance. Now, get her off me!"

He doubled over as the car came to a stop. The passengers couldn't seem to get off the car fast enough. No idea why. The attendant stood there, waiting for me to disembark.

"Ma'am, do you need help?"

"Can you just give me a minute?" I asked.

"I have to load the next group of passengers."

"Okay, you go get them, and I'll just stand here and reflect on the beauty in front of me."

Angel fell to the floor, laughing so hard, he had to draw his knees to his chest. Little shit.

"I'm going to beat you to death with a frying pan."

"Oh, please, *pendeja,* you don't own a frying pan." He wiped his eyes and tried to sober. "That girl's messed up in the head. Just heal her. You can make her cross."

"I tried that. Now I have a girl stuck to my face. I can only barely see through her. How am I going to go through life with a girl stuck to my face?"

And again with the fit of laughs. The next group of passengers were boarding. I had to get off this car now. I gave it one more shot. I reached out to her, into her, let my energy meld with hers until I found her huddled in a dark corner of her mind. I wrapped my energy around her, cradled her, and coaxed her closer. That was when I felt it. The trauma of what had happened to her.

"If you're staying, miss, you need to disembark now," the attendant said.

"I'm staying," I said breathlessly, the agony inside her seizing my lungs until she finally relaxed and slipped through.

She'd crossed, but when that happens, I see things. I catch glimpses of the departed's life. What their favorite pet was or what their first snow cone tasted like. But I didn't get that with this girl.

"Ma'am, I need to close this door. We're on a schedule."

I was still in the middle of her crossing. Images flashed bright hot in my mind, hateful and terrifying. The unimaginable things she suffered through had left her forever scarred, the abrasive texture of her memories undeniable proof. She'd been abused by her mother and ignored by her father, never seen, never cared for, and completely abandoned on the day he committed suicide, leaving her in the sole care of a monster. Even her brother ignored her, most likely because he was scared to incur their mother's wrath as well. So, instead of standing up for his sister, he joined in, laughing when her mother called her stupid, turning a blind eye when her mother tripped her and she fell with a pot of boiling water. She'd burned her hands and face in the water. Those burns were still visible when she died.

These were the things I didn't want to see. The things I couldn't wash away, no matter how much scrubbing I did. Miranda—her name was Miranda—was the product of a failed system. While I didn't see her death specifically, it was crystal clear she'd died at her mother's hands in a way that was so horrific, so nonsensical, my mind rebelled, my stomach contracted, and the world pitched to the side. I stumbled when I tried to get off the car. Angel caught me and lifted me to him. No, not Angel. A man. At the moment, I didn't care whom. I accepted the help, grabbed on to the tan jacket sleeves, and hefted myself up. I just needed to get through the worst of it. Despite everything she'd been through, the most prevalent emotion that she'd carried even into her death was a deep and abiding love for her brother. The same brother who looked the other way when her mother came at her.

I swallowed back bile as the images began to fade. Not that they would ever fade completely, but I needed to find Amber and Quentin. I would have fallen out of the car if not for the man holding me. The attendant hurried over, and I waved him away before pushing out of the man's grasp and lunging toward the corner of the landing. I grabbed hold of the railing and proceeded to empty the paltry contents of my stomach onto the wood platform. Sinking to my knees, I almost hyperventilated as my stomach convulsed way more times than was necessary, dry heaving until it became embarrassing.

After a solid minute of that crap, I wiped my mouth on my jacket sleeve and took out my phone to dial Amber.

She picked up immediately. "Are you here yet?"

"I'm here," I said, filling my hot lungs with the cool air of Sandia Peak. It was always several degrees cooler at the top of the mountain, and it felt good. Helped calm my stomach and clear my head until I could at least see to ascend the dozens of ramps that led to High Finance, the restaurant at the top of the peak.

"We're sitting outside the restaurant, against the back wall. Please, hurry, Aunt Charley. Something's wrong and I can't understand him. He's signing too fast for me to understand."

"I'm almost there, sweetheart," I said, bolting to my feet.

The man held out a hand and I looked up to thank him, only to come face-to-face with Captain Eckert. He'd followed me. Had he been in the same car? I never saw him. He was wearing a tan jacket and knit cap, clearly a master of disguise. Then again, I did have a girl stuck to my face on the ride up.

I could tell by the disappointment lining his features he hadn't wanted me to see him. I longed so very much to confront him right then and there, but at that moment, I needed him.

"Come with me," I said, grabbing on to his jacket again for stability. I dragged him until we were both running up the ramps, rushing past the sightseers enjoying the gorgeous scenery the Land of Enchantment had to offer. Eckert helped me every step of the way, catching me when I stumbled, picking me up once when I fell hard onto my right knee. My vision was still impaired by Miranda's memories. I couldn't quite navigate the uneven grounds right. The world tipped perilously onto its side over and over. I kept expecting the captain to ask me if I'd been drinking, but to his credit, he kept his mouth shut.

Angel was still there, too. He followed behind us.

Uncaring of anything the captain thought about me anymore, I spoke to him. "Go find them, hon, and tell me exactly where they are."

"Already did." He dashed past us and led the way. "Over here," he said when we topped the stairs to the restaurant. He pointed and I rushed over to Quentin and Amber.

"Aunt Charley!" She ran into my arms. "I'm so sorry. Something's wrong. He won't talk to me anymore."

Quentin sat against the back wall of the restaurant with his head between his knees, his arms covering himself protectively. Miranda had been creepy. I'd give him that. But this was more.

I touched his arm, but he didn't respond.

"What's wrong with him?" Amber asked. "We were just going to ride up here and look around, then be back before school let out."

"When did he start getting upset?" I asked her.

"On the ride up. He got real nervous and then just kind of shrank into himself. He couldn't look out the windows and kept waving me away from him. A lady asked me if he was afraid of heights, but he said he wasn't."

"No, hon, he wasn't," I said. I barely took note of the captain hovering nearby. Whatever he was up to, whatever he was planning, he could bite my ass. I rubbed Quentin's shoulders, trying to coax him back to me while I fought the aftereffects of Miranda's memories. I squeezed my eyes shut and shook my head to clear it. Her agony was so great, so all-consuming. She'd loved her mother so much and never understood why the woman who gave birth to her didn't love her back. But the fault surely rested on her shoulders. She'd been so certain. She'd caused her own misery. She deserved it.

It didn't matter now. She was in greater hands than mine. Hands that truly knew how to heal. He'd help her understand that none of that was her fault.

And if he was as just as I hoped, her mother would spend eternity burning for her transgressions.

I fought so many things at once. Pain, agony, helplessness, and anger. The anger was all mine. I clenched my jaw so tight, my teeth hurt.

After swallowing hard, I tried again with Quentin. "Angel," I said, waving him closer.

"I'm sorry about that girl, Charley. I didn't know."

"I didn't either, hon. But what can I do for Quentin?"

"I don't know. He's still alive. That's not really my area." When I turned back in disappointment, he said, "But he's like the girl. He's not thinking right. Maybe you could do what you did with her."

I started to argue with him but stopped and rethought his suggestion. It was certainly worth a shot. I petted Quentin's blond hair and let my energy gather in my core. Let it build and swell like a rising storm. But before I could send it out, Quentin looked up, his cerulean blue eyes glistening with fear and uncertainty. I let the energy inside me disperse and touched his handsome face. As though it took him a moment to recognize me, he furrowed his brows, then blinked and rushed into my arms.

We sat like that a long time, on the back deck of the restaurant, swaying to the music streaming from inside. Well, I swayed to the music. After a long while, I glanced at my gang. Amber was standing close by, wringing the knit cap in her hands. Angel was sitting against the wall next to us. He seemed very curious about Quentin, and I couldn't believe I'd never introduced them.

Captain Eckert was leaning against the bright red railing that encircled the restaurant in thick wooden planks. It was a beautiful place and a stunning view.

"What's wrong with him?" the captain asked.

I pasted on my best glare. "I'll deal with you later."

Though the captain wasn't used to being treated so harshly, especially by one of APD's lowly consultants, he didn't argue. He didn't threaten. He just stood there, observing, probably taking notes and weighing the possibility of getting me fired for mental instability.

After a while, Quentin finally pulled back and told me he couldn't get on the cable car. He couldn't go home.

"Is it the girl?" I asked him.

A look of surprise flashed across his face, but it didn't last. He knew who I was, what I was, and that we had a lot in common. He nodded.

"I saw her, too," I signed. "She was scared and lost."

He gaped at me. "*She* was scared and lost?"

"Yes, she crossed through me. She didn't want to at first, but I . . . convinced her. She was very hurt by her family."

"They abused her?" he asked.

I nodded. "Bad."

"Like hit her?"

"And worse. She was so scared."

He looked down. "I could feel that, too. I could feel how dark her world was. How empty. It made my stomach hurt."

"Mine, too, but how did you feel that?" I was beginning to realize Quentin could do more than just see the departed.

"I didn't tell you."

"So, tell me now," I said. I reached over and ruffled his hair.

That got his attention. He smoothed it into place, peeking at Amber, then did the same to mine, ruffling my chocolaty locks while wearing a mischievous glint in his eyes. My hair was a mess anyway, so I just left it.

"If the spirit touches me, I can see how it feels," he said.

"Wow. That's crazy."

"It's messed up. I don't like it." He shrank back when he thought about it.

"I'm sorry. Sometimes the departed carry a lot of baggage."

"Like suitcases?" he asked, confused.

I chuckled. "Sorry, hearing idiom. Like they have a lot of problems weighing them down."

"Oh, yeah. Just like people, I guess."

"Yeah, but that's super cool that you can do that." When he stabbed me with a dubious stare, I said, "Try it on Angel."

"Screw that, *pendeja*." Angel jumped up, but I took his arm before he could vanish on me and jerked him back down. "This is Angel."

Angel graced him with the ever-popular head nod, then stuck out his hand to shake. Quentin shook his hand, then asked him, "Do you know ASL?"

Angel shrugged, so I interpreted.

"No, man, I'm sorry. I wish I did."

I relayed that message but added, "He will learn."

Angel's brows shot up, and he nodded in agreement. "That'd be cool."

"Okay, now that that's settled, did you feel anything when you touched him?"

Quentin shrugged. "He's pretty happy. It's nice."

"It's because he has me," I said, then winked at them both.

"I want to learn that stuff," Angel said, now very into the idea. "You have to teach me."

"I ain't teaching you anything," I said, speaking and signing at the same time. "Go hang with him at the school in Santa Fe. You'll learn all kinds of signs."

"That's true," Quentin said; then he looked up at Amber. The minute he did, she fell to her knees in front of us. "I'm so sorry," he said to her.

"Please, don't be," she signed. I was so proud of her. She'd learned a lot in the last two weeks since meeting him. Kids. Freaking little sponges. "I understand. You see things I can't. I want—" She struggled with the next words, then added, "—I want me and you to be the same. I want to see what you see."

He frowned. "No, you don't. It's not fun."

"I know it's not easy. I've known Charley for a long time. She always tries to help dead people and gets in trouble. I wish," she voiced but didn't know the sign, so she started that sentence again. "I want I could help her."

I made sure to put it into my next sentence so she'd pick it up. "I wish we were off this mountain. Your mother is going to kill me about fifteen minutes after the nuns trample me to death trying to get to you. They are all worried sick."

Their guilt hit me in one rock-solid wave. Good. Served 'em right. Then a thought occurred.

"Wait a minute," I said as we stood and gathered ourselves. "How many times have you two done this?"

"This is the first time," Quentin said, his expression full of earnestness.

"I meant, how many times have you two skipped school?"

Their gazes instantly locked; then Amber's dropped to the ground in guilt.

"Quentin!" I shouted. Or, well, signed really fast. "Amber is twelve years old."

"I'll be thirteen next week!" she said.

"I'm thirteen," Angel said.

I ignored him. "You are sixteen, Quentin. That is so wrong."

He gaped at me. "You think—?" He stopped and shook his head at me. "No way. She's just a kid. We're friends."

Well, I'd put my foot in it. Amber winced at the pain that overtook her. His words had hurt. Clearly she thought they were more.

I turned to her and voiced my next words, holding my hand up to block Quentin's view so he couldn't read my lips. He tried to see past it, but I spoke fast. "He's lying," I said to her. "Whatever you do, for the love of all things holy, please don't let your mother know you two have kissed."

Quentin may have been able to hide that one, but there was no way Amber could have managed it. Guilt once again radiated out of her.

I gasped and turned to Quentin, appalled. "You kissed her?"

"What? No."

Amber caught on. She stamped her foot. "Aunt Charley, you tricked me."

I was still busy being appalled at Quentin.

He stuffed his hands into his pockets before he said another word.

"Wise decision," I said before stalking away. Or trying to. The world toppled again and I tripped, flying headfirst into Captain Eckert. Oh, well. Better that than pitching myself off the side of a mountain. And he'd be fine once his cracked ribs healed.

12

I have a perfect body.
It's in my trunk.
—T-SHIRT

I was still wobbly on the way down. Captain Eckert stayed close until he gave up and just wrapped one of his arms around me, holding me tight to his side as we descended. Not that the ramps were that steep. I was just that wobbly. Though the captain and I had a lot to talk about, now was not the time.

He held me all the way to the bottom of the tramway and walked me and the kids to Misery. I left him there with a warning scowl when he asked if I was okay to drive.

I dropped Quentin off at the convent to—just as I'd suspected—a horde of frantic nuns. They rushed out in one solid mass. They reminded me of penguins attacking. Our only hope was to drop into a fetal position and whimper. That stopped them in their tracks. Worked every time. Quentin didn't follow my lead, but that was okay. I was very willing to sacrifice my dignity for the both of us.

After barely escaping with life and limb, I took a very nervous Amber home and dropped her at her door. It was on the way. Cookie was busy pretending to get ready for her date. Pretending to be oblivious of the fact that Amber was two hours late. She wasn't the least bit angry. Fear and worry had swallowed any anger she might have had. The anger would hit later. Hopefully I'd be very far away when it did.

We walked back to her bedroom, where she was in the middle of spritzing perfume onto her neck.

"Mom?" Amber said, her voice thin and fragile.

"Oh, hey, hon. You're late."

Amber hesitated, then looked down at her feet. "I went to Paula's house. We made cookies."

And there it was. The spike of emotion I'd been waiting for, but instead of anger, I sensed a spasm of pain. She was hurt that Amber had just lied to her. "Go do your homework. I'm going out for a while."

"'Kay."

The little fairy princess shuffled off, feeling more miserable for having lied. She'd figure that out soon. I had complete faith in her. But Cook was hurt by her deception. No idea why. I lied to her all the time.

The second Amber was out of earshot, Cookie rushed to close her door and whirled on me. "What happened?"

"Sit down first."

She did as I asked and I explained the entire event in detail, including the part about Captain Eckert. And what he'd been up to. He had to be behind all the panhandlers and the cop with the camera.

"What is that man's deal?"

"I wish I knew, but I wanted you to be aware of the fact that Amber behaved beautifully, Cook. She never left Quentin's side. And she's learning so much sign. I'm terribly proud of her."

"She just lied to me."

"Yes, and I promise you, she feels worse about it than you do."

She turned a hopeful gaze on me. "Really?"

"I give it a day. She'll tell you the truth. She wants to talk to you about what happened so bad, Cook."

The corners of her mouth crinkled in a relieved half smile.

I got up to leave. "Before I forget, I want you to find out everything you can about the girl in the cable car. Her name was Miranda Nelms. I want to know if they charged her mother and brother with anything."

"Her brother, too?"

"Long story. You don't want to know."

"No," she said, holding up a hand in lieu of a stop sign, "you're right. I already know more than I want to. I'll get on it first thing tomorrow."

"Perfect. Are you ready for your date?"

And the apprehension was back in full force. "I just don't know what to wear." She tossed aside the pair of pants she'd been holding.

"I would definitely suggest keeping the pants, but you do what makes you most comfortable. Besides, your date is gay."

Surprise lit her face, and the apprehension she'd been feeling dissipated. "That's great. I don't have to worry about impressing him. He wouldn't be into me either way, right?"

"Right. He works for APD dispatch, but I doubt Uncle Bob knows him or the fact that he's gay." I snorted. "That would suck. All of our hard work would be down the drain if that were the case."

"And you're meeting Robert there, right? To make sure he sees us?"

I checked my watch. "In one hour on the dot. Are you okay with leaving Amber by herself for a while?"

"After what happened? No. I'm leaving the cop Robert sent over with her. And I've asked Mrs. Allen to check on her as well."

"Cook, the last time Mrs. Allen checked on her, Amber ended up in the hospital."

She nodded before saying, "It wasn't Mrs. Allen's fault. She was just trying to check up on Amber."

"In the dark, with a her hair in curlers and a Scandinavian mud mask on her face. Amber tried to run from her and ran face-first into a doorjamb. I'll never understand why Mrs. Allen didn't just turn on a light."

"It's okay." She patted my leg consolingly. "All the swelling is gone now, and I've asked Mrs. Allen to just knock and wait for the plainclothes to answer the door."

"And you think that'll work, do ya?" I chuckled. It sounded maniacal. It didn't quite have that refined edge of psychosis that I was going for, but it worked. I pointed to her closet. "Pants? Not that I don't appreciate a nice pair of pantaloons as much as the next girl, but most restaurants require they be covered."

I gave Amber a hug before I left and suffered the long trek back to my place. Five steps later, I pried my door open with a hefty nudge from my shoulder, then stumbled inside when it gave. Reyes had patched it temporarily—at least I could open and close it now—but I'd need a new doorframe. That man did not know his own strength. Of course, he hadn't considered the fact that my door had been unlocked when he decided to crash through it. I righted myself and stopped. Something was different about my apartment. What could it be?

Oh, yeah. My place had been ransacked. Son of a bitch. Every drawer I could see had been turned inside out. Every item I owned upended.

I jammed my fists onto my hips. "Mr. Wong! Didn't we talk about this? You are the worst guard ever."

The scene was strangely familiar. I went from room to room, but nothing else had been disturbed. Only the living room and kitchen had been upended. The intruder must have found what he wanted and—

Zeus!

I ran to my kitchen and tore through the knife drawer. Carefully, because it was the knife drawer. I figured hiding the dagger in a drawer full of kitchen knives was ingenious. I was wrong. It was gone.

It would seem that one Mr. Dealer of Souls had decided to visit while

I was out. The little shit. He'd pay. Literally. I wasn't cleaning up this mess. I'd hire a service or something, and make him pay for it. Damn it.

I picked up my bag and went to confront a demon in human's clothing.

After finally getting Artemis to scoot over enough for me to fit in, I started Misery up and summoned Angel. I was headed to the last place I'd seen the Dealer and asked Angel where the Daeva lived. I'd assumed he lived close by where the game had been held. According to Angel, I was right.

Artemis decided my lap looked more appealing than the seat Mr. Andrulis had recently vacated. I was going to miss that man. As a result of Artemis's fussiness, I drove down Central and up San Mateo with a fully grown Rottweiler on my lap until I reached a residential district off a side street. She caught sight of a cat—the horror!—and bound off me, using my ovaries, Beam Me Up and Scotty, as a launchpad. I had to admit, it hurt.

The Dealer's house was nothing like what I'd expected. It was kind of nice, for one thing, with xeriscaping in front and rich terra-cotta walls with thick wood trim. I walked up to a carved natural wood door with a patina knocker shaped like a deer skull, but he opened the door before I could use it.

"I want the dagger back."

A smile that was so pretty, it stunned me flashed across his face. The kid was gorgeous. No doubt about it. He wasn't wearing the top hat. It sat perched on a wall hook just inside the door. And his long black hair hung just a tad past his shoulders.

He widened the opening. "Come in." When I stood my ground, he added, "Please."

Okay, he said please. How dangerous could he be? Conceding, I stepped across the threshold and said, "I mean it. I want that dagger."

"So you can use it on me?" he asked, closing the door. "So you can sink it into my chest?"

"Duh."

He strolled into the open living area. It was very plush with lots of beiges highlighted with a soft Mediterranean green.

It was hard to imagine he actually owned this house. While I realized he only *looked* nineteen, he still *looked* nineteen. He still looked like a kid who should be flipping burgers at Macho Taco—or, well, burritos—when in truth, he was thousands of years old.

"You own this?" I asked him.

"Nah." He tossed a throw pillow aside and gestured for me to sit. "I killed the owners and ate their souls for breakfast." When I deadpanned, he shrugged and said, "It's a rental."

"The knife."

"What makes you think I have it?"

"Please," I said, scoffing at him. "What if I promise not to use it on you?"

He sat in a wingback chair across from the sofa, stretching one leg out and hitching it on the bottom of a beautiful iron coffee table.

"I would offer you something to drink—"

"I would just decline it." I sank onto the sofa.

"Figured as much. That knife could be very dangerous in the wrong hands."

"Like yours? Is it dangerous in your hands?"

He didn't answer. Instead, he studied me, a curious gleam in his eyes, and it reminded me he had a certain power. He was charismatic and charming, no doubt, but he also had a magnetism that went beyond the average supernatural being. The other demons I'd encountered were nothing like him. For starters, he didn't have slick black scales or razor-sharp teeth.

"You can stop now."

"What?" I asked, surprised when he pulled me out of my musings.

"Trying to figure me out."

"I was just contemplating the fact that you don't have scales and pointy teeth."

"I wouldn't be too sure about that," he said, accompanying his statement with a dimple.

"How were you able to get the knife? Demons can't even touch it without it infecting them."

"Good thing I'm not a demon."

Right. I knew that. Technically, he wasn't a demon. "So, it won't kill you?"

He lifted one shoulder in a half-hearted shrug. "I wouldn't go that far."

So, he could touch it, but it could still kill him. The same thing could be said about my relationship with knives. Or pretty much anything. Or anyone. "You said the knife had a glow to it. What does it look like in your eyes?"

"I don't know. It just has this soft sheen that I could see even through your pants. Kind of what a human soul looks like."

"Like an aura?" I asked.

"Well, yeah, but more like the soul itself."

"Oh."

When it didn't sink in, he asked, "Can't you see them? Human souls?"

"Not really. Not like you. Not until they've passed. Then I can see the dickens out of them."

He straightened in his chair. "Surely you can see your own light. It's blinding."

I shook my head. "Not so much."

"How can you mark souls if you can't see them?"

That threw me. "Um, I didn't know I was supposed to."

His surprise turned to anger. "You're kidding me."

I reached down and waited for Artemis to appear by my side. She rose up from the floor into my hand. I scratched her head absently as the Dealer took her in.

"What is your name?" I asked, changing the subject. "I only know you as the Dealer."

"Is that what you told her, Rey'aziel? That I was a Dealer?"

Only after he said that did I feel Reyes. He materialized more fully, and his heat rushed over me in a scorching wave. Naturally, he was angry.

He stood in his hooded cloak directly between the Dealer and me. "What are you doing?" he asked, his voice cold and hard like marble.

I rose to my feet, but Reyes still towered over me, his robes undulating around us. I couldn't see his face within the folds of unending darkness that enshrouded him. "The Dealer took the dagger. I was trying to get it back."

"You would come here, you would face this thing, alone? After everything we talked about?"

"Apparently."

My humor did not amuse him.

I sighed. "Believe it or not, you are not helping this situation. I knew I'd have a better chance of getting it back without you here."

"You have a better chance of losing your soul to him, that's for certain."

"Can you just have a little faith in me, Reyes? I'm not stupid."

His cloak disappeared, falling around him in a cascade of smoke and fog to reveal his requisite jeans and a navy button-down with the sleeves rolled up, exposing his sinewy forearms. He looked really good. He walked up to me until we stood a couple of feet apart, coming dangerously close to invading my personal space. "That, my dear, remains to be seen."

He continued forward, and just as we were about to touch, he dematerialized in a burst of smoke, his essence enveloping me for just a moment.

But I went from flirty to furious instantly. I looked at the Dealer. "He did not just say that." I knew Reyes was still there. He hadn't left. He wouldn't, I knew. But he was giving me as much privacy as possible.

One corner of the Dealer's mouth tilted up. "He has a point, you know."

I sat down, my back stiff. "You're on his side?"

"On this, yes, I am. You take your role too lightly."

A sigh slipped past my lips. "My role in what? Taking down the monsters in the basement?"

"No. The only monster that matters. It's imperative that you live."

"It's imperative that you give me back the dagger."

"What will you give me in return?"

Uh-oh. "This is the bargaining part, right? Where you try to steal my soul?"

"If I wanted your soul, I'd have it."

"I have to give it over willingly."

"Oh, you would." The grin that spread over his face was a little disturbing. "Quite willingly. It would be easy. Too easy. And that's what makes me nervous."

No one had any faith in me whatsoever. What would it take to convince them I was competent? Maybe if I stopped getting tortured and beaten up every few days. That would be a good start, anyway. I made a promise to myself. No more getting tortured for—I counted on my fingers—two, no *three* months.

"Why are you so invested in this?" I asked him. "What do you have against Lucifer?"

"The fact that he enslaved me isn't enough of a reason?"

"Okay, that's a pretty good one, but I've come up against his slaves before."

"The mindless creatures who came after you? Do I seem mindless?"

"Not especially. Or you didn't until you broke into my apartment. You're paying to have it cleaned up, by the way."

He lifted an acquiescent shoulder. "If I give you back the dagger, you have to do something for me."

"And what would that be?"

"You have to let me be a part of this. A part of the fall of Satan."

Sounded easy enough. "Look. You seem to know a lot about all of this. It's been kind of like hands-on training for me. I just . . . what am I supposed to be doing? Reyes wants me to figure it out as I go, but—"

"Rey'aziel is afraid of you," he said. "That's why he doesn't want you to know everything. That's why he wants to put off your knowing every-thing as long as he can."

I snorted. "He's not afraid of anyone."

"You're not just anyone. You're not even just a reaper. Your heritage is proof of that."

"Fine. I get it." I really didn't, but I wasn't about to let him know that. I had every intention of diving into my past, of digging up every ounce of my heritage I could get my hands on. If it existed. Garrett was look-ing into the prophecies, but I wanted to know more, and I knew how to get it. I was going to blackmail my nigh fiancé. If he wanted my hand, he had a lot of explaining to do. And while this kid seemed to know a great deal, I just didn't know if I could trust him or anything he told me.

"You don't believe me?" he asked. "Ask him what your name is."

"Speaking of which, your name is?" I reminded him.

His expression impassive, he said, "You can ask Rey'aziel that as well."

This was getting me nowhere fast. "You know, between Reyes's cryptic answers, that Cleo guy's ambiguous prophecies that Swopes is looking into, and your mysterious quips, I've had about enough of the lot of you. Can you just give me one straight answer?"

"I'll give it my best shot."

I didn't miss the fact that his response guaranteed absolutely nothing. "Wonderful. Okay, what am I dying to know?" I looked up in thought, then said, "Some . . . entities have suggested that Reyes was sent to this plane for me specifically. To kill me specifically. Is that true?"

"It is."

My chest contracted instantly. He could give a straight answer, as disturbing as that answer was. "He told me he was sent for a portal to heaven. That his father wanted a way into heaven."

"He lied."

The room grew hotter. I ignored it. "He told me you were the ultimate liar. That you were so good at it, even demons would fall for anything you had to say."

"True. But look at it this way: Why would the prince's father want a way into the very place that could destroy him?"

He had me there. "I don't know. To take it over?"

The Dealer chuckled. "The odds of Lucifer taking over heaven are astronomical. You've seen eighteen-wheelers on the highway, right?"

"Of course."

"If it hits a mosquito, what do you think the odds are the mosquito will crush the truck?"

"Astronomical."

"Exactly."

"So, are you telling me Satan is no threat to heaven?"

A soft laugh rumbled out of him again. "Honestly, it's like talking to a child."

I felt the same way. I stood and started for the door. He followed me. "I didn't mean to insult you. I'm just surprised, not only at how little you know, but how much of what you know is so impossibly wrong."

"Then how about you help me understand?"

"I can try. What else would you like to know?"

"Okay, if what you say is true, why would he want me? Satan? If not for access to heaven?"

"Rey'aziel has kept a lot from you. I'm surprised, considering we have the same agenda."

"What would that be?"

"Like I said before, to take him down. To end him once and for all."

"And you think I can do that?"

"No. I don't. I only know that you are a key player. Somehow, some-way, you are the key to it all, and Lucifer knows that. God, as humans like to call him, did what he said he would. He cast Lucifer and all like him from heaven. Now it's just a game of souls. Like chess."

"And humans are the pawns."

"For Rey'aziel's father, yes. Not for God. Comparing the two is like comparing the feelings a mother has for her child to those that a serial killer has for the same child."

"But you don't know what my role is exactly?"

"Sadly, I do not."

"Okay, then, what did you mean by marking souls?"

Now he was looking at me like I'd lost my mind. "Um, your job."

"My job is to mark souls?"

"Yes."

"But I'm a portal. I thought my job was to help people cross."

"That's only part of your job. You can see guilt, deception, malicious-ness for a reason, Charlotte."

"So, I mark them as liars or murderers or what?"

"You'll know when the time comes."

"But I don't have the right to judge people. I'm pretty sure the Big Guy upstairs would be upset if I went around judging his flock."

"You will not sentence the guilty. You simply filter their passage after death. You sift through them and prepare them for their final journeys. Think of yourself as one of those machines that sorts coins into the right slots, separating the quarters from the dimes."

"I'm a sorter?"

"Of sorts," he said, flashing his teeth.

"No," I said, mentally stomping my foot. "I want it all. What is my job, exactly? What can I do, exactly?"

"You realize when your human body ceases, you will be shown everything."

"I'll get a crash course in grim reaperism?"

"Something like that."

"But what about until then? While I'm still here on earth?"

"Your only job as far as I'm concerned is to live. This isn't usually a problem for reapers. No reaper has lived as long as you have. Ever."

"I'm only twenty-seven."

"Exactly. And that's about twenty-two years longer than most have ever lived."

"Reyes told me that, too. That most reapers' physical bodies passed quite young and they did their jobs for the next five hundred years or so incorporeally. I'd always wondered how they knew what to do. I didn't realize it would be downloaded into my brain when I pass."

"So, he's not keeping all the fun facts to himself. Just the important ones."

Another wave of heat suffused the room.

The Dealer glanced up. "I felt that."

"Lay it out for me," I said. "Let me have it. Marking souls is my job? That it?"

He leaned back in his chair again. "I could tell you and piss off Rey'aziel, an entity we most definitely want on our side if we are going to win this thing. Or I could take his lead and let you figure it out as you go."

"I vote for option A."

"I can only assure you that when you're ready, you will see souls. You will know how to mark them. You already know when to let people cross, when to help them or force them across. You're already on your way." He studied his hands. "While you are the key player in all of this, Rey'aziel holds the most sway in your destiny."

"Why?"

"He's the Thirteenth beast. Or didn't he mention that?"

Reyes appeared again in all his cloaked glory, the darkness that undulated like a black ocean of night filling the room to capacity. I was getting good intel. I didn't need him disrupting this font of information.

"Reyes isn't a beast, and he's certainly not a hellhound."

"Close enough. He was only slightly more civilized than the Twelve. Why do you think Lucifer sent him to kill you?"

"Then why? Why does Satan want me dead so bad if not for the lock and key thing?"

"What lock and key thing?" he asked.

"It's just, that's what I thought this was all about. They told us that if the key is inserted into the lock, we would open a portal straight from hell into heaven. Blah, blah, blah. And now you're telling me that has nothing to do with it?"

He lowered his head in thought. I'd thrown him. His brows slid together and he chewed on a nail as his mind raced. Like any human might do. It was hard to see this kid as anything but a kid. I knew from past experience, though, how big a mistake that would be.

"I don't know," he said, scanning me from head to toe. "If you're the lock and the key is—"

Dawning showed on his face. I saw it, and felt it, the moment it hit him. He took a wobbly step back, absolute astonishment knocking the air out of him.

I glanced down at myself. Chocolate brown top. Black jeans. Killer boots. "What?" I asked him.

"I can't believe I didn't see it. You said this friend of yours has the prophecies. Do you mean Cleosarius's prophecies?"

"Yeah. And?"

"If I can see them, I'll give back the dagger."

"Deal. But, seriously, what?" I gestured to myself.

He winked and led me to the door, encouraging me to get out with a light shove. Even light it was rude. "By the way, I didn't ransack your apartment."

Surprised, I just kind of looked at him.

"I didn't need to," he continued. "I could feel the dagger. Went straight to it. Your apartment was like that when I got there."

Well, crap. I could only hope the ransackers got syphilis. I wondered if there was a hashtag for that.

13

*Sometimes I write "drink coffee" on my to-do list
just to feel like I've accomplished something.*

—STATUS UPDATE

I made it home just after sunset, holding the title to my soul in one hand and a mocha latte in the other. Surely Reyes would see the bright side of that. The soul thing. How angry could he be that I'd gone to see the Dealer? I chose not to dwell on Reyes or his anger while searching for him. After checking his place and my place and everything in between, I headed for my office and finally found him outside in the alley between the bar and the apartment building, his legs sticking out from under the front end of the sweetest black muscle car I'd ever seen. I slowed my pace to take in the work of art before me. Then I checked out the car. The emblem on the side said it was a 'Cuda. Whatever she was, she melted my knees upon impact. She was stunning, and I decided right then and there to become a lesbian.

"Is she yours?" I asked him as I walked up. He was tooling around with her engine, which was clean enough to eat off of, shiny enough to apply makeup by, and big enough to make the earth shake, I was sure.

A soft thunder rumbled in the distance. I glanced up at the clouds that had rolled in, their grayness haunting against the dark sky.

Refocusing on Mr. Angry Pants, I bent over the engine to see what he was doing. He had one of those droplights, and I could see a portion of his face as he worked under the car. He ignored me and kept ratcheting something. Something that I could only hope actually needed ratcheting, because he was really into it. His signature heat wafted up and around me. I put my elbows on a shiny part and propped my chin in my cupped hands.

"Are you going to be mad long?" I asked him.

He ratcheted again, refusing to meet my gaze, so I let it drift over the front of the car to his spread legs, lean and powerful, his slim hips crafted to perfection, and his rock-hard waist, rippled and taut. His T-shirt had ridden up to reveal several inches of deliciousness above his jeans, and my mouth watered in response.

"Which part are you mad about?" I asked, realizing he could be mad about any number of things. I tended to rack up the shit-list points.

He finally spoke, drawing my attention back to him. "You are investigating what you think was my kidnapping."

That was what he was mad about? Wait, did he just say—? "What I think was your kidnapping? You mean, the baby that was kidnapped from the Fosters wasn't you?"

He put down the ratchet and picked up another, equally foreboding tool. "Yes, it was me, but I was hardly kidnapped."

I leaned closer to him, trying to see him past the engine. "What do you mean?" My thoughts staggered into each other as I reviewed the case in my mind. "I don't understand. You weren't kidnapped?"

"Not that time." The car dipped with the pressure he was putting on her.

"Reyes, please explain. Were you kidnapped from the Fosters or not?"

"It doesn't matter what I tell you. You'll take that information and do whatever you want with it. You never think about the consequences of your actions."

"You are so wrong." I lowered myself onto my knees and bent to look at him under the car. His biceps strained against the thin fabric of his T-shirt as he worked. "That's all I consider. I do what I can to help—"

"Strangers," he said, turning the wrench so tight, the car dipped again. "People you don't know. You don't think about the people who are closest to you. What your actions could do to them."

I was appalled that he would even say such a thing. "Do you think I don't care about my family? My friends?"

"I think you care for too many. You're spread too thin. You take on too much, risk too much, and you cannot possibly win."

He was changing the subject on purpose, bringing up an old argument to urge me off the trail of his kidnapping. "Reyes, were you abducted from your biological family or not?"

Breathing hard, he lowered the wrench and finally looked at me, his eyes glittering in the artificial light. "Yes. I was."

"So, the Fosters are your biological family. The family you chose to be born with on earth?"

"No." He went back to work, and I pressed my mouth together, struggling for patience.

"So, the Fosters' child was abducted, but he wasn't you."

He squinted as he struggled with the car. "Wrong. And wrong."

I found myself mesmerized by his actions for a moment. The shadows between his muscles shifted every time he flexed. "Okay, so if this is opposite day, the Fosters' child was not abducted and—" I strained to think about how I'd put it. "—and it was you. You were the Fosters' kid."

"Closer."

I threw myself onto the pavement as dramatically as I could manage without incurring injury. "Oh, my god. I will give you a million dollars if you will just tell me."

He examined the wrench thing he was holding. "You don't have a million dollars."

"Fine," I said, rolling onto my back and patting my pockets. I brought out what I did have: three ones, some spare change, and a watermelon Jolly Rancher. "I'll give you three dollars, fifty-two cents, and a Jolly Rancher."

His mouth softened as he gave me his full attention. "I was going to say no, but since you threw in the Jolly Rancher." He scooted out from under the car and stood before helping me to my feet. "If I tell you, will you give me your word on something?"

"I'll give you a lap dance. On your lap," I said, shaking out my hair.

"Deal. I wasn't abducted from the Fosters."

I swiped at my butt, but stilled when he continued.

"The Fosters were the ones who abducted me."

As I stood gawking at him, he lifted out the droplight and closed the hood of his car. While this was nothing like the times I'd tried to get him to open up about his childhood with Earl Walker, the monster who raised him, I could tell he did not especially want to talk about this part of his life either. He wiped his hands on a rag, completely ignoring the fact that he was covered in dirt and oil. He defined the word *sexy*.

I stepped to him, put a hand on his arm to get his attention. And, well, just to touch his arm, because damn. "Can you explain? I don't understand."

He studied the rag as he spoke. "I'm not a reaper. I can't remember everything from my birth on like you. But from what I've been able to gather, Mrs. Foster abducted me from a rest area in North Carolina."

"North Carolina?" I asked, taken off guard.

He nodded. "I think it was a crime of opportunity. She'd just found out she couldn't have children. She and her husband were driving home from yet another doctor's appointment. My mother's car overheated. She pulled off at a rest area, and since I was napping in the back, she locked the car and walked five feet to get the water hose. When she came back, she opened the door to check on me and cover me with a blanket. She forgot to lock it back. Mrs. Foster was watching the whole thing from her car as her husband used the facilities. She took it as a sign from God that I should be hers. Any mother who would leave her child alone like that . . . She couldn't believe that a mother so undeserving of a child could have one while she could not. As my biological mother was behind the hood, filling the water reservoir, Mrs. Foster walked up, opened the door, and took me. It all happened so fast. My mother stepped around to check on me again, and I was gone."

He was talking as though he'd read it from a police report. "But you know, then? You know who your biological parents were?"

"Yes. As I got older, I started remembering more and more. Most of it didn't come to me until I was in prison, but slowly I remembered their names. That was it. That was all that came to me."

"Then how did you put all of that together?"

"I hacked into the FBI database and read the reports."

"You hacked the FBI from prison?" When he simply lifted an arrogant brow, I shook my head, astonished. I'd forgotten how good he was at those things. "What happened after that? If Mrs. Foster abducted you, why did she then turn around and . . . and, what? Have someone else abduct you back?" I struggled to understand. "That makes no sense."

"It was one of those cases where everything just kept going wrong. After Mrs. Foster took me, she convinced her husband it was meant to be. But they could hardly just show up with a three-month-old baby. So they left the state, moved around for a bit until they ended up in Albuquerque, which was weird on a whole other level."

"Why?"

"Because my biological parents were supposed to move here. It was why I chose them. Then, after I'm abducted, I end up here anyway?"

I leaned against the thick lamppost. "That can't be a coincidence. What happened next?"

"The Fosters were here for a while. They'd met the neighbors. Joined a church. Started making friends. But Mr. Foster's family started getting suspicious. They wanted to see him. They never liked his wife and were worried she was dangerous, so they planned a trip to visit. And since the Fosters suddenly had a child the exact age of the abducted child from their state, they realized they'd get caught. So, they sold me."

"They just . . . up and sold you? Like, on eBay?"

"That is one piece of the puzzle I haven't quite figured out yet. Maybe Mr. Foster met someone who helped them. Who knows? Either way, I think the plan was just to sell me and be done with it, but a neighbor saw a suspicious-looking man leave out the back door with me. She thought I was being kidnapped, so she called the police. They showed up, the Fosters panicked and said, yes, their baby was gone, and the rest is history."

"Reyes, this is insane. What about Mr. Foster's family? They didn't catch on that he'd also had a mysterious child abducted?"

"Believe it or not, it never reached them. Children are abducted all the time. How many have you seen, especially from across the country? Even today, during the age of information, we hardly ever see the faces of missing children. Did you know there are over two thousand people reported missing every single day? How many do you see in the news?"

"Still," I said, completely taken aback, "how did the cops not make the connection? You had the markings, the map to the gates of hell on your skin."

"Yes, but when I was born, they were very light. So light, they were impossible for the naked eye to see. They grew darker as I got older. By the time the Fosters sold me, they resembled a very light birthmark. Nothing like they are now."

I lowered myself onto a box just as the first drops of rain fell from the sky. "This is just insane. The Fosters seemed so nice on paper and in their interviews." I shook an index finger, remembering what Sack had said. "Agent Carson said her father got a bad feeling from that whole case, like something else was going on that he couldn't quite put a finger on."

"Sounds like he was a good agent."

"You were going to end up here anyway? So that we'd grow up together and go to the same schools?"

He packed up the tools he'd carried out and looked up at the sky. Droplets of rain left tiny rivulets on his face and arms. "My biological father was going to be transferred to Albuquerque. But after I was abducted, they decided to stay in North Carolina and hope the police found me. They never left."

I jumped to my feet. "They're still there?"

"Yes."

"Have you gone to them, Reyes?" I stepped closer as he looked down at me. "Have you told them who you are?"

The expression he gave me stopped me in my tracks. "Why would I do that?"

"Why would you—?" I stopped, flabbergasted he had to ask. "Reyes, they should know that you're okay. They have the right to know that."

"They have a right to live out their days happy and none the wiser."

I could not believe any of this. "Why would you leave them in the dark like that all these years?"

The heat of his anger warmed the cool drops of rain as they fell softly to the ground. "They aren't my real parents, Dutch. You know that."

"But you chose them."

"I chose the woman to be a vessel, that's all."

There was more to it than that. I could feel the mixed emotions swirling inside him. I could feel anger and resentment and doubt. "That's not entirely true," I said to him.

His emotions were too strong to block, and that angered him even more.

He turned away from me to pick up the toolbox, but I stopped him, took his hand into mine, brought it to my face to caress it. "Reyes, you have to tell them. You have to ease their pain. Their uncertainty."

Raindrops dripped off his impossibly long lashes, his dark eyes glittering underneath them. "Why would they want me, Dutch? What would it do to them to know my true identity?"

While I completely disagreed, I just wanted to convince him to open up. To tell them. The rest could come later. "You don't have to tell them what you are."

"I don't mean just that." He turned away from me. "I've spent the last ten years in prison."

I stepped around, forced him to face me. "For a crime you didn't commit."

"I still have the stench of prison on me. Inmates are different. They act different. Their social skills aren't exactly up to par. They would know."

"Please tell me you're kidding."

"I'm not." He took hold of my arm, his demeanor changing on a dime. "And I don't want you to tell them either. This is my life, Dutch. I do not want you to interfere, do you understand?"

No matter how much I wanted to, I had to respect that. If he didn't want to meet his biological parents, I could not force the issue. He had every right to his privacy, but the thought of them still in pain after all these years, still not knowing what had happened to their baby, broke my heart. There was a lot to be said for closure. Leaving it as it stood was like leaving a gaping wound, well, gaping. Surely there was a way around his wishes, of just letting them know that their son was safe and doing well—very well, in fact—without giving away his identity.

"Promise me," he said, taking hold of my other shoulder.

Before I could make that promise, another thought hit me. "Oh, my goodness, what about the son they have now? The Fosters? Is he even really theirs?"

"I have no idea." He let go of my shoulders and crossed his arms. "I have a feeling he was abducted as well, since he is blond and they're both dark."

"Holy crap on Communion bread. This is just so wrong. They have to be stopped."

"Is this your way of getting out of promising me you'll keep that little nose out of it?"

"What? Me? Wow, look at this rain."

"Dutch," he said, his deep, sexy voice all deep and, well, sexy. The soft rain had molded the once-white T-shirt to him as though it were form-fitted to the expanse of his shoulders, to the tapering at his waist. "You may regret looking at me like that."

My gaze bounced back up to his face. It didn't help. "I could never regret looking at you."

He frowned as though he didn't understand. "Why?" he asked, completely serious.

And I was lost. I leapt into his arms, quite literally, and pressed my mouth to his. He fought a smile for a moment, returned my kiss enthusiastically, then backed me against his car. One hand instantly sought out the weight of Danger. He coaxed her to attention with a thumb. His mouth, so hot against mine, left to suckle her crest and only then did I realize he'd unbuttoned my shirt and released both Danger and Will from their confines.

The fact that we were outside didn't even register. The blistering heat of his kiss engulfed me as he suckled Danger. She tightened under his ministrations, hardening so fast, I almost cried out. The jolt of ecstasy was overwhelming. He switched to Will and then back again, offering them both the same amount of attention. Each time he drew on a pink crest, I felt a cutting bite of arousal lance through me. I looked down at him as he kneaded and suckled, his exquisite mouth beautiful against my pale flesh. But it was his teeth grazing across their hardened peaks that was my undoing. In one quick burst, the bittersweet sting of orgasm rocketed through me, colliding like fire and ice during a hurricane.

A scream I could not stop wrenched from my throat. Never. Never in my life had I ever climaxed in such a way. I gasped in utter astonishment as the orgasm pulsated through me like a waterfall of pleasure. It slowly ebbed, leaving me quaking in its wake, and yet I wanted more. Always more when it came to Reyes Alexander Farrow.

His mouth descended onto mine and I wrapped my arms around his head as he laid me back, easing me onto the hood of his car. Before he could rise off me, I reached down and fondled the erection that his pants could barely contain. He sucked in a sharp breath, the air it stirred suddenly cool against my lips, causing another wave of raw desire to ripple through me. Before I knew it, he had peeled off my pants. How he managed that stuff without my notice amazed me, but I lay on his car, half naked, gasping and spent when, without the slightest bit of fanfare, he entered me in one long stroke.

I seized and clutched him to me, the sharp spike of need obliterating my self-control once again. He stayed there, buried inside me, allowing my body to adjust to the fullness of his erection until I grabbed handfuls of hair, bit his shoulder, and shoved my hips against his, forcing him even deeper.

He growled against my ear, wrapped one arm under a knee, and drove into me again and again with quick, short bursts, coaxing the heat in my abdomen to swell, to swirl and churn, building with each thrust like the pressure from a volcano of molten lava about to erupt. My nipples were still sensitive. They rubbed against his chest with each thrust, doing their part to milk me to the edge once again.

The muscles in Reyes's powerful shoulders flexed under the strain of his efforts. His breaths grew ragged, more and more labored as he forced me to still under his viselike grip. I dug my nails into his flesh, urging him faster, begging him not to stop. Never to stop. His expression was one of agony as he bit back his own need to coerce me into another explosive climax. I buried my face in the crook of his neck as the fever inside me rose and burst like a floodtide crashing through a dam. Reyes growled again as his own climax shuddered through him. He trembled against me, his anguish just as powerful as mine, just as intoxicating. He held on to me so tight, it was almost painful and served only to send the crest of my orgasm higher. I rode it, reveling in the exhilaration that flooded me body and soul until ever so gently it ebbed, dissipating completely over the span of several heartbeats.

Reyes's breathing slowed, as did the rain. It tapped out a soft, melodic pattern against the 'Cuda as we lay there, limbs tangled, clothes askew. What little we had on, anyway. He leaned up and kissed me then, long and hard and deep, as though to thank me. As though to reinforce the fact that he needed me as much as I needed him.

When he rose, I brushed my fingertips over his cheek and whispered, "That was somewhat amazing."

His teeth flashed brilliant in the darkness. "You are somewhat amazing."

I'd take it. I was totally busy staring into his eyes when I heard a chime. It registered somewhere in the back of my mind, but didn't quite make it into conscious thought until I heard the sound again.

"That's my phone," I said to him.

He eased me off the hood and kept hold of me until I gained my balance. It took a moment to locate my pants, but once I did, I fished my phone out of my pocket, prayed the rain hadn't ruined it, and checked my texts. An expletive I couldn't repeat in public splashed across the screen. I screeched, covered my mouth with one hand, then said through my fingers, "I forgot about Uncle Bob!"

14

The fastest way to a man's heart is by
tearing a hole through his rib cage.

—T-SHIRT

I hurried in through the back of the bar, soaking wet and squishy, and found Uncle Bob sitting at the bar. After spotting Cookie with her "date" in a dark corner, I began to grow worried, wondering if Ubie had seen them. That was the whole point, after all. Both seats beside Ubie were taken, and there were only a couple of seats to be had at all. And zero, absolutely zero, tables left. I took a seat one over from him. In between us sat a fortyish man with a nice suit and too much cologne. He perked up when I sat down, then looked at me and changed his mind, deciding his drink was more interesting. I glanced in the mirror behind the bar and understood. Not only was I a mess, but my makeup was smeared (on only one eye), my hair (which had been pulled up) was lopsided and hung off to the side like a deflated balloon, and my shirt was on backwards. And it was a button-down. How was that even possible? Did I take off my shirt?

"Hey, Uncle Bob," I said over the guy who stiffened and leaned back a little, suddenly uncomfortable.

"Hey, pumpkin. Where've you been?

"Out back."

"That wasn't you having sex in the alley, was it? We got a call."

Alarm pushed my stomach into my throat. I lunged forward, practically lying across the guy's lap. "Really? Someone called the cops?"

"No," he said into his drink. "It was a hunch. I'm good at hunches."

"Uncle Bob!" I said, my voice a mere squeak.

I needed to know he saw Cookie without him knowing I needed to know. If he just looked at me, he'd see her. She was to my right. No way could he miss her, but he was busy nursing his drink. I cleared my throat and spoke above the crowd while summoning Teri, the bartender. "What did you find out about the woman in WITSEC?"

"Not a lot. They don't just give out that kind of information. But I did discover one thing about your guy."

"My guy? I have a guy? Can I get a coffee with extra coffee?" I asked Teri when she got to me.

She winked and poured. "Sure thing, hon."

I fell a little in love with her at that moment. "What's that?" I asked Ubie.

"He sells a lot of cars."

"Okay, but that doesn't really help me." He still would not look my way. I cleared my throat again. Coughed. Had a small seizure. The man was doing it on purpose. Realization washed over me. That was *why* he wasn't looking at me. He *had* seen her.

Uncle Bob's phone rang and he picked it up. I glanced over at Cookie. She had a where-the-fuck-you-been? look on her face. I shrugged. She shrugged back. I pointed toward the door that led to the alley, wriggled my brows, then did the universal sign for sex, poking an index finger through the hole I'd made with the other hand. Both she and her date started laughing before he gave me a thumbs-up.

The man beside me spoke. "Would you like to switch?"

"Absolutely, but I don't think you can wear my clothes. You're more of an eight, maybe?"

He was even more uncomfortable. And confused. And he clearly had no sense of humor. "I meant stools. Would you like to switch barstools?"

"Oh!" I snorted. "Okay, sure."

We switched seats and I was now closer to my beloved uncle. A fact that I had to emphasize by stealing sips of his whiskey. Straight up. Holy moly, that stuff burned all the way down. That time when I coughed, it was for real. So was the seizure. Without interrupting his conversation, Ubie patted me on the back. Hard. Hard enough to knock me forward into the bar. He was so sweet.

I decided to stick with my coffee. We loved each other, Joe and I. We would have a quiet wedding on a beach with only a few friends present, and I would be secretly praying for a blender. Surely someone would get me a blender.

Three women sat at the table right behind us. They were louder than most and difficult not to hear. I couldn't help but catch their conversation as I waited for Ubie to get off the phone. After a quick look-see over my shoulder, I realized it was Jessica's friends minus Jessica. Too bad. I really missed her.

"He drives a muscle car," one of them said, clearly talking about Reyes. I could not believe he was still the main attraction. He'd been there two weeks. When would they get enough? I had a feeling even if I said yes to his proposal and slapped an engagement ring on him, they'd still come, their hearts full of hope and dreams. How could I possibly blame them? If he weren't mine, I might do the same.

"I haven't heard from her all day," one of them said.

"Text her."

"I have. She's pouting. She does this."

Were they talking about Jessica? If so, they couldn't have been more right.

"She's missing out," one of them said, a purr in her voice.

Of course, I knew Reyes had come in. I felt his heat the moment he walked through the door.

"And, oh . . . my . . . god," one of them said. "He's . . . he's wet."

The room quieted as it often did when he walked in. I turned to him.

He walked right up to me and the fact that we were both soaking wet spoke volumes.

"Of all the gin joints in all the world."

"You forgot something." He tucked something into my hands. A bra. My bra!

What the—? I wiggled my shoulders, testing Danger and Will. Yep. No support whatsoever.

He watched me for a sec, then said, "Want me to put it on for you?"

"Okay, but I doubt it's your size."

I lifted Uncle Bob's firewater and stole his napkin to pat Reyes's face. He studied me from under his spiked lashes, his deep, coffee-colored irises glistening in the incandescent light. His mouth, full and sensual, tilted up at one corner, exposing the most charming dimple I'd ever seen, and I stopped, just to absorb him, just to memorize every line of his face, every curve. After we stared into each others' eyes a long moment, he sobered and asked, "What's wrong with your uncle?"

"What?" I was still staring. I shook out of it and said, "I think he's upset about Cookie's date."

"Ah. That makes sense." He ran a finger over the back of my palm. "Is he ever going to ask her out?"

"If he doesn't, I'm going to beat him to death with wet noodles."

"Does he know that?"

"He will soon enough. It'll be a long, slow death. Arduous and labor intensive. Hopefully I won't get a repetitive motion injury." I couldn't help but let my hand rest on his hip. I hooked a finger in his belt loop and pulled.

He eased forward, a willing participant. "I saw your apartment, by the way."

"I thought that was compliments of your Dealer. Now, I'm not so sure."

"Why?"

"He said he didn't do it."

"Ah, right, I remember. And you believed him." It wasn't a question, but I answered anyway.

"Why would he lie? He has the dagger. He freely admitted to taking it."

"Dutch, they lie because that is what they do. That is who they are. They lie when the truth would sound better. So, can I sever his spine yet?"

"No, you can't. I think he could be an asset."

"You're partly right. He can be an ass."

I gave him an admonishing glare. "Are you here to cook?"

"Nah, Sammy's got it covered. I'm just here."

Oh, how nice. "You mean just the two of us? Like on a real date?"

"If our dates are going to include your uncle and your best friend, then yeah."

I laughed out loud, and asked, "Okay, why are you really here?"

"Just keeping an eye on you."

"Reyes, you can't babysit me forever."

"Would you like to bet on that?"

"I mean, you have a life. I have a life. We both have lives."

He glanced toward the man in the seat beside me. It was just a glance, nothing more. But the man stood immediately, excusing himself. Reyes sat down and pulled me closer to him, leaning in like we were lovers having a flirtatious conversation. But what he said next was anything but flirtatious. "Have I explained fully what the Twelve is?"

"Yes. They're mean, horrible beasts who want to eat me for breakfast."

"Wrong," he said. "I want to eat you for breakfast. They want to rip you apart and hand your soul over to my father on a silver platter."

"I don't get it. If your father imprisoned them, why would they want to do him any favors?"

"They're the Twelve. There is no understanding them."

He'd rested his hand on the bar. As I leaned toward him, he let his fingers brush across Danger's nipple. She sprang to life, pushing against the restraint of my blouse, craving more of his touch. I couldn't blame her.

"We have an audience."

When his words sank in, I finally realized that we did indeed have an audience. Half the room was staring at us. I started to lean back when Reyes said, "Not them."

He nodded toward Uncle Bob.

I turned to him. "Oh, sorry, we were just talking about how lovely this rain is."

"I bet." His disposition had changed. It was weird. He looked over at Cookie and her date, and instead of anger and jealousy, there was just anger. And some of it seemed directed at me.

"So, about Brinkman and his cars."

"Yeah, it seems that his dealership is a front to launder money. He runs way more through it than he sells, but he hides that by duplicating titles."

"And they are just finding this out? What does that mean?"

"What that means is that if they can get him for that, they may not need Emily Michaels to testify against him. Agent Carson is working toward that goal."

"You're working with her?"

"More like consulting. We have a plan. Maybe you could help?"

"I am so there."

He nodded, but his anger was still present, simmering just under his curmudgeonly surface. "Are you okay, Uncle Bob?"

He looked pointedly at Cookie. "I'm fine. I have to get to a meeting."

When he left, I turned back to Cookie and shrugged. She shrugged back at me, thanked her date, and nodded toward the back door, indicating she was headed home. I followed her out, my shoes still squishy.

"Your uncle seemed upset," she said when I caught up to her.

"He did, didn't he? Oddly upset, but in the wrong way."

We passed the alley where Reyes's muscle car had been only a little while earlier. I wondered where he was keeping her parked. Any man who would risk his paint job for the feel of a woman was a winner in my book. I decided to check on him before hitting the sack.

The next thing I remembered was Reyes smiling down at me as the sun filtered into his apartment, his hair mussed, his lids hooded with the thick remnants of sleep. I stretched as those three little words that every girl longs to hear slipped from his mouth with effortless ease. As though they did it every day. As though they didn't mean the world to me.

With one corner of his mouth tipping sensually, he asked, "Want some coffee?"

And I fell.

I fell hard.

15

The most important thing is to not be on fire.
Ask someone who is on fire, and they will tell you
that the most important thing is to not be on fire.

—TRUE FACT

The first thing on my agenda, besides finding out who trashed my place, was to confront Captain Kangaroo. Oh, and I had to get ahold of Garrett and set up a meet with the Dealer so they could do their homework together. They were taking Vague Prophecies and Muddy Supernatural Innuendos 101, but that class didn't really get interesting until the second semester in VPMSI 102.

Now that my mind was on the subject, I'd never managed to figure out where Garrett found the knife. He said his acquisition of the dagger wasn't one of his finer moments. That could've meant anything from a museum heist to an illegal excavation of a dig in Romania to a con to swindle it out of an elderly investor.

Or maybe he stole it from a temple. Of doom! That would be cool.

His vagueness only made me all the more curious. Like he didn't know that would happen. The butt. I wanted so very much to ask him about his family, too. Another area he'd been very vague about. According to the research Cook and I had done behind his back, his great-grandmother was a true voodoo princess, quite a renowned one. She was born in New Orleans and practiced her art openly to become one of the most famous voodoo priestesses in history.

Our research uncovered the fact that his grandmother's gift was passed down to an aunt of Garrett's and possibly his sister. A sister! It was hard to imagine Garrett with a sister. Still, I wondered if a little of that gift hadn't been passed on to him. He was such a skilled tracker. His methods often went beyond the average interviews and Internet searches. He seemed to have a sixth sense where his job was concerned. Something a voodoo prince might possess, as it were.

He didn't talk about his family much, but that didn't stop me from finding out about them. Honestly, he couldn't tell me something like some of his family was sensitive to otherworldly occurrences and expect me not to follow up on that. Seriously? Did he not know me at all?

When I arrived at the police station, I was told the captain was in a meeting and that I would have to wait in the lobby. Fine. I could wait him out. If I had to sit there all day, I was not leaving this station until I knew what the captain was up to.

I dived into my bag and fished out my phone so I could at least do something semi-productive while I waited. After I found my favorite icon, I waited for *Bejeweled* to load and proceeded to kick some sparkling ass.

A voice filtered toward me through my mesmerizing grid of jewels.

"Your aura is very bright."

I glanced up at the woman sitting across from me. She looked normal enough, with short blond hair and sensible shoes, but most people who mentioned auras weren't that normal.

"Thanks," I said, going back to my game.

"I've never seen anything like it," she continued, despite my super big hint that would suggest she not.

"Really? That's weird."

"Actually," she said, "I know who you are. We're a lot alike. I'm here to help them with a case, too."

I nodded.

"What I mean to say is, I know you're psychic."

I finally paused the game and asked, "Are you punking me?"

"No, that's what I'm trying to tell you. I'm psychic, too."

"Is Pari punking me?"

She pulled her bag closer to her chest. "No."

"Is Cookie punking me? It's not in her nature to punk, but I find everyone has a little bit of punk buried deep down inside them."

"No."

"Is Swopes punking me?"

"No, I actually am a psychic."

"Is—?"

"No!" she said, her voice echoing throughout the room A nice couple who looked like they'd done one too many hits of methamphetamines looked over at us. She lowered her voice to a hissy whisper. "Nobody's punking you!"

"Gah, testy."

She loosened her hold on her bag and smoothed her pants with one hand. "I just thought maybe we could work together sometime. We both provide a service for law enforcement. Like the case they called me in for. We could team up and solve it together."

I decided to fess up, to give her a chance to come clean or suffer the consequences. "Look, I know who you are, too, Ms. Jakes. I've seen your show." Wynona Jakes was getting very rich off her *abilities,* and it made my skin crawl every time I thought about it.

"You've seen my show?" she asked, brightening.

"Sure have. You're what I like to call a con artist, a person with a natural talent for reading people coupled with some fairly good acting skills."

"Well," she said, straightening in her seat to show me how appalled she was, "I thought you of all people would understand what it's like to be accused of deception when our gifts are very real."

"I know exactly. And I'm certain you don't. I've seen what happens when your 'predictions'—" I added air quotes to emphasize the euphemism. "—don't pan out. I saw a young couple lose their home because they believed you when you told them to invest everything they had in their crazy uncle's pilot project."

"That was hardly—"

"And I saw a mother praise you because you said her son, who'd been in a motorcycle accident and was in a coma at the hospital, was going to pull through." I leaned forward and looked her square in the eye. "He died while she was at the studio listening to your garbage. Do you know what that did to her? The guilt she felt? The shame and devastation?"

She turned away from me, the remnants of her outrage rolling out of her like a summer heat.

"Look," I said, trying not to feel guilty for calling her on what boiled down to fraud, "I get it. You're looking for a book deal. To each his own. I'd be angrier if you were legit and using your gifts immorally, but in answer to your question, no, I won't team— Wait. Did you say they called you in to help on a case?"

"Yes." She raised her chin and smirked. "A Detective Davidson called me. He said he saw my show and wanted to consult with me on a missing persons case."

"Detective Dav—?"

"Ms. Jakes?" the desk sergeant said before I could sputter out the rest of Uncle Bob's title.

She rose. "Yes."

"Detective Davidson will see you now."

My jaw dropped to the floor. The desk clerk pointed the way to Ubie's office just as my backstabbing uncle stepped out to wait for her. He shook her hand when she got to him, then placed his other hand at the small of her back and led her inside.

I was jealous for me and for Cookie. Mostly for Cookie. He was always too nervous or too reserved to do something like that to her. And he'd called this woman in on a case? A charlatan?

Not on my watch. I stood to go prove to Uncle Bob she was nothing more than a fraud when the captain stepped out of the conference room and saw me. He motioned me to his office. After a longing glance toward Ubie, I swallowed hard and followed the captain into his man cave. And what a manly man cave it was. Awards and certifications littered his walls and counterspace, along with files and stacks of paperwork.

"Are you feeling better?" he asked.

"Not so much."

"That's too bad." He sat behind his desk. "Because you are about to feel a lot worse."

He gestured for me to sit in the vinyl chair across from him. I didn't. "I want to know why you are having me followed, who those people were, and what you plan to do with those pictures."

A grimness thinned his lips, like he was about to deliver some very bad news. He stood, retrieved an envelope from his top file drawer, pulled out a stack of photos, and tossed one onto his desk for my inspection.

It was a candid shot of me making what looked like a drug deal outside my apartment building. The photographer made sure to capture the vagrant looking over his shoulder as though watching for a cop as he handed me over something unidentifiable. At the same time, I handed him a few bills, which was very identifiable.

"That's Chris Levine, a known associate of a man they call Chewbacca, one of the biggest meth dealers in the city." He tossed another picture down. In it, I was in Misery passing a homeless man a couple of dollars through the window. He was the one who'd handed me the old plastic flower, but that wasn't in the shot. Naturally. "And that's Oscar Fuentes. His arrest record is as long as my left leg and reads like a pulp fiction novel. He owed me a favor." He tossed another one. In this one, I was just getting out of Misery and, once again, handing a man a few bills. I try to be nice, and look what happens. "That's—"

"I get it," I said, holding up my hand to stop the tour. "I've never bought drugs in my life, and you know it."

"Sure you have." A smile that reminded me of sloe gin spread across his face. "And I have the evidence to prove it. Who do you think they'll believe?"

"All they have to do is test me. I'll test Pine-Sol clean, bitch." I was being backed into a corner and did not like it there.

The edges of his mouth twitched. "Oh, I'm very aware of your drug-free existence. I just need insurance."

"For what?"

"Your silence."

"You couldn't just ask? You have to blackmail me?"

"For this I do."

"That's so very wrong."

"True, but just remember what I have on you when I explain my . . . situation. If I go to prison, you go to prison. I'm just making sure we both have a very good reason to keep quiet."

"You have my complete attention, Captain," I said, a cautious anger simmering beneath the surface. "What do you want?"

"I'm not a good person," he said, seeming to regret that fact.

"Ya think?"

"When I was a kid, my oldest sister was raped by a boy from her school. She was intellectually challenged and he took advantage of that. He was a popular kid, very well liked, from an affluent family. All the things that would allow him to get away scot-free."

"So he got away with it."

"For a while. But I'll get to that. After she accused him of sexually assaulting her, it became a big thing in my hometown. I was from a small suburb near Chicago. Nobody believed her, because why would a kid like that need to rape a handicapped girl? When he could have anyone? The town turned against us. The school turned against her, and what was a little teasing here and there became full-on everyday bullying."

I could feel the heartache that caused him. I didn't want to. I didn't want to have an ounce of empathy for a man who would set me up so frivolously, so I fought it. I buried it under a mountain of resentment.

"A few weeks later, she couldn't take the bullying anymore and killed herself."

That time, a wave of guilt hit me. It had a smooth, pure texture. Zero conflict. Zero doubt. He felt responsible for his sister's death. In a word, he hated himself, and I realized that had been the odd emotion I felt every time I met him. I just figured he hated me. I got that a lot. But his feelings were directed solely toward himself. That was new. In general, people can't handle guilt. Their minds won't let them for very long. So they make up excuses. Excuses work like a salve, allaying the guilt, letting you forget the real problem. For example, every time an abusive husband says something like, "You made me hit you," he's twisting the guilt—she didn't have dinner on the table, so hitting her was surely his wife's fault.

"It tore my family apart," he continued, standing to stare out his window. "My parents split up. My mother sank into a depression. I rarely saw my dad. Within six months, my world had been turned inside out."

"I'm so sorry, Captain."

He turned back to me. "It gets better. And this is the part you need to keep very, very quiet."

"Or you'll burn me."

"I'll bury you. You will spend years behind bars."

Just when I was beginning to sympathize with him. "How about you stop with the threats and get on with this?"

He walked over and leaned against the desk in front of me, towering over me, making sure I knew he was top dog. After studying my face—my perturbed face—a solid minute, he said, "I was seven when I hunted that kid down and killed him."

I stilled. He was confessing a murder to me. That was there in the back of my mind, but even more salient was the fact that he was only seven when he did it.

"Did you know that they rarely suspect a seven-year-old of murder? I wasn't even questioned."

The shock I felt surely showed on my face. As I'd demonstrated many times in my life, my poker face was virtually nonexistent. But my fight-or-flight response was top notch. He'd just confessed to murder. I wasn't going to make it out of that room alive. I couldn't help a glance toward the door.

"No one's stopping you," he said, nodding toward my escape route. He didn't seem particularly concerned. Of course he wouldn't be. He had evidence of me buying drugs all over town. My accusations would be in retaliation after his attempt to arrest me. He'd really thought this through.

Then again, would he risk someone knowing his deep dark secret? That paltry evidence wasn't enough. Any good lawyer could get the charges dropped. He had to know that.

"Is this the part where you kill me?" I asked him.

Of course this was the part where he killed me. He would never let me leave here with that information. Would he say that I went for his gun? That we fought and the gun went off? That's what I'd do.

"No. As I told you, I have enough evidence on you to put you away for a very long time."

"That evidence is all circumstantial. You'd need testimonies. Eyewitnesses," I argued. Why was I arguing this? Making the case for him to just kill me and get it over with. Perhaps it was because when I did leave here—*if* I did leave here—I didn't want to have to worry about him changing his mind. Would I get a bullet to the back of my head when I least expected it? I didn't want this hanging over my head for the rest of my life. "You'd need credible witnesses," I added before pointing to the photographs. "Not that crap you sent me in the streets."

One step ahead of me, he said, "Bought and paid for."

Damn, he thought of everything. At least he was thorough.

"I also have footage of you constantly talking to yourself. Arguing with air. Shaking some invisible friend's hand. Hugging someone only you could see. Everything together adds up to a lengthy sentence in prison or the nuthouse. I'm good with either."

Holy crap. I knew that stuff would come back to haunt me. Damn it.

He leaned closer. "As long as I stay out of jail, you stay out of jail."

I was beaten. He won. I crossed my arms over Danger and Will. "Why go to all this trouble? Why confess something so incriminating to me now? After all these years? You don't exactly like me. Or trust me."

"I do trust you to a degree. I see the lengths you go for your clients. It's noble. Stupid at times, but noble. But you're right. I'm fairly certain I don't like you. And I need to know."

"If you like me?"

"If he did it. The kid. When I was— When I killed him, he swore he didn't do it. Over and over. He swore he never touched my sister. But I'd seen the bruises on her. The blood. I also saw the mark she left on her assailant. She said she bit his wrist. He had a bite mark on his wrist days later. But I need to know the truth. I have to be certain."

If he killed the guy, how was I supposed to find out the truth? Just how much did he know about me?

"I need to hear it from the dead kid, and you are just the person to ask him."

I shifted in my chair, suddenly uncomfortable. Or, well, *more* uncomfortable. "And how am I supposed to do that?"

"I don't know. Call him. Channel him. Do whatever it is you do."

"That's crazy talk," I said, inching up out of my chair.

He didn't move to stop me, but put a hand on the sidearm at his hip. "I'm an excellent shot."

I plopped back down. "You're psychotic, is what you are. I am so telling Uncle Bob. You want me to talk to a dead kid? Now who's going to the nuthouse?"

"Spare me. I know everything."

He couldn't possibly know everything. Wait— "Did you bug me?" I asked, appalled. He'd done every other kind of surveillance. Surely he threw in a few bugs for good measure.

"A little."

"That's so illegal!" I bolted to my feet.

"So is framing you for crimes you didn't commit. I think we're beyond that right now."

He had a point. And despite everything he just told me, I felt nothing malicious coming off him. I did feel an odd mix of emotions, but I doubted he harbored any ill will toward me. This was a means to an end.

"How do you know I won't lie to you?"

"I don't. So I'll need proof. You talk to this kid, ask him how I killed him, then ask him if he did it." He tossed another picture at me, only this one was an old school picture of a blond kid, about fourteen years old. "Do whatever it is you do to talk to dead people. Ask him."

I gave in. "Captain, I can't just talk to dead people."

He glowered. "Don't bullshit me. I will have you in lockup with enough charges to make your lawyer's head spin before you can say frame job. And I might toss in some charges on kiddie porn to spice things up. I will destroy your reputation in any way that I can."

He was serious. He was actually serious, but again, reluctantly so. He would do what he had to do, my life be damned.

I blinked in absolute shock. "That's so not fair."

"Life's a bitch that way. His name was Kory. Do your thing or get used to the idea of spending the rest of the decade behind bars."

It could happen. Reyes was living, breathing proof that people went to prison for crimes they didn't commit. But the odds of this kid still being on earth, on this plane, were zero to nil. It just didn't happen that way. Once the departed crossed, I couldn't talk to them. They were gone. On the other side.

"You're going to have to indulge me a moment."

He shrugged a shoulder.

I summoned Angel.

"What the hell?" he said, complaining as ever. "I was in the middle of something."

"I need you to go to the other side and talk to somebody for me."

"I can't just go to the other side and talk to somebody, *loca*."

"Angel, I really need this. If you can't pull this off, I'm going to prison on drug possession and kiddie porn." I showed him the picture. "I need you to find this kid and ask him a couple of things for me."

The captain watched me with those eagle eyes of his. Not a lot got past him, I could tell. And I certainly no longer cared about what it looked like when I talked to my invisible friends.

"I can't jump over and back. Nobody can do that." He dusted off his shirt. No idea why. "Except you."

"I can't jump over either. Do you think Reyes can?"

"I don't think the son of Satan would be very welcome in heaven. Even if he could get there."

I collapsed onto the chair. This was an impossible situation.

"Why don't you just summon him?"

"Angel, if he's already crossed, I can't summon him."

"You never listen to me," he said. He took off his shoe and dumped sand out of it and onto the carpet.

I looked at it, watched it fall through the floor.

"How did you get sand—?"

"It doesn't matter if they've crossed. You're the stinking reaper."

I had no idea if the captain knew that part, so I clenched my teeth to demonstrate my annoyance to Angel, and whispered through my teeth so the man couldn't hear me. "I know I'm the stinking reaper, but I can't just summon someone back from the other side."

He put his shoe back on and took off the other, dumped out the sand, then put it back on before leveling a stare on me dripping with attitude, and said, "Yes, you can. I've been telling you that forever. *Oh, mi Dios.*"

"Don't bring God into this, and really?" I stood and sidled up to him. "I really can do that?"

"Of course." He shrugged, and if I didn't know better, I'd say his glare was accusing me of being a moron. "That's what I've been trying to tell you."

"So, like, how?"

He pulled out his pockets and shook them to get the sand out of them as well. How on earth? Incorporeal sand? Clearly there was a lot I had yet to learn.

"How what?" he asked.

"How do I summon someone from the other side?"

"*Qué demonios,* how should I know?"

When he shook out his hair from behind the wide bandanna tied around his forehead and sand fell all over the captain's desk, I took hold of his shoulders. "Angel, focus, my freedom and my access to coffee 24/7 could be compromised. How do I do that?"

"You just do," he said with a shrug.

I looked at the captain and shook my head in helplessness. "He's not helping."

"Bullshit. I told you. You just do it."

"Just like I have powers and I can mark souls and I can save the world?" I threw my arms wide. "I think I'm defective. I think something went horribly awry and they sent the wrong girl."

He chuckled. "Still, I don't know why you're asking me all this."

I pointed to the pic of Kory. "Because I need to talk to that kid. I told you."

"So why do you want to know how to summon someone back from the other side?"

I grabbed his shoulders again and shook them. He was pretty solid, though, and I actually shook more than he did. "Because I need to talk to that kid."

"Yeah, but he's not on the other side. Not yet."

I stopped, blinked three times, then gaped at him for at least sixty-seven seconds, long enough for Angel to clear his throat and shift his weight, squirming in discomfort.

"You couldn't have told me that ten minutes ago?"

"You didn't ask me that ten minutes ago. You asked me how to summon someone from the other side."

He had a point. I prayed for patience, then asked, "How do I summon this kid since he hasn't crossed?"

"*Que Dios me ayude.* Charley, what did I just say? See, you never listen. You're like those kids who poke forks in electrical outlets."

"I have never poked a fork in an electrical outlet."

"Is this conversation going anywhere?" the captain asked.

I whirled around and glared. "Really?"

He held up his hands in surrender.

"Just do your thing," Angel said. "You know, like you do with me."

"But I know you."

"You know everyone. You're the grim reaper."

Wow, okay, fine. I'd give it a shot. What could it hurt, besides my crumbling pride?

I took the picture, closed my eyes, and said, "Kory, I summon you."

When I opened my eyes, Angel was doubled over with laughter. "Really?" he asked, holding his stomach. "That's all you've got?"

"What?" I stomped my foot. "What am I doing wrong?"

"Do it like you do me. I know you don't say, 'Angel, I summon you.'"

"No, I say, 'Angel, get your a punk ass over here.'"

"You do not." When I raised my brows, he said, "No, really, you don't say that, right?"

Without answering, I closed my eyes again and thought about how I summoned Angel and Artemis and even, on occasion, Reyes. I just imagined them there, summoned their energy, and brought them forth. So I thought of this kid, sought his energy, found it in the distance, a luminous glow in the darkness, and brought him forth.

I opened my eyes and before me was a scared kid, hands in pockets, a bullet hole in his chest as well as one in his pant leg. His shoulders were concave, his chin tucked in fear. And despite every attempt to the contrary, my heart went out to him.

"You were a good shot even then," I said to the captain.

He stood and glanced around before saying warily, "What do you mean?"

"You shot him in the knee. That takes a steady hand even at close range."

Surprise and awe washed over him. "I was aiming for his head."

"Oh, then you kind of suck."

"Is he—is he here?"

"Yes."

"Did he do it?" he asked. "For certain he did it?"

"I haven't gotten to that part yet."

"Are you God?" Kory asked, his voice soft.

"Um, no, but I appreciate the compliment. I'm Charley."

He nodded and studied me from head to toe.

"I need to know something, Kory. Did you assault that girl?"

"Cindy," the captain said.

"Did you rape a girl named Cindy?"

"No," he said, shaking his head.

"Why are you even asking him?" Angel said. "You just have to see it. He can lie to you, but your vision won't."

See it? "I see people's lives when they cross. Is that what you mean? He should cross?"

"They don't have to cross for you to see them, to see what they've done. Just do your thing."

"What thing?"

"Your reaper thing. Just do it."

I was growing very tired of being told to just do it. Angel, the captain, the Dealer, Nike. Who next? The Pillsbury Doughboy? Actually, I really liked the Pillsbury Doughboy.

"You need to be honest with me, Kory. Did you sexually assault Cindy Eckert?"

He bowed his head. "No. Maybe. I don't know."

"What does that mean?"

"We saw her at the park after school. She was alone on a swing and everyone told me to go talk to her, to pretend to be into her."

"You're not winning any brownie points here, Kory."

"Just wait. I didn't— I was just kidding with her." He shoved his hands farther into his front pockets. "She told me she'd always had a crush on me, and I told her the same thing back."

As Kory spoke, I relayed what he was saying to the captain.

"She told me she had a special room in the woods just beyond the park. She wanted to show it to me. Everyone was teasing me, telling me to go with her."

The captain's anger rose. "That was not in the report," he said. "No one ever said that. According to the police, no one ever saw him with her."

"Then they lied," I said to him. "For Kory."

Kory kept going. "When we got there, she wanted . . . she wanted to show me . . ."

"I don't really want the details," I told him. "I just want to know what you did to her."

"She started it," he said, shame making him flinch every time he started to talk. "She rubbed me and told me to—" He stopped, unable to explain. "Then, right in the middle, she changed her mind. She told me to stop. I— I finished anyway. She didn't really fight or anything. She just bit me. But, yes, I did it with her. She said no and I did it anyway."

"That's very wrong. You know that, right?"

"I didn't mean for it to go that far. By the time she changed her mind, I was already in her. I just needed a minute. Then she killed herself. I wanted to die. I'd lied to everyone. They all thought I was so cool. Too cool to sink low enough to have sex with Cindy Eckert."

"Because she was mentally challenged?"

After he nodded, he repeated, "She killed herself because of me."

"And because of how she was treated afterwards."

"Exactly, because I didn't have the balls to confess to what I'd done." He looked up at me then. "No one would have messed with her if I'd just told them not to. They did it thinking they were doing me a favor. Am I going to hell?"

I shook my head. "I don't think that's how it works."

"That's enough," the captain said. "That's all I needed to hear. I had to know if I got the right guy."

"And if you hadn't?"

"I would have gone after the right guy. But since I got him, I can get on with this. Thank you, though," he said, tossing the entire envelope of pictures to me. "I won't be needing those anymore."

"Wait, how do you know I'll hold up my end of the bargain?"

"It won't matter. There are some things you can't outrun. Your past is one of them. Can you ask your uncle to come in here, please?" He sat behind his desk and started straightening papers.

"Why?" I asked, suddenly suspicious.

He tapped a pile of folders until they stood in perfect alignment, just like everything else on his desk. Pristine. Orderly. Everything in its place. "I'm going to turn myself in."

"What? Why would you do that? That was, what? Thirty years ago?"

"Thirty-five. My mother died last week. She was the only one I was protecting by keeping this secret. Now I can own up to what I've done and put it behind me."

"He doesn't need to do that," Kory said. He crossed his arms tightly over his chest, the JV letter jacket he wore crinkling. "It won't make any difference." Then he brightened. "Maybe if I fix this, I can go to heaven."

"What do you mean?"

"I think I'm supposed to make amends, but there's just no way to do that. But maybe if I stop Cindy's brother from making a big mistake, I can get in."

I wanted to tell him he could probably get in anyway, but I decided not to.

"He's a good guy, right?" Kory asked.

"Yeah, he's a pretty good guy. Or he was until he set me up like a bowling pin on league night at the alley." I scowled at him, but only a little, since he was taking the charges off the table. And he'd killed someone. Did I now have a moral obligation to see him brought to justice?

I was torn. On what to feel. On what to do.

Then another thought hit me. "Maybe you are paying for what you've done," I said to him as he straightened yet another stack. "I mean, you help people every day, right? Maybe that is your way of paying society back."

"But what about Kory's family?" He stood, put his jacket on, then walked to the door to face the firing squad. "My mind's made up, Ms. Davidson. If you won't get your uncle, I will. It's time this ends."

"Do your thing," Angel said.

"What thing?" I asked him for the bazillionth time.

"Your reaper thing. Only you know the hearts of men on earth."

"Trust me, hon, if there is one thing I do not know, it is the hearts of men. I know they like sex. That's about it."

"No, I mean, humans in general. You can see their intentions, and you mark them."

The captain opened the door, and I couldn't help but think he was making a huge mistake. I felt it deep inside. This was wrong.

"What do I do?" I asked Angel. The captain was getting away. So to speak.

"Ask him about the dog!" Kory called out to me.

Without another thought, I called out, "What about the dog?"

He stopped, hesitated, executed a slow, military-style about-face, and waited.

I tossed a sideways glance toward Kory. "What about the dog?"

Kory shrugged. "It's just, I don't get why he's so hell-bent on turning himself in for a crime he didn't commit."

My eyes widened. Before this got too out of hand, I stepped to the captain, grabbed his jacket sleeve, took a quick peek toward Uncle Bob, who was still talking to the psychic wannabe, and dragged the captain back inside his office.

"Just hold on," I said, closing the door. "Kory, what are you talking about."

He shrugged. "This is wrong. He didn't do anything wrong. I was the stupid one."

"In what way?"

Exhaling superfluously, he sat against the windowsill and said, "It wasn't even his gun. It was mine. Or, well, my dad's. I took it from his drawer. Trying to be all cool and shit once again. When Van found me—"

"Van?" I asked the captain. Even though he seemed to believe everything that was happening, my knowing that surprised him.

"When he found me, he was madder than a diamondback during roundup. He hit me and I pulled the gun on him. He just wanted me to confess. This kid who meant nothing to me. He wanted me to confess to what I'd done. When I refused, he got so mad, he was crying and shaking. He was a tiny shit." He looked the captain up and down. "I can't believe he turned out that big. We started fighting and my dog jumped on us. The gun just went off. Hit me square in the chest. He wanted to help me get to a hospital, but I screamed at him to leave. If my dad found out I'd taken the gun, he would've killed me."

"If you were shot in the chest, how did you get that wound?" I asked, pointing to his knee.

"When I was trying to find a place in our barn to hide the gun, I was in so much pain that I got really light-headed, and I shot myself in the leg on accident. Van didn't have anything to do with that."

I turned to *Van*. Who named their kid Van? "I know exactly what happened," I told him, my expression stern.

"Yeah, but his family doesn't. I killed him. I pointed the gun—"

"That's not the way Kory remembers it. He said you two wrestled for the gun and it went off. It was an accident."

He looked down in thought.

"You were only seven, Captain. And it all happened very fast, I'm sure. You didn't do this."

"Look," he said, clearly having made up his mind, "I've made up my mind."

Nailed it.

"Nothing you say is going to change that," he continued. "His family deserves to know what happened."

"Screw that," Kory said. "If he goes forward, everyone really will think I did it."

"You did do it, Kory. You did sexually assault an innocent girl."

He bowed his head and whispered, "Yeah, but they don't know that. They always believed me."

"So, it's okay for her name to be run through the mud, but not yours?"

"What will it change? He could go to jail for something that was my stupid fault."

I had to agree with him. Even if he didn't go to jail, his career would be over. He was good at his job. "Give me some dirt," I said to Kory. "I need something to blackmail him."

The captain crossed his arms over his chest in bored contemplation. "Dirt? I didn't know him. He was just a scrawny kid."

"Darn." I looked at the captain in desperation. "I'll help you," I said, scanning my memory for any bit of information I could use on him. Something popped up immediately. "I'll help you with the Loretta Rosenbaum case."

He gave me a dubious look. "That case has been cold for a decade."

"And I'll warm it up. I have connections," I said, wriggling my brows. "I can get to people you can't."

"Ms. Davidson—"

"Okay," I said, raising my hands when he tried to get past me, "let's tell all this to Uncle Bob, just like you said, and get his opinion. Just hear him out, yes?"

He nodded. "I'm going to tell him either way. I would prefer that he arrest me instead of Marsh. Marsh is a dick."

I almost chuckled at his reference to a detective nobody in the office liked. Poor guy. "I agree."

I stepped out and waved Ubie over to us. The fake psychic was gone, and though I was dying to ask him about her, I had bigger fish to can.

16

Uncle Bob had been distant when he walked in and was even more so now. It was very, very unlike him. We explained the entire situation, even the part where Captain Eckert manufactured evidence and the fact that he knew my deepest, darkest secret. Well, okay, not *that* deepest, darkest secret, but the one right next to my deepest, darkest secret. My ability to communicate with the departed. If only they knew why.

Uncle Bob listened with a quiet resolve, his poker face excellently placed and maintained throughout, and then he said the unthinkable: "Charley, can you leave us alone for a minute?"

I gaped at him. It was like he was speaking a foreign language—except I knew them all, so that wasn't the best analogy. "I'm sorry?"

"The captain and me. Can you leave us alone for a minute?"

"I don't understand." Ubie had never asked me to leave the room. He usually argued incessantly to let me stay in every situation.

"We need to talk in private."

"No," I said, completely offended. "I'm in this thanks to Van over there, and I'll stay right here, thank you very much."

Ubie raised a hand and gestured for a uniformed officer to come in. I didn't recognize him, but he was big and blond and big.

"Could you escort Ms. Davidson out of the building, please?"

I balked. "It's—it's that fake psychic chick, isn't it? You think she's going to solve cases for you? She's as fake as your hairline."

Ubie scowled at me. I scowled back, all the way to the front door of the station, where I proceeded to wrench free from the officer and brush myself off. "That was so uncalled for," I said to him. He stood there and watched me go.

My phone rang when I got to Misery.

"Are you okay?" Cookie asked.

"Yes. I'm fine."

"You don't sound fine."

"I'm fine."

"You don't sound fine."

"I'm so not fine!" I said, collapsing into a blob of sniffling nerves. "Something is up with Uncle Bob. I think he's . . . he's mad at me."

Cookie gasped. "Robert is never mad at you."

"I know. I just don't know what to think."

"Me neither. On the bright side, you can talk it over with your therapist. Your appointment is in half an hour."

"I can't go to therapy. That woman needs more therapy than I do."

"Most therapists do, hon. You still have to go. If you miss again, your sister will kill you."

"Cook, I have a thousand cases going on at once. My life has been threatened. My apartment has been ransacked. A half-human, half-demon stole a priceless dagger from me and won't return it until he gets together with Swopes so they can talk prophecies. And I was just almost arrested for drug possession and kiddie porn."

"Your sister won't care."

"My sister is at a conference in D.C."

"And you think that would stop her?"

I changed lanes to head back the direction I'd come. "Fine. I'll go."

"Good girl. We need coffee and creamer at the office."

"Okay."

"And I need an orange bra and a tennis racket. It's a new home-defense thing."

"Okay."

"And I thought about having sex with Garrett on my desk."

"Okay. But really, why do you think Ubie is mad at me?"

"I don't know, hon. He adores you. He'll get over it."

"He even called in a fake psychic. When he has me! You're going to do what, where, and with whom?"

"Just never you mind. Go to your appointment."

"Okay."

I sat through another pointless session of talking about my feelings when all I could think about was Uncle Bob. Hopefully, he'd talked the captain into putting his plans on hold, but I wondered if I was doing the right thing. There was still a dead kid. True, he died thirty years ago and his death was accidental, but wouldn't his family want to know what happened to him?

I had Cookie track Garrett's whereabouts and parked at my apartment building to walk the block and a half to the Frontier. He was sitting at a booth in the middle room of the meandering restaurant, reading the paper, a green chile burger with fries and iced tea on his table.

I sat across from him and decided to get right to the point. "What if you knew someone killed someone else decades ago, but it was more like an accident and now the person who accidently killed the other person wants to turn himself in and ruin a pristine career in law enforcement."

He didn't look up from his paper. "I'm assuming there's a question in there."

"Yeah. What would you do? What would you recommend he do?"

"It was an accident?"

"Yes," I said, stealing a fry off his plate.

"And this was how long ago?"

"Thirty years, give or take. They were just kids. But the man has done a lot to help people. He's a good person. If he goes forward, he'll ruin his career and negate all the good he's done over the years."

"That's a tough one. If it's eating him alive, that tells me he probably is a good person. He can do more good in law enforcement than in jail, if he went to jail."

"See. That's what I was thinking, but my moral compass doesn't always point north. You said earlier, right after I almost plummeted off that fire escape to my death, you had a condition? You scratch my back, I scratch yours."

"And why am I scratching your back again?" he asked.

"I need you to meet with someone for me. He's very knowledgeable and wants to work with us on all this prophecy stuff. Just do not let him talk you out of your soul. He's really good at that."

"I doubt he would want my soul."

"Okay, so you have a condition as well?"

He put down the paper and took another bite of his burger. "I do, but it will be tricky."

I shimmied down in my seat. "I like tricky. Tricky is my middle name. No, wait, that's trouble. Trouble's my middle name. My bad."

"Do you remember the woman I told you about?"

I knew we would get back around to this. I'd been dying to know more. "The one who used your body then threw you away like a toothbrush you had to use to clean the toilet because you couldn't find your scrub brush?"

"Well, yeah."

"And then you saw her out a year later and she'd had a baby who just happened to have your eyes?"

"That's the one."

"No. I don't remember you mentioning her. You should go order a sweet roll. Those are to die for. And a *carne adovada* burrito."

His mouth thinned. "Should I order something else to drink?"

"Yes! A diet whatever. No! A mocha latte. No!" I held up my hand to put him in pause so I could think. "Yes. No. Yes, a mocha latte."

"Are you finished?" he asked, rising to go place his order. He was really hungry.

"Yes. No! Yes. I'm good with that. I have a busy afternoon ahead of me, and I need all the energy I can get. And I need you to be my wingman."

"This should be interesting," he said, sauntering off like he owned the place.

By the time he got back, his fries had disappeared. It was weird.

"So, what about her?" I asked.

"Marika," he said, scooting into the booth. "That's the sticky condition."

I leaned in and did my best Italian accent. "You want I should off her?" I slid my index finger across my throat in the universal gesture for murder.

"Not exactly."

"Wait!" I said, holding up my hand before he continued. "What's your number? I'll keep watch for you so your food doesn't get cold."

He checked the receipt. "Fifty-four."

"Got it. Okay, hit me with the sticky."

"I need you to get samples of both Marika's and the boy's DNA."

I took a long moment to stare in disbelief. He stared back, but his stare was more matter-of-fact.

"Are you insane?" I asked him at last, considering it a real possibility. "How the bloody hell am I supposed to get DNA samples from them?"

He lifted a shoulder. "Not my problem."

Making a mental note to ask my therapist how I got myself into these situations and accuse her of sucking at her job because I was clearly not getting better, I said, "Have you put any thought into how it could be done?"

"Not really. Why do you need a wingman?"

"I have to go talk to a notorious crime lord and accuse him of sending men after me and trying to put a hit out on his ex-girlfriend, who is the only witness to a murder he committed."

"Do I have time to finish my burger?"

"I guess. But why are they called crime lords? Why not crime douche bags? Or crime asswipes? Why do they have to sound so cool?" I glanced up at the marquee. "Oh, your number's up."

He scooted out of the booth again. It was kind of charming.

"And hurry up before your food gets cold."

He turned the corner and flipped me off at the same time. See? Men could multitask. I was so proud of him. Since I sat there with nothing better to do than watch the man in the next booth argue with his ketchup, I summoned Angel. I told him about my latest dilemma, gave him some rather explicit orders, then listened to him curse in Spanish before he asked if he could see me naked. When I said, "Only if you can navigate time and watch my perilous journey through my mother's birth canal," he vanished to do my bidding.

"Why me?" Garrett asked when he sat back down with his food.

I took a bite of his burrito. "Wow," I said, rolling my eyes in ecstasy, "excellent choice. And why you what?"

"Why not get your boyfriend to be your wingman?"

"He's cooking this afternoon. Sammy had to go get his cast off." The regular cook had broken his leg trying to ski off his roof. Tequila often gave people the desire to tackle the impossible. It did not, however, make the impossible possible.

"Who's the crime lord?"

"Phillip Brinkman."

"The car salesman? He's a crime lord?"

"Apparently." I stopped and gaped at him. "Did you just take a bite of your sweet roll?"

"I paid for it."

"And?" I took the plate and slid it out of his reach. Not really, though, because he had a ridiculous reach, which he demonstrated when he stole another bite with effortless ease. Thankfully, their sweet rolls were big enough to feed a small country.

"If Mr. Car Salesman of the Year was going to send men to my apartment carrying suppressed Glocks, the least he can do is offer me a discount on a new Porsche."

"Should we, I don't know, devise a plan?"

"Do you think that's wise? I've always just kind of winged it."

"No," he said, his faux surprise chafing.

I strolled into the dealership wearing the wire Garrett had pinned to my bra between Danger and Will. Thankfully, Reyes never had to know that little fact. After pretending to browse a few minutes, and turning down a very enthusiastic salesperson, I made my way back to Phillip Brinkman's office. The man was facing murder charges, and yet there he was at work, nary a care in the world. He was a cool one. And he looked about as much like a crime lord as my great-aunt Lillian. He looked more like an accountant with dark hair, pale skin, and eyes too large for his face.

I took a seat across from his desk. He looked up from his paperwork, a little startled. No, that was fear in his eyes. A lot startled. He'd either had too much coffee or he was expecting someone else.

He scanned the area past his office then asked, "May I help you with something?"

"You may. If you're going to send men in black masks to my apartment and have them point a gun at my head so I'll find your girlfriend, I suggest you pick better men."

I'd confused him. The fear was still there, but I'd definitely confused him. Damn it. He had no idea what I was talking about.

"I don't know what you're talking about," he said.

Back to square one. Then again, this guy was up for murder. And the men in masks wanted the whereabouts of the woman set to testify against him. That was a little more than a thin connection.

I frowned at him. Maybe if the cops had a body, it would help their case.

I leaned forward, and a wave of fear washed through him. His poker face was worse than mine. His too-large eyes rounded exponentially. "Where's the body, Brinkman?"

"Are you a cop?"

"Depends. Would you be more likely to tell me where the body was if I were?"

"No."

"Nope. I am not a cop. Not even a little. Now, where's the body?"

"They're looking for Emily?"

"Depends. Who's Emily?"

"My girlfriend."

"Oh! Right, then yes they are." Fear and something painfully close to a full-on panic attack rolled out of him in waves. "Are you gonna talk or am I going to have to—?"

"Why would they go to you?" he said, interrupting. Dang it, and I had a really good threat planned. It involved fire ants, sandpaper, and a cement mixer.

I crossed my legs. "I don't know. Maybe because I have a sign on my head that says 'aim here.' Or it could be because I have access to information through different sources. They must think I can get her address. But it's WITSEC we're talking about here. It doesn't matter who I know, I am not getting that kind of info. You need to tell them that."

He rubbed his mouth and kept his hand there a long moment. Sweat ran down his temples, and his stomach churned in protest to the stress.

"Look, Phillip," I said, changing my tactics, "you made a mistake. It happens. Trying to kill your girlfriend will not rectify anything."

He nodded. "You got one thing right," he said absently, "I made a mistake. Lots of them, but Emily was not one of them. Is she—is she okay?"

He was genuinely concerned about her. Clearly, he had no involvement in the attempt to locate or, most likely, kill her.

"As far as I know, she's fine, but she won't be for much longer. If you'll just tell me what happened, where to find the body, I can help you, Phillip."

He grew wary. "I thought you weren't a cop. How can you help me? Did he send you? Is this a setup?"

The word *setup* seemed to be appearing a lot lately. I shook my head. "No setup. I'm just trying to help put you away so your girlfriend can get on with her life and not have to worry about those goons trying to kill her."

He opened his desk drawer, pulled out a bottle of Jack Daniel's, and took a hardy swig. Hardy as in half the bottle. Because he might be more inclined to help me if he were drunk, I didn't stop him.

"But you seem genuinely concerned about her. If you didn't send those men, who did?"

After another swig, he wiped a shaking hand over his mouth. "You need to leave," he said, his voice cracking.

"Oh, I get it. Watch your own back but no one else's. Am I in any real danger?"

He scoffed. "Let's just say you do not want to be on their naughty list."

"What happens if I get on it?"

"Not death, if that's what you're worried about. But you'll pray for it before they're through with you. This has just gotten so out of hand. So much bigger than we'd planned."

"We?" I asked, letting him take another drink before answering.

"I just wanted out."

Now we were getting somewhere. "You're being investigated for fraud. Is that what this is all about?"

"I'm being investigated?"

"Well, yeah, for that and murder, of course."

He leaned back in his chair and scrubbed his face with his fingers. If anyone was in over his head, it was Phillip Brinkman. I couldn't imagine what he'd gotten himself into. Maybe the death was self-defense or even accidental. Maybe his girlfriend was lying.

"Phillip, I can help you if you'll let me."

"Mr. Brinkman?" a pretty brunette said from the doorway. "Is everything okay?"

The fear I'd felt earlier came back full force. "Yes, Lois," he said, his exterior a picture of serenity, "everything is fine."

"Can I get you anything?"

"No. No, I'll just be a minute." After she left, he glared at me. "You need to leave. Now."

"'Fraid I can't do that. Those men are planning on killing a friend of mine if I can't come up with your girlfriend's whereabouts." I hated to bring out the big guns, but he'd practically handed them to me, locked and loaded. "I need answers, Phillip, and if those men come to me again and I have nothing to give them, I'm telling them you and your girlfriend were in it together."

"What?" he asked, appalled. "Emily has nothing to do with this."

"Yeah, but they don't know that. You seem to want to stay under their radar. What'll happen if they think you two set this whole thing up?" What thing, exactly, I had no idea.

He raked his fingers through his hair.

"Just talk to me," I said, my voice placating. "I promise you, whatever you've gotten yourself into, I can help you get out of it. I'm a private investigator. I have connections."

After a very long stare into the bottle of Jack, he said, "Not here. There are eyes and ears everywhere."

The possibility that he might actually talk to me sent a sharp thrill racing over my skin.

He wrote quickly on a piece of paper and handed it over to me. It had an address on it and the words, *Meet me here in half an hour. Alone.*

I shook my head. "So I can suffer the same fate as that poor man you killed? I think not."

He leaned over and whispered, "It's a friend's apartment. He's out of town."

"And that's supposed to set my mind at ease?" I whispered back.

"I'll tell you everything."

"Meet you there in thirty." I rose and walked out the door. When I passed by his secretary Lois's desk, I opened up to get a full read on her. Burning curiosity was all I got. She was curious about me. She lifted her phone and pretended to text, but I was about 90 percent positive she snapped a shot of me. I'd executed that very move a hundred times, only just now realizing how fake it looked. No one texted like that. I'd have to get a new technique.

I climbed into Garrett's truck. "Did you get all that?" I asked him.

"I did. Where we meeting him?"

"At an address on Candelaria near Lomas."

He started his truck. "What did you get off him?"

"The more important question is what *didn't* I get off him." When he raised his brows in question, I said, "Guilt."

17

Oh, my. What a lovely shade of bitch you're wearing today.

—T-SHIRT

We waited in front of the apartment for Phillip to show. He was over fifteen minutes late, and I was beginning to worry we'd been stood up when he pulled around to the side of the building. The two of us got out and walked over to meet him. But when he spotted Garrett, he started to rethink.

He was about to get back in his car when I got to him. "This is a colleague," I said to him, holding up my hands in surrender. "He's also a PI and the best tracker I've ever met. You can tell him anything you'd tell me."

I felt a wave of appreciation drift off Garrett. It was so much nicer than the annoyance or frustration I normally felt come off him.

"This was a mistake," Phillip said, edging back into his car.

"I'm sorry to do this, Phillip, but I will tell those men anything they want to hear if you don't let me in on this." I decided to hit him with my big question and gauge his reaction. "Did you kill that man?"

He raised his chin. "Yes, I did."

I gasped and glared at him. "You're lying. You never murdered any-one."

He jammed an index finger over his mouth to shush me. "Do you want the whole neighborhood to hear you? You're going to get us all killed."

What the hell was going on?

He took hold of my arm and led me to a lower-level apartment.

After pouring himself a stiff one, he offered a glass to Garrett. Thank-fully, Swopes shook his head. This was no time to be getting rowdy with the boys.

When he sat down, I said, "Okay, Brinkman, spill. Why is your girl-friend saying she saw you kill someone?"

He released a hapless sigh, then said, "Because I needed a way out. Things were getting too unstable. Too unpredictable."

"Does this have anything to do with the fact that you run way more money through your business than cars?"

His head snapped up. "How did you know that?"

"Told you, connections. What gives?" I asked, kicking a dirty sock away from me.

He collapsed onto the sofa and leaned his head back. The guy was about five minutes away from a nervous breakdown. I kind of felt sorry for him.

"I launder money for the Mendoza family."

Garrett stilled. Clearly that name meant something to him.

"The Mendoza family?" I asked, completely out of the loop.

But before Phillip could answer, Garrett said, "The Mendozas are one of the biggest crime families from Mexico. They have been responsible for hundreds of deaths there, including cops and judges."

I glanced back at Phillip. "How did you get involved with them?"

"They came to me, offered to help me get the business back on its feet, promised to make me a rich man. They did both of those things, but the Mendozas aren't the most stable people I've ever met."

"I still don't understand what a murder has to do with anything."

"It was Emily's idea. I'm hoping that once I go to prison, they'll forget about me."

"So that's the plan? Go to prison for a crime you didn't commit? If you aren't scared to go to prison, why not just turn yourself in?"

"Do you know what they would do to me if I did that? To my children? I moved my ex-wife and kids across the country to get them away from these guys, but their reach doesn't exactly end at the state line. They wouldn't hesitate to hurt them to keep me doing what I do. Or worse, kill them. This way, I go to prison for something completely unrelated. I lose everything, including this business. They have no more use for me, and my kids will be safe."

"So, there was never a murder? Your girlfriend never saw anything?"

"No."

"Then who are they looking for? Who did you supposedly kill?"

"My best friend from college. He agreed to disappear for a price."

"Dude, he will show back up eventually."

"No, he has no family here. No deep friendships, besides with me."

"That's terribly risky."

"Believe me, I understand that more than you can possibly know. And I have a contingency plan."

"Which is?"

"I have a man on standby who will take my ex and children into hiding. I've put back millions for that purpose."

"Who all knows this?"

"No one. No one but Jeff, the guy I supposedly murdered, and my girlfriend. And now you. Damn it." He chewed his lower lip in thought. "I knew this probably wouldn't work. I just can't risk Emily's well-being. She's so smart. And she's brave. She knew they'd go after her." The thought of her brought a smile to his face. "I've never met anyone so willing to risk everything, including her life, for me."

"So, whose apartment is this?" I asked him.

"Jeff's."

"The guy you supposedly killed?"

"The one and only."

"This is kind of creepy."

"Really?" Garrett asked, his expression deadpan. "*This* is creepy?"

"Let me look into this, Phillip, see what I can find out and what can be done."

"Nothing," he said. "The game's over. If they knew I was trying to lose the business on purpose, they'd go after everyone I've ever loved."

"We're not going to let that happen."

"Look, if they sent men to your apartment, I promise on my life, they're bugging you."

"They definitely bugged. That whole gun-to-the-head thing was very annoying."

"No, bugs. Surveillance. Watch everything you say. If you repeat this—"

"No, I gotcha." The captain had been bugging me, too. Literally and metaphorically. "I need to clean house anyway."

I called my friend Pari on the way home. "I need you to do my apt."

"I'm just not that attracted to your apt."

"I think I'm being bugged."

"Like I am? Right now?"

"Kind of, only less metaphorically. Do you still have that equipment to detect stuff like that?"

After a very long pause, she said, "No. You know I'm not allowed near anything like that. I am adhering to the conditions of my probation, thank you very much."

"Okay, but really," I said.

"Oh, are you asking me if I have that can of bug spray you loaned me?"

I could visualize her winking at me in a blatant attempt at subterfuge. But seriously, who loaned out a can of bug spray and expected it to be returned?

"Um, yes," I said, playing along. "Do you still have that can of bug spray I loaned you?"

"It will take me a while to comb through my back room, where I have nothing even remotely related to computers and/or electronics-related paraphernalia."

"You can't even have electronics-related paraphernalia? What the hell did you do?"

"Not what," she said, dropping the guise. "But who."

"Okay, then who did you do?"

"I kind of accidentally on purpose hacked the White House's phone system."

"No."

"Yes."

"Do you think that was wise?"

"Not anymore, you can bet your ass on that. They take that stuff really seriously."

"I wonder why."

I hung up, then gave my driver—whom I'd temporarily renamed Fitz because Garrett didn't sound like a driver's name at all—my full attention. "Have you found out anything else on the Twelve, Fitz?"

"A little," he said, rolling with it. "I told Dr. von Holstein to focus on them, see what the prophecies say."

"And?"

"He's still working on it, but one thing he's found that's very interesting is that there are mentions of two sets of Twelve with one defining force in the middle, the thirteenth beast."

"Really?" I asked, suddenly very interested.

"The way I understand it, there are the Twelve, aka the darkness, but there are also twelve sentient beings of light to balance the scales, sent to protect you, the daughter."

"That seems like a lot of trouble to go to. And the thirteenth?"

"He is the single being that will tip the scales either to the light or the dark."

No kidding.

By the time I got back to my building, Pari was there waiting on me. She lived only a block away, which made it nice, especially when I needed her help with something. Or when I needed a back rub. She had incredible hands.

I'd tried to call Uncle Bob, but he didn't pick up. I needed to know how it went with the captain. And if he really hired that fake psychic. She totally bleached her hair. I also called Quentin on video chat. He was doing fine as well and asked about Amber.

"Just don't go around her mother anytime soon. You'll be skinned alive."

He winced, and signed, "I understand. I'm really sorry."

"I know you are, sweet boy, and if Cookie gets ahold of you, you'll be even sorrier."

"Okay."

I blew him a kiss and hung up.

Pari had put on her sunglasses, as she did whenever she was around me. She could see my light, said it blinded her. She spotted Garrett as we got out, and her eyes danced a bit before asking, "So, what are we doing?"

"I'm being bugged by everyone from APD to the Mendoza crime family."

"You do like to piss people off."

"I didn't do anything to either one of them. The Man's got it in for me."

"I'm sure you're right," she said, offering yours truly a tender-ish pat on the back. Either that or she was trying to dislodge my larynx.

I coughed and introduced them. "Pari, this is Fitz. He's my new driver. I've decided I need a driver at my beck and call, and he's really cheap."

"I'm Garrett," he said when he took her hand.

She surveyed him from head to toe.

"Fitz, this is Pari. She's a killer tattoo artist and has only been to prison twice."

"I've never been to prison," she corrected, unable to take her eyes off him. "You have an incredible aura."

That was it. I'd seen enough to feel slighted for her main squeeze. "What about Tre?" I asked her, appalled. She'd been dating her employee for a while now. The whole thing screamed sexual harassment lawsuit, but they'd seemed happy.

"His aura is fine. Garrett's here, however, is quite unique."

"Really?" I asked, squinting my eyes. I could see auras. Kind of.

"Quite unique."

"My bugs?" I asked her.

"Oh, right." She unloaded her bag and brought out a handheld device that I assumed swept for bugs. Then again, she could be a total charlatan. How would I know?

"I am thinking about adding surveillance of some kind. Like motion detectors and cameras. I'm tired of people breaking in without so much as a by-your-leave."

"Normally, I'd say a camera was a bit much, but in your case, I'd recommend two and possibly some type of explosive booby trap."

She turned on the device and started waving it over and under the most obvious places to hide a bug. She found one almost immediately and reached under my windowsill. It looked like a small black button.

"Very state of the art," she said. She handed it to Garrett, who agreed with a nod.

"I doubt this came from your captain," he said. "The government would never spring for such high-dollar equipment."

"The Mendozas?" I whispered, not wanting them to hear me.

He held it up to the light and turned it in his fingers, admiring it. "Most likely."

"Okay," I said to Pari, "put it back exactly as you found it and make sure it still works. I'm going to need it later."

She gave me a thumbs-up, then whispered, "It's extremely sophisticated. It has a range of—" She stopped and let her gaze slide past me.

"Of?" I asked, before realizing she'd spotted my roomie.

"What is that?" she asked, straightening.

"That is a Mr. Wong. He's my apartment mate."

Pari had been able to see the departed since a near-death accident when she was twelve, but she could see only a slight disturbance in her vision, a light grayish mist.

"He's a departed?" she asked.

"Yeah. He just kind of hangs in my corner. All day. Every day. He doesn't get out much." When she didn't reply, I glanced back at her. She'd removed her sunglasses and stood transfixed. "What?" I asked. "You see the departed all the time."

"You sure that's what he is?" she asked.

That got my attention. "What do you mean?" I stepped closer to Mr. Wong. "He looks like every other departed I've ever seen. Maybe a tad more monochrome." He was awfully gray.

"No, he's not like every other departed," she said.

Garrett watched our exchange, more interested in the receiver he was holding than in anything supernatural. He liked things he could see. Things he could touch and explain. For a guy who hailed from a family of practicing voodooists, not to mention went to hell and back, he was not very comfortable discussing the supernatural realm.

I squinted again, trying to see what she was seeing. "How do you know? What are you seeing?"

But she just stood there, her eyes glazed over, her face alight, her expression reverent. Pari wasn't the most reverent person I'd ever known. Covered in tattoos, with her long dark hair styled in bold waves, she liked thick black liner and thin black skirts. If I had to describe her in one word, it would be *rebellious*.

"What?" I asked again. I turned my head this way and that. "What are you seeing?"

"Nothing," she said, blinking out of her stupor. "Nothing at all." She scanned the rest of the area. "But I do think I found part of your problem." She pointed into my bedroom.

"Really?" I hustled to her side, stood there a moment, then walked into my room. Despite my earlier assessment that my bedroom hadn't been disturbed when the intruder ransacked the place, something seemed to be missing. I rested my hands on my hips and looked around, trying to put my finger on it. My dresser hadn't been disturbed. My closet seemed okay, considering it was my closet. My bed sat untouched, the Bugs Bunny comforter lying exactly as I'd left it that morning: in total disarray.

But something wasn't right.

"Reyes. Alexander. Farrow," I said.

Seconds after I spoke his name, Reyes walked into his bedroom, and I looked across the open space directly from my room into his.

He waited for me to continue.

"I feel like there's something missing from my bedroom."

A dimple appeared at the corner of his mouth. "You don't say."

"Any idea what that might be?"

He glanced around my room as well, then shrugged. "I can't imagine."

"Oh, wait," I said, stepping from my room into his, "wasn't there something here? Like, I don't know, a wall or something?"

He looked up. "You could be right. I do seem to remember a barrier of some kind here."

"Yep," I said, stepping closer, "I definitely remember a partition separating our apartments." When his only response was a mischievous tilt of his full mouth, I asked, "Where did you put my wall?"

He crossed his arms over his chest and leaned against his doorframe. "What makes you think I took it?"

"It was there this morning."

"And that means I took it? Maybe you just misplaced it. Where exactly did you see it last?"

I pressed my lips together. "You tore down my wall."

The smile he wore could've charmed the panties off a nun. Completely unrepentant, he admitted, "I tore down your wall."

I stepped closer and he locked his long arms around my waist. "My apartment isn't a safe place," I warned. "It gets broken into a lot, it's haunted, and it has a terrible aversion to cinnamon schnapps. Long story."

"And you think taking down this wall was a bad idea?"

"Well, now that there is no barrier here, the curse that has been cast upon my humble abode has now seeped onto your side, too."

"This is a non-seepage opening."

"Really? Because it looks pretty seepy."

"Seepy?"

"Seepy. And now we have this really long bed," I said, nodding toward our two beds butting up against each other, no headboards in between. Then all the wondrous possibilities took shape in my mind. I beamed at him. "We can play Twister on it!"

"Twister."

"And we can have massive pillow fights. I will, of course, kick your ass."

"Will you?"

"Wanna bet on it?"

"I think you've done enough betting for a while," he said, referring to my pathetic attempt to cash in at the poker table.

"That was with a lying, cheating demon. You can hardly blame me for losing to someone who eats souls for dinner."

"I think your friend is upset."

I whirled out of his embrace to check on Pari. She was staring again, only instead of the reverence she had when looking at Mr. Wong, she was regarding Reyes with a wariness that, if I wasn't mistaken, resembled trepidation. She was terrified.

She took a deliberate step back when Reyes looked at her, then another and another until she backed up against Sophie and could go no farther.

"Pari," I said, inching toward her, "this is Reyes Farrow, my, um, neighbor." I didn't know how to introduce him. Was he my boyfriend? Lover hardly seemed appropriate. And he wasn't my fiancé. Yet. Still, boyfriend just didn't seem right. "Pari?"

She snapped out of it and began gathering her equipment. "I'll get to work on this ay-sap."

Garrett had stepped to the doorway and was inspecting the new construction. It was uncanny. No one would ever have known a wall was ever there. It had been finished and painted to match and simply looked like one long room.

He turned to Pari. "Don't worry, Farrow scares everyone."

I scowled at him as I stepped past. "Are you okay?" I asked her, but she didn't look up at me.

"I'm fine."

I realized she was panting, but the emotions pouring out of her were only partly fear. There was so much mixed in there, I couldn't decide which one was causing her the most grief.

I put a hand on her arm. "Pari, hon, sit down."

She looked up at last, cringed against the light, jammed on her sunglasses, then said, "No, it's okay. I'm fine."

I led her to my sofa anyway. "You guys play nice," I said, my tone warning. Not that it would do any good with those two, but they didn't always get along. Once we got settled, I spoke softly to Pari. She was not the type to get rattled. I didn't think she *could* get rattled. "What's wrong?" I asked her.

She pulled in her lower lip, then leaned over to me and whispered, "What is he?"

She was the second person to ask me that lately. I didn't know how much to tell her. She knew what I was because she could see me, my light, but what was she seeing with Reyes? "What does he look like to you?"

"He looks like, I don't know." She dared a quick look over my shoulder. "Have you ever seen the sky at night when the stars weren't out but it was crystal clear, the sky such a deep dark black that you were sure you could drown in it, it was so beautiful?"

I nodded knowingly. "Yes, I have."

"He's that." She slammed her eyes shut as though picturing him in her mind, afraid to look again. "He's the deep, dark kind of beauty that you'd sell your soul to have."

Wow, she was good. "I can't argue with you there."

"I've never seen anything like it. Like him. He's made of fire. A black fire that's so dark, so intense, instead of giving off light, he absorbs it. Bends it to his will." She gave me her full attention then. "This is your Reyes," she said, matter-of-fact.

"This is my Reyes."

She cleared her throat, swallowed hard, and adjusted her collar. "I can see the appeal."

"You seemed scared, Pari."

She nodded. "Oh, I was. I am. Don't get me wrong, but holy shit, there's nothing sexier than something that beautiful, that enigmatic, and that deadly all rolled into one. Well," she added, "as long as he's not trying to kill me."

I chuckled. "Can I give you a proper introduction?"

"No!" She started gathering her things again. "I mean, no, thank you. He's just so— He's too— I'm just not sure—"

"Gotcha," I said in understanding, but burning with curiosity on the inside. I wanted to see exactly what she saw.

I looked over my shoulder toward him. He was leaning against his own doorway, and Garrett was leaning against mine. It was a standoff as old as time, when cavemen would challenge each other to a fight to the death with clubs. One of them had to be the alpha, and neither was willing to accede to the other. I squinted at Reyes, concentrated, gave it my all. Nope. He was just the hot guy next door. No starless nights or black fire.

"Oh, your phone is probably most definitely being tapped. Stop by and I'll give you a clean one. You can use it for anything you don't want them to hear, but just remember, they can hear you even when you're not on your phone. Phones are the fastest and cheapest form of surveillance out there. If you need to have a conversation that you don't want them to hear, you must take the battery out of yours. Don't just turn it off."

"Call me later," Pari said to me before tossing a wave to Garrett and hurrying out of my apartment.

"Okay. Don't be a stranger."

I realized Reyes was watching me when I stood to show Pari out, but the girl was fast, so I turned my attention back to the problem at hand. The wall thing. Seriously, who did crap like that?

Pinching Garrett's ribs as I passed, I walked up to Reyes and stood with my arms crossed.

"Yes?" he asked playfully.

"This wall thing is not over."

He hooked a finger in the top of my jeans and pulled. "We have a wall thing?"

My hands instinctively rose to his chest, the hard expanse smooth under my fingers. "We have a wall thing."

"Charley!" Cookie called out.

"In here," I called back, mesmerized by the dimples at either side of Reyes's mouth.

She rushed in, winded with flushed cheeks. "What do you think of this outfit?" she asked, spinning in a circle until she noticed Garrett. Whom she'd just charged past. "Oh, hi, Garrett."

"Cookie," he said with a nod.

She'd been getting ready for the third and final date in Operation Punk Ubie. If this didn't work tonight, she might have to do something drastic, like—gasp!—ask the man out herself. But she was a knockout. If this didn't work, he was an idiot who didn't deserve her.

"I was just getting ready for a date. Thing. Not really a date, but—" She frowned. "Where's your wall?"

I jammed my fists onto my hips and glared at her. "That's what I'd like to know, missy. Speaking of which," I said, turning back to the wall thief, "why on earth would you tear down my wall?"

He shrugged a shoulder. "You live next door."

"Yes," I said, acknowledging that tidbit of info, "but why did you tear down my wall?"

He grew serious, studying me from beneath hooded lids. "You live next door."

"Oh." His meaning sank in at last.

Cookie sighed. "That's what I want, damn it." She pointed to us and questioned Garrett. "Is that asking too much?"

Garrett looked horrified by the thought.

"Okay," I said, walking to her and straightening her scarf, "I found this guy in an ad in the back of the *Weekly Alibi*."

"Wait, you don't know him?" she asked, appalled.

"No, but he's an actor. We need an actor for this one. Someone who can, you know, act."

She groaned. "This could backfire in so many ways," she said, and she was right, naturally, but I had to see the coffee cup half full. We were doing this for a reason. It would work. And unicorns sparkle in moonlight.

18

*Remember, it's all fun and games
until somebody loses an eyeball,
and then it's, "Hey! free eyeball!"*

—T-SHIRT

As I busied myself putting all my numbers in the phone Pari had loaned me, Cookie's date showed up. Right on time. We ran through the script and told him that the whole thing was being taped for a new hidden-camera show that could be picked up by HBO. "If you want it to air," we told him, "you really have to sell it."

He was tall and well built if a bit too young and too clean-cut for what we were asking of him, but he'd agreed to our little skit and to the fact that we were more or less punking the man we were setting up.

"I wish you were going to be there," Cookie said to me.

"Me, too, but if he sees me there, he'll know something is up."

By the time they left for the date, Cookie looked a little green in the gills.

"Chin up, hon. This is our last try."

"But is all this really necessary?" she asked, clearly wanting to back out. "Again, if he wanted to ask me out, he would have, right?"

"Do you even know my uncle Bob?"

"Okay, you're right."

She took her date by the arm and let him lead her down the stairs to a waiting limo. This would be good.

Minutes later, it seemed, my new phone rang. Reyes and Garrett and I had been discussing the prophecies and the Dealer. Garrett agreed to meet with him, to try to figure out what on earth was going on. But for now, I had an untraceable phone calling my name.

I slid my finger across the screen to answer. "Hey, Cook, how's it going?"

"Charley," she said, almost screaming at me, "get down here, now! Robert's going to kill him!"

I scrambled to my feet. "What? Where are you? What happened?"

"They're fighting. Robert confronted us, and your actor guy thinks it's all part of the script. Robert's going to kill him! Get down here!"

I was running out the door before I knew it. "Where are you, exactly?" I asked, taking the stairs down three at a time. Garrett and Reyes were right behind me.

"We'll take my truck," Garrett said, heading in that direction.

We followed him and hurried inside as he started the engine.

"Where are we going?" he asked.

"They're behind that little Italian place by the theater."

"Which theater?" he asked as he pulled out. I sat in the middle between Garrett and Reyes, trying to calm Cookie down.

"Put Uncle Bob on the phone," I said to her.

"I tried. He won't listen. He's furious, Charley. He thinks this guy is some kind of stalker or something."

"Did you tell him what we talked about?"

"Yes! I did everything just like we discussed. I called Robert and told him I was on a date from that online service, but that my date was making me very uncomfortable. I told him I didn't feel safe and asked if he would come pick me up. That was it! I didn't say anything else, but Robert stormed in when he got here, put the guy in a choke hold, and dragged him out. They're arguing now. Just hurry, Charley. Please!"

"We're almost there," I said, thanking the creator for giving Garrett a lead foot. "Just try to get Uncle Bob on the phone. Tell him it's me."

"O-okay, I'll try." I heard arguing in the background, then Cookie trying to talk to an insane man who went by the name of Robert Davidson.

"Just stay back, Cookie," he growled at her.

Then I heard scuffling and Cookie screamed and I buried my head in my hands. What had I done?

"Charley!" Cookie cried into the phone, "He has a gun!"

"What?" I couldn't believe this was happening. "No! No, no, no, no, no! Cookie you have to tell Uncle Bob it was all an act. Cookie?"

In the next instant, a sharp crack splintered the air, and the phone went dead.

I scrambled over Reyes before Garrett came to a complete stop, but Reyes grabbed my arm and held me until he could get out, too, and run over to the melee with me. Cookie stood in the lamplight behind a shopping strip by the theater complex. A crowd had gathered, and I heard sirens in the distance as I came to a screeching halt beside her.

She was in tears, her head down, her shoulders shaking.

Then I saw Uncle Bob. He was covered in blood, and Cookie's date was unconscious on the ground. I threw my hands over my mouth to stop a scream from escaping.

Cookie must've really sold it. She must've convinced Uncle Bob she was scared of this guy, and Uncle Bob reacted. I never dreamed in a million years he would react so blindly, with so much rage.

I stumbled forward to check the guy's pulse. His heart raced beneath my fingers and I almost passed out from relief. I immediately tore open his shirt to look for the wound. Perfect, unmarred skin gleamed in the lamplight. I saw no wound. No gushing blood. No sign that a near-fatal struggle had just occurred.

I heard Uncle Bob's voice in my ear. He'd leaned down, his mouth at my ear, and whispered, "Is he dead, or do I need to put another bullet in him?"

The words faded as I sensed a more salient emotion. Something wasn't right.

I turned to look up at Uncle Bob; his expression was grim, and the emotion pouring out of him matched that look. But it wasn't him. It wasn't Uncle Bob I was feeling, his usual cautious reaction to any adrenaline-spiking situation. He was a seasoned cop.

And he smelled wrong.

While his shirt was covered in blood, my olfaction did not pick up its signature coppery scent. It picked up—I sniffed the air—tomatoes. Ketchup, to be exact. Then I realized it wasn't rage flowing through Uncle Bob's veins, but resentment. And the man I was examining felt anything but fear. Or agony after having been shot. That was what was wrong. Different.

I'd been duped.

I scrubbed my fingertips over my face and looked up at Ubie. "When did you figure it out?"

He reached down and helped Cookie's date, who was grinning, up off the pavement. "If you're going to set Cookie up with a date to make me jealous, the guys you set her up with should at least be straight." Cookie's second date was with a friend of mine. A gay friend. How had Ubie known that?

I stood and brushed myself off. Cookie glanced between us, partly relieved and partly confused. "You picked up on that, did you?"

"Yes, Charley, I did."

"How did you know this was all a setup?"

"Give me a little credit. I *am* a detective. And neither one of you could lie your way out of a paper bag." He turned and glared at Cookie. "You need to take a class or something."

"We are excellent liars," I said, defending our honor. "And this was my idea, Uncle Bob. Cookie didn't even want to go along with it." Had I just blown Cookie's only chance to hit it with my uncle?

"Believe it or not, I figured that out as well."

"How?"

"Cookie would never come up with something this harebrained."

I folded my arms over my chest. "I resent that remark."

"And she would never go so far as to hire an actor."

Troy, the actor in question, grinned some more. "How'd I do?" he asked Uncle Bob.

"You have a fine career ahead of you, son."

"And," Cookie said, completely offended as well, "Charley may be a horrible liar, but I'm an expert."

"You keep telling yourself that, sweet cheeks."

"But how—no when—did you two get together?" I asked him, indicating both Ubie and Troy.

"I subpoenaed your phone records and got the number off them."

I gasped to show how indignant I was. "That is illegal!"

"So is just about everything you do on a daily basis," he said to me. "I felt I needed to put you in your place on this one, hon. That's why I called in Wynona Jakes."

"You mean the fake psychic was a setup?" I asked—so appalled, I was almost speechless. Almost. "I can't believe you'd set me up like that."

"And how does that feel?"

Again, I was almost struck speechless. Almost. "Uncle Bob, we were doing this for your own good. You needed a swift kick in the rear, and you got one. If you'd just asked her out in the first place—"

"Is this an example of that whole 'blaming the victim' thing you're always ranting about?"

I shut my mouth, refusing to answer.

He turned to Cookie, who stood in both shame and humiliation. I sucked so bad sometimes. I thought for sure this would work.

"Well?" he asked her, holding out a hand.

"Well?" she asked back.

"We going out or what?"

Her mouth opened, then closed again. Then opened. Then—

"Yes!" I said for her, sidling up closer to my curmudgeonly uncle. "Yes, you are going out."

A pink hue blossomed over Cookie's face. "Yes, we're going out, Robert. Right now before you change your mind."

His grateful expression warmed the cockles of my heart. As Cookie retrieved her purse from another onlooker, I wrapped my arm in his and leaned my head against his shoulder. "So it worked, then."

He pressed his mouth together under his trim mustache, loath to admit it. "Yes," he said at last, "it worked. But you guys sure went to a lot of trouble for nothing."

Cookie had stepped forward, and I handed him off to her. "Not nothing," she said, rising onto her toes and kissing his cheek. "Not even close to nothing."

A fiery blush suffused Ubie's face the exact moment a wave of nausea washed over me. I took that as my cue to skedaddle.

After Garrett dropped Reyes and me off, I brushed my teeth, washed my face, and put on my favorite pair of pajamas. The bottoms were baby blue with little red fire engines all over them, and the bright crimson top read LIFE'S SHORT. BITE HARD. After forcing a goodnight kiss on Mr. Wong's cheek, I strolled to my room and pulled back my Bugs Bunny comforter.

My room felt so big now. So open. It was weird.

I snuggled deep into the covers, adjusted my pillow until it was just right, then lay down until the top of my head rested on Reyes's shoulder. He was in the exact same position, only upside down on his bed. We lay facing each other, nose to nose, our breaths mingling. The scent of him reminded me of rain in a forest. I raised a hand to his face, let my fingers brush down his cheek and over his mouth.

He did the same, pushing my hair back with a large hand, tracing my jaw with his fingertips. "Don't think that just because there's no wall between us you can take advantage of me."

"Oh, I wouldn't dare."

He fell asleep cradling my head, his heat rolling over me in scalding waves, and yet I wasn't too hot. I fell asleep wondering how that was even possible.

I could sense the sun coming up over the horizon the next morning but fought my body's natural inclination to rise with the chickens. It was still early; I was certain of it. Surely I could get in another half hour before duty—or the need to visit the little *señorita*'s room—called. Then I felt it. The undeniable knowledge that someone was looking at me. Someone was sitting and breathing and fidgeting in my space bubble.

I let my lids drift open to reveal the smiling face of a little girl.

"She's awake!" she screamed, and I bound upright, trying to blink the sleep from my eyes.

A little boy ran into the room and scrambled up on the bed beside his sister. "What happened to your wall?" he asked, his huge dark eyes wide with wonder.

But now the little girl sat with her tiny arms crossed over her chest, stabbing me with a scalding glower, albeit an adorable one. Oh, yeah, she wanted me dead.

"Why do you have two beds?" the boy asked next. He was bouncing on his knees, clearly wanting to jump. "You look older than the last time we saw you," he added. "And you have bedhead."

"Oh, my goodness." A woman rushed into the room to scoop up the two children and set them on the floor. "I am so sorry, Charley."

I waved a dismissive hand at Bianca. She was married to Reyes's best—and pretty much only—friend, Amador. The two little munchkins at her side, one beaming and one glaring the heat of a thousand suns, were their children, Ashley and Stephen.

Amador walked in, nodding his head in approval. "Hey, Charley. I like what you've done with the place."

"Thanks," I said, climbing out of bed and smoothing my pajamas. Nothing like greeting guests in my pajamas.

Amador read my T-shirt, raised his brows playfully, then said, "Reyes told Ashley about the you-know-what."

I walked around the bed and gave his lovely wife a hug. "The you-know-what?"

"You know," he said, coming in for his own hug before I scooped up the rascal doing jumping jacks at my feet. "The, er, Post-it note."

"Oh." I looked down at her.

"No, '*jita*," Bianca said, kneeling down to scold her daughter, "you don't glare at people that way. It's very rude."

Reyes walked in, two cups of coffee in hand and an impish expression on his face.

Amador slapped him on the back. "No, I do," he said, surveying the area. "I like the blending of two cultures, the definitive lines separating the two: minimalist and, well, not minimalist."

"Oh, heavens," Bianca said, "you will never get hired at *Architectural Digest* if you don't learn the lingo." She glanced around my area of our connected rooms and nodded, having made up her mind. "Minimalist and lavish."

I laughed softly. "I like it."

She took Stephen from me so I could accept the coffee Reyes had brought me. She must know me better than I thought.

"Can we do our beds like this, Mama?" Stephen asked Bianca. "Pleeeeeease?"

I hid a look of amusement behind my cup as I took a sip. Then I stifled a shiver of delight.

"Are you going to say yes?" Ashley asked me accusingly. Her lower lip quivered as I bent down to her.

"I'm still thinking about it. What do you think I should say?"

"I think you should say no. You're too old for him anyway."

"How old do I look?"

"I'm so sorry," Bianca said, her smile suddenly nervous.

"Is that yours?" She pointed to a tiny doll made out of strands of soft rope. My sister, Gemma, had given it to me when we were kids.

"It sure is." I took it down as Reyes and Amador discussed the finer points of Reyes's décor, or lack thereof, in his room. Clearly my side outshone his, and Amador felt bad for his friend. It probably wouldn't take long for my stuff to leach over to his side anyway. Poor guy. He was the one who took down the wall. He removed its only protection.

"Do you like it?" I asked Ashley. Maybe I could bribe her into liking me. I was so not above bribery.

"I guess."

"I got two words for you, *pendejo*," Amador said to Reyes. "Eight ball."

Reyes tossed me a grin before he and Amador went to his luxurious pool table in the room adjoining his living room. Barely visible from where I stood, it was carved from dark woods with a rich cream-colored top. Good thing he knew the owner of the building. Neighbors rarely appreciated the noise of a billiards table in an apartment building.

It was good to see Reyes's friends over. His life was slowly becoming normal. Or, well, as normal as his life could become. I couldn't say *returning* to normal, because as far as I could tell, he had never had anything near a normal life. I studied him from my vantage point and wondered what he would consider normal. Was it a family with 2.5 kids? He had been a prince. A general in hell. A severely abused child. An inmate. Could he adjust to what we humans considered normal?

I sat on the bed and patted the mattress beside me. Ashley climbed up and took the doll to study it.

"What if I said yes to Reyes? Would you be very mad?"

She shrugged one slender shoulder. "A little."

"Because he is supposed to marry you?"

"Yes. He promised."

"Well, what if I only kept him for a little while? And when you grow up and become as pretty as your mother, you can decide then if you still want someone as old and grumpy as Reyes Farrow."

The corners of her mouth tipped up. "He'll always be pretty, though."

She knocked that one out of the park on her first swing. "Yes, he will always be pretty."

"Boys can't be pretty," Stephen said, squirming out of his mother's grip. She lowered him to the floor and he ran to see what the menfolk were up to.

"Can so!" I called out to him.

Bianca chuckled and sat beside her daughter. "Sometimes, God gives us something even better than what we want. You have to have faith that he will give you someone just as pretty as Uncle Reyes."

She eyed her mother, bewildered. "There's *not* anyone as pretty as Uncle Reyes."

And another homerun for the little lady in the pink sundress. She was good. I might have some serious competition when she got older.

―――――

After a long and fruitless talk with Ashley, I took a quick shower, dressed in my best PI attire, then waited for my neighbor—my other neighbor—to make her morning appearance.

And waited.

And waited.

I made more coffee, said my good-byes to the Sanchez family, and waited some more.

"You're worried about her," Reyes said, accepting a cup of coffee from my side of the playground. He looked good on my side. He had dressed in a pair of jeans, white T-shirt, and heavy boots. His dark hair, still wet from his own shower, curled over his forehead and around an ear. I longed to tuck it behind said ear, but it was just an excuse to touch him, to feel him beneath my fingertips.

But Cookie was officially very late. It was almost eight o'clock. She was always over by six thirty. Seven at the latest, and Amber had to be to school in about five seconds.

"Go check on her," he said, crossing back to his apartment. "I have an order coming in."

"Wait a minute," I said, my tone a little sharp.

He turned back to me, one brow hitched in question.

"That is my cup you're taking, mister."

His dimples appeared as he walked back to me. "I'll give you a dollar for it."

"It's my very favorite cup."

He stepped closer until his mouth was at my ear, until his warmth coiled around me and soaked my skin. "Two."

"I've had it since I was a kid."

After a quick glance at it, he asked, "Your cup predicted there would be a television show called *Downton Abbey*?"

"You don't know that. Downton Abbey could be a real place in England."

"It has the show's logo."

"It could be the house's logo. Like its crest. The show used it for authenticity."

"And a picture of the cast."

"That could be anybody. It's grainy."

He set the cup down and leaned onto the counter, bracing one hand on either side of me. "Why don't you tell me what you really want?"

"Your mouth on mine," I said before I could stop myself.

And before I could retract my request, he bent his head and slanted his mouth across mine.

"I'm late!" Cookie barreled in, her clothes askew and her hair a tad more spiky than usual. She rushed over, took my cup of coffee, and downed it in three gulps. It was still pretty warm, so I couldn't help but be impressed.

Then she noticed the fact that I was wearing a suit made of hunky man flesh.

"Oh, Reyes, hi." She stumbled back.

"I'm late!" Amber said, following in her mother's footsteps. Her hair hung in tangles down her back, her long limbs covered in wrinkled and mismatched clothes.

"Oh, my god," I said to Cookie. "You're wearing off on your daughter."

Reyes straightened when Amber's eyes alighted on him. She beamed brilliantly at him. "Hey, Aunt Charley," she said, her focus fixed on Reyes. "Hey, Reyes."

"That is Mr. Farrow to you," Cookie said, realizing the depths of Amber's attraction. "Go get your backpack. I'll drop you off before I go to work."

Amber lowered her head. "Okay."

When she left, I asked, "She still hasn't fessed up?"

"No."

"She will, hon. I know Amber. It will eat her alive." Cookie nodded, but before she could leave, I asked, "How was your date last night?"

A soft pink blossomed over her face.

"That good, huh?"

"It was—" She thought about her words carefully. "—nice."

"I'm glad. You guys didn't, like, make out or anything, did you? Because that's just wrong. He's my uncle, Cook. How am I going to be able to look at you?"

She turned and said over her shoulder, "I'm not discussing this with you right now."

"Okay, but that means we'll just have to go into more detail about it later. You'll be embarrassed."

Reyes chuckled. We stayed behind. Put off work as long as we could and talked. Just talked. We laughed about Amador's poor sportsmanship when he'd lost miserably to Reyes that morning, about Ashley's insistence that Reyes wait for her, about Cookie's blush and Amber's guileless adoration of him. It was nice. Everything about that morning was nice.

I knew it was too good to last. My forty-eight hours were up, and I still had no clue where Phillip's girlfriend was. Not that I was about to hand her over to the bad guys, but I needed to talk to Agent Carson. To fill her in on my latest findings and my newest plan. Surely it would work. What could go wrong?

So, after a wonderful morning with my main squeeze, I realized time and tide wait for no man. Or woman. I called Special Agent Carson on my way over to my office. I couldn't tell her what Phillip Brinkman told me just yet. I needed to talk to his girlfriend first, to get her side of things. If Carson pulled the plug on everything because of Emily's testimony, the Mendozas would know that Brinkman was just trying to get out from under him. Everything would be lost.

It amazed me that he would rather go to prison than turn on them. That told me just what kind of people the Mendozas were, and that they were not to be trifled with.

Then again, I liked trifling. Trifling was my middle name. Charlotte Trifling Davdison. Let Papa Mendoza bring the fight to me. I was ready. And I had a fab supernatural entity who could sever his spine in the blink of an eye, should it come to that. So there.

"Carson," she said when she picked up. I liked it. Clear. Concise. To the point.

I decided to try it myself. "Davidson."

A loud sigh filtered to me. "Charley, you called me. You can't just say Davidson."

"What are you, the phone greeting police?"

"What did you get for me?"

"I didn't get you anything," I said, starting to panic. "Are we exchanging friendship bracelets already? I can go get one now."

"What do you have?"

"I had chlamydia once. Thank God for antibiotics."

"Did you talk to Brinkman? What did you get off him? Have you heard from his men? Have they threatened you again?"

She was so serious. "Yes, I talked to Brinkman, and no, they haven't threatened me again. I need a little more time. And I need to talk to Brinkman's girlfriend, Emily Michaels."

"Charley, I told you, that is not possible."

"Do you remember the last two—no, three—cases I closed for you? Where's the trust?"

"I trust you implicitly. But the men who want Emily Michaels dead are not quite so trustworthy. And either way, I'm not giving you her location."

"Then can you set up a meet?"

After a long, thoughtful moment, she said, "If it will help this case, I can do that. It will take a couple of days."

"I only have a couple of hours. I need to see her now."

She cupped a hand over her phone, and I could only imagine the expletives flying around her. "Give me thirty minutes. I'll see if I can perform miracles."

"I have complete faith in you," I said, giddy with hope. Once I had Emily's side of things, maybe I could talk some sense into her, since it didn't work with her boyfriend. There was simply no reason for him to go to prison for a murder that never even happened. He might have to do some time for money laundering, but I'd leave that up to Carson.

I headed down to the restaurant to grab some breakfast when Cookie came in. She seemed devastated. We sat in a corner booth so we could talk, not that anyone was in. The place didn't open until eleven, and it was barely eight thirty.

Since none of the servers were in yet, we were served by a very sexy cook whose dimples seemed to calm Cookie down a bit.

"She broke down on the way to school," Cook said, her heart hurting. "That incident with Quentin really scared her."

"It scared me, too," I said, stirring my coffee.

"I guess I didn't realize how serious it got. I was just so upset that she would skip school and leave campus like that."

"I was a little surprised as well, but they really like each other. It has me a tad concerned."

"Why?" Cookie asked, surprised. "Quentin is a lovely boy."

"And he's four years older than she is."

"Three. Amber will be thirteen next week." She shook her head. "It's so hard to believe that. She's just growing up so fast."

"I'm a little surprised you aren't more concerned."

"I would be, normally. He is too old for her, but have you seen that girl?"

Amused, I said, "She's a knockout, I know. Which is reason enough for my concern."

"Yeah, but again, Quentin is wonderful, Charley. I've never seen Amber so smitten. Except when she sees Reyes Farrow."

"She does like them older, doesn't she? Speaking of Quentin, what about the girl in the cable car? Miranda. What did you find out about her?"

She looked into her glass of water and took a drink before answering. "I meant to tell you. We've just been so busy. I left the case file on your desk."

My interest piqued. "And?"

"It looks like she had a very hard life, Charley. I didn't get very far with the file, but I managed to get a copy of her autopsy, the investigation of her disappearance, and the court transcripts of her mother's trial."

"Where is she now? Miranda's mother?"

"She's in the women's correctional facility outside Santa Fe."

I nodded in thought. "Looks like I'll be making a trip to Santa Fe very soon. Did they give you a cause of death?"

Cook took another drink. "They said most likely blunt force trauma to the head. She was there over a month before they found her body, so it was hard to get an exact cause."

Since Cookie wanted to talk about Miranda's case about as much as she wanted her fingernails pulled out with pliers, I veered back to the subject of Amber. "I'm glad that rascal of yours admitted the truth."

Cookie relaxed the tight grip on her glass. "I am, too. She was more worried about my reaction to her lying than her skipping school and leaving campus with a boy."

"Told you," I said with a wink. "I knew it would eat her alive."

"Yeah, I totally played it up like she'd broken my heart and I would never be the same again."

"And she fell for it?"

"Hook, line, and sinker."

19

Do you believe in love at first sight,
or should I walk by again?

——T-SHIRT

Having just received a delivery, Reyes came in from outside with a woman following in his wake. A very familiar-looking woman. One with a determined gait and fire in her eyes. The minute those eyes landed on me, I ducked under the table, my head landing in Cookie's lap.

"Tell her I'm not here!"

Cookie coughed, then glanced around frantically. "What? Why? Who?"

"Mrs. Garza. Tell her I'm not here."

"She already saw you," she said through gritted teeth. "She's coming this way."

"Pretend like I passed out and call an ambulance."

"I am not calling an ambulance to cover for you."

"No, really, it'll work."

"Charley Davidson, they have better things to do with their time than—"

"I can see you from here, Ms. Davidson."

From underneath the table, I could see Mrs. Garza, too. Though only her bottom half. She had a killer bag slung over her right shoulder, turquoise with a woman's face painted *Día de Muertos* style, and if I wasn't mistaken, she was wearing an amazing pair of Rocketbuster boots. One of which she was tapping impatiently.

That woman had the best clothes. Then again, I was probably paying for them, thanks to her son, aka my investigator, Angel. She'd recently figured out I was the one sending her money every month and insisted I tell her what was going on, why I was depositing five hundred dollars into her account every month. That was until Angel blackmailed me into a raise. Now it was a cool $750, but I figured he was worth it.

But Angel didn't want her to know. He was so adamantly against it, I couldn't help but comply. What he didn't take into account was the fact that his mother was smart. She knew there was no uncle the minute Angel and I concocted the excuse. But what else could I have said? He just did not, under any circumstances, want her to know the truth.

He said it was because his death had devastated her and he didn't want her to have to go through that again, but she seemed to handle the prospect of another explanation better than he did. Could there have been something more to Angel's reluctance? I'd wondered that a lot since she came into my office that day. It had been only two weeks. She wouldn't be put off for long. I could tell by the determined set of her jaw. She wanted answers. Answers I could give her only if I betrayed Angel.

She finally had enough of waiting and leaned down to peer at me under the table. "I'm not leaving until you talk to me."

I crinkled my nose, busted beyond belief, then popped up out of Cookie's lap, wondering in the back of my mind what that would look like. "Oh, hey, Mrs. Garza! I didn't see you."

After taking a long moment to fold her arms over her chest, she said, "You sent more money this month."

"Right, um, your relative's estate was larger than we'd originally been told."

"It magically got bigger?" She was such a stunning woman. Even at fifty, she had an amazing body and fantastic hair. Combine that with her thick Spanish accent and her rich, husky voice, and she was what Garrett would call a TKO.

"It did get bigger. Weird, huh?"

"Right," Cookie said, nodding in agreement. "Totally weird. That was one eccentric aunt you had."

"Uncle," I corrected her.

"Uncle. Aunt," she said, going in for a save. "I think he was a cross-dresser."

Not bad. Not bad.

Mrs. Garza slid into the booth with us. "I'm not here to cause problems, Ms. Davidson."

This was not going to end well. "Call me Charley," I said. "And this is my assistant, Cookie."

She blinked at her. "Your name is Cookie?" she asked her. No one had ever questioned that, but she was right. It was an odd name. And yet it fit her so perfectly.

"Sure is." She held out a hand, and Mrs. Garza shook it.

"I am Evangeline."

"Oh, we know," Cookie said. "We make out a check to you every—"

"So," I said, interrupting her before she said too much, "what brings you to our neck of the woods?"

"You. This money. This *tío de tu imaginación*."

Well that was uncalled for. "I have a couple of imaginary friends," I said, correcting her, "but my uncle is very real."

"No, *my* uncle," she said.

"Does your uncle know you think he's imaginary?"

Just when I thought she might grow frustrated enough to storm out of the room, she stopped and implored me. "I just have some questions. For him. For Angel," she said, pronouncing it *Ahn-hell*.

"I don't know anyone named Ahn-hell."

Cookie shook her head, too, completely baffled. She was getting really good at this stuff. Of course, she was not lying. She'd never seen the little punk, though I'd described him to her on several occasions. Every time, a starstruck expression would come over her face. She liked the kid. So did I. Usually.

Evangeline held up hand. "Spare me. I know who you are. I know what you can do."

I kept waiting for the subject of our conversation to pop in. He always seemed to sense what his mother was up to. While I wanted to tell her, to let her know what a great kid she had and how well he was doing, Angel was so vehemently against it, I didn't know what to do.

"Charley," she said, leaning in to me, "I insist."

Maybe if I just explained why I couldn't tell her. Then again, that would be confirming her suspicions, but I had a feeling she was like a pit bull with a stuffed Elmo. No way was she giving up until everything was out in the open, polyester guts and all.

There was one place Ahn-hell wasn't allowed. "Follow me," I said, scooting out of the booth and leading her to the women's restroom.

"Is he in here?" she asked, kind of appalled.

"No, that's why we are. He is no longer allowed in the women's restroom."

She stilled. I'd just confirmed all her suspicions. All her hopes. Who wouldn't want to be able to talk to a lost child? I couldn't imagine what she went through when Angel died. He told me she was devastated. Understandably so. But the thought of the agony she'd suffered tightened around my chest as I watched her face. Every emotion known to mankind flashed across it.

"So, what everyone says about you is true."

"I wouldn't go that far. That whole chess-team thing was a big misunderstanding."

I didn't amuse her. She was lost in her thoughts. In her hopes and, deep down, her dread. "You can speak with the dead."

"I can, but only when they want me to, for the most part. Evangeline," I said, knowing I was going to regret everything I was about to say. Angel was going to kill me. "He doesn't want you to know he's . . . he's still with us."

A hand with impeccably finished nails covered her mouth. She leaned against the counter, clearly afraid her legs would give. I let her absorb, mull, and otherwise process everything she was going through. After a long while, she said, "Why—?" Her voice hitched. She swallowed and started again. "Why doesn't he want me to know about him?"

"He's afraid you will mourn all over again."

"All over again? I've never stopped." After a moment, she asked, "Is he well?"

I bit down, not wanting to give her any more information than I absolutely had to. "Yes, he is. But like I said, he is vehemently against me telling you any of this. If he finds out, he will be very angry with me."

Her chin rose. "It's my right, Ms. Davidson. I have more of a right to know about him than you do."

"No, I agree. It's not me, Evangeline. I don't know why he—"

Before I could finish, a young male voice filtered toward me, its tone even, calculating. "You did not just do what I think you did."

He appeared across from me by the women's stalls. I didn't know what to say. If I spoke to him, she'd know he was there. He rushed toward me, absolutely livid, and literally wrapped a hand around my throat, pushing me back against the wall. The paper towel dispenser bit into my back on impact, but I let him be angry with me. He had a right. I'd promised him. I'd promised him I wouldn't say anything. Ever.

"You did not tell her about me."

Evangeline said something, but it was drowned out by the blood rushing in my ears. He was furious, uncontrollably so.

I felt Reyes, but he didn't appear with his raging anger like I was worried he would. He revealed himself slowly, methodically.

Dangerously.

I had no idea what he could do to Angel, nor did I want to find out.

Placing my hand on the one he had wrapped around my throat, I spoke softly to Angel, soothingly. "Sweetheart, I know you're angry. But she figured it out on her own, hon. Just like I told you she would."

Reyes moved closer and I raised a hand, silently begging him not to hurt Angel.

Angel sensed him. He glanced to the side, applied one last ounce of pressure to my throat, then pushed off me, turning and letting his anger consume him.

"I'm okay," I said to appease Reyes, but he stayed put right where he was, hovering incorporeally close by.

Evangeline looked on, a slight rush of terror surging inside her.

I held on to my throat and shook my head at her. "I'm okay. I just swallowed wrong."

"Please stop lying to me, Ms. Davidson."

Lowering my head, I took several deep, calming breaths, then focused on Angel. He had never, in all the years we'd been together, raised a hand against me. He'd never even come close.

The cat was out of the bag and I was no longer going to pretend otherwise. I would take full responsibility, but I would not be treated that way. "Why are you so against this?" I asked him. "What the hell, Angel?"

"My Ahn-hell?" Evangeline asked, hope sparkling in her eyes. "Is he here?"

"Tell her no," he said, glowering at me. "Tell her he's not here. He's never been here."

"I won't do that. She already knows." I stepped to him. "She's smart, hon, just like you told me."

"Too smart," he said, working his jaw in resentment. "She'll figure it out."

"That you're here?" I put a hand on his shoulder as Evangeline held both of hers to her heart.

The glare he cast me was so toxic, so full of vehemence, my lungs seized under the weight of it. "That I'm not her son."

It was my turn to be surprised. He'd knocked the wind right out of my sails with that statement. I stood unmoving, trying to absorb what he'd said. Trying to figure it out. "What are you talking about?" I asked him at last. "Then just who are you?"

I felt it the minute the thought came to his head. He was going to disappear on me. I could just summon him back, but he was not getting away that easily. I grabbed his arm before he could go.

He tried to pull out of my grip, but I held fast and asked, "What are you talking about?"

He suddenly seemed embarrassed, as though he'd been caught with his hand in the cookie jar. It took him a long time to talk, but I waited, rather impatiently, refusing to let him off the hook.

"My middle name is Angel. Her son's first name was Angel, and we both had the same last name: Garza. We took that as a sign that we were supposed to be brothers. I loved him more than anyone. I lived at the home with all the other outcasts." When he looked at me, the pain in his eyes swallowed me whole. "With all the other kids whose parents didn't want them. Mrs. Garza was always so nice to me. We'd pretend that she was my mom, too. I loved being at his house. I loved that she looked at me like I was any other kid. Not like a kid from the home." He turned away again. "How do you think she would look at me if she knew I was the kid who killed her son?"

Despite my determination to hold my reactions at bay, I gasped. Evangeline wanted to ask me what was happening, but she knew enough to keep quiet for the moment.

"Angel, what happened that night?"

He stuffed his hands into his pockets. "We got in a fight with a group of neighborhood kids over some ice cream bars. Angel, the other Angel, wanted to scare them. He stole his mom's car and the gun she had under her mattress and we went looking for them. I drove. I was a better driver than he was. When we found them, he started shooting, but there were kids there. Little kids. I told him to stop, but he wouldn't. Or maybe he didn't hear me. He wasn't really trying to hit them. He just wanted to scare them, but I was worried he would accidentally shoot a kid. So I wrecked the car on purpose."

I stepped to him and touched the wound on his chest. "This is a gunshot wound," I said, trying to understand. He'd told me years ago they'd struggled for the gun and it went off. He never told me the other kid died as well. He'd definitely never told me he was the other kid.

"No. I flew out of the car and landed on something sharp, like rebar. But Angel died, too. I didn't think it would be that bad. I just thought the crash would bruise us up or something. But I killed us both. I killed my brother."

"Is he still here, like you?"

"No. Angel crossed the minute he died. Went straight to heaven. I watched him go, and I figured I'd go to hell for killing him, but I never did. I was just there. I was so lost and alone until you came along."

I covered my mouth with a shaking hand. "Angel."

"And then I thought I could make it up to his mom. I figured, when you offered me a job, that I could help her out."

"So, all the aunts and uncles and cousins you tell me about?"

"They were his. Not mine. I never had anyone. I just wanted to make it up to her. To all of them."

My heart broke into a million tiny pieces. He died trying to do the right thing, and the guilt had been eating him alive all this time. "What is your real first name?"

"Juan. Juanito Ahn-hell Garza. Angel."

I pulled him into my arms. He didn't want me to. He didn't want my forgiveness. But after a moment, he broke down and cried into my hair, his shoulders shaking softly.

Together, we told Evangeline the truth.

"Your son is in heaven, where he should be," I told her, worried she would resent my making such a bold statement when she'd only wanted to talk to him.

But she didn't take the slightest bit of offense. Her face brightened after a moment. "Please tell him that I never blamed him. I knew my son, Juanito," she said, her eyes bright with emotion. "Don't you ever feel like that was your fault. We know what you did. We know you were trying to do the right thing."

Angel put a hand over his eyes.

"Angel?" I said. "Is there anything you want to say to her?"

"I always wished she was my mom."

I delivered the message to a tearful and overjoyed acceptance. "And I always wished you were my son," she said.

If ever there was a time I wished a departed could touch the living, it was now. They both could use a hug. I did the next best thing and pulled them both into my arms.

"I came here for a reason," Angel said after Evangeline left.

Even after everything, I got the impression he was still embarrassed. "Do you still want me to call you Angel?" I asked.

He nodded. "I was going by Angel, too, before I died."

"Okay. Why did you come here?"

"I found that Marika chick and her kid. They're at the Target on Lomas and Eubank buying diapers."

"Oh." I looked at my watch. "Okay, are they still there?"

"Yeah. They just got there a few minutes ago. She had some errands to run."

The departed didn't always have a good sense of time, so I hoped he was right.

I put a hand on his cheek. "I am so proud of you."

He shifted away from me, uncomfortable. "Why would you be? I told you, I killed my best friend. And I lied to you for years."

"You did not kill him, Angel. It was an accident that occurred when you were trying to do the right thing, if you'll remember. I'm proud of you whether you want me to be or not."

"Then can I see you naked now?"

"Why would I let you see me naked now?"

"Because I'm hurting inside."

I barked out a laugh. "You're going to be hurting a lot worse when I'm done with you."

He lowered his head. "I'm sorry I lied to you."

"It's okay. I lied to you, too. I never slept with Santana." Carlos Santana was his idol, so naturally I'd told him I'd had sex with him after a concert once.

"Oh, that's so wrong!"

"Dude, you've been committing identity fraud for over a decade. Don't talk to me about wrong."

"No way. That's wrong. You can't just talk about Santana like he's a piece of meat."

Oy.

20

*There should be one line at every store
for people who have their shit together.*

—TRUE FACT

I rushed over to Targé and wandered to the diaper aisle. No Marika. Or, well, no woman with a baby. Garrett had described her to me, but I'd never seen her. They were probably already gone. I had no idea how I was going to get DNA off them. The baby wouldn't be a problem. I could swab his bottle while Mommy wasn't looking. But how would I ever get hers?

This was going to get messy; I could tell.

I walked the entire store three times before giving up. I didn't want to summon Angel to help. He needed some time. Surely I could handle hunting down one mother and a baby without him. Or not. I'd missed them, or so I thought. As I headed out of the store, I spotted a dark blond woman with a baby in the store's tiny cafeteria. She was drinking a soda and reading a book as the baby nursed a bottle in his stroller.

I walked up and ordered a coffee, chancing the occasional glance over my shoulder. She was a very pretty woman, and yet for some reason not what I figured Garrett would go for. She just looked like a mom. Probably because she had a baby. Maybe that was what was throwing me. Imagining Swopes in a domestic capacity was a little more than my brain could handle.

She tucked a long strand of hair behind her ear as I sat in a booth across from her. Clearly a woman of good taste, she was reading a historical romance. I loved historical romances. And contemporary romances. And paranormal romances. And young adult romances. Pretty much anything in front of the word *romance* would do it for me.

"Is that good?" I asked her, referring to her book with a nod when she glanced at me.

"Oh, yeah, it is." She closed it and offered me a better view.

"It looks awesome. I love that genre."

She turned to her son when he cooed at her. "Me, too."

"And your baby is adorable."

A brilliant smile brightened her face. "Thank you."

I rose a couple of inches for a better view into the stroller. Garrett had been right. Her son was clearly multiracial. I wanted a better peek at his eyes and was just about to ask for one when the store manager walked over to her.

"Hey, little guy," he said, pretending to steal the boy's bottle until he laughed. Then the man turned to me, and the resemblance to Garrett Swopes was uncanny. Dark skin. Silvery eyes. "Hello," he said, tipping an invisible hat before kissing Marika on her cheek and sitting down with his family.

I called Garrett on the way home. "So, I just saw your ex and her adorable baby. Clearly you are not the father."

He was not amused. "Did you get the samples?" he asked.

"No, I did not. It's going to be a little difficult to just walk up and swab her baby's mouth. And even more awkward when I start swabbing hers. What am I going to say, Swopes? 'Excuse me while I take a DNA sample for my paranoid friend'?"

"Did you even look at him?"

"I did," I said, "and I agree. He is multiracial and has your eyes, but guess what."

"What?"

"So does her boyfriend."

"What?"

"Yep. Her boyfriend looks very much like you. As in, same skin tone, same eye color, same facial features. Do you have a brother you never told me about?"

"No."

"Well, I don't know about you, but I'd bet my bottom dollar that baby is her boyfriend's."

"Charles, you did not see the way she looked at me that day. He's mine—I know it."

If anyone could read people, it was Garrett Swopes. "Okay, what if you are right? Then what? She clearly has a thing for guys with dark skin and sexy silvery eyes."

"But what if there's more to it than that?" he asked.

"Like what?"

"I don't know, but the way she looked at me, Charles. Like she was scared to death I'd make the connection. How did she seem with him?"

"Fine. I mean they seemed tight. I didn't sense any stress coming off her when he walked up. They looked really happy, in fact."

"Something's not right. I know it. You're not off the hook."

"Seriously?" I whined. "I still have to get their DNA?"

"Yes. And sooner rather than later. Now I'm even more curious about what she was hiding."

"Maybe she was hiding the fact that she finds you paranoid and delusional."

"I don't think so. That wasn't the vibe I picked up on."

"I'm sending you a vibe right now. Are you getting it?"

"That's not nice, Charles," he said before hanging up.

I'd never had to steal someone's DNA before, but I was sure I would suck at it. He was going to have to give me a damn good reason for taking such a risk.

Before I got too close to home, my phone rang again. It was Agent Carson.

I answered excitedly. "Well?" I asked, hoping for good news.

"Meet us at the Crossroads Motel in half an hour."

"What? You're keeping her in that dive?"

"No, we're meeting you in that dive. Do you really think I'd reveal the location of the safe house?"

"Oh, okay. Never mind. I'll be there."

When I pulled up to the Crossroads, Agent Carson got out of a parked SUV. "We are risking a lot, here, Davidson. If Emily doesn't testify tomorrow morning, Phillip Brinkman walks."

"I understand," I said, pretending to be working toward the same goal, the successful prosecution of Emily's boyfriend.

We walked up the stairs to room 217. Carson used the key. I was half expecting a secret knock or a password or something. Nope. She just used the key. It was all rather anticlimactic.

As we sat around the table, Emily explained what happened through a sea of unending tears. I sat stunned, completely impressed. The girl could lie. I wondered if she'd taken any acting classes.

"He just got so mad," she said, sniffing into a tissue. "I think he forgot I was there. He was mad at one of his men and he beat him to death with a tire iron while his other men just stood around and watched. Don't get me wrong. I could tell they were very uncomfortable, wondering if they were next. Something went wrong with a shipment, he said, and he just lost it. I've— I've never seen him like that."

I fought the urge to applaud.

After using every pleading word in my repertoire, I finally convinced Agent Carson to let me speak to Emily alone. She was not happy about it, and I got the feeling Emily wasn't either.

"Look, Emily, I spoke to Phillip. I know what's really going on."

She didn't trust me. Her gaze darted to the door, toward the FBI agents on the other side of it, as though wondering if I were setting her up somehow.

"They say they have someone from my inner circle and are holding her hostage. Everyone is present and accounted for, but I can't take the risk."

"We didn't know what else to do. They will kill him, Ms. Davidson."

"I know, hon. You're very brave for doing this. For risking your life for your boyfriend."

"I love him, Charley. He's a screwup, but he's my screwup. He never thought it would come to this."

"I understand, but if it's found out that you lied under oath—"

"I'm not worried about me."

"Well, that makes one of us. Can you stall?" I asked her. "Can you just hold out, don't testify tomorrow, but don't back out. Just—" I didn't have a clue what to tell her.

"Get sick?" she asked. "Because if I'm sick, I can't testify, right?"

That was perfect, but would they buy that? "It would have to be both severe and completely believable."

One corner of her mouth twisted up into a smirk. "Trust me, it will be both. I have an excellent gag reflex."

I nodded. If her puking-on-demand skills were anything like her acting skills, she'd nail it. "Okay, if you think you can get away with it, do it. Just try very hard not to get on that stand tomorrow without recanting anything just yet. If my plan works, you won't have to testify at all, and we can tell the FBI that you had to do it. I'll try to get you out of any charges."

"I'm not worried about me," she said again, and I realized just how much she loved Brinkman. "I can handle anything they throw at me. Just get Phillip out of this. I want him alive and well. That's all I care about."

"You're a good person, Emily."

She shook her head. "No, he is. He just got in over his head, said yes to the wrong people. But he is a very good person inside."

"I understand. The wrong people can be very persuasive like that."

Now that Emily had bought me some time, surely I could get some kind of evidence on the Mendozas without endangering her or Phillip Brinkman.

"Did you find anything on that case I asked you to look into?" Agent Carson asked as she walked me to Misery.

I didn't know what to tell her. How much to reveal, considering Reyes's insistence that I stay out of it. "You said your dad thought there was something iffy about that case."

"Yes, he did."

"I think your dad had incredible instincts."

She stopped and gave me her full attention. "What did you find out?"

"I'm still working on it, but can you just check into one thing?"

"Sure."

"Can you find out more about their son now? When and where they had him?"

"Why?" she asked, suspicion knitting her brows.

"I'm not sure. I just think it's very odd that he looks absolutely nothing like either one of them."

"I'll see what I can dig up."

I'd parked across the street from the Crossroads and waited. Agent Carson left a few minutes after I did with Emily Michaels surrounded by no less than three men in suits. I appreciated that she trusted me enough to let me meet with her star witness, especially when the woman's life was in danger. But now that I'd seen Emily, I was certain I could pass for her from a distance. I just needed a blond wig and some really big sunglasses.

The way I saw it, if we took Emily out of the equation, if her testimony was no longer needed, both she and Phillip would be safe. But in order to do that, I would have to get some kind of confession on tape. Some hard-core incriminating evidence that would convince the DA he didn't need Emily's testimony, nor did he need to prosecute her for making a false statement. She was trying to save Phillip, after all. He was willing to go to prison for a very long time to get out of his life of crime. Would that hold any weight with the DA? Would he take that into consideration when charging him with money laundering for a known crime family? He would almost surely want Phillip to testify, and that was the whole point. He simply couldn't, not without placing his ex-wife and children in terrible danger. Crime bosses didn't see the world through the same eyes as the rest of the world. They saw it and everyone in it as a means to an end, the end being wealth and power.

I went to the front desk of the motel and told them I'd lost my key to room 217. Getting another one didn't take too much finagling, once I showed them my PI license. Most people had no idea it meant next to nothing in the grand scheme of things. Now I just needed to get Garrett over there to wire me up and have Reyes on standby. When Mendoza contacted me, I would be ready.

I hurried back to my apartment for supplies and to begin the initial setup of my ingenious plan. I called Cookie on the way, making sure she was ready for phase two of said plan. Once I got to my apartment, I put the battery back in my regular phone, took a seat at my kitchen table, and waited for Cookie's call.

I parked Misery across the street from the Crossroads Motel at a medical clinic and started toward the room the FBI had conveniently paid for clad in a large sweater, a blond wig, and dark sunglasses. If the Mendozas were listening when Cookie called pretending to be Special Agent Carson, or Sack, as I'd called her several times throughout the conversation, they would believe that Emily Michaels was being held in room 217.

Garrett would show up soon, dressed in a suit. He would play my FBI protector when Mendoza's men showed up. It was a dangerous role, one he'd not only agreed to but insisted upon playing. I figured if we were going to work together, he should probably get used to the idea of my being used as bait. It just worked so well so much of the time. Reyes wasn't at the restaurant when I'd called over there, and he wasn't picking up his cell, but I figured whatever situation I got myself into, I could summon him in a heartbeat. As long as I wasn't concussed or drugged or bleeding out so profusely I couldn't focus. It would probably take hours for Mendoza to gather his forces and execute a plan.

I'd just put my foot on the first rung of the stairs when a car screeched to a halt behind me. Alarm spiked and dumped adrenaline. It was too soon. I'd only just called, and Garrett wasn't there yet. But sure enough, a man got out and encouraged me rather roughly to get into the car with them.

That was how I found myself in the back of a dark sedan, wondering if they thought I was Emily or not, and wondering as well if being Emily or just plain old Charley would be more dangerous in this situation.

The plan had been to lure Mendoza's men to the hotel, capture them, then get them to turn against their boss. So far, my plan wasn't going precisely according to specs, but all hope was not lost. I still had a supernatural nigh fiancé with a hair trigger and a penchant for severing spines I could call upon should the situation demand. I could do this.

"Would you remove that ridiculous wig," a man with a heavy Mexican accent said to me. I had no idea who. My sunglasses were so dark and the windows of the sedan had been tinted, so it was impossible to see. But I could tell as the tires screeched beneath me that I was facing the wrong direction.

We were in a stretched car with two backseats facing each other when someone ripped off my wig and glasses. It was very uncalled for. I could only assume the man sitting across from me was Mendoza himself. It surprised me that he would come in person.

"That was a nice try, Ms. Davison," he said as he clipped the end of a cigar.

He wore a white suit, impeccably tailored, and yet he didn't look at home in it at all. He was overweight and wore enough gold to require an armored car service to sport him about town. He was like cheap cologne on a billionaire. He didn't belong. Everything about him screamed cliché, like he'd taken his cues from '80s movies about Colombian drug lords.

I smoothed my hair down after having half of it ripped out by one of the men on either side of me. Clearly they had never heard of bobby pins. I'd wedged that wig on, thinking it would be there awhile.

Mendoza wasn't taking any chances with me. Both his men had pistols jammed into my rib cage, and I recognized one of the guns as the one that had been pointed at my head. I glared at the man holding it. He smirked.

We took the onramp to I-25.

"You were quite the challenge, but after everything I'd heard about you, I had expected no less."

"I feel challenging," I said for the sole sake of being a smart-ass. I could afford to be. And I didn't like being manhandled against my will.

Or having pistols jammed into my sides. One bump, one reflexive squeeze, and there would be no way to dodge a bullet from a gun that close, no matter how fast I could slow time. Perhaps it was time to summon my ace in the hole. But I still didn't really have anything incriminating on him. And I never would. All the recording equipment was back at the hotel room. If I could get to my phone, I could at least record our conversation, but how I was going to manage that with Dumb and Dumber on my ass, I had no idea. Maybe if I pointed out the window and said, *Look! A bird!*

Nah, that wouldn't give me enough time. I needed a major distraction. Where was a runaway semi when I needed one? The bad guys always confessed all their sins right before they killed the good guys on TV, and I had no way of recording it.

"Still," he continued as he lit the cigar.

I crinkled my nose. I actually loved the scent of cigar smoke, but I wasn't about to let him know that.

"You led us directly to her. I never dreamed you had that kind of pull."

I stilled. Directly to her? What was he talking about?

"You must have some kind of mojo to get the FBI to set up a meet. I didn't think it could be done."

The world fell out from under me.

"You don't have enough faith in me, boss," the gorilla to my right said. The one who'd held the gun to my head.

Stunned speechless, all I could think was that I needed to warn Agent Carson. I'd led them into a trap.

"No smart-ass comeback?" Mendoza asked. "And here I thought that was your thing. Didn't you tell me that was her thing?" he asked the other gorilla.

"It's her thing. She doesn't know when to shut the fuck up. I think you surprised her."

"I think I did," he agreed. He blew out a thick puff of smoke.

My eyes watered, but not because of the smoke. What had I done?

"Unfortunately for you, we had taken measures to make sure you'd give this little mission your all. Too bad they weren't necessary. Now we have to kill everyone involved."

We were driving south and took the Broadway exit, heading toward a sparse industrial area. After a few minutes of my mind racing, trying to figure out how to get to the phone in my bag, we pulled into a closed grain elevator. It had three tall cylindrical silos and a few other outbuildings scattered across the grounds. We stopped in front of an armed guard. There were two more armed men in the shadows of the elevator.

Mendoza slid down his window. "Where is Ricardo?"

"They're all still up there, boss. We didn't know what you wanted us to do with them."

Them? My head swarmed with worry.

"That will work. Tell Burro to save his ammunition. I want to see this."

The guard laughed and spoke Spanish into a handheld radio, telling the man on the other end to hold where he was.

The gorillas led me inside to an actual elevator. Mendoza followed and we rode to the top of the silos, taking a set of stairs up to the last level. When we emerged onto the cone-shaped roof of the biggest silo, I gasped and my knees buckled beneath me. Not because of the height or the fact that the wind pushed at us, urging us to the edge, but because they had two people up there with them: Jessica Guinn and Reyes Farrow. My Reyes Farrow. It was impossible. Was he messing around? Pretending to let them take him?

Both of them were covered in their own blood. Jessica had rope burns on the sides of her mouth, and one eye sported a nasty shiner. She sat on her knees on top of the metal structure, her hands tied behind her back, the wind tossing her hair about. Fear radiated out of her so strongly, I had a hard time seeing past it. Even more than the men with guns, even more than the fact that she was tied up and held hostage, I got the distinct feeling the height scared her the most. And she was precariously close to the edge of a pitched metal structure. One strong gust, and she would go over.

Reyes was tied to a metal ladder that went to the very top of the silo. He was barely conscious. His head hung, his long arms and wide shoulders limp against the ropes that bound him. My mind could not absorb what I was seeing.

When Mendoza spotted the disbelief in my eyes, he explained. "Several of my boys were in prison with him. They know what he is capable of. Better yet, they know how to take him down."

How to take him down? Even I didn't know how to take him down. How on earth?

"Tranquilizer darts," he offered when I only shook my head in incredulity. "The kind made for elephants." He walked to Reyes and jerked his head up by his hair. My instincts bucked, and I inadvertently summoned Angel. "What would kill a normal man barely brought this one to his knees. But it was enough to disorient him. Another dart brought him down, and still it took another to keep him that way. I don't know what he is made of, but whatever he is, he can be killed."

"You don't know me as well as you thought," I said to Mendoza. "Jessica and I are not friends. Enemies would be a more applicable term."

Jessica's eyes were filled with absolute terror.

"Then you won't mind when we toss her off the roof?"

I bit down, afraid to say anything. Afraid to risk her life.

"What do I do?" Angel asked. He took hold of my arm, as if he could keep them from harming me.

I shook my head. I just didn't know, but I looked at him regardless. "I need Reyes," I said. "Can you bring him back?"

He glanced at him. "I don't know how. He's out. Whatever they gave him worked."

"I need him, Angel."

Angel nodded and stepped cautiously toward him, facing his own fears of Reyes in that instant.

After Mendoza watched my interaction with air, one of his men said, "She does that a lot."

"I like you," Mendoza said. "I'll let you choose. Which one dies and which one lives?"

My vision narrowed and I swayed in the gorillas' arms. It didn't matter whom I chose. They were going to kill us all. If I could just buy a little time. If Reyes would just snap out of it.

I swallowed and pointed to Reyes. "Him," I said, my hand and voice shaking.

Mendoza shot me a delighted look, picked up a booted foot, and gave Jessica a soft shove. I barely had time to gasp before she toppled over the side. I lunged for her, as though I could catch her, but the gorillas tackled me and held me down.

She didn't scream. I'd expected her to scream, but there was only silence. I didn't even hear her fall. I only heard the wind whipping around us, howling through the metal structure.

"Surely you're not upset," Mendoza said, the smug look on his face the incarnation of evil. "You were enemies, after all, yes? But you'll get your wish. Untie him."

I tried to scramble to my feet as they untied Reyes, but they were still holding me down. This wasn't happening. Not to Reyes. Could he survive the fall? It had to be the equivalent of seven stories. He'd survived worse. But he'd been conscious. Able to prepare, to defend himself.

Before I could say another word, two of Mendoza's men dropped his listless form over the side and he fell quietly from my sight.

21

Misery loves company,
which explains my sudden popularity.

—T-SHIRT

I watched as Reyes fell, a scream I couldn't hear wrenched from my throat as I waited for him to do something. For him to react. To save himself. It was Reyes, after all. He could do anything. He could fly or dematerialize or grab on to something on the way down like they did in the movies. But there was nothing. Just the sound of the wind howling through the abandoned building.

Angel was in shock, too. He was standing on the side, looking over, his eyes round.

"Angel," I said to get his attention.

He turned to me, his mouth a thin line of regret.

"No." I shook my head at him. It was impossible. There was just no way.

"Don't look so worried," Mendoza said. "You can join him."

He nodded to his men, and they dragged me to the side. I could see two bodies, but they didn't look real. They were small from that vantage, like mangled action figures. None of this was real.

Mendoza said something I didn't comprehend. No one could have survived that fall. Not even a supernatural being. Not even the son of Satan. He lay there, unmoving, and I could not wrap my head around it. Any of it.

"Ready?" I heard at last.

Mendoza was the kind of man who enjoyed killing. He enjoyed the false sense of power it gave him. But he also enjoyed the part right before the actual death. The torment. The taunting.

I looked at him. And I did my job. I judged him unworthy of crossing into heaven.

He didn't like the revulsion he saw in my eyes. Where he'd expected fear, he found disgust. He turned me to face the edge again, put a hand on my back, and just before he pushed, he said, "No loose ends."

I stepped forward, but the roof beneath my feet disappeared. I was over. He'd thrust me over the side just as he had Jessica. Just as they had Reyes. And we would die together.

In one final act of rebellion, I twisted around to look at them and swiped a hand through the air. In that split second between dream and reality, I'd marked their souls for the Dealer, a bright archaic symbol emblazoned on their chests. They were all his.

Then I saw Angel. He grabbed for me. When I twisted around, I'd kicked out and he caught my boot and pulled. But there was nothing he could do. I weighed too much. Little did I know the shit had a plan. My foot caught on something. A metal brace protruded out from the side of the silo, and Angel wedged my foot there. But my body kept falling until the wedge took hold. Pain shot up my leg, and my ankle very likely broke as my body slammed against the side of the silo. My skull cracked against a metal rung. I grabbed hold of it and held on for dear life.

I hung there upside down, trying to gain my bearings, staring at the top of the silo, and waiting for the men to figure out I didn't fall. They would have to shoot me now if they couldn't reach to dislodge my foot. When they didn't appear immediately, I took another long look at the ground beneath my dangling body. Reyes hadn't moved. He hadn't flinched at all. A wave of grief overtook me, and tears fell up my face to mingle with the blood flowing there. I looked at my boot, wondering if I could move it a centimeter to the left with the ankle broken, just enough to dislodge it and finish the journey.

In that moment, the only thing I could think about was what it would be like to live without Reyes. It wasn't a life I wanted, and I suddenly realized how and why Emily Michaels could do what she did. How she could risk her life to protect the man she loved. Even prison was better than death, losing the ones we loved so desperately.

An agony that matched the shooting pain in my ankle consumed me so fully, I could think of nothing else but the fact that I did not want to go through life without him. I pushed on the metal bar and tried to dislodge my foot. I'd never been particularly suicidal, but I'd never been consumed with quite that much pain. Not emotionally, anyway.

"What are you doing?" Angel asked, peering over the side.

"Help me dislodge my foot," I said.

He shook his head and said, "Fuck you," right before he disappeared. Little shithead.

My teeth welded together as the pain of my busted ankle coursed through my body like electricity. Somewhere in the back of my mind, I registered the sound of fighting above me. I snapped to attention as gunshots ricocheted around me before an eerie silence thickened the air. As I fought the effects of blood rushing to my head and pain hammering into me, another dark-haired man peered at me from over the side of the building. But this time, it wasn't Angel.

"Reyes!" I shouted, reaching out to him.

"Sorry, sugar," the man said. "It's just me."

I blinked and tried to focus. The Dealer. What was he doing there? Had I summoned him when I marked the souls of Mendoza and his men? Was that even possible?

He showed his teeth and gestured over his shoulder with a nod. "Thanks for the grub, though."

I unclenched my stomach muscles and lowered my upper body to take in the horrific scene underneath me. Reyes was still unmoving. The Dealer reached down for me and grabbed hold of my pant leg, and in that moment, I honestly wanted to slip out of his grip. I considered kicking him with my other leg to loosen his hold, but he glowered and shook his head in warning.

"Uh-uh-uh. I keep telling you," he said, pulling me up as though I weighed nothing, "we need you alive. No thoughts of suicide just because that mutt of yours kicked off."

My heart contracted so fast and so strong, I felt as though a hulk made of rock had punched me in the chest. I would not survive the force of my agony. Even knowing he could still be with me incorporeally didn't help. I wanted him. I wanted Reyes Alexander Farrow in my arms, warm and solid and real.

The Dealer lowered me to the roof carefully, and a jolt of pain shot through me the second my toes touched down. My right leg collapsed, and the Dealer tightened his hold to keep me from falling. I bit down, pushed off him, and tried to rush to the access door for the elevator, but I just couldn't support my own weight. I stumbled before I took two steps. He caught me. That was when I noticed the bodies on the roof.

The Dealer shrugged. "I think after throwing those two off the roof and trying to throw you off, they got into an argument and killed each other. Who would've thought they'd do such a thing?"

"Works for me," I said, glaring at Mendoza's corpse. "Please, take me down."

He cradled me in his arms and carried me down the stairs to the elevator.

Holding me close, he said, "We need you alive, sugar. No more thoughts of joining the mutt, *capisce?*"

The Dealer's words dislodged the sobs I was holding on to, and I cried and screamed and railed against him. He pulled me tighter, and I felt true empathy radiate off him. Who would've thought a demon, a Daeva, could feel empathy?

When we got to the ground, the men there were dead, as well. "You could've marked their souls," the Dealer said as he walked where I pointed, right up to Reyes's body.

I scrambled out of the Dealer's hold and fell beside Reyes. He looked perfect. He had blood from being beaten, but otherwise, he looked perfect. Serene. His long lashes lay against his cheeks. I felt for a pulse at his neck. Waited. Repositioned my fingers and waited again. Nothing.

"Reyes," I said, urging him to open his eyes. "Reyes, please."

The Dealer put a hand on my shoulder and tried to coax me off him. I'd draped my body over his and was running my fingers gingerly over his face.

The Dealer's grip tightened at the same time I felt a presence. I looked up and watched as a darkness pooled near Reyes's body. It lifted and molded itself into the shape that resembled a human, but its proportions weren't quite right. Only after it had fully formed did I realize it was Reyes, but only partly so. His demon side had emerged. He was massive and towered above us as the Dealer moved between us.

I struggled to my knees as Artemis appeared beside me, her guttural snarls echoing around us. I held her to me as the Dealer slowly slid out the dagger from his boot. Every time he made a move, Reyes growled, his black gaze moving from me to Artemis to the Dealer. Every time it landed on me, it took everything in me to hold Artemis back. She didn't recognize him, the man she'd been sleeping with for the last couple of weeks.

He had all of Reyes's stark beauty, his fluid lines and smooth textures; only his eyes were deeper and blacker, and he had razor-sharp teeth, like the demons I'd seen. Was this what happened when his physical body died? Was this what all the warnings had been about?

Slowly, and with infinite care, the Dealer passed me the knife. "Kill him," he said, his voice soft, unhurried. "Or everyone dies." He turned back to me. "He'll destroy the world, sugar. And everything in it."

Rocket's premonition hit me hard. He'd said I would be the one to kill him. He'd warned me that there was nothing I could do to stop it, not without dire consequences. Was that what he meant? Would my not killing him mean the destruction of the world?

Before I could think on it much longer, Reyes knocked the Dealer aside and lunged for me. I slowed time, holding back both Artemis and the Dealer, who was already charging Reyes. I stood and marveled at the Dealer and Artemis. Even though I was holding back time, they were still charging forward, their essences a blur, they were so fast. But I was faster.

I stepped to Reyes, who was also a blur, and placed a hand on his handsome face. Even part demon, he was stunning, more dark and enigmatic than before. When he shook off my hand and gained precious inches, his teeth opening to rip into my jugular, I placed the knife at his heart and pushed, barely breaking the skin.

He stopped. Looked down at the blade. Back up at me. And recognition shone on his face. The knife was already spreading the poison that only a demon could feel. A blackness crept around the insertion point and began to spread, but his attention was fixed on me.

The demon side of him dissolved, and Reyes reemerged. He stumbled back and shook his head as though trying to shake out of the stupor he'd been in. I let time crash back and held Artemis to me to stop her from attacking. The Dealer realized what I'd done and stopped his advance as well. But when time bounced back like a train crashing through me, so did the pain. My knees buckled, and I fell back onto Reyes's body, but I did not take my eyes off his incorporeal essence. He fell to his knees, shook his head once more, then dropped it into his hands, trying to get his bearings.

"Come back to me," I whispered to him. I ordered him. "Rey'aziel, come back to me."

His gaze shot to mine, and he did as I'd asked. He came back.

Then he was in front of me, but Artemis had calmed down. When he touched my face, she whimpered and nudged his hand with her nose. He gave her a quick caress.

I'd looked down, my brows sliding together in confusion. "Come back to me," I ordered again.

He was grinning when I looked up again. "You have to kiss me, like in all of your fairy tales."

"Kiss you?" I questioned.

"First you have to say yes, then you have to kiss me."

I heard sirens in the distance and wondered who'd called the police. "I have to say yes?"

He sat beside me and nodded.

"And what am I agreeing to?"

"It's a simple yes/no question, Dutch."

His proposal. "You're blackmailing me." I couldn't help but feel appalled. And a little flattered.

He shrugged. "If that's what it takes, okay."

I looked down at his face, bloodied and bruised, but still so impossibly handsome, my heart ached. "Yes," I said, realizing how silly I'd been to make him wait for the answer I'd always known in my heart I would give. I could not live without him. It would be like expecting a sunflower to live without the sun. Without further ado, I placed my mouth on his.

He sucked in a soft breath from under my mouth. I leaned back. His incorporeal body was back where it belonged. "You look like heaven," he said.

"That's weird, because you look like hell."

He laughed, then winced in pain.

"Are you really okay?" I asked.

"He's fine," the Dealer said as though disappointed.

Then I heard another voice. A female voice. One with a distinct nasally quality to it.

"Well?" she asked, standing beside me and tapping her bare toes in the dirt next to me. "What are you going to do about this?"

I looked over at her body, an all-consuming dread coming over me. No way. No way in hell was I going to put up with that witch for the rest of my life.

"Cry?" I asked.

"I'm dead, aren't I?"

"Pretty much."

"This is your fault."

The sirens were getting closer. How was I going to explain all this?

"Jessica, look," I said, trying to rush her, "you have to cross. I can't do this with you."

"Cross? Through you?" She sneered at me. "I would rather die."

I started to point out the obvious, but she disappeared before I got another word out. Being haunted by a former best friend turned enemy number one was so going to suck like Tornado Alley in April.

I glanced up at the Dealer. He stood with arms over chest, his top hat perched to one side. "Mr. Joyce's soul," I said, reminding him that we had yet to settle a certain bargain.

He lifted first a shoulder, then one corner of his mouth, then the brim of his hat in a silent salute. "It's all his."

Relief washed over me, but it was short-lived, as a line of official vehicles raced toward us. Agent Carson led three other SUVs onto the scene. It had bullet holes in it when it swerved to a stop, covering me in dust. Her questionable act provided the perfect cover for me to quickly stash the knife, sliding it into the boot of my nonbroken ankle before the dust settled around us.

When she stepped out, I flattened the leg of my jeans and said, "You totally did that on purpose."

Her men bolted from the vehicles, and she rushed over to me as Reyes eased up. Someone told him to stay put, but he rose to his feet anyway. So stubborn.

"Carson," I said after she checked for a pulse on Jessica's throat.

I couldn't look at her. It had been a long, long drop, and it showed. I glanced around. The Dealer was gone, of course.

"There are more on the roof," I added as an agent helped me to my feet. I balanced on one foot to keep my weight off the broken one. It would heal in a few days. A cast would only annoy me, so I didn't let the extent of my injuries show. "I heard gunshots after I escaped them."

Agent Carson barked a few orders, sending men into the elevators before giving me her attention. "I suppose you have an explanation." She looked at me first, then Reyes, then back at me.

I pulled my lower lip between my teeth and shrugged. "I'm still working on it."

A plethora of cop cars were speeding onto the site, lights flashing and sirens blazing.

"Well, hurry," she said, ordering another of her men to guide them. "We've been tailing you, worried something like this might happen."

Reyes pulled me to his side, expertly taking my weight with skilled nonchalance. "Then you're late," he said, seeming annoyed.

Uncle Bob showed up then, as did the captain, and I wondered what it would be like to have him on our team. Would it be nice for Ubie to have someone to talk to? He used to talk at great length with my dad, but their relationship seemed to be cooling a little, much to my despair.

Maybe having the captain in on the whole departed thing would be good for him.

He rushed over, but before he could say anything, Reyes lifted me into his arms and carried me toward Ubie's SUV. No one seemed particularly alarmed that Reyes looked like he'd just fallen from a seven-story grain elevator. His clothes did, anyway. His dark skin was unmarred, flawless, and whether that was a result of our kiss or just his natural ability to heal at the speed of light, I didn't know.

"I'm assuming you have everything you need for the moment," Reyes said to Carson.

She started to protest, but one look at the determined expression on Reyes's face convinced her otherwise. "I'll need both of your statements first thing—"

"She needs to get home," he said to Uncle Bob, his tone brooking no argument.

Ubie nodded, offered another quick nod to Agent Carson, then walked over to open the door for Reyes, who he sat me inside, his movements gentle, unhurried. His profile was so strong, so amazingly perfect, it was hard not to stare. I wondered if I would ever get used to his exquisiteness. To his blinding perfection. Prolly not.

"Yes," I said, repeating my answer in case he didn't hear me the first time.

Despite the time lag, a charming set of dimples appeared at the corners of his full mouth. "You already said that."

"I know. I just wanted to make sure you heard me."

"Just remember that feeling a moment."

"Why?" I asked suspiciously.

He didn't answer. Instead, he motioned Ubie over to us.

"Would you mind obstructing the view?" Reyes asked him. Ubie's brows slid together in concern, so he explained. "She is going to start healing immediately. This has to be set."

I gasped when I realized he was talking about my ankle. It felt engulfed in flames, but it was nothing I hadn't been through before. Still, the thought of Reyes setting it—of it being set at all—filled me with terror.

Uncle Bob nodded and shifted his weight until his body was blocking the view of the officers on-site.

I gripped Reyes's arm, clawing at him as he slid off my boot. He almost brought me out of my seat as Ubie peeled off one hand and took it into his. After studying my lower extremities, a feat I couldn't bring myself to do, Reyes glanced back at me, his deep mahogany eyes sympathetic when he said, "Bite down."

Fear spiked like a nuclear explosion in my head. "Maybe we should—"

A sharp pop sounded in the small space, and the pain that shot through me evoked a gasp loud enough to turn the heads of those around us. Reyes's arms were around me instantly, and I clutched on to him, buried a scream in his shoulder as the pain—a pain that had risen so high and so fast, I'd almost passed out—ebbed. When it reached a level tolerable enough for me to trust myself not to cry out in agony, I eased my hold. Only then did I realize Uncle Bob still had my hand, his thick fingers engulfing mine until all that was visible were my fingertips.

22

*On a scale of one to stepping on a LEGO,
how much pain are you in?*

—SIGN IN HOSPITAL

Two days after the incident that would come to be known around the world, or at least around the office, as the Great Silo Tragedy, I quite bitterly hobbled to the entrance of the New Mexico Women's Correctional Facility, crutch in one hand, case file in the other. Cookie had managed to track down what happened to Miranda. She got a copy of the case file. It explained what had happened to her, why she'd chosen to haunt a cable car, and what became of her abusive mother.

I had a funeral to get to later in the day, but this morning was set aside for one woman and one woman only: Miranda's mother. The woman who had abused her daughter so severely, the girl could not escape the mental repercussions even in death.

I needed to know. What she did to her daughter was unconscionable. I needed to know if she felt remorse of any kind. If she took responsibility for what she'd done. If she knew how severely her actions had affected her gorgeous child. If she cared. How anyone could do such a thing was far beyond my realm of understanding. Did it take a socio-path? Or simply an utter bitch?

I pulled some strings, namely the one I had wrapped around Uncle Bob, and had him call the women's detention center to set up an interview. He told them I was a consultant working on a case for APD and needed to question Mrs. Nelms about an old case. Which would explain why I was sitting in front of a large pane of glass, waiting for Miranda's mother to arrive.

She was in prison, thankfully, for her daughter's death, but she'd never admitted to any wrongdoing. The court transcripts showed that she'd professed her innocence even after a jury of her peers had convicted her. Even after a judge had sentenced her to fifteen years in prison. She'd prob-ably be out on parole in a couple more years. If she failed my test, I'd be waiting.

A large woman stepped into the room. I was surprised. In the mug shot from her arrest record, Mrs. Nelms was painfully thin, the lines of her face hard and cracked like the plains of an unforgiving desert. She'd gained weight while in the big house and cut her horrendously bleached-out hair. She now wore it short and didn't look so much like a crack addict as the stalwart matriarch of a Russian girls' school. Neither look was appealing.

She sat in front of me, her regard curious as she picked up the phone. I did the same and, wanting a clean, unobstructed read off her, said one word only.

"Miranda."

Outwardly, she blinked and waited for me to get to my point. In-wardly, her defenses rose. Her pulse quickened. Her muscles tensed.

"Did you kill her?" I continued.

She pressed her lips together so hard, they turned white. When she finally spoke, it was with a vehemence I hadn't expected. "I did not kill Miranda."

I forced myself to be still as a wave of shock rushed through me. She wasn't lying. Not completely. But I knew from Miranda's crossing she had been horribly and unforgivingly abused by this woman. I went over the case file in my mind. They'd found Miranda's body in the Sandia Mountains, almost directly under the path of the tram. She was too decomposed when they found her to determine an exact cause of death, but the evidence pointed most strongly to blunt force trauma to the head. She had two cracks in her skull. Either could have caused a subdural hematoma. Either could have caused her death. She also had ligature marks on her ankles and wrists and multiple discolorations along her skin suggesting massive amounts of bruising.

That certainly wasn't enough to convict Mrs. Nelms. In fact, it would almost point to the opposite. Anyone could have taken Miranda. Anyone could have tied her up and killed her. But the prosecution had proved that Mrs. Nelms lied about how long Miranda had been missing. She'd reported her daughter missing two weeks before they found her body, but forensics showed she'd been in the wilderness at least a month. The fact that the timelines didn't match up combined with other circumstantial evidence, like the multiple fractures and repeated visits to the emergency room over Miranda's short life, was enough for a jury to find her guilty of a lesser charge of gross child endangerment resulting in death. The prosecution, knowing they probably couldn't get much more, settled for that.

"I had nothing to do with her death," she added. Though there was a boatload of resentment, there wasn't the slightest spark of guilt in her eyes. How was that possible? I'd felt it from Miranda. Sensed it when she crossed. This woman had caused her death. She had to have.

I leaned forward, more determined than ever to get to the bottom of Miranda's passing. "Then who did?"

"Is this why you came here? To question me on my case? The guards said it was for another case. I just figured it was about my son."

"Marcus? Is he in trouble?"

She glared at me, making it very clear she had nothing else to say.

Perhaps she was a sociopath, and the reason I felt no guilt off her was because she simply felt none. But she'd reacted when I mentioned Marcus's name. She'd flinched, the movement quick, almost invisible. And a wave of emotion sprang out of her. It wasn't what I'd expected. If I didn't know better, I'd say it was fear. The kind of fear that materialized when one had done something bad and didn't want anyone else to find out about it. Not that I had any experience in that area.

I suddenly had someplace else to be.

"Fine," I said, placing my elbows on the desk in front of me, "you may or may not have been directly responsible for Miranda's death, but you damn sure contributed. She's in a better place, a place where monsters like you can never harm her again."

Mrs. Nelms schooled her expression, refusing to say more. It didn't matter. I had what I'd come for. What I needed to see. She had zero remorse for what she'd done. Whether she killed her daughter or not, she was a monster, and I intended to make sure she burned in hell for what she'd done.

Just in case someone in the future dropped the ball and she got sent in the wrong direction after she died, I put my hand on the glass, relaxed my muscles, cleared my mind, and stepped back onto another plane. I'd been here before. I'd seen Reyes's eternal fire from this plane. I'd seen the flames that licked across his skin, that caressed every inch of him. And from this plane, I could see the true nature of the woman sitting before me. I could see her soul, cold and dark and empty like a giant chasm.

I swept my hand between us, brushing my fingertips along the glass partition, sweeping my essence across to her, and marked her soul. As I sat there, an energy took shape in the blackness within her. I had seen it before on Reyes. Not on his soul, but imprinted on his skin. It was part of the map to hell, a part of his tattoos, and I knew I'd sent Mrs. Nelms's soul to the right place.

I grinned and spoke into the receiver, my tone matter-of-fact, and somehow she knew I was telling the truth. I could feel her acceptance of each word that left my mouth as I said them. "You will suffer in hell for a very, very long time."

Fear spiked within her. She sat stunned a moment, then slammed down the receiver and stood to leave. I offered her a quick wink, then did the same. I had places to be and people to see.

The moment I got back into Misery, I called Cookie. "I need an address," I said when she answered. "Marcus Nelms. I need to know where he is right now."

I exited off I-40 at Moriarty, a small town about thirty minutes east of Albuquerque, and headed straight down Central. Marcus Nelms would be in his very early twenties. Cookie said he'd been in and out of jail since he was twelve for various offenses, but mainly possession of a controlled substance. After a few twists and turns that led me to a small mobile home park, I pulled to a stop in front of one just as my phone alerted me to a text. Cookie sent me Marcus's latest mug shot. He was a nice-looking kid who'd already led a hard life.

I stepped out and walked through milk- and ragweed until I got to a wobbly set of stairs and, after taking my life into my own hands, the front door. With no vehicle out front and no lights on inside, no one appeared to be home, but I knocked anyway. After my third and most aggressive try, I felt annoyance through the paper-thin walls of the mobile a few seconds before the door inched open.

A set of dark eyes peered through the slit. It belonged to one Mr. Marcus Nelms. I showed him my PI license to make myself seem more official, then asked, "Mr. Nelms, can I talk to you about a case I'm working on?"

"I'm busy," he said, his voice deep and groggy. I'd clearly woken him.

"Marcus," I said, trying to connect, "my name is Charley Davidson. I'm a PI. You're not in any trouble at all. I just need to ask you a couple of quick questions, then I'll leave. Can I come in?"

He hesitated, then released a loud sigh and opened the door. He stood shirtless, his jeans fitting low on his hips, revealing the fact that he'd decided to go commando underneath them. He was too thin, his unhealthy skin revealing long-term drug use, and his hair hadn't been washed in at least a week, though he didn't smell bad. I stepped inside the dark living room as he turned on a single lamp. It illuminated the place just enough for me to make my way to a rickety recliner.

I took a moment to absorb what I could, to get a better understanding of him. The frigidity I'd felt with his mother wasn't there. He wasn't all warm and fuzzy inside, but he wasn't cold. Calculating. He was . . . vulnerable.

"What's this about?" he asked as he cracked open an energy drink and took a large gulp. His Adam's apple rose and fell, his lack of fat tissue making it easily visible. He dropped onto the only other chair in the room, another rickety recliner, only with a little more stuffing than mine. After crossing his bare feet on the milk crate he was using as a coffee table, he gave me his full attention.

"Do you have roommates?" I asked, looking behind me, not wanting to be caught off guard.

"Not at the moment. My girlfriend left me a couple weeks ago." He peered into the top of the can. "Said I had commitment issues. Johnny send you?"

He took another long swig, so I figured I'd get right to the point. "I don't know who Johnny is, but I wanted to ask you about your mother."

He stopped drinking, coughed lightly, then said, "Bitch ain't my mother. You come to the wrong place if you think I'm going to answer anything about her. Ain't seen her in years, anyway."

I did feel hatred radiating out of him, but also something else. Pain. A thick, caustic pain that seared the back of my throat when I breathed in. Either that or he had a meth lab in the back and I was breathing in the toxic fumes. That would suck.

He looked out the dirty front window, rubbing his bottom lip with his thumb.

I waited a heartbeat, gave his emotions time to level out, then went for the jugular. "She says she didn't kill Miranda."

What hit me next felt like a fist in my gut, but he hadn't moved. I fought the urge to double over, his pain was so powerful, so suffocating. Yet he hadn't moved. His expression hadn't changed.

"She's a liar" was all he said.

"I believe you. I was just wondering if you could tell me what you remember about the time Miranda disappeared. It would really help my case."

"And what case would that be?" he asked. He turned a heated scowl on me. "She's in prison. What else is there?"

"There's justice for Miranda," I said, but it did no good. He was already deflecting, looking me up and down like I was his next meal, even though I felt very little interest emanating out of him. It was a ploy to change the subject. To put me on guard.

"What's your name again?"

I leaned forward as nonthreateningly as I could and spoke slowly, gauging his reaction to each word I spoke. "My name is Charley, and I would love for you to tell me what you remember about your sister."

Sister. That's when his grief, as hot and raw as if she'd died yesterday, hit me in the midsection again, and I suddenly understood why he did drugs. He was still hemorrhaging so much pain, so much guilt over his sister's death, self-medication was the only way he could deal with it. But there were better ways. I made a solemn promise right then and there to make sure he found them.

"She was missing for a month before they found her body. Do you remember what happened before she disappeared?"

He took another drink and went back to staring out the window, his jaw working under the weight of his guilt.

"Did your mother hurt her?"

He scoffed aloud before scowling at me, his eyes shimmering, a telling wetness pooling in their depths. "What makes you think I'm going to tell you a fucking thing when I didn't tell the cops shit?"

"I'm not the cops, and I'm in this for Miranda and Miranda only."

"She's dead. Ain't a fucking thing you can do about that, yeah?"

His torment was hard to see past. My own eyes were watering, too, remembering the frightened little girl in the cable car, remembering her despair, her utter hopelessness. Her belief that she had no value whatsoever. "You were a couple of years older than she was," I said. "Maybe you feel responsible somehow."

A slow, calculating smile appeared. He leaned forward, closed the distance between us until his face was in my hair, his mouth at my ear, and said, "I'm glad she's dead." His breath hitched in his chest, and it took him a moment to say more. "I wish she'd never been born."

As cruel and unusual as his words sounded, as vehemently said, they didn't mean what he would have me believe. I felt absolutely no hatred coming from him. No malice or contempt. I felt only a deep reverence and a debilitating, cutting guilt. That seemed to be going around a lot lately.

He pushed me away from him and stalked down the hall. After giving him a moment to gather myself, I followed. I could feel grief pouring out of him, so without knocking, I opened the door to a tiny bathroom. He was in a state of agony as he splashed water on his face. On the sink next to him was a bottle of prescription pills. According to his file, he'd been suicidal for years, and my guess was that those pills were a very powerful pain reliever. It took something powerful to mask that much pain.

I stepped in as he toweled off his face. "Marcus," I said as softly and as unthreateningly as I could manage, "you do realize you aren't actually responsible for her death, right?"

He granted me a flirtatious wink. "Sure."

He opened the bottle, dropped two large white painkillers into his palm, then popped them into his mouth. He swallowed, waited a moment, then sank to the floor as his guilt devoured him. It was why he'd turned to drugs in the first place. I suddenly understood all too well. He felt guilty for not helping his sister when he had the chance. He'd loved her. I could feel it course through him.

"Please tell me that bitch isn't getting out of prison anytime soon," he said.

I knelt beside him. Like his sister, he'd been taught from an early age that he had no value. No intrinsic worth.

My torso felt too tight as I inched toward him. "Can you tell me what happened, Marcus?"

"Why do you care what happened to her?" he asked. "Nobody cared. My mother only reported her missing because a neighbor started asking questions. She'd been gone more than two weeks." He looked up at me. "Can you imagine that? Two fucking weeks before she even considered calling the cops."

"Marcus," I said, putting a palm softly on his knee.

He had the towel in both hands, wringing it until his knuckles turned white. Dredging up the memories was taking its toll on him. He took the bottle off the sink and tilted it at his mouth, swallowing at least one more before setting it aside and covering his eyes with one hand. "We'd been evicted and were living in my aunt's house while she tried to sell it. She married some rich guy from California and said we could stay there until it sold."

That explained why Miranda was in that part of the city. The property around where she'd been found was upscale, and Mrs. Nelms didn't strike me as ever having money.

"Something wasn't right," he continued. His hand clenched around the towel. "She was acting different. She kept saying she wanted her sister's house but couldn't afford it—then this man in a business suit came over and I heard them talking. My mom was buying life insurance on us." He lowered his hand to look at me.

The bathroom had more light, and I could finally make out the color of his eyes. They were hazel green.

"She was going to kill Miranda. I knew it. From then on, every time she looked at her, she had this smile." He wiped at his cheeks. "No, this smirk. And she started talking to me about everything we were going to do with the house. She wanted a pool and a wet bar and a big TV. She said if her sister could have nice things, so could she. Then one night, she came into our room. Told us to get dressed. Said we were going to the lake. It was the middle of the night in the middle of January, but she wanted to go to the lake." His gaze slid past me. "She was going to kill her."

I sat as still as I could and listened. He needed to tell the story. Miranda's story.

"But we weren't packing fast enough, and she hit Miranda. Hard. I just remember blood. So, she told me to forget the lake, that she was going to take her to the hospital, but I knew that was a lie, too. I took Miranda and snuck out the back door. We were just going to hide until morning, until I could get help, but it was so cold. We didn't have our jackets. And it was so dark. We stumbled around, just trying to find somewhere to get warm when it started to snow. Miranda said she couldn't go any farther, so we huddled next to a rock." Fresh tears pushed past his lashes and streamed over his sunken cheeks. "She fell asleep in my arms and didn't wake up." He covered his face and bit back the sobs fighting to get past his closed throat. "I tried to carry her, but she was so heavy. I just left her there. Like she was nothing." A sob finally wrenched its way past his efforts, and he covered his face again.

"No," I argued. "Marcus, you were only nine." I swallowed past the lump in my throat and reached up to cradle the back of his head.

"I finally found my way back to my aunt's house the next day. Mom didn't even ask where we were." He cast me an astonished glare. "She didn't even ask about Miranda. Not once. Days passed, and we just never talked about her."

I bit my bottom lip, wondered what my chances were of getting the rest of the pills away from him. He tipped the bottle again, and I realized he had no intention of leaving that bathroom. Ever.

"And then a neighbor asked about Miranda?" I said, inching closer.

"Yeah. She figured she couldn't hide her disappearance much longer. She had to report her missing. That's when she told me to lie. To say Miranda was in her bed the night before and then was just gone the next morning."

I didn't dare blame him for lying. He was living with a monster. He clearly feared for his own life. But at the moment, I was more afraid for his life than he was. The drugs were taking the desired effect. He leaned his head back and let them swallow him whole.

I took advantage of the situation and reached for the bottle.

"Please, don't," he said. He seemed tired. Spent. "You won't succeed." A sadness settled over him as he picked up the bottle again. "It's okay. No one will miss me."

"You're wrong."

His laughter felt hopeless in the tiny room. Humorless. "Don't worry. This isn't some pathetic attempt to pretend to try to commit suicide only to make sure someone is close enough to call an ambulance in the nick of time." He held up the bottle, shook it to prove to me there was still one left. "This is my own version of Russian roulette."

"I don't understand."

"In the center of one of these pills, and I have no idea which one, is a lethal dose of cyanide. So I take one every so often."

I gasped and ripped the bottle out of his hand to check the label. Oxycodone. But I had no idea if that was what was really in there or not. I looked back up, gaping. He wasn't lying.

"The way I see it, if I'm worthy of living, I won't get the lethal one. If not . . ." He shrugged and leaned his head back again.

I patted my pants, but my phone was in my bag in the living room.

"You should leave," he said, the sad smile back on his face. "This is long overdue."

23

Bad decisions make good stories.
—T-SHIRT

Cookie and I stood along the outer edges of a small funeral procession clad in its best mourning attire. I was glad she'd come with me. The thickness of grief that surrounded us, the oppressive weight of it, made it difficult to breathe. And my ankle hurt.

Normally, I could shut down the part of myself that absorbed emotion, that siphoned it off the people around me like others siphoned vitamin D from the sun. Otherwise, I would be bombarded with the drama of everyday life nonstop. It took energy, but raising the wall was almost automatic now. I did it quite often before I even left my apartment in the mornings.

But here at the funeral of a beautiful three-year-old girl whose love for her two fathers lingered on the air still, my defense mechanism didn't work. I could only hope Jessica's funeral would not be as painful, as I had that one to look forward to.

Thankfully, I wouldn't have to attend the funeral of Marcus Nelms that week. I'd called 911, told them about the cyanide. They pumped his stomach, but according to the doctor on staff, even though they'd gotten there in time to prevent an oxycodone overdose, the cyanide would have killed him almost instantly regardless. The authorities checked, and the one laced with the lethal poison was the only one left in the bottle. And I suddenly believed in miracles.

Marcus would need a lot of help, and I planned to make sure he got it. I'd already talked to my friend Noni Bachicha. Noni offered to not only hire Marcus at the body shop but also to keep a very close eye on him and let me know how he was faring. Noni's support, along with the free counseling I'd talked my sister into providing, gave me hope that we could get Marcus out of the lifestyle he'd been living and into bigger and better things. He clearly had a huge heart. He so very much deserved another chance at life. Clearly someone else agreed.

Sadly, not everyone was granted a miracle. I had to focus on making it through the funeral without breaking down. The emotion radiating out of the friends and family of Isabel Joyce was strong. It came at me from all directions. I felt dizzy as we stepped forward in line to offer our condolences to the two grieving men. Isabel's fathers loved her so deeply, walking toward them through their grief was like pushing against a brick wall.

Seeming to sense my distress, Cookie took my arm in hers and inched forward. Attendants hugged the men, their sympathy sincere, their loss like gaping holes in their chests. Cookie sniffed and took the hand of Mr. Joyce's husband, Paul. He was a big man with a warm face and firm handshake, as I found out when it was my turn. Fortunately, he didn't ask how we knew his beautiful daughter. Cookie and I had come up with a cover story, but so far, we hadn't had to use it.

"Thank you for coming," he said, his red-rimmed eyes watering in the process. I could feel the suffocating agony he held at bay. Forcing the words out, any words out, was torture for him. He just wanted to go home and mourn, and my heart ached in response. I wanted to tell him that all the ceremonial stuff would be over soon, and he and his husband could grieve, and heal, together, but it was not the time or the place. Isabel's friends and family had come to pay their respects. To diminish that would be doing her an injustice.

Cookie squeezed my arm, and I realized I was still holding on to the man's hand. He didn't seem to notice. He was fighting tooth and nail to stay vertical. To keep from crumbling to the ground. Mr. Joyce's arm tightened around his husband's shoulders as they took a moment to let the sobs overtake them.

It was then that Mr. Joyce realized who stood in front of them. He glanced at his partner, worry flashing in his expression before settling his own red-rimmed gaze on me. I took his hand, leaned in, and whispered to him, "You'll be with her again. Your soul is all yours. Don't lose it again."

When I tried to pull back, he held me to him, buried his face in my shoulder as a fresh round of sobs engulfed him. I wrapped a hand around the back of his neck and fought for control over my own emotions. I hated funerals. I hated any rite of passage that emphasized how fleeting and fragile our physical lives were. I hated that children died. Even knowing what I knew about life and the afterlife and the momentary condition of our existence on earth, I hated it. It was better on the other side. I knew that. I'd been told by countless departed, but I hated this part nonetheless.

And just for the record, telling the living how their loved ones were in a better place rarely helped. Nothing helped apart from time, and even then, the long-term prognosis was sketchy. Most recovered. Many did not. Not really. Not fully.

After the funeral, I had one more errand to run before I could take the evening off to elevate my throbbing ankle. I felt a scalding hot bubble bath was long overdue. Combine that with a little candlelight, a glass of sparkling wine, and a real-life fiancé named Reyes, and I might have a wonderful evening. Only the fiancé named Reyes was still recovering from his fall. I had no idea how extensive the damage was as I'd fallen asleep the moment we got home, but having him so close to me, his heat permeating the sheets, enveloping me in a heavenly and healing warmth, sent me into a deep slumber. He was gone when I woke up that morning, his freshly showered scent bathing the area, making me crave at least a glimpse of him, but I'd been running late for the funeral, so I didn't get a chance to go to the bar before I left.

And seeing him would have to wait a little while longer. I pulled Misery to a stop in front of Rocket's place. The abandoned mental asylum had been cleaned, the grounds cleared, and a sparkling new chain-link fence bordered the entire area. I took out my key and glanced over at Cookie.

"Are you ready for this?" I asked her. She'd never met Rocket or his sister, Blue. Nor had she been introduced to Officer Taft's sister, Rebecca—or Strawberry Shortcake, as I liked to call her, mostly because she'd died in Strawberry Shortcake pajamas, but partly because calling her Strawberry was safer than calling her the plethora of other names that surfaced every time I saw her. She was a handful. And she had issues.

Cookie was gazing wide-eyed at the building. She nodded, then turned toward me, biting her lower lip, her nerves getting the better of her. "You'll have to interpret."

"I promise," I said.

After managing our way through the locked gate and the locks on the main entrance, we stepped inside cautiously. Cookie was cautious because she wasn't super fond of abandoned mental asylums. Especially haunted ones. I was cautious because the last time I'd seen Rocket, I wasn't very nice to him. He'd told me Reyes was going to die. I didn't

take it well. In fact, it was a fairly low point in my life, if one could measure low points by how many times one threatened to rip five-year-old
girls—namely, Rocket's sister, Blue—to shreds.

I cringed when I thought of it. Cookie noticed as I hobbled along
beside her. While the outside had been cleared and maintained to perfection, the inside was still in a state of chaotic ruin. Bits of the crumbling
plaster cluttered the floor, along with trash and other paraphernalia that
had been left throughout the years. Many a partier had celebrated life
here. Along with Rocket's scribbling and scratches was all kinds of evidence of how many times the place had been broken into. Spray paint on
the walls. Empty beer bottles and soda cans. The occasional used con-
dom, which evoked a gag reflex every time I saw one. This place needed
a good scrubbing.

"Has he ever been angry with you?" Cookie asked, referring to how
I'd left things with Rocket.

"No, but he should be now. If he's not, I'll feel worse than I already
do."

"So, you deserve his wrath, is that what you're saying?"

"Yep."

Before she could argue, a young, high-pitched voice echoed throughout the halls. I winced at the sound of it. It had a certain je ne sais quoi
nails-on-chalkboard quality that one didn't find every day.

"Just where on God's green earth have you been?" Strawberry appeared
before me, her long hair hanging in tangles around her pretty face. Her
pajamas had gotten soiled when she drowned, but they were still pink and
cute and sweet. Unlike, say, Strawberry.

I hesitated. She'd been there during my lesser moment, and I didn't
know if she was still mad at me or not. The departed could hold a grudge
like nobody's business.

"Hey, kid," I said at last.

In my periphery, Cookie was looking where I was, even though I knew she couldn't see the beautiful girl standing in our path. She was such a good egg, and way more handy than a crutch. This way I could lean my weight on her and not have to worry about dragging around a huge piece of metal. And Cookie finally got to see Rocket's place. It was a win–win.

"Well?" Strawberry asked. "Where have you been? He's very upset."

"Is he mad at me?"

She crossed her tiny arms over her chest. "He won't stop, and he has work to do. He's very behind."

Rocket's work, if one could call it that, was carving into the plastered walls of the asylum the names of all those who pass, which contributed greatly to their crumbling and dilapidation. Thousands upon thousands of names lined almost every inch of the interior of the asylum, a fact that Cookie was just noticing. She made a slow circle, taking in the décor. I had to reposition my hand over her arms and shoulders to keep my footing as she circled. It was quite awkward when I grabbed hold of one of her girls, but she didn't seem to mind.

"This place is incredible," she said.

"Isn't it?"

"It's just so creepy and yet cool at the same time."

"Right?"

Strawberry jammed her fists onto her slim hips. "Well?" she repeated. When Cookie took my arm into hers again, I refocused on Strawberry. "He won't stop what, honey?"

Her chin raised a notch. "I can't tell you."

I was getting used to this beguiling creature, much as I hated to admit it, and I asked, "Can you show me, then?"

One shoulder lifted and her attention flitted to Cookie as though just noticing her. "Who is that?"

"Oh, I'm sorry. This is Cookie. Cookie, this is—"

"Her name is Cookie?"

"Yes, and it's not nice to interrupt."

The corners of her eyes crinkled as she studied my BFF. "I like her."

"I like her, too. Can you show me what Rocket has been up to?"

After another one-shouldered shrug, Strawberry led the way, asking Cookie question after question. I held a flashlight and interpreted as we made our way through the perilous halls. By the time we found Rocket, Strawberry knew just about everything there was to know about Cookie, including the fact that she had a daughter. Strawberry wanted to meet her immediately and made me promise to bring her to see them.

We rounded yet another corner, which led to the infirmary, and found Rocket standing against a wall, scribbling another name into it. Rocket was like a human version of the Pillsbury Doughboy. He towered a solid foot over my head when we stood toe to toe, and he had kind, inquisitive eyes that never quite registered what was going on around him.

"He's very behind," Strawberry repeated, pointing to the wall he'd been carving up. But I wasn't concerned about the names on his list. I was concerned about him. About how I'd left things between us. I wouldn't blame him if he never spoke to me again. At least Reyes had bought this place for me, so I could keep Rocket and his sister safe here. While he was incorporeal, the property damage he did was quite corporeal. If this place was ever torn down, I didn't know where he would go.

"Rocket?" I said, inching toward him. He paused and glanced at the floor before continuing with what he was doing. He held a piece of broken glass in his left hand, scoring the wall with it until his scratching resembled a letter of the alphabet, only not ours, not English. I didn't pay much attention as I glanced around for a sign of his sister. It had taken me years to get a glimpse of her, and I'd scared the life out of her—so to speak—during my last visit. I would probably never see her again.

Though he was very aware of my presence, he continued working.

I let go of Cookie's arm and stepped closer. "Rocket, I'm so sorry about how I behaved. I had no right to get mad at you or to threaten your sister. I have no excuse."

"That's okay, Miss Charlotte," he said, keeping his gaze averted. "But he shouldn't be here."

He was talking about Reyes. "He died yesterday," I said. "And he came back. Was that why you wrote his name on the wall?"

"He's very behind. People are crossing over to the other side, and he's not writing their names down."

"Strawberry, he's working like crazy. See all those names?" I asked, pointing to Rocket's artwork.

"No," she said, growing frustrated. "Those aren't people who have died. Those are people who are going to die."

I blinked in realization. We were in the room he was saving. The only room that, until recently, had pristine walls. Not a scratch on them. Not a single name had marred their surfaces. He'd told me once that he was saving these walls for the end of the world. For when Reyes was going to end the world if I kept him here on earth with us. He'd told me his being here was breaking the rules. It went against the natural order of things.

Rocket spoke over his shoulder. "I told you not to bring him back, Miss Charlotte."

I stepped away from him for a better view. Strawberry was right. These were all new names, all new carvings. "I don't understand," I said to him.

He stopped scribbling at last and turned toward me. When he spoke, his words were a mere whisper echoing in the large chamber. "I told you, he's not supposed to be here. He's breaking the rules." He put an index finger to his mouth as though to shush me. "No breaking rules, Miss Charlotte."

"Who are these people, Rocket?" I asked, stepping forward to run my fingers along the jagged lines.

"They are the people who are going away soon."

I shook my head. "I don't understand."

"You didn't kill him. You were supposed to kill him. It wasn't your fault, but you were supposed to. Now they're all going away."

"How many people are going away?"

His mouth thinned as he scanned his work. "All of them."

"This can't happen, Rocket."

"You broke the rules, Miss Charlotte. You brought him back."

"Bullshit," I said, getting angry with Rocket again.

He took a wary step back as I drew in a deep breath, tried to keep hold of every ounce of calm I could muster. "I'm sorry, hon. I just don't understand. How is Reyes supposed to cause the deaths of all these people?"

"Not how," he said, reverting back to his old standby. "Not when, only who."

He could only tell me who died. Not how or when or why. Only who.

"No breaking rules," he said, his voice now shaky.

I narrowed my lids, the shards of anger that nipped along the edges of my psyche slicing through the barrier I'd put up and slid silently inside. "I make the rules, Rocket. How is Reyes supposed to cause the deaths of—" I glanced around. "—thousands of people?"

"Not thousands, Miss Charlotte. Seven billion two hundred forty-eight million six hundred twenty thousand one hundred thirteen."

Stunned, I shook my head. "How?" I repeated through teeth that were now welded together. "That's everyone on Earth, and that's not possible. How?"

He frowned and glanced down in thought. "Or one."

"What?" I said, blinking back to him.

"Or one. If one dies, everyone lives."

"Who, Rocket? Reyes?"

"No, Miss Charlotte. Not this time."

"Wait, I changed destiny, right? I brought Reyes back. But now someone else has to die?" When he nodded, I asked, "Who?"

We'd been here before, and it did not end well. Rocket didn't want to tell me, but he'd lost some of his innocence since our last encounter. He now knew better than to hold back.

He swallowed hard and whispered, the word like brittle paper in the air, thin and so fragile, I was afraid it would crumble before it got to me. But it didn't. It reverberated in my mind like a crash of thunder.

He looked at me, his eyes round, and said again, "You, Miss Charlotte."

And there it was.

24

Reyes and I lay in our respective beds, our faces centimeters apart, our breaths meeting in the middle, caressing. Though it was past midnight, he'd just showered and smelled clean, his earthy scent rich beneath the sandalwood soap he'd used. His hair, still slightly damp, curled at his cheek and around his ear.

I didn't get much more out of Rocket, but if I had to die to save the world, so be it. Timing would be an issue, but I planned on enjoying every second I had left with my fiancé.

"Want to come over to my place?" I asked him.

The sparkle in his eyes danced in humor. "I don't know," he said. "You live so far away."

I squeaked as he reached up and slid me down the length of him, caressing my stomach with his mouth as I passed, searing my skin with each kiss. I kissed his stomach back before turning over and curling into his side.

We settled onto his side of the beds. His was much more comfortable than mine anyway. I had no idea how different I'd feel after sleeping on a good mattress. I could totally get used to it.

I had this amazing gift for living in denial. Until I died, I was going to live each day like I had a million more after that one. And that started here and now.

"If we ever get divorced," I said into his neck as I trailed kisses over his pulse points, "I'm taking you for every mattress you have. Fair warning. You might want to consider a prenup."

"Are you planning on divorcing me?"

"Not at the moment, but I have a few movie-star crushes I'm still holding out hope for. If any of them call, you will be so yesterday."

"You know, it's sad how many movie stars die unexpectedly."

I gasped and rose so I could gape at him. "You'd kill my crushes?"

"Only the ones that hit on you."

"Fine." I rolled my eyes. "I'll tell Brad to stop calling. He's married, for God's sake."

"That would be wise." He nipped at my earlobe, causing a tingle to bolt through me.

I pushed a lock of hair out of his eyes. "You bought me a new Jeep," I said, noting that she'd been doing much better than before my run-in with Mr. Raving Lunatic two weeks prior.

"I was hoping you wouldn't notice."

"I figured."

"Noni did the best he could, but to drive her without completely replacing the frame would have been dangerous. It would have cost more, and you would've still had problems in the long run."

I understood. "Thank you. It's still Misery. I can feel her in spirit."

He patted my head like one would when consoling a child. "Whatever helps you sleep at night, Dutch."

He made me giggle, but he still needed to be punished for his insolence, so I bit his shoulder. Hard. He sucked in a lungful of air and rolled on top of me. Brushing the hair out of my eyes, he said, "You know, they say that those who know the real name of the grim reaper hold power over him. Or, in this case, her."

I sobered, suddenly more interested in the conversation than in his delicious shoulders. "They say that?" I asked, wondering what *real* name he would be referring to.

"Yes."

"And do you know my real name?"

He propped his head on an elbow and stared down at me. "I do, in fact. I heard it whispered on the voice of every angel in heaven when they sent you."

"And?" I asked, hopeful. I knew so little about that part of myself.

"You aren't supposed to hear it until you pass."

"Pass? Like, away?" I asked, surprised. That could be much sooner than either of us had expected.

"Yes. When you fully become the grim reaper."

"But you know it now, right? You could tell me."

He lowered his head. "I'm not sure what knowing it would do. Like I said, there is a power behind it."

"How can something as arbitrary as a name have power?"

"Your real name is anything but arbitrary. Just remember something, Dutch. You are not of this world. You never will be. Your human existence is just a microsecond in your life. A necessary state of being to ground you on this plane. At first, I thought that was why my father wanted me to wait for you. You can't just capture a reaper unless you can catch one in human form. There is simply no way to catch a portal otherwise. It's like trying to grab hold of smoke."

"You said, at first."

"Yes. I'm with Swopes. I think Lucifer lied to me and to him. I think there's more to it; I just don't know what. Either way, you still have a job waiting for you after your corporeal being ceases to exist. A job that will last centuries."

"And knowing my name will make me more powerful?" I asked, perplexed.

"Yes. It is part of your transformation. And since your family is so powerful, you even more so, I can't imagine what knowing it would do."

"So why are you telling me this now?" I asked. I'd been begging for information like this from him for months.

"I owe you," he said, matter-of-fact.

"You do? Cool. And just what do you owe me for?"

The seriousness in his eyes hit me hard. "Because you said yes."

I blinked in surprise. "You think because I agreed to marry you, you owe me?"

"You don't realize what that means. You are literally royalty, born to the king and queen of your kind. Your marrying me will be like a beloved princess marrying a street urchin."

I snickered, but his expression remained severe.

"But again, you are more special than any of your kind. More powerful. I'm beginning to understand you have a much higher purpose than I'd ever realized. For us to marry . . . let's just say your celestial, for lack of a better word, family would not approve."

"I would love to know more about them," I coaxed. When it became clear I wasn't getting any more out of him where that was concerned, I pressed him about his own. "What about your family? Are you ever going to try to contact them? I still believe they would want to know you are alive and well."

"Perhaps. Just as your parents would you."

I rose onto my elbows. "What do you mean?"

"Their sacrifice was a great one. Once one of their kind is sent, they lose all contact until the reaper's physical form passes. They have no idea how you are doing, what your life has been like."

"Wow. Our parents are more similar than I thought. Do you remember being born?" I asked him out of the blue. I'd always wondered about how he came into the world, both in the supernatural realm, when created by his outcast father, and here on earth.

"The memory of my human existence isn't like yours. I remember bits and pieces."

"What about your creation? What about when Lucifer created you?"

He lay back and rested an arm on his forehead. "*That* I remember well."

"Can you tell me about it?" I asked, resting my chin on his shoulder. He pulled me closer against his side.

"I remember the pain of creation," he said, his thoughts far away. "The heat of the fire. The color of my skin as it smoldered, as the muscle and tendon beneath it formed and solidified. I remember the being that created me—my father, as it were—and from the moment I took my first breath, I knew he had no love for what he'd created. He had dark machinations. He had a plan and I was a big part of it. But first I had to prove myself. And so the tests began." He came back to me and kissed the tip of my nose. "My childhood was not the stuff of fairy tales."

"I would love to hear about it."

"Then you're going to be disappointed. I can't tell you."

"Why?"

"Any love that you have in your heart for me would vanish."

"Reyes—"

"Dutch," he said, cutting me off. "Please do not ask that of me. It is a darkness I cannot share. I would lose you forever, and I've only ever wanted you. You are literally the light in my darkness, the redemption of my past. I waited centuries for you to be born on earth, for me to be able to bask in your glow. You are like a gravitational force that lures me closer with each breath you take."

I lay rather stunned.

"Imagine a canvas bathed completely in black. Only black. There is no shape. No purpose other than to bring darkness. Then splash on a brilliant white. Add some reds and blues, some yellows and greens. Suddenly it has meaning. It has a reason to exist. That is what you have done to my world. You brought me purpose. Light and color to fill the void of oblivion. Without you, there is only the darkness."

I pulled him closer and kissed his neck. He ran his fingers through my hair.

"That will be my gift to you on our wedding day."

I rose and regarded him with a questioning expression.

"The name I caught on the air as you were being brought into this world. The angels all whispered it, each and every one, but only once. They are forbidden to mention it again until your passing. Then one angel will have the honor of telling you and only you. I've kept it safe, locked away. It will be my gift to you on our wedding day. The power behind it is immense. The light it holds."

"I— I don't know what to say."

"I think we should work together."

"What?"

His eyes glistened in amusement. "With the Twelve coming, I've decided to hire a manager for the bar and work with you full-time."

"Um."

"I know," he said, ruffling my hair. "Your gratitude is all I need."

"Reyes—"

"No arguments. It's not safe to leave you alone anymore. If we work together, who will question it?"

Wow, my partnerships were multiplying like bunnies on Viagra. I guess I could take on three partners: Aunt Lil, Garrett, and Reyes.

We could be the Fearsome Foursome!

Or not.

"But I do have one question," he said, patting my head to his chest to let me know he understood how grateful I was that he would deign to work with me. Such a nice, humble guy.

I giggled under his playful arm and said, "Just one?"

"For now. Why a spork?"

It took me a moment to remember my response to the utensil question I'd asked him earlier. "Because!" I said, shocked he'd even ask. "Sporks multitask. They look unassuming, but pack a powerful purpose. Like a Swiss Army knife, only not quite that useful."

"Ah," he said, nodding in understanding.

"And it's such a cool word. Who can resist a good sporking?"

He laughed and was just about to kiss me when someone pounded on the door. Someone insane, apparently. Who would dare interrupt the son of Satan?

Well, besides me.

I tossed on Reyes's robe and rushed to his door. Once there, I found a harried Garrett Swopes, but he was knocking on my door.

The minute he saw me, he barreled forward, pushing past me to get inside. "I was wrong," he said, handing me a stack of papers. "Sorry about the hour, but I was wrong about everything."

Cleary, he needed consoling. And I was just the woman for the job. "Swopes. We're all wrong at some point in our lives. Can you say tie-dyed leg warmers? I used to live for those things. It was a dark time for me."

His pounding had awakened Cookie. I gestured her inside as well, trying not to giggle at her hair. Or the fact that she had on a green mineral mud mask. I was pretty sure she'd forgotten that fact.

She shuffled inside sleepily, her bright pink bottoms gathered between her butt cheeks. I'd skip that enlightenment as well.

When Garrett turned around, he took in her appearance and decided not to react. I knew I liked him for a reason. But only that one. No need to get crazy.

Reyes came out then, but didn't react as he took in his guests before heading to the kitchen. He put on a pot of coffee, knowing the late hour wouldn't matter to Cookie and me, and took out two beers as I glanced over the papers Garrett had handed me. Reyes had caught on to the routine and took it like a man. God, I loved him.

"You were wrong?" he asked Garrett.

Garrett nodded, his expression grave as he glanced between the two of us.

I looked up from the papers. "You've already told us all this," I said. "It's the prophecies from the von Holstein guy."

"No, A. von Holstein is the translator. He had a lot to wade through with the prophecies being written in a dead language *and* in code. I don't blame him for getting anything wrong. I just misinterpreted his interpretation. Your new friend, the Dealer, has come in very handy."

"That's good." I sank onto Reyes's sofa beside Cookie. She yawned, and I realized she must've had a late night with Uncle Bob. I was so not going there. I could only hope she'd put the mask on *after* the nightcap.

Garrett paced the floor, deep in thought, taking periodic sips of the beer Reyes gave him.

Reyes sat on the armrest beside me. "Coffee in two. Now, what did you get wrong this time?" he asked Garrett, badgering him just a little.

I jabbed my fiancé with an elbow, then said, "Swopes, sit down."

"It's about you, the daughter," he said, his agitation growing. "At first Dr. von Holstein and I thought you were the daughter throughout the prophecies. All the prophecies. That you had to face Lucifer."

"Okay," I said, trying not to drool as the scent of coffee brewing washed over my senses like baptismal water. I could face Reyes's dad. I had to die soon anyway.

"But there are two," he continued. "Two distinct references. Two distinct time periods."

"I'm getting dizzy," Cookie said as she watched him pace. She rubbed her forehead and I watched from my periphery as realization dawned. She brought her hand down slowly, her expression changing from one of exhausted but interested to one of utter horror. She sat in shock a few seconds, then slowly rose to her feet, glancing toward Reyes's bathroom.

It took every molecule of self-control I possessed not to giggle. Not in a mean way. Well, kind of mean. I wasn't so much laughing at her but with her. Only on the inside, because I didn't want to be backhanded.

Before she took two steps that way, another pounding sounded at the door. Our eyes met and our thoughts merged. Amber was alone. Did she wake up and get scared?

We both bounded for the door, but Reyes still beat us. Freaking supernatural beings.

But when he opened the door, a group of nuns stood before him. Which was unusual, especially considering the hour.

"Is the church collecting door-to-door now?" I asked as I hobbled forward to stand beside my man. My abstinent friends were dressed fairly normally, the veils on their heads the only giveaway that they were nuns. They parted to let a couple of them through, revealing the fact that they were practically carrying one of my besties, Sister Mary Elizabeth. She was almost limp in their arms, her forehead shimmering with a fine sheen of sweat, her eyes heavy-lidded, her gaze distant.

I rushed forward to help. Garrett did the same and we dragged the sister into Reyes's apartment. Once everyone was inside, Reyes shut the door behind us. Sister Mary Elizabeth dropped to her knees, clutched her head, and whimpered, insisting there were too many. Far too many.

"She's been like this for a couple of hours," the mother superior said, her demeanor far less intimidating than usual in the simple dress and short veil. She knelt beside us.

Another spoke up then. A Sister Theresa, if I wasn't mistaken. "She was screaming at first."

"Yes," the mother superior agreed, petting Mary Elizabeth's hair. It was the first time I'd seen it uncovered, and it was shorter than I thought it would be. Cut into a simple bob, it had clearly seen better days. It hung in matted clumps as though she just woke up and had been pulling at it in her sleep. The thick clumps entangled in her fingers confirmed that suspicion.

Another one spoke then, one I didn't recognize. "She's been wailing in pain and saying they were all talking at once."

"The angels?" I asked, pulling Mary Elizabeth's head to my chest. She calmed instantly, but stayed fetal, rocking against me.

"Yes," the mother superior said. "According to Sister Mary Elizabeth, something has them all upset."

"What?" Cookie asked, her green face shocked. "What could upset the angels like this?"

Before any of them could answer, Mary Elizabeth stilled. She unfolded herself and stood. I helped her, and Reyes helped me help her, as my ankle was still tender. I took her by the shoulders and tried to bring her terrified gaze to mine.

When she finally focused, her expression changed from terrified to shocked to sorrowful. She cupped my cheek in her hand, then looked down.

"Charley," she said at last, her voice soft, full of fear, "what have you done?"

"What?" I glanced at the other nuns, but they seemed as confused as I was. "What did I do?"

She sank to her knees and put both hands on my abdomen before refocusing on me. She took one hand away to cover her mouth as she looked from me to Reyes and then back again. "What have you done?" she repeated, her words muffled.

And then I understood. I touched my abdomen and knew. In an instant, like a flash of lightning, I knew. I felt it. A tiny spark at first. A warmth. A glow in my nether regions that welled up and filled me with such unexplainable joy. Such unimaginable ardor. Such unconditional devotion.

Reyes was the first to catch on. He stepped forward, his expression just as shocked as Mary Elizabeth's, and put his hand on my abdomen, covering both the sister's hand and mine at once. I felt a pulse, a wave, like a greeting from a new life, as his body connected with mine.

I looked up at Garrett. He knew, too. "The daughter," he said, his voice full of awe. He knew. The prophecies about the daughter of light were about me. But the ones about the daughter, *just* the daughter—well, those had been about . . . I looked back down at my abdomen. Cradled it as though holding her already. Reyes was emitting a combination of happiness and bewilderment.

Then I felt another presence. Another . . . admirer of the moment. We weren't alone. Reyes tensed, feeling the presence, too. Outside in the alley, I felt the Dealer, could practically see him smile into the darkness as we all began to understand. But he already knew. He'd always known.

What had I done indeed?

Excerpt:
Reyes's POV

I stripped off my clothes and crawled into bed, trying not to let this latest development in all things Charley Davidson bother me. It didn't help. It bothered me, and there wasn't a whole hell of a lot I could do about it. She would never listen. I had to realize that. And, admittedly, her stubbornness was part of her charm. Unfortunately, that charm was going to get her killed someday. I would do everything in my power not to let that happen, but when she disregarded my advice at every turn, she made that goal more and more difficult to achieve.

And she paid the price. Holy shit, did she pay the price. With all that she'd been through, one would think she'd at least try to avoid life-threatening situations. I heard her screams at night. I felt the fear that rushed through her when her dreams turned dark. It penetrated the wall between us like razor-sharp shadows that cut to the bone.

My ire rose once again with the thought. I swallowed it back, held it at bay. Dutch seemed to care more about others than about herself—and to an incomprehensible degree. It went against everything I knew about grim reapers. They didn't care about humans. They did their jobs and went about their days.

Dutch was different, unique, and I couldn't help the pride that swelled inside me with that knowledge. If she had any idea what she was capable of, I'd probably be in a lot of trouble. Grim reapers were not to be trifled with. She'd figure that out one day.

I felt her crawl onto her mattress. Our beds practically butted against each other, and the wall between us was growing tiresome. I'd have to do something about that soon. Still, feeling her so close, even with a wall between us, was like a salve. She calmed the seas that forever roiled inside me. Illuminated the darkness I dwelled in. I could not get enough of her. I could never get enough of her. Even growing up, I dreamed about her constantly. Had I known she was not just a figment of my imagination, I would have sought her out in the flesh way sooner than I did. Instead, I visited her in my dreams. Her energy, her vividness and blindingly bright soul, drew me to her every time I closed my eyes. For the most part, I kept my distance. I would make myself known only if she was in any kind of danger, which seemed to happen a lot.

But there were times growing up, in my loneliest, darkest hours, when the pain of my upbringing became unbearable, and I would search her out. She was the only reason I was still alive. Without her there to light my way, I would have been lost decades ago. I would have taken my own life, certainly, and quite possibly the lives of several others along the way. That was the simple truth of it.

I felt her then. I felt her cross the barrier between us, probing, searching. I tensed, wondering what she was up to. She had been hurt a couple of weeks ago, and I'd vowed to give her space and time to heal. Maybe she was better. Going by what I was feeling radiating off her now, she was a lot better.

The sensation of her grew stronger. She was reaching out with her mind, playing a game at which I was a master. I couldn't help but be amused and send out my own essence in response. I left my physical body and slipped through the wall as though it weren't there.

She was holding her palm against it, trying to reach out to me, to touch me as I was now touching her. I didn't materialize. Instead, I started at her wrist and worked my way down, sliding my fingertips along her arm, across her cheek, down her neck, until I lay atop her. She sucked in a breath, her chest rising softly with the action, stirring me to my core. I cupped a breast in my hand, its fullness soft and tantalizing. She moaned underneath me, writhed with pleasure as the friction caused me to harden against her. She was honest to God the sexiest thing I'd ever seen, and I'd seen a lot.

But she stopped. She opened her eyes, their gold depths glittering like water in the moonlight, and concentrated, fighting me mentally, struggling to reverse our positions. I was always the one to leave my physical body and come to her. I gained just as much pleasure from being with her incorporeally as corporeally. But the thought of her doing the same to me caused a jolt of pleasure at the base of my cock. Blood rushed to that general area lightning quick the moment I felt her brush over me.

She sent out her essence, letting the heat from her mental energy explore my body. No one had ever touched me that way. Her essence was warm and smooth like silk. She tested every inch of me, running her fingers over my abdomen, then—almost timidly—around my cock. I gritted my teeth, curled my hands into the sheets as I felt her mouth slide over me, encircling my erection. Her lips glided down, her teeth grazing over the sensitive skin there. But she wanted more. I could feel it. I could allow her to get only so close. To go only so deep. Anything more, and she could see things I didn't want her to see.

So, I stopped her. I raised a barrier to limit her explorations to those places visible to the naked eye. Then again, it was Dutch I was dealing with, the most powerful of her kind to be born in a millennium. She sharpened her touch, raked her fingernails over my skin, let them bite into my flesh. I bit back a curse.

"Dutch," I said aloud in warning, but there was no fighting her. She was too powerful, and she broke through my barrier in one quick strike.

Heat penetrated muscle and bone and burst inside me. A feeling I'd never felt before spread through every inch. It was hot, like lava, and burned from the inside out, coursing through my veins, rushing along my nerve endings. She pushed my legs apart and pressed into me, and the pleasure that rocketed through me almost brought me off the bed.

Our energies collided, the friction grinding, causing my hunger to grow stronger with every beat of her pulse. As she caressed me, I caressed her. I felt her energy engulf my cock in long, powerful strokes until I pushed her down and did the same to her. I felt her climax swell like a sea inside her, churning and swirling. I kissed her and sucked her and pushed into her so hard and fast, she burst into a cascade of shimmering lights. The moment she came, I exploded as well. Only I wasn't really inside her. I wasn't really on top of her, and I came on my stomach, my jaw clenched, my muscles convulsing with each spasm of pleasure.

When the orgasm died down, I threw an arm over my face and listened to the sound of my own labored breathing. That was one of the most incredible things that had ever happened to me.

I reached out to her again, the enigma that was known across the universe as the daughter of light. "Come sleep with me," I said.

She didn't answer, but I could hear her soft sighs as she panted into her pillow. So, I rolled out of bed to clean myself. I could feel her surveying me. I smiled. She kept watch until I crawled back into bed. With exhaustion quickly overtaking me, I repeated, "Come sleep with me."

I wasn't sure if she responded or not. Apparently, I fell asleep like I generally fucked—hard and fast—because I didn't remember anything else until I awoke to an overwhelming feeling of panic coming from Charley's apartment.